JUST
SOME
STUPID
LOVE
STORY

JUST SOME STUPID LOVE STORY

Katelyn Doyle

FLATIRON
BOOKS
NEW YORK

JUST SOME STUPID LOVE STORY. Copyright © 2024 by Katelyn Doyle. All rights reserved. Printed in the United States of America. For information, address Flatiron Books, 120 Broadway, New York, NY 10271.

www.flatironbooks.com

Designed by Jen Edwards

Library of Congress Cataloging-in-Publication Data

Names: Doyle, Katelyn, author.
Title: Just some stupid love story / Katelyn Doyle.
Description: First edition. | New York : Flatiron Books, 2024.
Identifiers: LCCN 2023040100 | ISBN 9781250328090 (hardcover)
  | ISBN 9781250328106 (ebook)
Subjects: LCGFT: Romance fiction. | Novels.
Classification: LCC PS3616.E279 J87 2024 | DDC 813/.6—dc23/
  eng/20231121
LC record available at https://lccn.loc.gov/2023040100

Our books may be purchased in bulk for promotional, educational, or business use. Please contact your local bookseller or the Macmillan Corporate and Premium Sales Department at 1-800-221-7945, extension 5442, or by email at MacmillanSpecialMarkets@macmillan.com.

First Edition: 2024

10 9 8 7 6 5 4 3 2 1

For Chris

PART ONE

PALM BAY PREPARATORY SCHOOL,
FIFTEENTH REUNION

November 2018

CHAPTER 1

Molly

If you ever find yourself hosting an event that requires a rented white tent, you can be certain that I, Molly Marks, will RSVP with regrets.

If your tent is festooned with off-season flowers, or thousands of fairy lights, or embossed linen place cards—if it's bedecked with a dance floor, a wedding band, a dais for the giving of toasts—rest assured I'll be there in absentia, cheering you, my dear friend, from hundreds of miles away.

It's not personal. I'm sure your event is momentous and that you're a wonderful host.

But the rented white tent is a monument to public displays of emotion, and sentiment makes me squeamish. If I must evince a feeling—and, gross—I want to do it at home, with the blinds drawn and the lights off, in a robe covered in frosting and dribbles of sauvignon blanc.

You can thus understand why, on this sultry night on this star-glimmered island famed for its champagne-colored beaches, I have the enthusiasm of a woman hobbling on heels to her tropical, waterfront grave.

For approaching us in middle distance in the pearlescent glow of the full Florida moon is the hungry white mouth of a tent the size of a cruise ship.

And beneath it, draped in fake bougainvillea and lit up in spotlights flashing from violet to rose, a banner proclaims in a jubilant font:

WELCOME TO YOUR 15TH REUNION,
PALM BAY CLASS OF 2003!!!

Three exclamation points. Lethal.

I will allow that under the right circumstances—if I were another person, for instance—the atmosphere that greets me beneath the billowing canvas might be called dreamy.

The air, after all, smells like jasmine, and orange blossoms, and the salty breeze rippling off the Gulf of Mexico. Tiki torches cover the dance floor in flickering light. There's a champagne bar and a lobster station. Carefully dressed men and women are embracing with genuine sincerity, beaming at each other. On a few faces I even spot tears.

I put my hand to my throat to feel my fluttering pulse. It was a mistake not to take a Xanax at the hotel. Perhaps I can hide in a lifeguard station.

"I can't do this," I whisper to my best friend, Dezzie, who along with her husband, Rob, is the closest thing I have to a date for the evening.

She squeezes my hand with immoderate pressure—a gesture meant to be either reassuring or painful enough to scare me straight.

"You *will* do this," she whispers back.

"This is how I know my wife went to an obnoxious prep school in Florida," Rob remarks, unperturbed by my nerves. "Her fifteen-year reunion looks like a destination wedding."

"Actually, this is ten times nicer than our wedding," Dezzie says, dragging me past a table of welcome bags full of sparkly flip-flops and bug spray. We pause to take in centerpieces that involve pineapples, orchids, and foot-long diamanté palm trees.

"That's what you get for marrying an impoverished social worker," Rob says. "Maybe we can hijack the reunion and renew our vows."

"If there is one thing worse than a high school reunion," I say grimly, "it's a high school reunion slash vow renewal. Besides, it is a law of the universe that every couple who renews their vows breaks up within a year. You guys are too well-matched to throw it all away for some coconut shrimp."

"I see we're in a chipper mood tonight," Rob says, reaching out to flick my shoulder.

Rob is lucky I'm too miserable to retaliate, or I would frog him right between the ribs. He and Dezzie have been together for so long that Rob and

I are almost like siblings. The kind who love each other dearly and show it through bickering and a touch of light physical violence.

"Being dour was Molly's brand in high school," Dezzie tells him. "She was voted 'Most Pessimistic' senior year."

I toss back my hair. "An accomplishment in which I still take pride, thank you very much. I had to work for that honor."

I paid in a teenage proclivity for panic attacks. But don't feel bad. I grew up and got a psychiatrist and am now a strong, fierce woman with a soothing cocktail of prescriptions for antidepressants and the occasional benzo.

"I can only imagine what Molly was like as a teenager," Rob says, accepting a tiny, caviar-dotted crab cake from a waiter. "Given how intolerable she is now, I'd guess . . . not great." He gives me a wicked smile, and it is my turn to flick his shoulder.

"Oh God, she was insufferable," Dezzie says, throwing her arm around me affectionately. "Just all sad poetry and black coffee and feminist rants at debate club. She was like the human embodiment of a Sylvia Plath tattoo."

"So, literally nothing has changed," Rob says.

"Not true," I counter. "I'm the life of the goddamn party. Just not this one."

Please believe me: this is true. I live in Los Angeles, and my career depends on my ability to strike up sparkling poolside conversations at absurdly large houses tucked into the Hollywood Hills while downing just the right amount of champagne. I can charm with the best of them, converse like an ingenue, network so effortlessly it's almost like I'm enjoying myself.

But that's real life.

This is fake high school.

"Well tonight," Rob pronounces, "we are going to get you so jazzed to see all your old friends they aren't going to recognize you. Aren't we, Dez?"

Dezzie scans the room, no longer paying attention to us. "Where are we sitting?"

"Let's snag a table in the back where no one will talk to us," I suggest.

She hits my arm with her clutch. It's a very good clutch. Dezzie has excellent taste. Tonight she is wearing a short, architectural frock that looks like Comme des Garçons but that, she assured me when I gasped in envy at the sight of her, is a creatively belted tunic from none other than the high fashion house of Amazon.com. Her glossy black hair is in a severe, shoulder-length bob, and her lips are a slash of red that perfectly sets off her pale complexion. Rob, meanwhile, is lucky that he is handsome and square-jawed, because his fashion sense can charitably be called schlump-core. He is in his usual rumpled tan chinos, which tonight he has dressed up, if you can call it that, with a tweed blazer far too warm for the weather and some scuffed black loafers that don't match his belt. They're an odd pairing, like Karen O meets Jim from *The Office*. But they have enviable chemistry.

"Oh my God, Molly, you *must* stop complaining," Dezzie says. "You haven't seen most of these people in fifteen years. You flew all the way to Florida, which you hate, from Los Angeles. I'm not letting you hide in your wineglass all night, texting sarcastic observations to me and Alyssa under the table."

"If you think I am going to drink something as low-proof as wine tonight, you don't know me at all," I say. "Besides, I saw there are signature cocktails. How can I resist a Palm Bay Preptini?"

"Oooh, what does nostalgia for a forty-thousand-dollars-a-year private school taste like?" Rob asks.

I grab a coupe glass from a passing waiter and down half the pale orange liquid. "Women sweating through their DVF dresses, aging drunk bros dancing to hip-hop . . . and, um, rum or something."

Dezzie makes a beeline for a table and trots back holding three place cards.

"I found us," she says, handing me one.

Molly Marks, Table 8.

My stomach drops. "Wait a minute. Seats are *assigned?*"

Dezzie shrugs. "Marian Hart planned this. She probably wants to encourage social mixing. You know what she's like."

Marian Hart was our class president and our prom queen. She has the relentless, upbeat energy of a cruise ship activity director.

"Please tell me we're at the same table," I say, grabbing Dezzie's place card.

Desdemona Chan, Table 17.

"Fucking hell," I mutter. "Alyssa better be at my table, at least." Alyssa is our other best friend, the third in the impenetrable trio we formed in second grade.

"Nope. I saw her card. She's at eleven. And besides, her flight got in late and she won't be here for another hour. She can't save you. You'll just have to *mingle.*"

"I can *mingle* fine," I shoot back. "It's false nostalgia and forced cheer I'm not capable of."

Onstage, the steel drum band of white guys playing Jimmy Buffet covers finishes "The Weather Is Here, I Wish You Were Beautiful," and none other than Marian Hart steps onstage.

Unsurprisingly, she looks impeccable. Her perfectly highlighted blond hair is pulled into an elegant chignon that is somehow not melting in the Florida humidity, and her arms look like they're sponsored by Goop.

"Guys!" she squeals into the microphone. "It is amazing to see everyone. We have a hundred and fifty-eight out of our class of a hundred and sixty-seven here tonight, can you believe it? And we are going to have So. Much. FUN."

Her blue eyes roll back into her skull with sincerity.

I bury my head in Dezzie's shoulder. "I already hate this. Why am I here?"

"You *wanted* to come, you hypocrite. Perk up. Maybe you'll have fun."

She's wrong. I most certainly did not "want" to come. I'm here because I was peer pressured. I'm the only one of our little circle who lives on the West Coast, and occasions to see each other are increasingly rare, now that Alyssa has kids. But I'm finishing a project, and I don't like to travel when I'm in writer mode.

"I should be at home, working," I say.

"You can take four days off," Rob says. "It's not like you're an oncologist."

I am very far away from practicing life-saving medicine. I write rom-com scripts for a living. Think meet cutes, splashy set pieces, heartthrobs choking back tears as they profess unlikely, undying love to a woman who purportedly works at a magazine and always has blown-out hair.

I'll wait for you to stop laughing.

My career is admittedly a departure from the misanthropic sensibility for which I am known. However, please note I'm surprisingly good at it. I had two indie hits back-to-back right out of grad school. Granted, that was eight years ago. But my producer is in talks with an A-lister to play the lead in the screenplay I'm finishing, and I think it could be a hit.

A big one, even.

Which my career could desperately use. I get steady work writing for hire, but after my success right out of the gate, I was vain enough to think I'd be the next Nora Ephron or Nancy Meyers, banging out stone-cold classics while minting money. Right now, I'm coming up short in the "millionaire voice of a generation" department.

"Appetizers are about to be served," Marian continues from the stage. "So if y'all can go find your seats now, that would be perfect. We're going to have this fabulous meal and then we're going to get down like we're sixteen again! To kick us off, there are icebreaker questions at each table. Chat through them while you enjoy your scallops. Now go have so much fun!"

I grab Dezzie's hand. "I can't believe I have to endure this alone."

"You're going to be great, princess," she says, detaching herself from my grip. "Knock 'em dead. If not with charm, then with that famed sinister glare."

"I already regret this."

"Look, here's our table," Dez says to Rob, pointing at a nearby eight-top already populated with that quiet guy who founded a hedge fund and Chaz Logan, the funniest boy in our class.

"Oh man, you got Chaz *and* the billionaire?" I whine, despite being thirty-three years old. "I'm legit jealous."

Dez scans the room. "Oh, I think your table will be interesting."

I follow her eyes to a smaller table toward the side of the tent, near the beach, with a seagull-shaped sign that reads: Table 8.

And sitting at it, alone, is Seth Rubenstein.

My breath lodges painfully in my esophagus.

"Oh for fuck's sake," I hiss.

CHAPTER 2
Seth

I'm having so much fun. I *love* shit like this.

We're one hour into my fifteen-year high school reunion and I've already recapped the last decade with my old chem partner, Gloria, and her wife, Emily (they're set designers in Hollywood, and they just got a dog), looked at twenty pictures of Mike Wilson's baby (cute little guy), threatened to throw Marian into the ocean (I love Marian, and she looks great), had two craft cocktails named after our high school (totally delish), and watched a snip of the Lightning game on Loren Heyman's phone (I'm not a hockey guy, but I think Loren thinks I'm someone else, and I like that about him).

I am now sitting at table eight, alone, because unlike the rest of my former classmates who are still milling about, I respect Marian's intricately choreographed event protocol. Besides, when you're the first at the table, you get to watch everyone's reactions as they realize they have to talk to you all night.

It's a blast.

I stretch out my legs with my back to the lovely Gulf of Mexico, sip my Palm Bay Preptini, and tap my foot to the opening of "Margaritaville" as I await my dining companions.

There are those addictively crunchy Parmesan twists sticking out from the breadbasket—yum—and I grab one and bite into it. A somewhat embarrassing amount of cheese crumbs falls on my chest.

I'm brushing the schmutz off my jacket when I look up and my stomach lurches.

It's Molly Marks, standing in the shadow of a potted palm, looking at me in horror.

I haven't seen her in fifteen years.

Not since the night we broke up.

Or rather, since she broke up with me, stunningly and without notice, in a way that I didn't get over until deep into college—or possibly law school, depending on how much PBR I'd been drinking.

I quickly jam the rest of the breadstick into my mouth and stand up with a huge grin on my face, still chewing, because Molly doesn't deserve for me to wait until I swallow.

"Molly Marks!" I call, opening my arms wide like there is no reason on earth she wouldn't step into them for a big old back-slapping hug. I am Seth Rubenstein, attorney at law, and I am going to *drown* her in my famous charisma.

She stands there with her head cocked, as if I'm a loon.

Look, I *am* a loon, I admit it. But I'm a *nice* loon, which Molly no doubt finds foreign and difficult to parse, being a cruel and chilling person.

"Hey, don't leave a poor guy hanging," I exclaim. "Bring it in, Marksman!"

She reluctantly steps into my arms and gives me a tentative *tap, tap, tap* on the shoulder—as if touching me with more than one finger would put her at risk of contracting a venereal disease.

Which I don't have. I got tested before I flew out here. Just in case.

I pull her in closer. "Hey, a little affection if you please, Marky Marks. It's your old pal Seth Rubes."

"Who?" she asks, deadpan.

I laugh, because I'm determined to exude the relaxed affability of a very chill dude who is not at all disturbed to be in her presence. And Molly was always funny, to those rare people with whom she condescended to speak.

"I can't believe you showed up to this shindig," I say, stepping back to look at her. She didn't come to our five- or ten-year reunions, to absolutely no one's surprise.

"Me neither." She sighs in that world-weary way that once drove me out of my mind.

"You look amazing," I tell her.

This is, of course, the obligatory thing to say to someone at a high school reunion, but in her case it's true. She still has that long, thick, dark brown hair straight down to her ass, which makes her stand out among the bobs and updos of our fellow Palm Bay Flamingos. She's even taller than I remember, with killer legs shown off to great effect by the short, flimsy black dress she has accessorized with a leather jacket in predictable contravention of Marian's "tropical cocktail" dress code. She is wearing somewhere between ten and twenty delicate gold necklaces, which fall at various lengths from her throat to the gap between her breasts, adorned with tiny pendants, like a thistle and the shape of California. I'm disappointed in myself to report that I want to take the necklaces off her, one by one.

She scans me up and down. "You look good too. I would have thought you'd seem older."

Um.

I try not to look sad.

I likely don't succeed because she claps a beautifully manicured hand over her mouth.

"I'm sorry. That came out wrong. I meant—"

"You expected me to wear the maturity bespeaking my innate gravitas?" I provide, to save her, as she looks like she wants to run off and bury herself in the sand.

I was never able to avoid trying to save her from herself.

Not that it ever worked.

"No, just . . . I mean, um, you haven't aged. Or, you have, of course, but not like commensurately with the others here? You look handsome and virile? God, sorry, apologies."

She still talks like a walking SAT study guide, but she seems genuinely mortified. I take pity on her.

"It's the Botox," I joke, "and I have a great surgeon." She doesn't laugh, unsurprisingly. She's always been stingy with her laughter. If you want to crack her up, you have to earn it.

But it's extremely gratifying when you do.

"Please, have a seat," I say, making a sweeping, gentlemanly gesture at the empty chair beside me.

It's empty because I did not bring a date. Or, more accurately, my date canceled at the last minute when she, my girlfriend of nearly four months, broke up with me over text the night before we were scheduled to fly here.

She said, as have the last five or six women I've dated, that things were moving too quickly. That I wanted more than she was ready to give.

Perhaps she was right. I tend to throw myself eagerly into courtship, hoping we'll both fall in love. Why hold back one's natural zest and affection when any woman might end up being the one? I'm looking for my life partner, my soul mate, my wife.

And I'm certain—*certain*—I'll meet her soon.

I do not share any of this with Molly.

"Who else is sitting here?" she asks, looking around the table.

"Marian," I say with delectation. Molly has always loathed Marian.

"God, she looks the same," Molly says. "What does she do these days?"

Trust it to Molly to not keep up with anyone from our class.

"She's an advertising exec," I say. "Specializes in feminine hygiene brands."

Molly snorts. "Marian sells tampons and shit?"

I shake my head. "Not shit. Just tampons."

This time, she does laugh.

"So how are you? What do you do?" I ask, even though I know exactly what she does, because she is, at least in our overlapping circle of high school friends, famous.

She grabs one of the Parmesan twists and idly breaks it in half, like it's a toy and not a delicious food.

If I'm not mistaken, she's nervous.

I'm making her nervous.

Delightful.

"I'm a writer," she says vaguely.

"Oh, that's so great. What do you write?"

"Films. Rom-coms."

She says this blandly, in the manner of someone who does not wish to invite further questions. Here is my opportunity to torture her, just a little bit.

"Miss Molly McMarks," I say, "you must be joking. *You*, of all people, write kissing movies?"

"Kissing movies gross upward of fifty million dollars opening weekend," she says. "Or, they used to, before superheroes started dominating the box office."

"I love superheroes," I say. "No offense."

"Of course you do. You always loved a simplistic battle between good and evil."

This is mean, but true, and I can't help liking that she's being catty. It reminds me of our romance. True love at sixteen is hardwired. To this day, I am hopelessly attracted to hostile women.

"I knew you were sentimental at heart," I say, which is true. She always refused to go to movies with me because they made her cry, and she has a phobia about crying in public.

"It's a job," she says and swallows down half of a Palm Bay Preptini.

"Careful, champ," I say. "There's five kinds of rum in those."

She flags down a waiter and motions for two more.

"Cheers," she says, offering me one.

I accept it and take a sip. "Yum."

"So what do you do?" she asks.

"Attorney. I'm a partner at a firm in Chicago."

I will admit that I say this with pride. I graduated law school at twenty-three and made partner by twenty-eight, unprecedented at my firm.

"What kind of law do you practice?" she asks.

I'm less eager to tell her this detail. I know she's not going to like it.

"Family law," I say, as vaguely as possible.

Molly stares at me in what looks like true disbelief. "You're a *divorce* attorney?"

She has a deep loathing for divorce attorneys. Justifiably.

But I try not to be like the ones who helped ruin her mother's life when we were kids. I pride myself on helping couples break up humanely—or better yet, heal.

"Not entirely," I say quickly, "I also handle prenups, mediation—"

Her lips crinkle into a menacing smile.

"That's hilarious," she says, without any mirth. "You were always such a hopeless romantic in high school."

"You would know," I say.

Her face turns the color of sand.

Whoops. I didn't mean to go for the jugular so quickly.

I meant to *draagggggg* it out.

Her awkwardness pleases me, nevertheless.

Before I can engage her in further reminders of what she did to me in our youth, Marian comes to the table, flanked by her ex-high-school-boyfriend,

Marcus; our French exchange student, Georgette; and Georgette's plus one, an intimidatingly handsome man who looks bored in the way only a Parisian at a Florida high school reunion can.

"Aww, look at you two!" Marian cries, taking in me and Molly. "Like not a day's gone by." She turns and addresses the French guy. "These two used to be quite the *amours*."

I throw an arm around Molly's shoulders and squeeze the living daylights out of her. "Still are."

Molly very subtly quivers with what might be disgust, or the chill of the ocean breeze, or a wave of nostalgic lust for me.

Okay, probably not the latter.

"Yeah, no," she mutters.

The French guy extends his hand to Molly. "I'm Jean-Henri. Georgette's husband."

"I'm Molly," she replies, shaking it. "Class bitch."

CHAPTER 3

Molly

It's difficult to pretend you're unaffected by seeing someone you hurt deeply and never apologized to when your hands are shaking.

I put them under the table and hope Seth doesn't notice.

Dezzie promised me he wouldn't be here. In retrospect, Dezzie is the type of person who has no problem lying to get you to do what she thinks is good for you, and she thinks facing my anxieties is good for me.

But Dezzie is a pastry chef, not a therapist. Her psychological interventions often fall flat.

Meanwhile, Seth has gone back to acting as if absolutely nothing is wrong. As if I did not callously break up with him after four years of dating the night of our high school graduation. As if it wasn't the night we had planned to lose our virginity, in a hotel suite he'd already filled with rose petals and four kinds of condoms, only to have me walk in, break his heart, and leave.

As if all that didn't transpire in under five minutes.

If I know him—and who could say, since I ghosted him fifteen years ago and haven't spoken to him since—he's toying with me.

But that's okay, I tell myself, trying to breathe normally. He deserves to.

I'm relieved when Seth falls into conversation with Marian and Marcus about Chicago, where Seth lives. They then turn to Marian's home in Miami and Marcus's in Atlanta, and their jobs in advertising and sports management.

I practice my French on Georgette, who now lives in Paris, is a stylist, and has the same disgust for scallops that I do.

"*Tu es avec Seth?*" she asks in a low voice, nodding at him.

"*Non!*" I sputter. "I came with Dezzie and her husband."

"Ah," Georgette says, with a very French puff of air. "*Tant pis.*"

Her tone has the slightest whiff of disappointment.

I shrug it off. Georgette only attended school with us for junior year. She is no doubt unaware of the sordid story of our breakup.

"Tell me," I say to her husband, "how did you two meet?"

At a photography opening at the bar on the roof of the Centre Pompidou, *bien sûr*.

I allow myself to become absorbed in the glamorous tale of their courtship. Or, perhaps more accurately, I feign deep interest in it so that I can swivel my body away from Seth, like Georgette's words are a force field that might protect me from having to talk to him for the rest of the night.

But then Marian stands up and reaches for a pile of cards at the center of the table.

"Time to do our icebreakers!" she chirps.

"Fun!" Seth enthuses, somehow making it into a two-syllable word.

He does not appear to be kidding.

I can't believe we used to date.

Granted, he was beautiful in high school, and has somehow become even better-looking—tall and lanky with wavy black hair, dark eyes that sparkle with mischief, and a nose that slightly twists at the bridge in a way I can only describe as sexual.

And then, of course, there is the fact that he was once infatuated with me, rather than alienated or scared like all the other boys at our school. And the small detail that I became a puddle of goo in those stolen moments when we were alone.

He's still the only person I've ever been in love with.

I shouldn't have sat next to him.

Even through the glaze of my anxiety and my attempts to concentrate on Georgette's anecdotes about Marion Cotillard, all those groping-each-other-in-the-backseat pheromones are rushing back, and I'm distracted by Seth's nearness. I'm caught between the urge to go to the bathroom to collect myself, and the urge to grab him and disappear under the pier where we used to make out.

Sex, you see, is an excellent balm against anxiety. It relocates you in your body, as it's difficult to be in a mental doom spiral when someone is touching your breasts. This phenomenon accounts for at least 70 percent of my otherwise inexplicable ex-boyfriends.

Seth's arm brushes mine as he reaches for his drink, and I feel his touch reverberate somewhere in the vicinity of my ovaries. My shoulders relax for the first time all night.

I sneak a look at him for any sign that he is overcome with vestigial lust too.

Instead, he's focused on Marian.

"First question!" Marian says, waving the card at us. "What's your favorite memory from high school?"

Oh God.

Marcus raises his hand. "That's easy. It was getting to be prom king next to this beautiful girl."

Marian blushes and takes Marcus's hand. He looks into her eyes, his gaze alit with something like wonder. You can *feel* the heat between them.

"That was my favorite night too," Marian purrs.

I accidentally catch Seth's eye. I wonder if, like me, he's remembering how I persuaded him to skip prom and go on a beach walk instead. How the night was exactly like this—ever so slightly sticky and lit up with a full moon. How we jumped into the ocean in our finery, and showed up at the after-party giddy, me in soaking wet sequins, him in a waterlogged tux.

We both look away.

Georgette takes the floor, describing scuba diving on a class trip we took to Costa Rica, and then it's my turn.

I blank.

The truth is that all my favorite memories from high school involve Seth. But I'm certainly not going to admit that. So I dredge up the first innocuous thing that comes to mind.

"I'll always remember this one night when Dezzie and Alyssa and I snuck out of a sleepover, looking for an old-school country-western bar we'd heard about out east, in ranch country. We stole Dezzie's mom's convertible and drove for like an hour down these dark, dusty roads blasting Patsy Cline until we found it. No one carded us and we ate barbecue and danced with a bunch of old cowboy-ish guys until two in the morning. It was incredible."

What I don't add is how that whole night, I wished Seth had been there. How Dezzie and Alyssa kept chiding me for calling him, so he could listen to the band through my cell phone.

"That's so sweet," Marian says, beaming at me.

"It truly is," Seth says. "Wish I'd been there."

Seth literally had wished he'd been there. He was sad I hadn't invited him. He loves—loved—country music. And dancing. He's one of *those* people.

I tried to take him there for his birthday a few months later, to make it up to him, and found that the place had closed down.

This could be a metaphor for our dynamic in high school: him always yearning for more. Me, always just a gesture short of the devotion with which he showered me. He had such an endless capacity for affection. And I already had the poison pill I still possess: an instinct to flinch and pull back just when other people most crave my love.

"Your turn, Rubes," Marcus says.

Seth leans back and casually wraps his arm around my shoulders.

"It was the day this one agreed to go out with me," he says.

He's definitely toying with me.

"We were at a speech and debate tournament in Raleigh freshman year," he goes on, eyeing me with what I can only assume to be mock-fondness. "Marks here won, of course. After that a few of us ended up in Chaz Logan's hotel room, and we were talking about the Supreme Court, because we were pretentious little fuckers. Molly went off on a very eloquent tangent defending Constitutional interpretation over strict constructionism, and she was so smart, and she looked so pretty—I thought my heart was going to just melt out of my chest. So when Chaz kicked us out to go to sleep, I asked if she wanted to go talk by the pool, since we were wired. We put our feet in the water, and I told her that all I could think about while watching her do her perfect oratory was how badly I wanted to kiss her."

Everyone at the table is looking at us like we're in a Hallmark movie. I want to wriggle out of my seat and run into the ocean, because being eaten by a shark would be preferable to the combination of shame and embarrassment that is currently choking me.

Seth chuckles, as if he is telling this story at the rehearsal dinner for our wedding. "And do you remember what you said, Molls?" he asks, staring pointedly into my eyes.

Everyone waits, smiling.

I clear my throat, hoping I can get out the words.

"I asked you what you were waiting for."

CHAPTER 4
Seth

Molly is squirming.

Admittedly, making her squirm was my intention, but now I feel slightly bad for her.

I assume everyone at the table knows how things ended between us.

How she deleted her AIM account and holed up at her father's ski chalet all the way out in Vail, and I commenced a six-week crying jag and lost twenty pounds.

How she never replied to my emails.

How she avoided all our old haunts on college breaks.

How she basically broke my heart and then threw it into a garbage can in some random park for good measure.

At thirty-three, I should be over this.

And I am!

At least, I thought I was. But I wasn't expecting to see Molly ever again.

Marian, who is a doll, cries, "That is so sweet! You two were adorable."

"Not as adorable as you two were," I say back, with a smile.

Marcus throws one of his buff, former-quarterback arms around Marian. "Want to sneak in a dance before the entrées, pretty lady?" he asks.

I wonder if they are rekindling something this evening.

I hope they are.

They're both single. Neither of them can stop touching each other. If I had to place bets on who from our class might end up together someday, it would be these two.

Georgette and the Frenchman also excuse themselves, leaving Molly and me alone to either pick at our scallops or find something neutral to talk about.

I would ask her to dance—I'm a total dance hound—except I have dignity, and the vibe is a little excruciating, now that I've brought up the unmentionable. Especially because I can't stop looking at her hair falling over her shoulders in that dress.

I need to get away from her.

"I'm gonna go say hi to Jon," I say, rising. Jon is one of my best friends from high school, and we hung out all last night with his boyfriend, Alastair, and our other BFF, Kevin. So there's no pressing reason to greet him, other than not wanting Molly to sense that I still, inadvisably, seem to have a crush on her.

I thought she'd be relieved to see me go, but instead she grabs my sleeve.

"Hey," she says. "Um, before you go, I just . . . I wanted to tell you I'm sorry."

All arousal flees my body. I feel uncomfortable. Being pretend-nice while internally seething with resentment is a position of power. Being apologized to makes me feel like a victim. Like the pathetic boy who got his heart broken.

"For what?" I ask, trying very hard not to seem vulnerable.

"You know, for how things ended. For disappearing."

Yeah, I *really* don't like this. I wasn't courting pity. I was trying to shame her for being a rat. Those are not the same thing.

Nevertheless, she still looks the way she did when we were alone together and she dropped that too-cool-for-school act.

I'm disturbed by how much I'm still touched by it.

I shrug. "It was fifteen years ago, kid. No worries."

She shakes her head. "It was shitty of me. I've felt terrible about it ever since. And I heard you were . . . not good for a while."

I lean back in my chair and stretch out my legs. I guess we're talking about this.

"I was pretty torn up about it for a minute." I spare her the details.

She nods, avoiding my eyes. "You might not believe me, but I was too."

She's right. I don't believe her.

"I kind of assumed you'd call, eventually," I can't help but say, probably because I've had four drinks. "Or write. Or like at least send a carrier pigeon letting me know you were alive."

She picks up her Parmesan twist and commences breaking it into quarters. It pains me. She's wasting good saturated fat.

"Yeah," she says. "That's what a normal person would have done. I can't really explain it. I was a jerk."

I don't believe that she has no better explanation than that. The truth is, despite her demeanor, she was never a jerk. She was sensitive, and she covered it up with cynicism. When she dropped her guard, she was so incredibly lovely.

"I don't think that's true," I say.

I expect her to dismiss me, but she takes a beat to consider this.

"I guess I was scared. We were going to schools a two-hour plane ride apart, and I thought you'd end up breaking up with me, and I couldn't deal with it. So I just snapped and ended things before they could get more intense."

It's a reasonable explanation. Better than me doing something awful to her I never knew about, or her not really loving me, or any of the other painful scenarios I brooded on over the years.

But it also seems like something she could have just told me at the time. A worry I could have hugged and kissed away, like I did so many of her other anxieties.

Whatever. I didn't come here to engage in retroactive couples therapy with Molly Marks.

I came here to slap backs and get drunk and maybe make out with a cute girl from the tennis team.

I need to change the subject.

"Look, Molls, no worries, okay? It's water under the bridge. Anyway, check out Marian and Marcus. I think they're in love."

"Wow," she says, eyeing the dance floor, where they are holding each other so tightly they may as well be one person.

In my capacity as an expert on relationships, I can say with authority that you don't dance that way to "Cheeseburger in Paradise" unless you are soul mates.

"I always thought they'd end up together," I say.

"Certainly seems like they will tonight. I'm not even sure they're going to make it to a hotel room."

"No, I mean I thought they would end up married or something. Look at them. You really don't think they're soul mates?"

"I don't believe in soul mates."

This throws me. Her movies are romantic and life-affirming. And in each one, an oddball finds their perfect match with someone equally odd and perfectly suited. I love her movies. They're funny and sweet and optimistic, but with an edge that gives you a glimmer of the wry sensibility of the person who wrote them.

(Not that it means anything that I've seen them both at least three times.)

I don't want to disclose how familiar I am with her IMDb page, so I just say:

"What! You're a rom-com writer who doesn't believe in soul mates? Unreal."

"Yeah, unreal." She leans back in her chair. "Exactly. Romance is a fantasy. This"—she gestures at Marian and Marcus—"sadly, is real life. And in real life, there are very few happy endings."

I refrain from suggesting she thinks this because she killed ours at an impressionable age.

"That's kind of cynical, kid," I say.

"I'm just reporting the facts. I'm an expert, right? Romance is a genre. It has a set of beats, like thrillers and detective novels. It starts at the meet cute and ends when things are finally going well. And as the writer, you hit the pause button there forever, leave the story in suspended animation. You don't show the part where he cheats on her, or she falls out of love with him, or their kids kill their sex life, or they die in a snorkeling accident on their honeymoon. You know? It's a fantasy. Just some stupid love story."

"God, that's depressing."

"Says the guy who destroys relationships for a living."

"Um, excuse me. Having presided over many divorces and seen many last-minute reconciliations, I happen to know that just because a relationship ends doesn't mean the love behind it wasn't real. Sometimes it just wasn't right. At this point I can tell when people are gonna reconcile, and when they need to go off and find their true love. Everyone is meant to find their person. Everyone is meant to have a love of their life."

"That's sweet," Molly says in a nice, dismissive tone—abandoning the all-consuming intensity of our conversation rather than conceding my brilliant argument. I can't even be annoyed because getting into it with her like that—like we're alone and the only thing in the world is our brains—has made me extremely nostalgic for when we were sixteen and obsessed with each other.

I roll my eyes at her. "Don't condescend to me, Marks."

"I'm not. It's nice that you think that. I just know you're wrong."

"Who hurt you?" I ask. I am completely kidding, but she winces.

Because someone did. Badly.

I shouldn't have said that.

"Let's just say I'm not cut out to be anyone's soul mate," she says.

Those words make me sad.

I don't know what to say.

She certainly wasn't cut out to be mine.

CHAPTER 5

Molly

Goddammit, Molly.

It is one thing to be brutally honest about my failings in my own head. But I try not to do it out loud.

At high school reunions.

To an ex-boyfriend who hates me.

What makes it even more excruciating is that Seth knows I'm right. He pities me for it. I can see it on his face.

"Sounds like you're pretty hard on yourself, Molls," he says quietly.

But I'm not hard on myself. I'm hard on the people who make the mistake of trying to love me. Because, unfortunately, I know how that ends.

"Marks!" someone yells from across the room.

It's Alyssa. Thank the universe.

"I'm just gonna go say hello—" I say to Seth, but he's already waving me off, like we were not just absorbed in each other. Like we were not just debating something more personal than the bullshit of rom-coms.

"Jon and Kevin and I have an appointment with some expensive shellfish," he says, gesturing to his two childhood best friends, who are standing in line for lobster rolls.

He waves at them. Kevin does a double take at the sight of me next to Seth.

I can't stand up fast enough.

I weave my way through the crowd over to the bar, where Alyssa is already ordering a San Pellegrino on the rocks with five limes. Her locs are piled on top of her head, giving her five-foot-ten frame an extra six inches of loft, and she's wearing a floor-length marigold wrap dress that sets off the gold undertones in her dark-brown skin and shows off her baby bump.

"Look at you," I squeal. I haven't seen her since before she got pregnant.

She puts a hand to her belly. "I know. Whatever happens, promise me you won't let me give birth on the dance floor."

"I don't know. If you do, I can steal it for a screenplay. Excellent set piece."

"How are you faring?" she asks in a low voice.

A guy she dated for ten minutes in tenth grade passes and high-fives her. "Go Flamingos!" he yells.

Alyssa was a track star. The pride and joy of our class.

"I'm losing my mind," I tell her. "Did you see who's sitting next to me?"

She smirks. "Yes."

"I'm dying."

"You look alive and well to me."

"Well guess what I'm going to do?" I say, flagging down the bartender. "I am going to get stinking drunk."

It is not difficult to make good on this promise. The tent is flooded with waiters circulating with champagne and, as the night goes on, trays of espresso martinis named—what else?—the Flamingo.

I conveniently skip the entrée to avoid filling my stomach with anything that isn't booze and, more importantly, to steer clear of Seth. I see him out of the corner of my eye, working the room, hugging nearly everyone he runs into, putting numbers into his phone, dragging people onto the dance floor.

He is so obviously happy that he seems to be singlehandedly lifting the serotonin levels of everyone in the tent.

Except mine.

"Hey!" Dezzie says, marching over to me and Alyssa, who has appointed herself my designated chaperone for the evening.

I'm actually not so drunk that I require adult supervision. My nervous adrenaline overpowers the alcohol. I feel like I'm on illegal stimulants, or at least Schedule II controlled substances.

"Come and dance with me, betches," Dezzie demands, holding out a hand to each of us.

"I am too preggo to dance," Alyssa demurs. "My ankles are like watermelons. And I have to call Ryland."

Alyssa's husband skipped the reunion to watch their two kids.

Lucky Ryland.

"I cannot dance," I say. "I simply cannot. For you see"—I point at the dance floor—"*Seth* is there."

"They exchanged words, and now she's a wreck," Alyssa summarizes on my behalf.

"A *wreck*," I emphasize, because I have consumed enough alcohol to lose all sense of proportion.

"Then come dance it out, honey," Dez says, grabbing my arm.

The DJ is playing hits from when we were teenagers, and it's a little bit hard to resist dancing to "Baby Got Back," even though I think it might be canceled. Dez throws her arms up in the air, dancing furiously, and before I know it, I am too. I discover that if I dance hard enough, and close my eyes tight enough, I do not need to worry about Seth Rubenstein.

A slow song comes on, and Rob materializes. "May I steal her?" he asks Dezzie, taking my hand.

Dezzie spins me into her husband's arms and grabs Alyssa.

"Come on," she urges her. "You aren't too pregnant to slow dance with me."

I put my hands on Rob's shoulders.

"Having fun?" I ask over the Céline Dion.

"This is a blast," Rob says. He's already drunk—he keeps lurching and throwing off my balance—but he's the infectiously jolly kind of drunk.

"Is it, though?" I ask, over the music.

"Yeah! I love your friends. Did you know Chaz is a professional comedian? He's gonna get me free tickets for his standup act next time he rolls through the Chi."

"Lucky you."

"And that hedge fund guy at our table was telling me he used to be secretly in love with Dezzie and was too shy to talk to her. Isn't that cute?"

"Yeah! She should leave you for him. He could buy her an island."

"I know! That's what I said. Oh, and I met those fun lesbians who live near you in LA."

"Gloria and Emily?"

"Yeah. And get this—they design film sets for movies."

"Uh, yeah. I know? Because we're neighbors? Like you said?"

"And I *love* Seth," he shouts, just as the song ends abruptly.

"Shut up," I hiss.

"What?" he asks with feigned innocence. "He lives in Chicago. We're going to get a beer when we get back."

"You know he's my ex."

"Yep. All the better."

"Traitor."

The DJ taps on the microphone. "And now a request and dedication to the lovely Molly Marks," he says in that goofy voice all DJs seem to have.

"Oooh," the crowd yells, every single person in the room knowing I hate any attention, especially the kind that involves dancing.

"Molls," Rob drawls. "You must have an admirer."

The iconic opening strains of "It's Gonna Be Me" by NSYNC blast out over the speakers.

I whirl around to Dez and Alyssa, who are laughing at me.

"Did you do this?" I shout over the music.

They shake their heads innocently. Alyssa gestures at me to turn around.

Seth is standing behind me, mouthing the words to the song.

He bends down on one knee. "May I have this dance, my lady?"

"You didn't."

He smiles, tickled with himself. "I had to. I *had* to."

This was the opposite of "our" song in high school. I loathed it so much that Seth would blast it in the car to annoy me when I was being a brat. I loathed it so much that he would make me dance to it when I was upset to channel my sadness into rage. I loathed it so much that he serenaded me with it every time we did karaoke, as some perverse mating ritual.

You know. Boyfriend stuff.

Seth grabs my hand and yanks me toward him. "C'mon, Marks. You gotta dance with me. It's tradition."

I have no choice but to follow him.

He catches me around the waist and brings me in closer.

"It's gonna be me," he bellows into my ear.

CHAPTER 6
Seth

I'm finally, *finally* over it.

After fifteen years of harboring low-grade resentment toward Molly Marks, I am now at peace. I feel light as a feather, if a little absurd for harboring a grudge for so long. But I forgive myself for that. I was holding space for pain.

After all, Molly was my first real love and she apologized, however badly, and I will likely never see her again after tonight, and I want to dance with her for old times' sake. To her favorite song.

Okay, maybe I want to torture her just a little.

The thing with chronically grumpy people is that sometimes they need to be tortured. Counterintuitively, it cheers them up.

Also, I've had a *lot* of Flamingos and I am *buzzing* with caffeine.

"This is cruel," Molly yells in my ear.

"Nope," I counter. "This is *fun.*"

I move her hips near mine—innocently enough distancewise, but with a rhythmic approach favored by horny teenagers at high school dances.

Mostly to troll her but also because, well. She's hot as fuck.

"Come on kid, put your hips into it!" I yell, shaking her shoulders into a shimmy.

"Gross," she yells back. But she obeys my command.

We are flesh against flesh.

"Do it for Justin," I whisper into her ear, putting my hand at the small of her back and spinning us around.

"Justin who?"

"Timberlake, baby."

She giggles, and I know I have won.

She's still the same as she was in high school. And I always intuitively got her in high school. We had instant chemistry—not just sexually but the intrinsic friendship kind, where you fall into conversation effortlessly and end up talking for hours.

Despite my long string of girlfriends, I haven't had a connection like that with anyone in a long time.

In a way, I still miss her. My Molls. My Miss Molly. My Marky Marks.

"Molls," I say, pulling her in a little closer.

"Yag?" (She might have said "yeah" but the NSYNC is *very* loud.)

"I'm sorry if I was intense earlier. I hope I didn't ruin the night for you."

She shakes her head. "I deserved it," she shouts.

I don't deny this.

"It's nice to see you," I shout back.

"It is, isn't it?" she mouths. I cannot hear her. I do not care.

Now that we've cleared the air, I want to dance.

I sing the bridge to Molly passionately while she leans away, laughing. I spin her around a couple of times, asynchronously with the music—just for fun.

By the end of the song, she's singing too. We're looking into each other's eyes, and our hips are now . . . dare I say it? . . . *grinding*.

It is fun and hot and when "Shake Ya Ass" comes on next she doesn't even attempt to get away. Instead, she commences booty dancing with me.

Is this happening? Is she rubbing her ass against my crotch and tossing her extremely long erotic hair in my fucking *face?*

She is, Your Honor. She is!

When the song ends we're winded, so I put my arm around her shoulders and lead her off the dance floor. "Let's get a drink," I say. "It's been at least twenty minutes since my last Flamingo."

We flag down a waiter and grab another round of deadly, caffeinated alcohol.

"Let's take a walk on the beach," I suggest.

I am no doubt pressing my luck. I brace myself for her to make her excuses and go moan to Alyssa that she accidentally enjoyed my company.

But she nods. "Great idea," she says. "It's so nice and balmy."

Kevin catches my eye from across the room and squints disapprovingly in the manner of an English nursemaid who has caught a child mainlining cake. He's friendly with Molly—they went to college together in New York—but he's protective of me.

Which is kind of him, but I don't need a hero right now; I need to kiss this woman who is clutching my hand and marching me off toward the ocean, whispering, "Come on. I want air."

I hope she means "I want *you.*"

I grab her hand and we stroll down the beach, stopping at the pier.

"Remember when we used to make out here?" Molly asks.

I play it cool.

"Yeah, totally. It's annoying that this beach has been discovered by tourists. Nowadays it takes an hour and a half to get here from town with the traffic."

"I know. My mom always wants to come here when I visit, but I refuse to compete with the tourists."

"Do you come back often?" I ask.

I do, but I've never run into Molly.

"Just once a year, if I can help it," she says. "I do Christmas here, and my mom comes to LA for Fourth of July."

I recall that she got very excited about the Fourth of July in high school. No matter how desperate things were at home, her mom would always host beach cookouts for their entire extended family. Molly moved through those parties with so much joy and confidence that she was hardly recognizable. I loved watching her like that—happy, uncomplicated.

"So no more beach parties?" I ask. It kind of makes me sad that the tradition no longer exists.

"They don't let you make bonfires on the key anymore," she says, shrugging. "And my mom got busy with her job and moved to the fancier part of the island, and my aunts and uncles are less enthusiastic about driving down here—they're getting older, you know? Plus the traffic."

Floridians hate traffic with a fiery passion—in part because our towns become overrun during high season with tourists and snowbirds whose driving skills are not at their peak. It is, consequently, a state prone to road rage.

I'm glad I now live in Chicago.

But I still like coming back.

"What's LA like on the Fourth?" I ask.

"Oh my *God,* Seth," she says, her voice full of something uncharacteristic, like excitement.

I too am full of excitement, because she has not called me by my first name in fifteen years. It literally sends tingles down my spine. *Seth.* It sounds like "sex," with a lisp.

"It's so beautiful," she continues. "It's the city's best holiday—everyone goes nuts with fireworks, and you see the whole valley exploding in these gorgeous lights from the canyons. I can't describe it. It's a little scary because, of course, fire risk and all the sonic booms echoing off the mountains, which make you feel like you're in the Blitz, but it's so full-body that it's almost sublime."

Apparently, it still turns me on when Molly is that rare thing: earnest.

"Are you a Los Angeles July Fourth evangelist, Molly Marks?"

"I guess I am. It's this pure, magical night. You should come sometime."

She seems to take in what she said exactly in tandem with me—it makes her visibly gulp, and makes me sweat a little.

"I mean, you know," she says quickly, "you should visit LA for the Fourth sometime, not—"

"Yeah, I get it," I assure her.

"Not to be rude, it would just be weird if—"

"Molls," I say, taking her by the shoulders and lowering my voice. "I get it. You're not inviting me to come stay at your house for Fourth of July. It's okay. I'm not offended. I'd rather visit you over Thanksgiving anyway. I make incredible pumpkin pie."

She relaxes.

And then we are standing in the moonlight, on a gorgeous beach, and I am holding her, and she is looking into my eyes, and she is so beautiful.

I know what I have to do.

It's the law, and I am an officer of the court.

CHAPTER 7

Molly

Slowly, Seth leans in.

Slowly, I step forward and put my lips to his.

And then 2002 takes over our bodies.

Seth knows exactly how to kiss me. Or perhaps he just invented the model, and now it's the standard by which I judge all other kisses.

Either way, he pulls me into him, wraps his fists in my hair, and jerks my neck a little bit—which is the end for me.

For such a sensitive guy, he was always surprisingly dominant in "bed"—or more literally under piers, in the backseats of cars, and in empty guest bedrooms at friends' house parties.

Manhandling works on me. It forces me to be, as my therapist says, "present."

To this day I keep my hair long so guys can pull it the way Seth used to.

I go at him hungrily, and before long we collapse onto the sand. This is bone-white, fine-as-sugar barrier island sand, so it immediately makes a film over our bare skin and lodges into our clothes.

We don't care. We are consuming each other.

"Wait," I gasp, coming up for air. He instantly stops the pleasurable—extremely, intensely pleasurable—thing he is doing with his fingers, which are underneath my panties.

"This is literally illegal. You're a lawyer. You could be disbarred."

"It might be worth it," he says hoarsely.

I sit up. "Hotel," I say. "We need to go to the hotel."

"Molly Marks"—I can hear the Flamingos in his voice—"are you inviting me to your room?"

"Use it or lose it, Rubes."

He hops to his feet (impressive core strength) and reaches a hand down to help me up.

"Do I look like I just did hand stuff on the beach?" I ask, trying to brush sand out of my hair—which is now tousled into knots from all the delectable pulling.

"Yes," he says. "But don't worry. It's late. Everyone will be too drunk to notice."

We slip back to the tent and walk around the perimeter, in the shadows away from the bar, and call an Uber.

"Couldn't take it anymore," I text Dezzie and Alyssa as we pull away. And that's kind of a lie, but kind of the truth.

I can't take any more sexual tension.

We make out all the way back to town.

CHAPTER 8
Seth

It will come as no surprise to you that I enjoy *making love*.

Give me some tender eye gazing, some Sade in the background, some massage oils, and I am a happy and sexually aroused man. (Just kidding about the Sade part. Let's be honest; I prefer the more intimate soundtrack of the breath.)

I'm sentimental, I know, but it's also a taste borne of practicality. The ability to have slow, present sex with someone without bursting out laughing is a good litmus test for whether you might fall in love.

But I don't want to *make love* with Molly Marks.

Tonight, I have more of a horny teenager energy.

I have two-virgins-desperate-to-finally-have-the-privacy-to-*do-it* energy.

Which is where we left off fifteen years ago, the night she broke up with me.

But let's not think about that. Heartbreak isn't great for virility.

So no.

I do not want to light candles.

I do not want to indulge in leisurely foreplay. My cock straining against my pants in that fucking endless Uber ride back to our hotel was the foreplay.

Now I want to fuck this girl fucking senseless.

I pull up her dress and pull down her panties. She's so fucking wet.

"You okay?" I ask, because consent is sexy even when you are reliving your sixteen-year-old desperation lust.

"Get it in," she replies, producing a condom.

Reader, I get it in.

And it is good.

More than good.

It is more than good three times before we pass out.

I awaken in Molly Marks's hotel room, which smells like her perfume and the incredible scent of whatever she puts in her hair.

Molly is lightly snoring, which I find adorable.

This whole thing would be idyllic except for my shattering, *phantasma-gorical* hangover.

I get out of Molly's bed (Molly's bed!), call room service, and order the works, charging it to my room. I pilfer around in the minibar and find one of those $18 packets with four tabs of Tylenol. I take two for myself and put two out for Molly, along with a glass of cold water.

She doesn't stir.

I open the sliding glass doors and make myself comfortable on her balcony overlooking the bay while I wait for our feast.

It's not hot yet, and there's a lovely breeze. I close my eyes to do my morning meditation. (I do it every day, no excuses. Discipline is the essence of self-care.)

I hear the knock at the door for our breakfast, and Molly rouses as I go over to open it. She hides all but her squinting eyes under the covers as the server unveils our spread of eggs, pancakes, green juice, orange juice, bacon, and croissants, and pushes down the steaming French press.

I tip him generously, and he leaves with a smile.

I turn to Molly, also smiling.

She pulls down the covers to reveal her mouth.

She is not smiling.

"You're still here," she states flatly.

My extremely good mood leaves my body and hovers just above my head, fluttering, not sure if it it's safe to come back.

"Oh . . ." I say, worried I have deeply misread the room.

Was this supposed to be a one-night stand?

Can it be, if you've waited fifteen years for it?

Was I supposed to slip out under the cover of darkness on a girl I've known since we were fourteen?

"Sorry," I say with all the casualness I can muster. "I won't linger. I just thought you might want something to mop up the booze."

She closes her eyes and rubs her temples. "Sorry, sorry," she says. Her voice is froggy, like she smoked a pack of cigarettes last night. I would say it's seductive except I'm getting strong vibes that seduction time has drawn decisively to a close.

"No, it's fine," I say. "I'll get out of your hair. I'm just gonna steal a cup of coffee because my head is protesting the twelve Flamingos I pounded last night. It was great to see you . . . and stuff."

She sits up. "No . . . Hey, Seth, I'm sorry. That came out wrong. You don't have to go. Help me with these pancakes?"

I relax a bit but not entirely, because it seems like she's pitying me.

"It's okay, Molls. I want to get a swim in before I pack anyway. I'll leave you to it."

She hops out of bed and walks to the closet to grab a long, hippieish robe that is so Los Angeles it recontextualizes her into the adult she is now, rather than the girl she still is in my mind.

Wait, that sounds creepy.

What I mean is that I know her through the lens of my memories. I don't have the slightest idea who she's become.

I'd love to get to know her.

I doubt, from the brisk way she cinches her robe, that it's mutual.

I really should go. I do possess pride, and she's damaged enough of it for one lifetime.

I stand up and grab my wallet from the dresser.

"Sit down, Rubenstein," she orders. "I can't eat five hundred dollars of room service alone."

"Don't worry, it's on my tab," I say.

"I'm not worried. I'm a lauded and well-compensated screenwriter. Sit down."

I sit down without further protest, because I am so fucking hungry that I'd rather eat than preserve my dignity.

"How *did* you end up a screenwriter?" I ask. "I always thought you'd be a lobbyist or a professor or something."

She was so *serious* in high school.

"I'm full of mystery," she says, piling scrambled eggs onto her plate.

Apparently, she doesn't intend to say more.

"Seriously," I prod.

"Well, I majored in communications, because I wanted to be White House press secretary. You know, a normal thing eighteen-year-old girls want." She laughs at herself a little. "But I had to take a couple of creative writing classes for my major to graduate, and I was really good at it. So I decided to do a screenwriting MFA."

"Why screenwriting?"

She dumps a huge blob of ketchup onto her eggs.

"Because screenwriting is more lucrative than toiling away at a literary masterpiece, and I like money."

"Strategic," I say. "But why rom-coms?"

In high school she could not abide the slightest whiff of anything romantic. She wouldn't even watch masterpieces like *Titanic*. She liked to cuddle up on the couch with popcorn and watch *Frontline*.

"They were way more popular, when I started, and easier for women to break into," she says. "And I wanted to write stuff I could sell. Plus, you can bang them out quickly because they all have the same arc and use similar tropes. It was just practical."

"You sound somewhat dismissive of your own genre."

And dissonant with the girl she used to be. Molly's interests were never "practical." She liked listening to Rufus Wainwright and debating the existence of trickle-down economics and reading slim volumes of Edna St. Vincent Millay.

"I'm not dismissive. I think rom-coms are an undervalued reflection of our culture. The conventions are a narrative vehicle reflecting the fantasies and anxieties underlying, you know, the primal biological will toward finding a mate."

"Oh, like, a *soul mate*?"

She groans. "Not this shit again. I mean the impulse to reproduce one's genetic material."

"It's not shit, it's true love. And it's what you're selling, isn't it? Soul mates? You must on some level find the idea attractive if you've devoted your entire career to it."

"What I find attractive is exploiting the inherent human desire for connection for profit. It's a job. I'm good at it. End of story."

I don't buy it.

"You're so full of shit, Molls. God, I can't believe I'm hearing this."

"Excuse me?"

She looks mad.

I guess we're not at so restored a level of closeness that I'm allowed to call her out.

Apparently, this is the part of her high school schtick she's still hanging on to: finding love corny.

I happen to know she actually doesn't.

I'd bet my life on it.

But for now, I'll bet something else.

CHAPTER 9

Molly

Seth looks very hot when he's provoking me. I'm torn between wanting to kick him out of my room and wanting to grab his hand and put it under my robe.

But I can't do that because I'm already soaked in shame that I slept with him.

Not because the sex was bad—it was, um, fantastic—it just feels like he wants this a little more than I do.

He always has.

"If you really believe I'm so wrong," he says in a lawyerly voice, "and true love is not real, and soul mates are Hollywood bullshit, then prove it."

He's sitting at full attention, knocking his knife against the table like this is very serious business rather than awkward posthookup conversation between two people who are never going to speak to each other again.

"Prove it how?"

"Let's make a bet. See who knows more about relationships: the romance writer or the divorce attorney."

"And how would we do that?"

"With evidence. Five couples, five years. We both predict who will stay together and who will break up. We'll meet again at our twenty-year reunion and see who was the most accurate. If it's you, I'll admit true love is a fantasy. If I win, you admit soul mates exist."

"You're just trying to get me to come to the next reunion."

He considers this.

"Well, I did enjoy fucking you."

Dear God.

"What?" he asks, watching me squirm. "You didn't like the sex?"

"I did," I concede weakly. "So much that it's annoying. *You're* annoying. Were you this annoying in high school?"

"Yes!" He grins at me. "C'mon, Marks. Are you scared you'll be cowed by my superior insight into relationships?"

I'm not cowed. I just feel discombobulated by the fact that my high school boyfriend is sitting across from me, the image of a successful, fit, confident professional, wearing no shirt (with thick, manly chest hair he did not have the last time I saw him in such a state), talking to me as though we are adults who just had sex. Really *good* sex.

I don't know why I'm surprised. We always had chemistry. But there's the kind of chemistry you have when you're grinding in someone's parents' guest-house during a rager—the kind of chemistry you have when you're trying to find furtive places to hook up, and every hour of not feeling each other's skin is a frantic torture—and then there's this.

This is . . . mature. Adult. Playful. Knowing.

It's like the meet cute in a rom-com.

Except I don't believe in rom-coms.

I learned at an early age what happens to so-called happy endings.

But I do believe in my ability to read people. When you write the tropes of romance, you can see people replicating them in real life. They can't help it. They breathe these narratives in with the air.

But people are not characters created in a lab to be perfect for each other.

As someone who studies these things for work, I can look at a couple and see the needs they can never possibly meet in each other. The irreconcilable wounds that will drive them apart.

I can see how it will end.

I'm not saying I *like* knowing this. I'm just saying if I could write my friends' relationships for them, I would.

So accept his bet?

No problem.

I could win it in my sleep.

"Fine. Five couples, five years. We each get a point for every couple we're right about."

"Deal," he says.

"Since I clearly have the advantage, you can pick the first couple."

He taps his lip, thinking.

"Marian and Marcus."

"What's your prediction?"

He laughs. "Are you kidding? They're obviously in love. They have been since we were teenagers, and the way they were dancing last night—I think they finally know it. I think that when we see them again in five years they'll be married with kids."

I don't buy it. Nostalgia for a high school relationship is not the same thing as compatibility. See: us. Seth is mistaking the second-chance romance trope for a real rekindled relationship.

"Nah," I say. "At best, they might date long-distance for a minute, but they won't end up together. She needs someone with a bigger personality. Besides, Marian is a planner. If marrying Marcus were part of her plan, she would have done it already."

Seth pulls out his phone and starts typing. "Marcus and Marian," he murmurs. "Rubenstein for, Marks against." He looks up at me. "Your turn to pick."

I go for one I know I'm right about. "Dezzie and Rob. They'll still be together. Those two are going to die an hour apart in the same bed when they're ninety-nine, squabbling after making passionate love."

Something dark flashes over his face. "I'm not sure about that."

"What? You're the one who believes in true love. Even my calcified heart can see that if anyone has it, it's them."

He winces. "Don't get me wrong—they're both lovely people. I just got a strange vibe from Rob. He was drunkenly flirting with everyone in the room last night. Actually, now that I think about it, so was she."

"That's just what they're like," I protest. "It's like a game to them."

He shrugs. "Sometimes games wear thin. Opposites attract, and they seem so similar they might combust."

I'm offended on behalf of my friends.

"They most certainly will not. Opposites attract is a tired old romance trope. In real life, people are drawn to human beings like themselves. Have you ever noticed how longtime couples begin to look alike?"

He literally guffaws. "Yep. And Dezzie and Rob look nothing alike. Did you see what they were wearing? My God."

Before I can point out that they are still in their early thirties and have plenty of time to age into one another's clones, he's tapping his phone.

"Anyway, that's two," he says. "My pick. I'm going for Alyssa and Ryland."

This one feels easy as well. "They stay together," I say. It would be unsporting of me to predict that my friend's relationship will fall apart, but in this case I really, truly believe that Alyssa and Ryland will outlast us all.

Seth raises his brows at me. "You're awfully optimistic for someone who purportedly believes that love is a mass delusion."

I shrug. "I didn't say it *can't* exist. I just don't think it's fated. And most of the time, it doesn't last."

He takes a sip of his green juice. "I think you're less cynical than you think you are."

"I think you don't know much about me."

"I think I know a *lot* about you."

"Because we dated fifteen years ago?"

"Yes. You still have the same world-weary affect protecting a vulnerable emotional core."

"Nope," I say, snatching a piece of bacon off his plate. "My emotional core is dead. Anyway, Alyssa and Ryland. What's your prediction?"

"They stay together. Obviously."

"Well does it count if we both think the same thing will happen?" I ask.

"No," he says. "Who's next?"

I don't know many of the people in our class well enough to prognosticate on their relationships, so I go with Gloria and Emily.

"They'll break up," I pronounce. "Probably soon."

He looks at me like I'm a murderer.

"Oh my God. No way. They're beautifully compatible. And do you see how they look at each other, with that gleam? We should all be so lucky."

I shake my head. "You don't know them as well as I do. Emily wants a baby. Gloria's going along with it for now, but the idea of being a parent obviously freaks her out. She doesn't even like having a dog. I don't think they'll get past it."

Seth looks at me like I'm delusional. "Gloria seems like she'd do anything for Emily—hence the dog. And it's not unusual to be ambivalent about parenthood. They'll work it out. You're being cynical again. And mean. Aren't they your friends?"

"I'm not being mean. I'm trying to win a bet. And you're wrong."

"No, I'm not. I can *see* these things, I told you. I just catch a vibe and I know: soul mates, or not soul mates."

Well if he's counting on magic, I am definitely going to win. And I like winning.

"Fine. Put it in your phone."

He tap, tap, taps away.

"I choose the next one," he says. "Jon and Alastair."

I would protest that this isn't fair, as Jon is one of Seth's oldest friends, except I pulled the same trick with Dezzie. And besides, I know who Jon is in love with, and it's not Alastair.

"No way," I say.

He looks up from his phone, surprised. "No way?"

"Yeah. Jon's been in love with Kevin since we were sixteen. I don't know if the two of them will get together, but I do know that Alastair's not going to last, given the way Jon was looking at Kevin last night."

Seth looks dumbfounded. "That's actually a rather romantic take. Offensive, but romantic."

"Offensive? What could you possibly mean?"

"I mean that just because they're friends and they're both gay, you think they have to be in love."

"Um, no. That is not even remotely what I'm saying. I'm still in touch with Kevin. And he mentioned Jon like eight times when I said I was coming to this."

"If you insist, Marks," Seth says. "You're wrong though. Jon's thinking about proposing to Alastair."

"Well, I would say it's unethical to use insider information to rig the bet, except a lot can happen in five years, and I'm absolutely certain I will be right in the end."

He types our predictions into his phone.

"Want to pick the last one?" he asks.

I do, but I wasn't paying enough attention to any of the other couples last night to have a strong read on them.

"Go ahead," I say.

He smiles devilishly.

"Me and you."

CHAPTER 10

Seth

If you have never experienced a gorgeous, half-dressed woman flicking a giant forkful of ketchup-drenched scrambled eggs at you, you're missing out.

The only bad part is picking the egg bits out of your chest hair.

I try to appear stern as I perform this elegant maneuver, but it's difficult, as Molly is so pleased with herself that she is literally crying with laughter.

I suppose this is my karmic punishment for playing her all that NSYNC.

"You think you're very funny indeed, don't you, Miss Marks," I say, dabbing my napkin into my water glass.

"That's what you get for trolling me."

I shake my head gravely as I sponge the ketchup from between my nipples.

"I'm not trolling you. Place your bet."

She rolls her eyes. "Seth, I hate to devastate you all over again, but this is the first and last time we're having sex. Enjoy the afterglow."

"I don't know about that, Molls. I have more condom . . . ments." Like the great dad jokers before me, I waggle a tiny jar of jam and a mini bottle of Tabasco at her.

"Don't make me throw more eggs at you. I'm running out."

I slide my plate across the table. "You can have mine."

"Okay!" She immediately dumps them onto her plate and splats more ketchup over them. "Anyway, this will never happen again. Sorry."

"And why is that?" I ask through a mouthful of croissant.

"Because you kind of hate me, and I kind of deserve it."

She's maybe a little bit right. But admitting it is not the point of this exercise.

Provoking her is.

"I don't hate you!" I protest. "And you don't deserve hatred. Well, possibly you do. Do you have a sideline in serial killing or design those tiny airplane seats or something?"

She smiles at me. "Both."

"I can forgive you. At least for the murders."

She leans back in her chair and crosses her legs, so that one thigh emerges from her silky robe.

"That's actually the problem with us, Seth."

I lean back too, aping her posture, and cross my arms. "What's the problem?"

"I broke your heart too young. I'll always be the one that got away. You'll never really get over me. So we couldn't date even if I wanted to, which I don't. The power dynamic would be too lopsided. You'd always love me more."

I can't tell if she's kidding.

"What a poignant monologue. I might cry."

She nods solemnly and licks ketchup off her fork. "Yum."

"You are so gross."

"You like it."

(I do.)

"Anyway, don't be sad," she says. "I'm sure you'll find some poor woman you can trick into marrying you eventually. Can you pass the salt?"

"You are in an astonishingly good mood this morning," I observe. "And I think I know why."

"Because the reunion is behind me."

"Nah. You always got uncharacteristically chipper after I gave you an orgasm. You're happy cuz I fucked you senseless."

She throws back her head and laughs. "You have a very high opinion of your sexual prowess."

"You also have a high opinion of it, if I'm not misremembering last night."

"Charming."

"Anyway, we're obviously sleeping with each other again at the twenty-year reunion. That's my bet."

"You think I can't resist you?"

"I think you're going to be my date."

She smiles at me with exaggerated pity. "No, I'll probably be there with my hot boyfriend."

"I'm probably going to *be* your hot boyfriend."

She laughs. "You're funny."

"I agree, but in this case I'm not joking. You see, I'm prime boyfriend material. Emotionally available and well-adjusted and open to commitment. But you, very sadly, are damaged. Because you never got over *me*."

I don't actually believe this part. I'm merely playing her game. The way she would take the negative and I'd take the affirmative in speech and debate, and we'd argue until our faces were blue about things we didn't really care about.

"And what makes you think that?" she says. "The fact that I haven't spoken to you in fifteen years?"

I giggle. It's so mean it's adorable.

"You're very cruel," I say. "And you take such delight in it."

"I know. You really want to date a wicked, self-amused woman?"

"Oh, Molly. You poor thing. I didn't say I *wanted* to date you. I'd be doing it as an act of charity. A mercy case."

She slurps down some coffee she's put so much milk and sugar in that it's basically tiramisu.

"And what is it you pity me for, that you would extend me such magnanimity?"

"Well, darlin', I'm obviously the nicest boy you've ever known. Our magical night together is going to rekindle your feelings for me. You'll remember what it's like to feel something. You'll go home and pine. Drag out your high school yearbooks and read my notes to you. Beg your mom to send you pictures of us from homecoming. Eventually, you'll get so desperate you'll show up at my door and plead with me to take you back. And because I am a generous soul, and I want to afford you some dignity, I'll agree to go out with you. Just long enough for you to have a date for our high school reunion."

"And then what?"

I smile, take her hand, and kiss her knuckle. "I'll break your heart."

She rolls her eyes at me, stands up, collects my shirt off the floor, and drops it in my lap with two fingers. "Okay. Breakfast is over. See you in five years."

I dress, kiss her on the cheek, demand that she give me her contact info, and make my way back to my room, humming.

When I get there, I can't resist writing her an email.

> From: sethrubes@mail.me
> To: mollymarks@netmail.co
> Date: Sun, Nov 11, 2018 at 9:54am
> Subject: You're welcome
>
> Hey Marks—
>
> Good to see you and know you biblically last night. Since I know you're a person of little integrity, here are the terms of our bet. No weaseling out of it, my slippery beauty.
>
> By the way, I still have sand in my teeth.
> —Seth

I paste in the list of our wagers, hit send, and begin packing up. It's not until later, when I'm at my parents' house, that I get a response.

> From: mollymarks@netmail.co
> To: sethrubes@mail.me
> Date: Sun, Nov 11, 2018 at 12:56pm
> Re: Subject: You're welcome
>
> Wow Seth, you really could not WAIT to email me. You know emails are time-stamped, right? Anyway, I'm glad the sand is in your teeth and not, like, your urethra.
>
> See you in five years!
>
> xo
> Molls

PART TWO
December 2018

CHAPTER 11
Molly

"We're here!" Dezzie calls as she lets herself in through the kitchen door of my mother's huge, vulgar mansion.

"Desdemona!" my mom says, rushing to embrace her on a cloud of jasmine perfume, trailed by the silk swirls of her flamingo-printed caftan. "You look stunning as always."

Dezzie's wearing a severely low-cut black one-piece bathing suit under a sheer cream linen dress. Her only nod to the fact that this is a Christmas party are her shoes, a pair of towering crimson espadrilles. Rob, by contrast, is sporting reindeer swim trunks and a Santa coat, complete with a bulbous belly.

"Merry Christmas, Miss Marks," he says, setting a box of Dezzie's elaborate Christmas cookies and a huge bag of liquor down on the kitchen island. "I brought ingredients for my famous polar punch."

My mom gives him a kiss on the cheek and hands him a cut-crystal pitcher. "Mix it quick. Alyssa just texted Molly that they're almost here."

Every year on Christmas Eve afternoon, Dezzie, Rob, Alyssa, Ryland, and their kids gather at my mother's house for a cookout. Ryland grills steaks and veggie burgers, Dezzie brings fancy desserts, my mom buys the kids a sickening number of presents, and Rob hands them out in a tropical Santa costume. At sunset we pile into my mother's eighteen-foot speedboat, and she captains us across the bay to the marina, so the kids can see the sailboats decked out in holiday lights.

It's a capitalist fantasy come to life, and one of my mother's great joys of the year. Given that I am her only child, she is bitterly divorced, and I have not provided her with grandchildren, she likes to spoil my friends with her great stores of affection and material wealth.

"Punch?" Rob asks, holding out the pitcher. I decline, knowing this concoction is mostly Captain Morgan with a dash of Sprite and maybe a thimble of cranberry juice. I'm not trying to get torn up for a kids' party and fall off my mom's boat.

Rob shrugs and chugs a glass of it.

"Jesus, slow down. It's eleven a.m.," Dezzie says, taking the glass.

"Santa has to stay toasty up in the North Pole," Rob says, waggling his eyebrows.

Outside, there is a bloodcurdling shriek.

"The kids are here!" my mom says.

She throws open the door, and Frankie and Amelia run in, passing all of us in favor of jumping on Rob. "Uncle Santa!" they cry.

Ryland is close behind them, juggling a stack of presents. "Whoa, guys, slow down," he says. "What did we talk about? Don't break Aunt Kathy's house."

My mom waves this away. "Oh, they're fine. How are you, darling?"

"Fantastic, now that I've seen you." He shoots her his killer smile—at once charming and sincere, like it emanates straight from his heart. She practically swoons. Not even Kathy Marks can resist his striking good looks—olive skin, expressive eyebrows, and just the right amount of stubble.

He looks over his shoulder. "You good, Lyss?"

Alyssa's walking toward the house very, very slowly with a hand on her belly, which is even bigger than Rob's.

"Don't worry. I'll be there in twenty minutes," she calls.

Dezzie and I rush out to meet her. She looks amazing, her skin all glowy from hormones or the Florida humidity or the effort it is taking her to walk.

"Look at you!" Dez cries.

"Yep. Fourteen months pregnant."

"Mama, come *on*," Amelia yells, sticking her head out the door indignantly. "Santa's here."

The next six hours are a flurry of Christmas-scented chaos as the kids open presents and the adults try to keep them from diving to their deaths at sea. It isn't until we get back from the marina, and the kids pass out in the guest room, that the adults get a chance to catch up in peace.

"So we have some news," Rob says. He's been steadily working his way through the polar punch and seems a little on the tipsy side.

Dezzie gives him the side-eye. "Hey. Don't—"

"Oh, come on. We're all family here." He raises his glass in the air. "Ms. Chan here and I are officially trying to get pregnant."

"Aww, guys!" I say. "That's amazing."

Dezzie and Rob have wanted kids forever, but they've been waiting for him to finish his master's in social work first.

"You should follow their example, Molly," my mother says. "Some of us aren't getting any younger."

"Um, I'm single?"

"Let's work on that," she says. "Do you all know any nice men?"

This question surprises me. My mother has never given me shit about my spinster status before. Given her own romantic history, I thought she was relieved I've never shacked up with anyone.

But actually, she's been acting funny all week. She keeps wandering off to take mysterious phone calls and coming back all distracted. And when a massive bouquet of holiday roses arrived, she snatched the note before I could read it and would only say it was from "a client."

Either she has a disease she's not telling me about—which seems unlikely, as she's in very high spirits—or she has the unthinkable: a crush.

"We don't know any single guys anymore," Alyssa says. "We've somehow become those people who only have parent friends."

"Well, Seth says hi," Rob says impishly.

"Seth?" my mom asks.

"Rubenstein," Dezzie says.

"Seth *Rubenstein?*" my mother repeats, like she's said something ghastly. "Well there's a name I haven't heard in a while. Whatever became of him?"

She never warmed up to Seth. We dated during the worst years after her divorce, and she thought we were too serious too young. That he would either get me pregnant or break my heart.

She was relieved when I broke up with him before he got the chance to do either.

"He lives in Chicago," Dezzie says. "Molls didn't mention we saw him at the reunion?"

Mom gives me the eye. "She did not."

"They had a nice, long *chat*," Alyssa says. "Didn't you Molly?"

"You didn't!" my mother yelps, because Alyssa is evil, and my mother is not dumb.

"No!" I lie. "We just caught up. And get this: he's a divorce attorney."

She narrows her eyes into slits. "He *isn't*."

"Yep. A partner at some big firm."

"See. I was right not to trust him," she says. "To think he could do that when he saw what happened to you."

I don't disagree that it's kind of a weird life choice, since I was a walking case of divorce trauma for four straight years. But whatever. Seth's career is not my business. Even if I have thought about him a somewhat alarming number of times since we saw each other.

A very small part of me was tempted to email him to ask if he was going to be here this month. But I don't want to give him the wrong idea about our trajectory. Bet or not, his assertion that we'll sleep together again implies he thought that night could be more than a fling—that he read it as a meaningful beat in a romance narrative that will have an ongoing arc.

It wasn't.

I don't fraternize romantically with nice people. I'm not built for it.

And I don't want to hurt him again.

Alyssa yawns, apologizes for yawning, and yawns again. "I think that's our cue," Ryland says. Everyone stands up and half an hour of hugs, last-minute asides, holiday wishes, inside jokes, and more hugs commences. When everyone's gone, my mom kisses me good night and goes up to bed.

I go to the kitchen and check my phone, which I left to charge while we were out on the boat.

There's a missed call and two texts from my father.

Dad: Hey tootsie.

(He knows I detest being called tootsie.)

Dad: I need a rain check on tomorrow. Call me.

I was supposed to go to his house at eleven for brunch with him and his (fourth) wife, Celeste. Canceling Christmas is ice-cold, even for him.

Not that this is surprising. He's the kind of parent you always have to call first (unlike my mom, who would happily call me five times a day if she thought I'd pick up), and the kind of human who thinks nothing of flaking on long-term plans, or, for that matter, marriages. He's been this way since I was a teenager, and for the most part I don't take it personally.

But blowing me off on the birth of our Lord Jesus Christ is a new one.

I don't call him back, because if I do, he will hear the dismay in my voice. Instead, I send him a text.

Molly: What's up?

There's a flurry of typing bubbles, which I guess is a compliment. Usually, it takes him days to reply.

Dad: Celeste is sick and I feel a little under the weather too—can't do tomorrow.
Dad: Let's try for drinks on the 26th instead.

Try for drinks? I am this man's only child.

Molly: I'm leaving on the 26th
Molly: My flight's at 8am
Dad: OK—I'll be in LA next month for meetings. I'll take you to dinner.

How lovely.

Part of me wants to call and yell at him to, like, at least *pretend* he is disappointed by this. But if he knows I'm angry, he'll just be defensive, and that will make me angrier, and I'll start crying, and hate myself for crying, and he'll tell me I'm being childish, and I'll hang up on him.

Speaking speculatively, of course.

So I just type "ok."

Dad: Merry xmas!

I don't reply. Suddenly, I'm gripped with anxiety. Nothing triggers me like my father's rejections.

I consider waking up my mother to commiserate with me on what an incurable asshole he is—her favorite subject outside of real estate prices—but then I'll end up ruminating all night.

I don't want to think about him; I want someone to hold me and make me forget.

Fuck it, I think.

I pull up my email and search for Seth's address.

> From: mollymarks@netmail.co
> To: sethrubes@mail.me
> Date: Mon, Dec 24, 2018 at 9:02pm
> Subject: Hey
>
> You in town?

CHAPTER 12
Seth

I am not in town. I am in Nashville, at my brother's house, with my family.

But I am very tempted to sneak out, charter a plane, and fly to Florida, just for the pleasure of replying to Molly Marks's email in the affirmative.

My brother Dave walks into the den, where I am holed up, attempting to assemble a tricycle for my nephew.

"Need help?" Dave asks, looking skeptically at the sea of bolts and screws and random shiny red metal bars scattered on the floor around me.

"I might just throw it away and write him a check," I say. "How much do you think? Five hundred?"

"He's *three*."

"All right. See if you can attach that wheel with that metal thing over there."

"The *Allen wrench?*"

Dave is a mechanical engineer. My lack of familiarity with tools pains him.

Within minutes, and with scarcely a cursory glance at the inscrutable diagram that passes for instructions, he has assembled the mini red bike, handlebar tassels and all.

"We should get some sleep," he says. "The boys will be up at five, and we can only hold them back so long."

I can't wait. I love Christmas here. We didn't grow up religious—my mom's a lapsed Catholic and my dad's a secular Jew—so as kids, the holidays were mostly about presents and latkes. But Clara, my sister-in-law, is a big Christmas person. She has three trees of varying themes, pays professionals to cover their entire house in twinkle lights, and hosts Christmas dinner for twenty.

I am not quite ready for bed, however.

I want to gloat.

"Hey, guess what," I say.

"What?"

"Molly Marks emailed me."

After we hooked up at the reunion, Dave told me I'd never hear from her again.

I enjoy it very much when he's wrong. Especially when the matter concerns girls I have crushes on.

His face immediately darkens. "*No.*" He shakes his head so vigorously it's like he's been possessed by the devil. "Delete it. She's not good for you."

The extremity of his reaction gives me pause. Objectively speaking, he's almost certainly right. But that's not enough to dampen my excitement. Molly's thinking of me. That means something.

"It's been fifteen years," I object. "You can't *know* she's bad for me."

"Yes, I can. She treated you like shit. She doesn't get a second chance after that."

His protectiveness is heartwarming, but I'm not convinced he's right. People can change.

"We were kids when that happened. I had fun with her at the reunion."

"And then she blew you off. A nice little reminder that she's still the same person."

"She didn't blow me off, she just said she'd see me in five years. Would it be *so* bad to just—"

"Okay, yeah, write her back. Hell, fly her out here. Get married by a justice of the peace on Christmas morning. I'm sure you two will be very happy."

I sigh. It is my opinion that he is not giving me, or her, enough credit.

"You don't get it," I say. "You have a wife and family and *love* and I have . . . lots of friends and a gym membership and a really big office at a law firm. I'm lonely. So why not take chances when they present themselves?"

He inhales long and deep, like we've already had this conversation two hundred times.

Which, of course, we have.

"Your problem," he says, "is that you think a woman is going to miraculously make you happy. You keep jumping into all these relationships, talking yourself into thinking you're in love when you're not. I'm tired of watching you get yourself hurt."

"Well, what do you suggest I do? Stop dating?"

"No. I want you to find someone. We all want that. But you act like love is going to solve all your problems, so you make bad choices. And Molly Marks? That's a bad choice."

I shouldn't have said anything to him.

I hold up my hands in defeat. "Okay. Point taken."

He nods warily and says good night.

I wait for him to close the door and then immediately pick my phone back up to exercise my allegedly terrible judgment.

> From: sethrubes@mail.me
> To: mollymarks@netmail.co
> Date: Mon, Dec 24, 2018 at 9:35pm
> Re: Subject: Hey
>
> Merry Christmas, Sir Marksalot.
>
> I'm in Nashville at Dave's with the fam. I take it you're in Florida, pining for me?

I can't stop grinning as I wait for a response, which arrives almost immediately.

> From: mollymarks@netmail.co
> To: sethrubes@mail.me
> Date: Mon, Dec 24, 2018 at 9:37pm
> Re: Re: Subject: Hey

Yes, desperately pining. By which I mean hoping you might be around for a quick bout of meaningless sex. Oh well, YOUR LOSS. Merry xmas etc

I'm sure she would be content to let our exchange end here, but I'm in too good a mood at the idea she wants to sleep with me again—even in a booty-call fashion—to let it drop.

From: sethrubes@mail.me
To: mollymarks@netmail.co
Date: Mon, Dec 24, 2018 at 9:39pm
Re: Re: Re: Subject: Hey

Someone is sure eager to lose our bet. Which, by the way, you are. Look what I came across on the socials from your best friend Marian:

> Marian Hart. . . . . is with Marcus Reis. . . . . at The Gulf & Yacht Club. . . . . Feeling bliss!!!
>
> What a lovely holiday season I had here in my hometown with such a beautiful group of friends and family. Basking on the catamaran with the one and only Marcus—is there anything like an island sunset with one of your favorite people?

Not to panic you, of course.

I press the send button, knowing her competitive nature will leave her powerless to ignore me.

From: mollymarks@netmail.co
To: sethrubes@mail.me
Date: Mon, Dec 24, 2018 at 9:41pm
Re: Re: Re: Re: Subject: Hey

You must be feeling very smug. But please remember I allowed they might briefly date before ultimately going their separate ways. I do have five years to be right. (Including about us.)

Enjoy your sex-free Christmas cheer.

Dave pops his head back into the room.

"You're doing it, aren't you?"

"Doing what?"

"Emailing her."

"Well, when a woman admits her desire for a late-night assignation, it's only polite to reply."

"Don't make me confiscate your phone."

"Respectfully Dave, fuck off."

He rolls his eyes and shuts the door.

But he's right.

I already feel that tingle of *what if* setting in. That obsessive part of me that meets a woman twice and starts naming our babies. If I embark on an extended email flirtation with someone I have this much history with—someone I still like so much—it will only get my hopes up. Despite my chronic optimism, even I know that I can't put myself in an emotionally vulnerable place at this time of year.

The Dark Times are coming. By which I mean: New Year's.

You might think that a person like me—a man known for his perennial pep—would rejoice at the start of a new annum. You would think I'd be a resolutions man. A "this year I'll run a seven-minute mile and climb Kilimanjaro" type of guy.

I'm not.

As a rule, I'm rarely depressed, but something about the start of the year bums me out. The dread begins around now and gets worse as we approach New Year's Eve, a holiday I find overrated and disappointing.

It could be a comedown from the holidays. Christmas at Dave's is always great, his unwelcome opinions on my love life notwithstanding. I roll around with the boys, douse them in presents, joke around with the fam, destroy everyone at UNO. And then I leave—always by the twenty-seventh, to avoid overstaying my welcome. And I go back to Chicago, which is invariably frozen, and I stare at the calendar and wait for the sadness to set in.

I am never as lonely as I am in the aftermath of being so happy.

On the surface, my life is packed to the brim. I have interesting work, a bustling social life, no shortage of women to date, and a calendar of sports and cultural events I keep full.

But it's full of the wrong things.

I want what Dave has. I want my own cute kids and my own smart, funny wife and my own loud, peanut butter-smeared house in the suburbs.

There were many years when this wasn't such an ache. When my law firm was my true north. Being an attorney was my dream from the time I was in junior high. I've built a reputation as one of the best family lawyers in Chicago.

But I'm bored. And worse than that: unfulfilled.

I keep finding myself wondering if I should be doing something different—volunteering, or making a lateral move, or even starting something of my own—and then I get too busy with work and too distracted by my quest for true love to pursue it.

I'm probably just frustrated. I have everything I want professionally. And once I have a family, work won't matter as much.

Besides, this feeling always fades by the middle of January, as work jolts back to life (the postholiday season is a popular time to file for divorce) and the Christmas lights come down and everyone gets back into the routine of existence.

I'm happy again. It's like magic.

But that week of comedown is brutal.

This year proves no different.

The tricycle is a hit with Max. My mother and I make an eighteen-pound turkey. Clara leads her full house of dinner guests in a caroling session, complete with printed songbooks and an accompanist from the music school at Vanderbilt.

I don't email Molly, even though I think about her.

But then I fly home, back to the tundra. I unpack in my pristine apartment. I turn on the gas fire to approximate some form of the cheer I just left, and it flickers like a mockery of my empty home.

I stay in New Year's Eve, dishonestly pleading exhaustion, and twist the knife by waking up in the morning and opening Facebook to peruse all the joyful times other people were having.

And that's when I see it.

A rare social media post from Molly Marks. It's dated from a few days ago, but it's not so old I can't use it as an overture.

I snap a screenshot and paste it into an email.

> From: sethrubes@mail.me
> To: mollymarks@netmail.co
> Date: Mon, Jan 1, 2019 at 11:09am
> Subject: Congrats!
>
> Hey Mollson—
>
> Happy New Year! I just saw your news. Congratulations—I loved her on Headlands!
>
> > BOXOFFICEGOSS.COM: Golden Globe winner Margot Tess attached to rom-com from producers 6FiftyX
> >
> > *Tess, who took home Best Actress in a Drama Series for her role as Rhathselda in the sweeping historical epic* Headlands, *has signed on to star in and executive produce* Daughter of the Bride. *The rom-com, about a woman searching for love at her own mother's wedding, was written by Molly Marks. Simon Larch is attached to direct.*

I should absolutely end this email here—keep it casual, let her either write back or not. But I'm happy for her, and I want to let her know that she deserves to be proud of herself. I suspect it's not a feeling she indulges in often. So I add:

> I have to confess something: after the reunion I went back and watched (okay, you got me, rewatched) your movies. I love how I can relax and not worry someone is going to tragically die and tear my heart out. And I can always hear your voice in them—that sarcasm that lets me know a foul-tempered wretch is responsible for all the happiness on-screen.

Congrats, champ. You're doing God's work.

Hugs.
—Seth

I hit send and then freeze.

Hugs? Why did I write that?

I spend a few minutes poking around to see if my email app has some sort of "I regret sending that please delete before the recipient sees" function, but no dice.

Oh well. Hugs!

CHAPTER 13
Molly

I wake up at 1:00 p.m. on the first day of this blessed year with a hangover and acute postparty anxiety. I brought in 2019 at Margot Tess's annual bash at her estate in Los Feliz. She's a big deal right now, and the crowd there was glitzier than the industry people I usually hang out with. Consequently, I networked my face off and am now a crumpled ball of emotional toilet paper.

My relationship with parties is complicated. I dread going to them, because I'm an introvert who prefers to spend her time alone or—once socially starved—with the same four to six close friends. But since so much of my job is reliant on networking, and social and business relationships are so intertwined in LA, I do have to force myself out of the house when the occasion arises.

And then, I'm like that guy from *The Mask*. I glam myself up and walk into a room and remember that I'm attractive and funny and good at banter. I dole out compliments, offer favors, introduce people, fetch cocktails, and collect numbers until I'm in a fizz of party energy and don't want to go home. I am the girl who ends up at the after-party bumming cigarettes and slinging take-it-to-the-grave gossip with the die-hards. By 4:00 a.m., I have eight new best friends.

But then—*then*—I wake up in the morning (or, in this case, afternoon) and second-guess every single thing that I did. Was it rude of me to introduce myself to that producer? Did my manic energy make me seem drunk, or crazy? And, oh God, what do I do with all these numbers I collected? Should I follow up with invitations to coffee or drinks? And what on earth will I do if my new acquaintances say yes?

I drag myself out of bed, grab a sugar-free Red Bull from the fridge (an unparalleled hangover cure), and settle myself on the couch to reread my texts from last night in hopes of remembering who I ensnared in my web.

Seven people. Sob.

I brace myself and check to see if I did any more damage by email.

Seth's name is at the top of my inbox.

I didn't expect to hear from him again after my deranged decision to contact him over Christmas. I open it, and it's a sweet message about my new movie.

I consider not replying. As someone who had no business contacting him in the first place, I really don't want to give him the wrong idea. But the gesture is so kind that I owe him at least a quick response.

From: mollymarks@netmail.co
To: sethrubes@mail.me
Date: Mon, Jan 1, 2019 at 1:45pm
Re: Subject: Congrats!

Thanks, Seth—that's nice to hear. My last couple of scripts have been trapped in development hell for years, and producers are pivoting away from original screenplays and optioning books instead, so this is the first big gig I've had in a while. I'm excited about it.

I consider deleting all this—my hangover jitters are making me a bit too sincere—but this is Seth, who is a thirteen out of ten on the sincerity scale, so I keep it, and just add:

You good?

xo
Molls

I close my inbox and move on to sending dreaded follow-up texts to my new friends and associates and eating soothing, delicious carbs.

I'm just about feeling normal, if tired, when I get a text from my father.

Dad: HNY toots
Dad: Saw your news re the movie. Not bad.

Not bad. I smile, despite myself. This, from him, is the compliment of the century.

No one is more dismissive of my career than my father. He thinks rom-coms are "fluff" and tells me I'm wasting my time with "indie bullshit" when I should be going after "the big stuff." He considers himself an expert on such matters because his books have been adapted into movies. Specifically, they've been adapted into a huge blockbuster film franchise that grosses hundreds of millions of dollars a picture.

I suppose here is where I should disclose that my father is Roger Marks. Yes. The guy who writes those sleazy potboilers about Mack Fontaine, the Florida private eye who's always catching serial killers in swamps and seducing hot blondes with dangerous pasts. The one whose books you've seen at every supermarket checkout line in the country.

Because of his status as a premier author of novels with one-page chapters and plots about exotic pet–smuggling rings, he also credits himself with my success as a screenwriter. He loves to tell me I get my talent from him, and to imply that the Marks name has gotten me where I am.

It has not. I'd rather die than name-drop Mack Fontaine, and my father is a narcissist.

But in my darker moments, I wonder if he's at least a little bit right about the talent part. It's possible I do get my best professional qualities—my creativity, my ease with words, my ability to be charismatic at parties—from him. And this worries me. Because if I've inherited his best qualities, there is a strong possibility I've also inherited his worst. His incurable sarcasm. His ice-cold approach to relationships. His ability to hurt people without even noticing.

I don't text him back. I'm already on edge, and engaging with him will only make it worse. Instead, I check my email to see if there's anything new from Seth. A hit of his optimism might level me out.

And there is a new message. But it's surprisingly lacking in perkiness.

From: sethrubes@mail.me
To: mollymarks@netmail.co
Date: Mon, Jan 1, 2019 at 6:52pm
Re: Re: Subject: Congrats!

Am I good? Well let's see. I'm at the office, even though it's 9pm on a national holiday.

Not by choice. I had dinner lined up with a buddy tonight, but he canceled this afternoon and I nearly wept. Well, not really. But it hit me harder than a rescheduled dinner should have. Probably because I'm not dating anyone at the moment and my friends are occupied with their families, which they have been busy creating while I have, despite my best efforts to find the human connection I crave, instead billed millions of dollars drafting ironclad prenups.

I need to get a life, Molls. I hear there's more to human existence than conference calls about custody hearings and eating extremely expensive takeout sushi at your desk.

This is not the Seth Rubenstein I know. He sounds despondent. Worryingly so. I don't even think about it. I just write him back.

From: mollymarks@netmail.co
To: sethrubes@mail.me
Date: Mon, Jan 1, 2019 at 6:55pm
Re: Re: Re: Subject: Congrats!

Poor lonely old man. You know, you can call me if you need a shoulder to cry on. It's only 7pm here, and I love miserable people.

555-341-4532
xo

My phone rings almost immediately. I hesitate for a second. Are we really going to talk on the phone? Like in high school, when we would have those long, emo chats that would go on for hours?

Probably not. I'll just say hi and make sure he's okay.

I pick up on the second ring.

"Wow," I say. "That was fast. Good to know you still have no cool."

"Molly Marks, have I ever once pretended to be cool?" There's a smile in his voice. A wry one I can picture. Good. He must not be as miserable as I thought.

"You're right," I say. "You've always been very honest about being a dork."

"Thank you."

There's an awkward pause. I'm not sure what to say. So I go with, "I'm sorry you're stuck at work."

"Oh, it's okay. I'd rather be here than at home. What are you doing?"

"Not much. Contemplating making pasta."

"I thought people in LA didn't eat pasta."

"Hungover people do."

He laughs. "Big night last night?"

"Huge."

"Was it at least fun?"

"Yeah, but all that socializing makes me jittery the next day. Plus, my anxiety is always worse around New Year's. I hate this time of year."

"I hate it too," he says. "All the pressure to start fresh and be better."

I am floored that Seth is not a New Year's person. You would think he'd be champing at the bit to practice mindfulness and give up sugar and sign up for marathons.

"I'm surprised you're not into it," I say. "But yes. Achievement fetishizing. Gag me."

"I like setting goals in other contexts. But there's something about doing it just because it's January that makes me grumpy."

The idea of him as anything other than sunshine and light is so novel it's adorable.

"I bet you're cute, all grumpy," I say.

Flirtatiously?

Should I be flirting? Is that wise?

I'm not sure what I'm doing. I'm not sure what this is.

"Not especially cute, I'm afraid," he says. "There's soy sauce on my shirt."

"There's probably a woman out there who likes that."

"Good, can you give me her number?" he says.

Uh, yeah. We are definitely flirting. I need to regroup.

"I bet you make resolutions anyway," I say. "Admit it."

He sighs. "Of course I do. You have to. Otherwise you have nothing to talk about at the office."

"Not me. My office is in my house, and it's currently littered in Hershey Kiss wrappers."

"I thought you didn't like chocolate."

He remembers.

"I don't, but Alyssa sent me a bag of 'New Year's kisses' because she pities my spinster existence. And hangovers make me hungry. Anyway, what are your resolutions?"

"You'll make fun of them."

I probably will.

"I promise not to."

"I don't believe you. But my attraction to your scorn is deeply ingrained."

It gives me no small measure of satisfaction to hear him acknowledge that I'm not the only one who's still attracted.

"Try me."

"Spend less time at the office. Find a girlfriend. Get married. Have a baby by thirty-six."

I whistle. "Damn. You have work to do."

"I know. It's crippling," he says.

"Maybe if you didn't pressure yourself so much it would be easier to just, like, live?"

"But I don't want to just live, Molly Marks. I want to suck the marrow from the bones of life and fulfill all my most mundane heteronormative fantasies."

It feels oddly intimate that he is disclosing this to me.

"Do you want me to show you how Tinder works?" I ask, trying to lighten things up.

"Oh, believe me, I know how Tinder works. I feel like I've dated every woman in Chicago. But they keep breaking up with me."

"I have trouble believing that," I say nicely, because he sounds sad.

"It's true. Dave claims I'm a serial monogamist who plows into doomed relationships because I romanticize love as a cure-all."

"Hmm," I say. I don't want to hurt his feelings, but this kind of tracks. "Do you?"

"I don't know. Every time I meet a nice gal, I get very excited. It always *feels* real."

I can't imagine this problem won't sort itself out soon enough. He's hot, rich, and good at sex. He's just had bad luck.

"Well, don't worry," I say. "You're an eligible bachelor. It'll happen. All that wifed-up stuff is easier for men."

"Is it?"

"It certainly is in LA. We ladies get put on the shelf young."

"Are *you* dating anyone?"

I pause before answering. I'm worried this conversation is getting too personal.

"No. I broke up with a guy a few months ago, before the reunion."

"Why?" he asks.

"Uh, I found out he owned a sword."

"Are you *serious?*"

"No. He was a boring careerist. I got tired of him droning on and on about his finance job."

Belatedly, I realize Seth also has a professional job, and might worry that I find *him* boring. Which I don't.

"I'm sorry it didn't work out," he says. "If you wanted it to."

"Thanks. I didn't. We were only together a few months. No big deal."

"Do you want to find someone? Like, get married and have kids and all that?"

I don't really think about it that much. I don't put much stock in relationships to dictate my future. But I guess, if some miracle happened, I wouldn't be opposed to it.

"Uh, maybe. If I found the right person."

It occurs to me that we're having a conversation about marriage and life plans. I need to back off.

"Um. Is this weird?" I ask.

"Is what weird?"

"You know, talking about our *feelings?*"

"I don't think so. It's nice."

"It's kind of intense, actually," I say.

"Well, you can hang up if you can't handle the heat, Marks," he says with a sharp laugh. "I know you sometimes have trouble finishing what you've started."

Whoa.

That was needlessly barbed from anyone I'm trying to be nice to—let alone *Seth*.

"Excuse you," I say, not hiding my offense. "What's that supposed to mean?"

"Just a joke."

But we both know it isn't.

"Really? It sounded like a dig."

"No, I was just referencing what you said at the reunion. That you're scared of intimacy."

"Wrong," I shoot back. "If I recall, I said I was scared of losing you in high school, so I broke up with you to avoid being hurt. That's not the same thing."

"Are you sure?"

I don't appreciate this Socratic method bullshit. If I wanted to be criticized, I'd have texted my dad back.

"Seth, I was talking about my behavior when I was a teenager. Are you really going to extrapolate that to who I am now, having interacted with me for about ten hours in the last fifteen years?"

Bizarrely, he doesn't back down.

"Remember how I'm a divorce attorney? And I deal with breakups eighteen hours a day? You're a type, Molly. You're a bolter. You get scared of feelings and run away."

I should hang up. This is not the light conversation I wanted to have with him.

"Do I have to pay you your hourly rate for this, counselor?" I ask.

There is a very, very long pause.

"I'm providing it pro bono because I like you," he finally says. His voice has gone soft. Almost tender.

I feel unsteady. I don't know what to do with this.

"You *like* me?" I repeat.

"So much, Molly."

"You know, I'm not terribly likable," I joke, because I don't trust myself to follow where this is going. "You could be forgiven for saying no."

"See, you're doing it," he says. "Deflecting. When the conversation gets earnest, you make a joke or some self-deprecating comment."

I know he's right, but I don't want to admit it.

"Maybe I just do that with you."

"I highly doubt it. You did it when we were teenagers. And it correlates with a personality type in a relationship. You probably check out when things scare you. Intimacy shuts you down."

What am I supposed to say to this? He likes me "so much," but he's criticizing me for how I act in relationships?

"Why are you being like this?" I ask. "I offered to keep you company. I'm not looking for a psych diagnosis. Believe me, I have enough of those."

"I'm sorry," he says quickly. "It's the lawyer in me, I guess. Can't stop arguing. I'm being a dick."

But that isn't quite it. None of this comes off as mean. It comes off as too honest.

"You're not being a dick," I say. "You're being awfully presumptuous about me though."

"You're right," he says. "I want to get to know you better."

Yeah, it's time to end this.

"Listen, I need to eat dinner and get some sleep," I say.

There's another long pause. Then he says, "Marks, you're abandoning me in my hour of need?" His tone is lighter. He obviously senses that he's freaked me out.

"What did you think you were getting?" I blurt without thinking. "Hours of phone sex?"

He lets out a shocked laugh. "A boy can dream."

My cheeks are red, and my eyes are shut so tightly that they hurt. "Sorry."

"Well, save my number in case you change your mind. It's good to talk to you, Molls."

"Uh-huh. Sweet dreams."

Sweet dreams?

Am I the most awkward person in all of Los Angeles?

I hang up before he can say goodbye.

I wish it wasn't too late to call Dezzie or Alyssa to dissect this conversation.

Although, if I tell them what happened, they'll think I'm obsessing and read into it.

Which . . . *Should* they read into it?

What am I doing, telling a man I somewhat recently had sex with to call me late at night when he's sad, if not suggesting there's something between us?

I *did* suggest it, tacitly at least, then backpedaled in terror when he acknowledged what was happening. Which is maybe why that stuff about my habit of bolting stung.

I console myself with pasta. A lot of pasta. The entire box of pasta.

I won't even get into the amount of wine I wash it down with.

Suffice it to say, enough to text him in the middle of the night.

Molly: I know it was my idea but I don't think we should talk anymore

I pause, and then type one more line.

Molly: sorry

There, that should settle it.

Usually when I make a decision, especially one involving a man, I am unequivocal. I break off relationships like a bodybuilder snapping a pretzel in half, and then I pop that pretzel into my mouth and savor the salt like I would the taste of his tears.

But this time, it doesn't work.

I lie awake, clutching my phone until my hand starts to ache, staring at my own text bubble.

I feel like I wrote the wrong thing.

Am I allowed to write something else after requesting cessation of contact? And if so, what do I say? *Sorry, Seth, you called it. Intimacy freaks me out! Please make yourself available for light banter only lest I panic and . . .*

And what?

What do I think I will do?

Well, exactly what he said I would.

Run away.

I can't help it. It's in my DNA.

I get up and put my phone in the other room where I can't stare at it or, worse, use it to text Seth something else. I pick up the eight-hundred-page Norwegian novel I'm slogging through and, thanks to the gods of mind-numbing Scandinavian autofiction, fall asleep within minutes.

I wake up to warm California sunlight streaming through the windows and feel good until I remember what I did. I force myself to get up and make coffee before I grab my phone off the charger.

There's a message from Seth. It's time-stamped brutally early in the morning, so he must have sent it as soon as he woke up.

Seth: Hey Molls. Don't be sorry—I get it. You were just trying to be nice and keep me company and I was totally out of line. I hope you don't think I was criticizing you or that I harbor ill-will over high school. I promise I'm not carrying a grudge.

Seth: The thing is, I think I might be carrying a torch. I really enjoyed our time together at the reunion and getting back in touch with you. I've thought about you a lot since we saw each other, and how much fun I had with you, and how beautiful you are, and how hot it was when we had sex.

Seth: I know it's juvenile playground stuff to antagonize a girl you like, and maybe that's what I was doing last night, and I'm sorry. If you want to try talking again, I promise to do nothing but flirt with you and tell you how pretty you are. But I hear you, and I won't bother you unless you tell me it's okay . . . at least not until I collect my winnings at our 20th reunion. Take care. —Seth

Trust Seth to be the type of person who writes entire perfectly punctuated paragraphs by text message, and signs them with his name like my mom. The nerdiness of his prose styling, however, does not stop me from doing a deep textual analysis of his every word.

It's the "carrying a torch" that gets me. It's got a nice ring to it—courtly with an ache of regret, like it's torn out of a Lyle Lovett song. There's a large, wicked part of me that wants to tell him to keep sending me softhearted paragraph-length texts about how lovely I am.

But his sweetness is the clincher. I'm just not nice enough for him.

I wish, for a moment, that I was. That I believed in the logic of rom-coms: that Seth could shore up my faith and sand down my rough edges, and

I could brace him with realism until we evolved into each other's missing piece.

But that's not how it works.

I send Seth one more message.

Molly: You're sweet. But I can't.

PART THREE
October 2019

CHAPTER 14

Seth

Is there anything like a cold beer in a thirty-dollar novelty cup at a baseball game? What is it about that translucent hard plastic that makes beer taste so much better? So *crisp.* So *fun.* So *American.* And not the bad, dog-whistle kind of American. The America's pastime, Fourth of July, peanut shells on the floor of the ballpark, type of American.

The only problem with novelty cups is the difficulty of carrying two of them, plus a giant tub of popcorn and a hot pretzel with extra mustard, back to the stands. Especially at a playoff game where everyone is screaming and stomping and jubilantly (or despairingly) bumping into one another.

I bid good day to the cheery concession stand worker, balance the pretzel over the popcorn, pinch two beers by the rim in my other hand, and begin my Herculean trek back to my seat.

I am lucky. It is a very, very good seat. Even though I am rooting for, some might say, the wrong team.

I am at Dodger Stadium, in Los Angeles, cheering on the Chicago Cubs in the seventh game of the National League Championship Series. Whoever wins goes to the World Series. It's the sixth inning. The game is tied, 2–2. I am losing my mind. I had to leave and get snacks so I don't have a stroke.

My seat is approximately thirty steps down a narrow staircase, so I'm panicking a little about how to maneuver past the throng of highly charged fans. I feel vulnerable yet proud in my Cubs jersey. I know Dodger fans will throw popcorn, or worse, at me as I descend. I need to be physically and emotionally prepared. I take a deep breath.

"Seth!" someone calls from behind me. I pause but do not turn my head, because if I do I will spill something, and besides, all the people I know at this game are down in our seats. Surely no one is talking to me.

I take a few more precarious steps, pretzel wobbling on its perch.

A finger taps my shoulder.

I slowly turn around to see my high school friend Gloria and her wife, Emily.

Somehow, *somehow*, I manage not to spill my haul of concessions on any passersby as I say hello.

"I *knew* it was you," Gloria said. "I'd recognize those ears anywhere."

My big stupid ears are indeed recognizable. And I just got a haircut, emphasizing my least comely feature. Which is fine, as I don't think my levels of physical hotness are particularly pertinent to two married lesbians. One of whom, I notice, is quite a bit pregnant.

"You're expecting!" I squeal. "Congratulations!"

Emily puts a hand on her belly. "Twin boys. Can you even?"

I can even, as they will be wonderful parents. And I cannot help but experience a small pang of vindication that they have bonded their union by starting a family—as it aligns with a bet I made with a certain woman who shall not be named.

"You two will *destroy* parenting," I say.

"Is that a good thing?" Gloria asks.

"So good," I assure her.

"What brings you here?" Emily asks.

"The Cubs, obviously," Gloria says, gesturing at my jersey. "This rat has the nerve to root for the enemy on our turf, and not even call to say he's in town."

"Horrible man," Emily agrees.

"I'm sorry!" I say. "I just got in this afternoon. I was going to text you, I swear. Do you think I *don't* want to hang out by your pool overlooking the canyons?"

"How do you know we have a pool overlooking the canyons?" Gloria asks. "Are you stalking us?"

"Yes," I say solemnly. "I actually live in a car outside your house. I have this telephoto camera that lets me see *right* through your windows."

"Good," Gloria says. "I was hoping for a reason to have you thrown in jail. Where all Cubs fans belong."

I laugh, and it throws off my balance. I grip the plastic of my novelty beers harder. I can't spill Coors Light on a pregnant lady.

"Who are you here with?" Emily asks.

"There you are," a voice says from over my shoulder. "Sorry, the bathroom line was eleven point two million people long. Also the sinks are crusted in blue face paint."

I careen around at the sound of that voice.

The pretzel flops onto my chest, smearing my shirt in mustard. I try to resettle it and the popcorn goes flying, raining down like edible confetti on myself and—who else?—Molly Marks.

"Fuck!" I cry. "I'm so sorry."

One cup slips, and I try to catch it, but instead bat it in the air, spraying all eighteen ounces over the clavicle, cleavage, and Dodgers tee of a woman who told me to stop texting her after I told her I had feelings for her.

Spectacular.

Molly stands there, shocked and silent, for about fifteen seconds. And then she looks down at the beer dripping into her bra, dabs a drop with her finger and delicately puts it to her tongue.

"Hmmm," she says. "Taste of the Rockies?"

"Oh my God," I moan, unsure what to do to help this situation, as my hands are covered in mustard.

"I would have pegged you for an IPA man," Molly says, dripping.

"They don't have it in the collectible cups," I say, wanting to actually weep.

"I'll go get you some napkins," Gloria says. She darts off toward the snack bar.

"Do you want me to help you wash off in the bathroom?" Emily asks Molly.

Molly laughs. "I'm afraid the public restrooms at Dodger Stadium are not equipped with showers. But it's fine. I enjoy smelling like the bar. It reminds me of my youth."

"Molly, I cannot apologize enough," I say. "I'm going to buy you a new shirt."

"Yeah, and maybe also yourself one," she says.

I look down at my mustard-stained torso. "Why is it that whenever I get near you I find myself smothered in condiments?"

"Oh, the mustard's fine. I was referring to your Cubs jersey. You'll be taking that off as your punishment for ruining my outfit."

Gloria returns with the napkins and hands them to Molly, who begins cleaning herself up.

"Don't worry about me," Molly tells her. "You'll miss the beginning of the seventh. Seth here is going to give me carte blanche at the Dodgers merch store. I'll meet you back at the seats."

"Seth, I'll text you," Gloria says. "We're having a baby shower on Saturday. If you're still in town you should come."

"I'd love to," I say miserably.

"Don't cry," Molly says with mock solemnity. "You're going to get through this. Come on."

She grabs my hand and starts leading me through the crowd along the curved walkway of the stadium toward, I assume, the gift shop. The intimacy of this gesture confuses me. Which is not to say I don't like it.

"So why are you here, anyway?" she asks.

"To watch the Cubs beat the Dodgers."

"No chance."

"Want to bet?"

"I don't gamble."

"Except on your friends' relationships."

She frowns. "I suppose you must feel quite smug. Two to zero. For now."

I'm confused. "Uh, what?"

"Well, Emily and Gloria seem quite happy and are with child. And Marcus and Marian are always posting lovey-dovey updates on Facebook."

I smile the way a man does when a person he feels mild animosity toward does not know something he does.

"Molly, Marian is in a relationship, but it's not with Marcus."

"Oh. Then who is it?"

I squint out at the game on a nearby flatscreen and locate the Cubs' star outfielder. A ball comes flying at him and he leaps and catches it right against the stadium wall. The camera zooms in on his handsome face, grinning.

"That guy," I say, pointing.

Molly cocks her head like a confused parrot. "Javier Ruiz?"

"Yep," I say.

"You have to be fucking kidding me. Isn't that guy worth like two hundred million dollars?"

"Yep," I say.

"Okay, wait. How does Marian even *know* a professional baseball player?"

"Marcus introduced them. He's Javier's agent."

"Jesus Christ. But she doesn't even live in Chicago."

"They're long-distance."

"How do you know all this?"

"I'm here with her. She invited me because she knows I'm a huge Cubs fan."

"You're here with *Marian Hart?*"

"Yes. Who is a lovely, generous, thoughtful person kind enough to think of me. It's quite an experience, being here with the team. Did you know there's a whole suite for the visiting team with free drinks and catering? I had prime rib and a Manhattan before the game."

"Well, good for you. And good for Marian. I would fuck that guy right into the ground."

I try not to choke at the thought of this.

"I thought you were a Dodgers fan," I say.

"I can be bought."

We arrive at the merchandise store, crammed wall-to-wall with Dodgers paraphernalia.

"Anything you want, Marks," I say. "On me."

She takes her time perusing this and that, showily checking the price tags and declaring things like, "No, no, not expensive enough."

I stand sheepishly in my mustard-covered Cubs jersey, watching people eye me with hostility, confusion, and mirth.

She finally comes to me with her selections: a hoodie ("it might get cold later—this is the desert!"), a jersey ("this color looks great on me"), a baseball cap ("it's too bright out"), four key chains ("for my cousins in Iowa") and two T-shirts: one a men's large and one a women's small.

"One for you and one for me."

"Molly, I'm not wearing a Dodgers shirt."

"Yes you are. It's your punishment for pouring beer all over me."

"An accident."

"It's not the intent, it's the harm."

"I'm literally sitting with the families of the team. As the guest of the star outfielder."

"Well, explain to them that you're being gallant."

I sigh. I suppose I can wear the shirt backward and inside out.

I take her selections to the register and proffer my credit card to the tune of $473.12.

"So," I say as I hand her the bulging bag. "How are you?"

"Me? Fine, fine. You know. Writer's life. Just type, type, typing away. And you?"

"I'm *great*. Thanks *so* much for asking."

"Are you being sarcastic?"

"No, enthusiastic. You wouldn't be familiar."

I'm trying to be casual, but I feel awkward. What do you say to a person who has flatly stated they don't want to speak to you? Has she forgotten?

"Well, um, we should probably go change," I say. "It was nice to see you."

She furrows her brow. "You aren't going to invite me down to see Marian?"

I furrow my brow back. "You don't . . . *like* Marian."

"But I like *you*," she says, stopping my heart.

She seems taken aback that she said that—like it just slipped out.

It still robs me of breath.

"Uh, well. We're in section H, row thirty-one, by the aisle. The ones wearing Cubs shirts and getting booed. Come say hi if you want."

CHAPTER 15

Molly

I enter Seth's seats into my phone so I don't forget, and wave goodbye as he walks away.

There's a dry breeze cooling the sweat in my hair as night descends. The floodlights cast shadows over the stands, making the light-up novelty wands in the crowd glow brighter. The stadium feels alit with opportunity. And so do I.

Seth. Here. What are the odds?

I have to tell Alyssa and Dez about this. I open our text chain.

Molly: Holy. Fucking. Shit.

Alyssa: What????

Molly: I'm at a dodgers game and I just ran into seth rubenstein!

Molly: He spilled beer all over me and I made him buy me $400 worth of sweatshirts?

Dezzie: What

Molly: IDK!!!!! I panicked

Alyssa: Ok, first of all, what is Seth doing at a Dodgers game?

Molly: They're playing the cubs

Molly: And get this: he's here with marian hart, who is dating JAVIER
      RUIZ
Dezzie: Wait. The Javier Ruiz who used to be married to that super-
      model?
Molly: Precisely that javier ruiz!!!!
Alyssa: What is happening?!?!
Alyssa: Chaos in the universe!
Molly: I have to go clean beer out of my cleavage
Alyssa: Be nice to Seth
Dezzie: But not *too* nice, Molly

I shove my phone back into my regulation transparent plastic bag before
I can disclose that I already told Seth I *like* him.

Obviously, when you discontinue communication with someone after
they tell you they have a crush on you, the courteous thing to do is stay out
of their orbit. You can't reject someone and then jet pack around in their
airspace, skywriting compliments with your exhaust.

Besides, there were one trillion other things I could have said when Seth
asked why I would want to see Marian. Like "I don't want to seem rude."
Like "I want her to set me up with a millionaire baseball player." Like "You're
right, I don't like Marian; never mind, good luck with the mustard stain."

There must be something seriously wrong with me.

The problem is I really *do* like him. When I saw him my stomach did a
flip-flop as acrobatic as the one performed by his pretzel.

I go to the bathroom, wet some paper towels to sponge off the beer warming
in my belly button, and put on my new T-shirt. I smile at my reflection in the
mirror. I *love* dressing up in team-centric apparel. I truly am a fan.

My mom grew up watching baseball with my grandpa, and our area of
Florida is home to several MLB teams' spring training grounds. Tickets are
dirt cheap. After my dad left, we would go whenever we had the chance,
sneak in a bag of microwave popcorn, buy a huge Coke to share, and spend
hours losing ourselves in the rhythm of the game.

To this day, I love that feeling. The energy of the crowd is infectious, as
reliable a burst of serotonin as an extra half-dose of Lexapro. I delight in the
fans singing along to the songs that they play at top volume—"We Will Rock
You," "Seven Nation Army," "Sweet Caroline." Plus, when the Dodgers win,
there are fireworks all throughout Echo Park.

I go back to find Emily and Gloria. Our seats are bad—we decided to come last-minute, and the nosebleed section was all that was left. They are squinting at the field, trying to make out what's happening.

"You look cute," Emily says.

I toss her a baseball cap. "Courtesy of Mr. Rubenstein."

"Ahem," Gloria says. "What do I get?"

I dig in the bag. "Want a sweatshirt?"

She narrows her eyes at me. "It's one hundred degrees."

I shrug. "But it's a dry heat. And it's free."

She takes the hoodie.

"So, guess who Seth's here with," I say.

"Who?" Gloria asks.

"Marian Hart! She got tickets because she's *dating* Javier Ruiz."

Emily looks at me blankly, but Gloria leans in closer.

"The guy from the Cubs?" she asks.

"Uh-huh!"

"Are you making this up?" Emily asks.

"I don't lie, Emily. Lying is boring."

"If Marian is here, why didn't she text me?" Gloria asks. "Why doesn't *anyone* text me?"

"I text you, my love," Emily says, kissing her cheek.

"Marian didn't text me either," I point out.

They both give me long-suffering looks.

"Maybe because she can tell that you don't like her?" Emily suggests.

"Why does everyone keep saying that?"

"Because you are very bad at hiding your feelings."

Like, for instance, when I blurt out *I like you!* Point taken.

"Well, I told Seth we would walk down and say hi."

Gloria stands up immediately. "Oh, we certainly will. Javier Ruiz? I have to hear about this."

Emily insists we wait for the inning to end—excruciatingly, no one scores—before we make the trek down to Seth and Marian's glamorous seats in the Loge. Marian is wearing a sparkly red jacket with RUIZ appliquéd on the back. She and Seth are surrounded by other women in matching jackets bearing different players' names, all of them so preposterously glossy and well-groomed that I want to excuse myself to call a dermatologist, a colorist, a facialist, and a liposuctionist for emergency appointments.

"Marian Hart!" Gloria yells over the din.

Marian turns around, and her face lights up. "Glor! Get over here!"

Gloria prances down the vertiginous stairs in her platform mules, making me fear for her life, and throws herself into Marian's arms.

Marian, as always, is radiant. She smiles and waves over Gloria's shoulder. I wave back, doing my goddamn best to evince warmth and enthusiasm.

Seth laughs at me from behind Marian. "Good job," he mouths.

"I would have called you, but I'm only here for the night," Marian is saying to Gloria.

"Swooping in with your *man*, I hear," Gloria says, poking her in the ribs. "Tell us everything."

Marian giggles the giggle of a woman in love. "Marcus introduced us a few months ago. He's Javier's agent. We met, and it was just thunderbolts. We went on one of those dates that last all day and"—she blushes—"all night. And we've been together ever since."

"Isn't it hard if you're in Miami and he's in Chicago?" I ask, because I have a constitutional need to question other people's joy.

Marian waves this off. "He travels so often it doesn't really matter where he lives. We make it work. It's so *worth* it."

"I don't suppose he has a friend for this one," Emily says, pointing at me. "She could use a man with strong arms."

"Excuse me!" I cry. "I have many suitors."

I sneak a glance at Seth. His face is studiously neutral.

"Well, we should get back to our seats before the inning starts," Gloria says. "But, Seth, see you at the shower on Saturday? It starts at two."

"I'll be there," Seth says. "Text me the address."

We get back to our seats just in time to see Tom Beadelman hit a home run, breaking the tie for the Dodgers. Gloria, Emily, and I scream until we're hoarse. I exchange a high five with the heavily bearded gentleman to my right and a low five with his tiny daughter, who is whipping around one of those commemorative sweat towels they give you for free during the playoffs.

I bend down and offer her one of the Dodgers key chains Seth bought me. (I don't actually have cousins in Iowa; I just wanted to run up the tab.) She smiles shyly and lisps out "thank you." Emily side-eyes me like "who are you?"

I don't care. The DJ is blasting "Don't Stop Believin'," the entire stadium (sans, I imagine, the sullen Cubs fans) is singing along, and I, for once, am happy.

My phone buzzes in the pocket of my cutoffs.

I pull it out to see a text from Seth.

Seth: Fuck.
Seth: We're gonna lose, aren't we?
Seth: I blame the Coors Light.

Above it, I can still see the bubble of my last conversation with him.

January 2

Molly: You're sweet. But I can't.

He had to read *that* before texting me, and he did it anyway.

I hope he's texting me because enough time has passed since that awkward phone call in January, not because I said *I like you.* But either way, seeing his name in my phone adds to this strange feeling of joy.

Molly: Don't worry. Y'all have another inning to further humiliate your-
selves
Molly: And it's not the cheap beer. It's that we're a way better team
Molly: Also you SUCK at being a fan! You're supposed to be ride or die,
not just GIVE UP because we're ahead

My phone vibrates again.

Seth: I can't believe I'm getting (accurate) fandom lessons from a woman
who once wrote a term paper at a Tampa Bay Lightning game out
of boredom.
Molly: That's because hockey is puerile and vicious

I put away my phone and try to focus on the game. The inning ends. Bottom of the eighth and the Cubs have a chance to tie it up. Emily grabs my hand. "Say a prayer," she demands.

I pull out one of my Dodgers key chains, kiss it, and hold it up to the heavens like a sorceress. The fellow fans around me clap.

I get a text.

Seth: Now it's MY time to shine. Eat shit, Molly Marks.
Seth: God, ugh, sorry. My attempts at pro sports machismo are . . . ungallant. I take that back. Please don't eat shit.
Seth: Unless you have pica or something.
Seth: Although actually you could still get dysentery so better not.
Molly: STOP
Seth: Yep. Good call. Stopping.
Molly: Anyway use your attention to focus on losing the game

Just then, none other than Javier Ruiz walks up to the plate, and my phone goes quiet.

"Strike out, strike out, strike *out*," Gloria is murmuring. The pitcher lobs a ball. Not ideal.

"It's okay it's okay it's okay," Emily murmurs like an incantation. "We got this we got this we got this."

Ruiz swings and misses. Strike one!

We cheer.

Another strike.

We cheer harder.

"Strike him out!" I shout as the pitcher reels his arm.

We all hold our breath.

Ruiz cracks that fucker deep, deep into the stands.

"Goddamnit!" I yell. The fans around me moan similar sentiments.

My phone buzzes.

Seth: You know what? I spoke too soon. We're definitely going to win this.

I can't manage a sassy reply. I'm too stressed-out.

The Cubs don't score again, and then the Dodgers are back up at bat. The whole stadium is taut with tension.

The first player strikes out.

I'm dying.

"Come on, Lanzinella," Emily is screaming. "Tie it up, baby!"

The friends we've made during the game chime in with her. "Tie it up! Tie it up!" we all chant.

Lanzifuckingnella ties that motherfucker up, and we all lose our minds.

That is until Woo, who's up next, strikes out.

We have one out to break the tie, and then it's their game to lose.

Madison's up next, and he gets on base. "We Will Rock You" blasts over the speakers, and I almost wish they would turn it off because I want the players to focus and win this thing.

Next up, Robinson, who is not known for his batting.

Emily erupts in uncharacteristic rage. "Are you kidding me? No pinch hitter?"

The woman behind her spits on the ground. "MORON BITCH," she screams at, presumably, the coach.

Robinson hits a foul immediately.

Every part of me that can clench clenches.

Robinson hits another miserable foul.

I unclench, because I can see where this is going. And it's not to the World Series.

The Cubs pitcher lines up. Time slows. And then, the most beautiful sound rips through the stadium.

The crack of the bat.

I strain to see against the floodlights as the ball lists *just inside* the foul pole and into the stands.

It's a home run. Lanzinella rounds the bases with Robinson right behind him. Damn if we are not up by two going into the top of the ninth.

I hug Emily and Gloria, screaming.

When we are done jumping up and down, I take out my phone and text Seth:

Molly: Bad night to have to hang out with a professional cub
Seth: Nope. We got this.

They do not got this.

They lose.

The stadium basically levitates. People are dancing in the aisles, hugging each other, throwing popcorn in the air. The sky lights up with the silver whorls and golden spiders of fireworks, and we all stop and gasp.

In the distance, you can see smaller, amateur fireworks going off—reds and greens and golds crackling like thunder, echoing off the mountains.

"God, it's so beautiful," I say to no one in particular.

My phone buzzes.

Seth: You were right about fireworks in LA. Magical.

I smile down at my screen.

"Shall we go celebrate at Izzie's?" Gloria asks.

"Definitely," I say. Izzie's is a cute little bar right down the hill from the stadium in Echo Park. It's close enough to walk to, and it's our tradition to go there for cocktails after a game.

We slowly make our way behind the crowd seeping out of the stadium and into the parking lot. People are tailgating, dancing. The sky is still booming with fireworks. The air smells like sausage and peppers from the guys barbecuing on the sidewalk, selling hot dogs and cold beer to fans walking home.

I wonder if Seth is taking this in, the enchantment of my city on this warm fall night.

I take out my phone and reply to his last message.

Molly: They are pretty, aren't they? Glad you could see them
Molly: And sorry for your loss :(

He replies immediately.

Seth: Can't say it doesn't hurt. But at least I'm best friends with Javier Ruiz now.

I laugh at the idea of Seth hanging out with an A-list celebrity. But I guess it's no less absurd than Marian dating one.

I consider for a moment, and then decide *fuck it.*

Molly: Hey—emily and gloria and I are going to grab drinks at a bar nearby. want to come?

Molly: And of course marian, should she deign to fraternize with the enemy

Seth: Aww, thanks for the invite! Can't though—we're going back to the hotel on the friends and family bus to mourn.

Of course. It was stupid of me to suggest it. No one wants to hang out with the jubilant fans of the opposing team.

But I kind of thought he might want to hang out with *me?*

"What's wrong?" Gloria asks.

I realize I'm staring glumly at my phone.

"Oh, nothing!" I say. I shove my phone back into my pocket and try not to be disappointed.

But as we get down to the bottom of the hill, my pocket buzzes.

Seth: But I'll see you at the baby shower, right?

CHAPTER 16
Seth

Gloria and Emily's house is the kind of place people move to LA for—a mid-century modern on a Silver Lake hillside overlooking Hollywood, complete with palm trees, a pool, and the smell of orange blossoms on the breeze. Inside is just what you would expect from a pair of set designers. The bathrooms alone are more beautiful than any room in my entire condo.

"You made it," Gloria exclaims as I walk into the backyard, where about twenty intimidatingly stylish people have congregated around a long table surrounded by electric pink bougainvillea. I scan the crowd for Molly. She's not here. I dislike how much this disappoints me.

I hold up two sparkly gift bags—one from me, and one from Marian—to the mothers-to-be. "For you."

"We said no presents!" Emily objects. "Childbearing is so commercialized. It's sickening. All the twins are getting are cribs and some swaddling cloths."

"No diapers?" I ask innocently.

"Nope." She laughs. "I hope that's what you brought me."

"One's from me and one's from Marian. She was so bummed she couldn't make it."

"Ooooh, open the one from Marian first!" Gloria says.

I point to the purple bag. "That one."

Emily fishes inside and then bursts out laughing. "Oh my God, that *tramp*."

"What is it?" Gloria asks.

Emily holds up two tiny Cubs jerseys with RUIZ on the back.

"Well Lordy me," Gloria says, shaking her head. "I would never have imagined she could be so devious."

"They're signed," I say sheepishly.

"What's in yours?" Emily asks, grabbing the other bag. "It better not be matching hats."

She pulls out a copy of *Goodnight Moon*.

"Awww, that's more like it," Gloria says.

"It was my favorite growing up," I say. "I can't wait to read it to my kids someday."

Gloria kisses my cheek.

"You're cute, ya know that?"

"It's my only good quality."

"I'm glad you're here, Seth. It's always a delight."

"I'm glad I could come too. It's great to see your place in person. It looked fabulous on Insta but wow. That pool. If I lived here, I would do nothing but lounge on a swan float drinking piña coladas."

"Did you bring your swimsuit?" she asks.

"I wasn't aware this was a baby shower slash pool party."

"This is LA," she retorts. "Every party is a slash pool party. And don't worry, you can skinny-dip. LaCroix?"

I accept a coconut-flavored sparkling water that tastes deliciously of sunscreen.

Gloria's sister, Eliana, emerges from inside the house, with Molly in tow. Wow.

Molly looks so beautiful with the sun glinting off her curtain of dark hair that I have to look away. My days of admiring Molly's beauty should be decidedly behind me. This is just a reflex.

"Elle!" I cry, getting up to give her a hug. "I had no idea you lived here."

"Oh God, I don't," she says with an exaggerated shiver. "Never *ever*. I'm in New York with the sane people. I just flew in to host this shindig."

"And what a host you are. So positive and full of joy," Gloria says. "And only forty minutes late."

"Sorry, I overslept. But just wait 'til you see what I have in store for you. You'll *wish* I were less fun."

Molly slings an arm around Elle's shoulders. "Miss Gutierrez here is always fun. You should have seen her last night at the bar. Threw back like ten tequilas and took home a twenty-four-year-old Australian surfer."

"Um, you matched me on tequilas and spent all night flirting with a fireman," Elle retorts. "Did you get his number?"

"Been texting with him all morning," Molly chirps. "We're going out for drinks tomorrow at that new cocktail bar on Fig."

I try not to wince at the idea of Molly in the buff embrace of a heroic firefighter. Or in the buff embrace of anyone. The buff embraces in which Molly chooses to spend her time are most certainly *not* my business.

"Don't brag," Eliana says. "Anyway, now that I'm here to be master of ceremonies, shall we begin?"

"Do we have to play games?" Gloria asks. "Can't we just sit here in the shade and eat cupcakes and have civilized conversation?"

"My dear sister, I did not spend upward of twenty minutes on TheBump.co researching baby shower games for us to be civilized."

"I agree," Emily says. "Let's see what horrors Elle has concocted."

Eliana is a notoriously sardonic person who might have out-cool-girl'ed Molly in high school, were she not three years younger. She is now an A&R executive for an indie music label. She has neck tattoos. (I am equally scared of and aroused by neck tattoos.) That she was tasked with planning a baby shower is shocking.

"One moment, please," Elle says. She disappears around the side of the house and comes back dragging a giant plastic bin full of balloons.

"Oh God," an elegant man in short shorts and a sheer caftan exclaims. "Are those *water* balloons?"

"Correct," Elle says. "Our first game is called Baby Bumper Cars."

"Dare I ask?" Gloria groans.

"I will divide us into two teams. Everyone puts a water balloon under their shirt to be their baby."

Elle demonstrates, shoving a balloon beneath her T-shirt. The balloon is not large. She does not look pregnant so much as afflicted with a small abdominal tumor.

She waggles the fake belly around, causing it to undulate.

"Gross," the caftan guy says.

I'm inclined to agree.

"What next?" Gloria prompts her.

"A person from each team runs at each other and bumps bellies to try to break the other's balloon first," Elle says. "Whichever team breaks the most bellies wins."

Emily claps her hands in delight. "I *love* this game."

"You would, since you don't have to play," Gloria grumbles. "Much too violent for a pregnant person."

"Precisely," she says.

Elle splits up the table into two teams, and we all pass around balloons.

"All right," she says. "Team one on the left side of the yard, team two on the right. Emily, you're in charge of documenting this for posterity and blackmail."

We form two single-file lines on our opposing territory, with twenty-odd feet between us.

Molly catches my eye and jiggles her belly menacingly. "I'm gonna get you and your little fetus too, Rubenstein!"

I clutch my water baby protectively. "Keep your hands off Seth Junior," I call back. "He's my best prospect for an heir."

"On your marks, get set, go!" Eliana cries.

At her command, twenty well-groomed thirty-something adults go careening toward each other. I sprint as fast as I can at Molly, clutching my belly so it doesn't go flying out into the grass. Hers is secure beneath her tight one-piece bathing suit, giving her the advantage of speed.

She comes right at me, belly first. Our balloons collide. I cradle mine protectively, choosing a defensive strategy.

"Cheater," she cries. "Stop that."

"There are no rules!" I yell, dodging her attempt to smack into me.

"Okay then." She waves her long nails at me, which are elaborately manicured into pastel-flowered talons. She comes at my stomach, claws-first.

I bend down to my knees to avoid her hands and attempt to pop her belly between my palms.

I use too much force and it surges up toward her boobs instead of bursting.

She lunges and pulls up my shirt. My baby falls into the grass, but remains intact. She lifts her foot to stomp on it but I grab her shoulders and press her into me, tight, to put pressure on her balloon. The balloon pushes up above her cleavage.

I know what I must do.

I bend down, take the balloon between my teeth, and chomp.

It bursts all over both of us.

Molly scream-laughs. "I cannot believe you just ripped my baby apart with your teeth."

"Victory tastes sweet. And slightly rubbery."

I wring out my shirt, which is drenched and clinging to my torso.

"Never pegged you for a wet T-shirt contest guy, but you pull it off," Molly says.

"I guess I can go swimming after all," I observe, trying not to focus on the suggestive nature of her words and the way she is openly eyeing my chest.

Around us, most of our fellow competitors are still swinging balloons at each other. But I barely clock them, because suddenly the air between me and Molly feels thick.

Too thick.

I step back, but Molly takes my hand and yanks it up into the sky.

"Rubenstein vanquished me," she yells to Eliana. She turns back to me. "Let's go in the pool."

Without waiting for an answer, she shimmies out of the cutoffs she's wearing, kicks off her sandals, and goes running. She jumps in without a moment's hesitation, creating a splash that douses half of my teammates.

"Come on," she yells at me. "It feels amazing!"

"No suit!" I yell back.

"Who cares?" Emily interjects, getting up and stripping off her cover-up to reveal a two-piece and a very adorable baby bump. "We have a clothing-optional pool policy."

There is no way I'm taking off all my clothes in front of an audience of mostly women at a *baby shower,* but I figure boxer briefs are close enough to swim trunks.

"Okay," I say, "but only because it's ninety-nine degrees. How do you guys live this way in October?"

"Isn't it already, like, snowing in Chicago?" Molly retorts.

I take off my clothes and hang them on the back of a chair to dry in the sun. I'm going straight to the airport after this and don't want to throw them wet into my suitcase.

I jump in close enough to Molly to splash her. The water is warm from the sun and the heat, but cool enough to still be refreshing.

I swim toward Emily in the shallow end, but a hand grabs my ankle, and my head goes under. I hear the muffled sound of laughing and look down to see Molly's mermaid hair swirling around my feet.

She lets go of me and surges toward the surface. I chase after her, grab her shoulders, and dunk her below the water.

She's laughing and coughing as she comes up. It reminds me of all the pools of our Floridian youth. When Molly and I were dating, we'd often do homework together and then horse around for hours in my parents' pool. It was a very convenient way to be almost-naked and touching in a parentally sanctioned way.

Molly's hands reach out to my hip bones and she begins to pull me toward her, but I scoot backward and swim out of her grip.

I try not to like this attention, but it feels good on my ego. Restorative.

She comes at me again, and I pick her up out of the water and hold her above my shoulders.

"I'm going to throw you in if you don't behave," I threaten.

"I dare you," she says.

I don't need further encouragement. I send her flying to the deep end, and she lands with a splash. "Oh, you are going to get it," she yells, power swimming back to me with a murderous glint in her eyes.

"Okay, children," Eliana calls. "That's enough Tom, Dick, and Harry."

I look up and realize every single person is staring at us.

No one else is in the pool, except for Emily, who is sitting on the steps of the shallow end, smirking.

"Let's play the next game, if Molly and Seth are quite done with their horseplay," Elle says.

"I think I'm pregnant just from watching them," the caftan guy says to a soaking wet woman beside him.

My cheeks go hot. We've been acting like teenagers.

Flirty teenagers.

Completely unacceptable.

"Sorry!" I call, paddling very, very far away from Molly Marks, and lifting myself out of the pool.

I'm better than this.

Gloria throws me a towel. "What's the next game?" she asks Elle.

"Baby Bucket List," Elle says. "It's where we go around in a circle and write down an activity we think you should do with the babies in their first year. I'll compile them all into a book, and you and Em can write little notes about the experience on the back of the cards, to remember."

"Oh, that's so sweet!" Emily says.

"I know." Eliana laughs. "It's sickening."

We all gather around the table, and Elle passes out Sharpies and yellow cardstock embossed with the words *In your first year as moms . . .*

"Okay," Elle says, "I'm setting a timer for five minutes. Let's do this."

We all bend down over our cards. I try not to drip water on mine. This is important. They'll probably keep these for the rest of their lives. (Or, at least, I would.)

I rack my brain for an idea. Then I remember when my nephew Max was born. He was a fussy baby, and when I came out to visit Dave and Clara, they were desperate for any break they could get. So I used to strap him to my chest in their baby carrier and walk him around the hiking trail near their house. Some days we'd do it for hours, just me and him. I loved the feeling of him tucked against my chest, his tiny feet dangling on either side of me.

I take care to make my terrible handwriting legible.

Hike with them close to your chests on a beautiful trail on a beautiful day.

When everyone is finished, we take turns reading them aloud.

Elle suggests feeding the babies her and Gloria's mother's recipe for arroz con leche. A pink-haired woman in a linen jumpsuit suggests making copper molds of their hands and feet and turning them into a mobile to hang over the crib. (She offers to do it herself; unsurprisingly, she's an artist.)

I read mine aloud and successfully avoid choking up, even though the game is making me emotional.

Molly goes last. I expect her to say something glib or sarcastic, since mushy topics repel her. Maybe something like "Make breast milk cheese and bring it to a cookout for your neighbors," or "Remember: don't shake the babies—too hard."

She clears her throat, and her voice is softer than usual. "So, when I was a baby, and really until I was nearly grown up, my mom would sing me lullabies while I was falling asleep. And it was so soothing that to this day I still have a lullaby playlist I listen to when I have insomnia. So my suggestion is to sing your babies to sleep together." She pauses and twists her lips. "Yeah. So that's my, um. Yeah."

Gloria puts a hand over her heart. "Molly! That is so sweet."

And it is. It really is.

I can't help but think of tough, flinty Molly curled up in bed with her earbuds, drifting off to a lullaby.

Or better, Molly cradling a baby of her own, singing her child to sleep.

It makes me regret that it will never be me singing with her.

CHAPTER 17

Molly

One of the problems with almost never being earnest in public is that you fail to develop a graceful way to be sincere.

Other people seem to be able to express poignant sentiments without awkwardness. They can say, for example, "Wow, what a cute baby," or "That piece of music was very moving," and not want to throw themselves off a cliff. But people like me—people who are more comfortable treating life like everything's a low-key punch line—become flustered when forced to acknowledge we experience human emotions. We don't have the muscles to pivot back to normalcy. Instead, we dangle in the excruciating vulnerability.

Like I am now, after admitting my addiction to lullabies. My heart is racing, and my cheeks are so hot it feels like I'm having an allergic reaction.

Gloria's friend Mona puts a hand on my arm. "That was such a beautiful story. It makes me want to call my mom and tell her how much I love her."

Oh, God, make it stop.

"Yeah," I sputter. "Thanks."

No one else speaks, but everyone is looking at me.

I put my phone up in front of my bright red, miserable face. "I'll text you my playlist, Glor," I say.

A text comes in while I'm fumbling with the app.

Seth: Can you send me the playlist too?

I look up at him over the edge of the phone and he's smiling at me, like he's sending me emotional support with his eyes.

Ugh, I hate how well he knows me.

Molly: Why, are you pregnant?
Seth: Yes.

I pop the URL into the text thread.

Molly: Here ya go. Mazel tov

"Who's ready for cake?" Elle asks.

Not I. I'm baby-showered out. I wish I had an excuse to leave.

Seth stands up. "I actually can't stay," he says apologetically. "I've got to get to the airport. I'm just going to change and then call a car."

Don't let him get away, a desperate voice in my brain wails.

I jump up. "Wait. Don't do that. It's so . . . expensive. I'll drive you."

Once again everyone looks at me. It is a rare Angeleno who impulsively volunteers to brave LAX traffic. To do so when one is on the Eastside, an hour away at this time of day, is unheard of.

But part of me already misses him. Regrets we didn't get a chance to catch up. Regrets blowing him off in a fit of panic however many months ago.

"I'm meeting friends for an early dinner in Venice, so I need to head that way soon anyway," I lie.

"Are you sure it isn't out of your way?" Seth asks.

"Nope. Go ahead and get changed. I'll meet you out front."

I give Gloria and Emily big kisses and make my way around the table, saying my goodbyes.

Eliana grabs my arm as I reach the door to the kitchen.

"Wait," she whispers. "Is something going on with you and Seth?"

"No!"

She raises an eyebrow. "Really? Cuz you sure looked like you wished there was in the pool."

"Oh come on," I say. "Can't a girl tease her ex-boyfriend?"

"I kept waiting for you to drag him into the pool house to ravish him."

"I guess I'll do that in my car."

She smirks. "That's what I thought. Boy still can't take his eyes off you. Get it, sis."

I try to act as though this information rolls off me.

"Okay, gotta run and try to beat the traffic. Let's get drinks before you leave."

She pulls me in for a kiss on the cheek. "Love ya."

"You too."

When I get outside, Seth is standing there with a rolly bag.

"Where to, captain?" he asks.

"I'm the white Lexus."

He scans the road until his eyes alight on my SUV. He laughs. "I didn't expect you to drive a suburban mom car."

"I *love* my car," I huff. "Suburban mom cars are spacious and practical. And if you want the privilege of riding in one you will apologize to my dear Laurel."

"Your car has a *name?*"

"Of course she does. I spend more time with her than anyone else."

I pop open the back and he lifts in his bag and then climbs in next to me.

"Ready?" I ask.

"Yep."

This is self-evident from the fact that he is in the car with the door closed wearing his seat belt. But now that I have extricated myself from the baby shower, I realize I've created another conundrum: What to talk about for the next hour?

I wanted this. But now my mind is a vast, anxious blank.

"So, how long is the drive?" Seth asks.

"Let's see." I plug in my phone and the maps app reports it's a mere fifty-eight minutes.

"Oof," he says. "You're sure I'm not taking you out of your way?"

"Positive."

In actual fact, the airport is in the wrong direction, I have no friends in Venice, and getting back will take even longer.

It's worth it. For some reason, I really do want to do this.

Besides, now that we're on the road, I feel calmer. I love driving in LA— the musical ebb and flow of traffic on ten-lane freeways brings me a kind of peace. People here aren't aggressive on the road like they are in New York or in Florida, but they are quick and assured and competent. It's like the whole city has made a gentleman's agreement to get everywhere as quickly as possible without killing anyone. (In New York it feels like they would not at all mind if they killed you. In Florida it feels like they actually want to.)

"So what have you been up to since the game?" I ask.

"I went to the beach in Malibu."

"Ah that's nice. Too cold to go in though."

"Not for me," he replies. "I love a cold swim. I go to the beach in Chicago all the time."

"Chicago does not have beaches."

"It most certainly does."

"Those little patches of sand on Lake Michigan don't count."

"They most certainly do."

"You really go swimming in Lake Michigan in the winter?"

"Not in the winter, but this time of year it's still bearable. A nice polar swim."

"You are so wholesome."

"I know."

"You should have called me. I could have given you some bars and restaurants to try. Taken you out."

He leans back in his seat.

"Molly," he says slowly. "Not to be awkward. But I got the distinct impression you didn't *want* me to call you. Like, ever again."

I'm quiet. I know, of course, that I've been inconsistent with no explanation, and that this is likely confusing to him. But being clearer would require me to process my own emotions—which is something I find highly distasteful, as my long-suffering therapist can attest.

I drum on the steering wheel, grateful that the traffic frees me from the obligation of looking at him.

"Yeah," I finally say. "I regret that."

"You do?" he asks. There's an intensity to his voice that tells me this information is not nothing to him.

That he really *cared* when I told him not to contact me.

There's a long pause while I gulp down my innate resistance to even the faintest hint of vulnerability. But I owe it to him.

"I do," I make myself say. "I've been debating whether to get in touch with you for months to apologize. For overreacting that night."

He's staring at me.

"I would have liked that," he says. "I didn't . . . realize you felt that way. Obviously."

"Yeah." I look determinedly ahead. "I've missed hearing from you."

He shakes his head and laughs softly. "Wow."

"And when I saw you at the game," I confess to the rearview mirror, "I realized how dumb it was not to just get over myself, because I was really happy to see you. I mean, how many times in my life have I been grateful to Marian Hart?"

He snorts, but his voice goes soft. "I'm touched, Molly."

For a moment, we're both silent. I gather the courage to glance at him, and he's looking at me sadly.

"But, you know," he says, "I *am* aware I was out of line during that conversation. It was . . . too much. I understood why you felt the way you felt."

Floating underneath his words is the unspoken thing he said. *I'm carrying a torch for you.* I wonder if it's still true. If I dare ask.

No. That's not the kind of thing one asks. It's the kind of thing one has to earn back.

I fiddle with the air conditioner vent instead of saying anything.

The truth is I have no idea what to say.

Being a more socially adept person than me, Seth changes the subject.

"So how are you?" he asks.

"Right now? Kind of damp."

"I mean generally speaking."

"I'm doing okay."

"So specific and expressive."

I shrug, because I'm not going to tell him I'm exhausted from the nonstop social maneuvering of scrounging up work, and bored of the oppressive October heat, and lonely from my latest string of empty hookups.

"I'm fine," I say. "Not much to report."

"Oh come on. How's your movie with Margot Tess going? I want to live vicariously through your glamorous life."

I really, really don't want to talk about this. See: scrounging up work. But I'm not going to lie to him. So I say, "Not happening. At least, not with me."

He looks at me with the kind of disbelief that a person with a normal job has at the vagaries of a career in film. "No! What happened?"

"Margot decided she wants to take the script in a more 'mainstream' direction. Thought my voice was too 'prickly.'"

I'm sure he, of all people, can understand what she meant.

"Jesus, Molly. I'm sorry."

I shrug. "I mean, I still get paid for my work on it, so it's fine. But it would have been nice to get something big into production."

"I agree! I want more Molly Marks joints for my own selfish enjoyment."

"How is your work?" I ask, because I don't want Seth Rubenstein's pity, nor further reason to dwell on my current career drought.

"You know, I'm a little bored, if I'm being honest."

"All those divorces got you down?"

He winces. "I know you think I'm a shithead for practicing family law, and I get it, but you're actually part of the reason I do what I do."

I momentarily take my eyes off the road to narrow them at him.

"You were inspired by my childhood trauma to spend your peak earning years causing emotional devastation and financial ruin?"

"No, I wanted to help people. I'm serious."

"I'm not sure how you could be."

If I'm honest, it really *does* hurt me that he would go into that field, after seeing what happened to me and my mother. My dad left her when I was in eighth grade, and Seth was there for the fallout. He saw how my dad's lawyers and business manager fucked my mom over by moving his money around offshore, and then kept her tied up in court for years when she tried to prove it. He saw how hollowed out we both were by the experience.

I mean, to be clear, we didn't starve. My father paid his court-ordered child support and my tuition. My mom began cobbling together a new career in real estate. But it took her years to rebuild her finances. The two of us had to move to a shitty apartment, and every time the car broke down it was a roll of the dice over whether we had the cash to fix it. And that's not getting into her yearslong depression, or my nonstop panic attacks.

Meanwhile, if you're keeping score, my father bought the first of many sailboats, moved to an oceanfront condo, remarried a person seven years older than me, and saw me one weekend a month.

So yeah. Divorce lawyers. Not a fan.

"I thought there had to be a more humane way to dissolve marriages," Seth says. "So when I made partner, I hired an in-house family systems psychologist who specializes in divorce, and I encourage all of my clients to work with her. I also steer them toward private mediation. It's not always pleasant, obviously, but we've had a lot of success in guiding couples to amicable resolutions outside of court, even in situations that begin acrimoniously."

I'm not sold.

"Good for you. You'll have to forgive me for being skeptical."

He meets my eyes in the rearview mirror. "I'm sorry for what he put you through. With your mom. I've never forgotten it."

He's alluding to the fact that my mother had a complete nervous breakdown during the divorce, and my father left me, his pubescent daughter, as her primary emotional support system. She's apologized for that—the two of us even did family therapy. But it made my teenage years incredibly difficult.

"Thanks," I say. "She's great now. She started *dating* someone last year. She won't really say how serious it is, but suddenly she's been on me to 'let my guard down and open myself up to love,' like she's Oprah."

He laughs. "Good to hear it."

Talking about myself in relation to romantic attachment is making me uncomfortable.

"Anyway," I say, "why are you bored?"

"Well, I'm pretty much at the top of the game. But I feel a little bit like I've plateaued."

"Can you do something else? Like, say, not divorces?"

"I've toyed with the idea of starting a nonprofit legal clinic. Or my own firm. But I don't want to get really busy with work and then have kids and no time for them."

I get a strange twinge of affection that he's thinking of this. Taking care of his future children. He's so . . . *good*.

"Got it," I say, because Seth's quest for a family is another unsettling topic to be discussing.

And that's where the flow of conversation dries up.

There's a pause so long I almost consider turning on NPR. It eats at me that I can't seem to sustain a comfortable chat with Seth, a person I have never been unable to talk to. In fact, several of the best conversations of my life have been with Seth. Which is saying a lot, given we were under the age of eighteen when we had them.

But he seems as reticent as I am on the topic of his future.

"How is your family?" I finally ask, feeling like I'm checking off conversational boxes. Next, I'm going to be inquiring into his fitness routine and sleep schedule.

He smiles. "Amazing. I was actually with Dave and the kids last month. We drove up to Pigeon Forge and went to Dollywood. It was wild."

"You did not! It's my *dream* to go to Dollywood."

He smiles at me wryly. "I don't know. You have a pretty rocky relationship with theme parks, if I recall."

"Oh God. Don't bring that up."

He is referring to when we went on an "ironic" date to a cheesy, second-rate water park in Central Florida and I almost died.

"Only you would commit a near-fatal error getting onto a water slide," he says.

I rolled my ankle trying to get on a raft, slipped into the water, and was nearly sucked down the steep tube of "rapids" on my ass. Luckily Seth grabbed me, and I wasn't hurt, but I think I am single-handedly responsible for millions of dollars of additional safety features at the Ocala Splash Attack.

I still feel emotional thinking of that day. How Seth held me as we climbed off the ride, me crying, him squeezing water out of my hair. It was romantic teenage trauma-bonding at its finest—like we were inside a John Green novel. We really do have the profile of two romance tropes. Seth the sensitive, cinnamon roll of a boy, and me the manic pixie dream girl. (Or manic pixie nightmare, more accurately.)

"I genuinely thought you were going to drown," Seth says. "I couldn't breathe for hours. Maybe days. Actually, I kind of can't breathe right now, remembering it."

He puts his face to the air conditioner vent and takes exaggerated gulps of air.

I pat his back. "Easy there. Head between your legs."

He laughs but stiffens under my touch.

I quickly remove my hand.

"You were so sweet afterward," I say.

He glances at me. "I was always so sweet."

It chastens me.

"You were. You spoiled me. I'm not sure I ever thanked you for that."

He shakes his head. "You don't have to thank people for being nice to you."

"Maybe you should when you're bad at reciprocating it."

I don't just mean in high school. I mean in life. But especially with him.

"You *were* nice to me, Molly. You just have a different way of showing it."

"Yeah. An alienating one."

He gives me a long look. "Are you okay?"

"What do you mean? Yeah. Of course."

"You seem like you might be depressed or something."

"I'm actually not depressed," I lie. "Which is a rare and momentous occasion for me."

"Good."

"I guess I'm just doing the thing you told me I do. Deflecting my feelings."

"What are your feelings?"

Sadness that I let him get away.

"Oh, I don't know," I say. "Nostalgia for the past, perhaps."

He nods. "I suppose we bring it out in each other. Talking to you is like fanning through my high school yearbook while listening to Dashboard Confessional."

"Pretty sure that's not a compliment."

"Oh come on. You loved emo."

"I did not! That was all you, Rubenstein."

"Oh right. You loved NSYNC."

"Don't make me turn this car around."

"You wouldn't dare. Then you'd be stuck with me."

Stuck with him. God, I wish.

I'm so stupid. He's been here for days, and instead of trying to reach out I just looked at my phone a lot, wondering if he would text me. And now he's leaving, and things are weird, and all I want to do is tell him the feelings he confessed all those months ago turned out to be mutual.

I'm carrying a torch, too.

We pass the first sign for LAX.

I don't want to let this man out of my car.

"You know, Seth," I say quickly, before I can lose my nerve. "You haven't been here for very long, and it sounds like you could use a longer break from work. You don't have to leave yet. I have a spare room . . . You could stay and I could show you around the Eastside. Or, ooh, even better, I could drive you out to Joshua Tree and we could go hiking and eat greasy bar food and buy expensive incense. My friend Theresa has a gorgeous place out there. It's only two hours—"

"Molls," he interrupts, laughing a little in a way that seems forced. "That's super nice of you to offer, but I have to get back."

I want to die at this very reasonable rejection, but I've got momentum now, and I know I'll regret it if I don't just fucking say it, so I gather my courage and take a deep breath and plow on. "I guess I just think it would be nice to spend some time together. You know, we had a great time at the reunion, and then things went sideways, which might be my fault because, as you pointed out, I sabotage things and get in my own way. But I guess what I'm saying is . . . I like you, and I miss you, and I wish you would stay."

I can't look at him. I'm frozen, waiting for an answer. *Praying* I haven't just embarrassed myself as much as it already feels like I have.

Seth puts a hand on my shoulder, and it sends my cortisol levels back down. His touch has always had an incredible, miraculous power to make me feel calm.

I gather the courage to glance at him, and something is flickering in his face, and I hope.

I *hope*.

When he doesn't immediately say yes, I stutter out more. "Or, I could grab a flight to Chicago. Stay with Dez. We could hang out, and maybe—"

"Molls," he finally says, so very softly, so very kindly, "I've met someone."

The breath rushes out of me.

"Oh!" I say. "Oh, okay, sorry!"

"No worries." He takes his hand off my shoulder. "You're sweet."

Sweet. Kill me.

I merge into the lane for departing flights.

"What airline?" I ask. I arrange my lips into a flat line, and check in the rearview mirror to make sure that they don't quiver.

"American," he says.

I nod.

It takes fifteen excruciating minutes to weave through the traffic to his terminal, and neither of us says another word.

I stop the car.

"Well, this is you."

He bends over and kisses my cheek. I close my eyes.

"Be well, Molls," he murmurs into my ear.

I manage to wait until he grabs his bag from the back before I start to cry.

PART FOUR

February 2020

CHAPTER 18

Seth

Her name is Sarah Louise Taylor, and she's absolutely perfect for me in every way.

We met back in August, at a Legal Aid fundraiser. She's a Cook County public defender, a stressful, low-paying job that she adores because she loves justice, fairness, and equality with her whole heart. She inspires me. With her encouragement, I'm putting the steps in motion to open the nonprofit legal clinic I've been toying with starting for years.

She's a distance runner—she qualified for the Boston Marathon this year for the *fourth* time—and we get up early every Saturday morning and go on long runs together. (My pace is quite leisurely by her standards, but she's helping me improve. I now have the lung capacity of an eighteen-year-old.)

She grew up working on her parents' farm in Kansas, and is an incredible vegan cook devoted to using local produce. This is obviously difficult in the long Chicago winter, but you would not believe what she can do with pre-served lemons and roasted beets. I haven't eaten meat in months.

She's an only child and longs for a big family with kids and dogs and relatives running around. She can't wait to get pregnant—she thinks she'll love the experience of creating a life inside her body, being so close to someone she loves so much. We spend a lot of time talking about what we'll name our kids. (Current favorites are Jane, after Sarah's mom, and Sam, after my godfather.)

She's generous and intuitive in bed, and on Sundays we stay in and make love. She likes to lock eyes, go slow, check in. The first time we had sex, she cried, and it made me cry too.

Her apartment is filled floor-to-ceiling with pictures of the people close to her—frames crowding on frames of treasured friends and family. Because who could meet Sarah Louise Taylor and not fall head over heels in love with her?

Certainly not me.

Currently, Sarah is in Milwaukee at a conference, which has afforded me a prime opportunity for a boys' weekend in New York with Jon and Kevin. Sarah thinks I'm here to enjoy restaurants and theater with old friends. In fact, I'm here to buy her an engagement ring under the guidance of two people who have much better taste than I do.

It's only been six months, but we are both ready to settle down. I know she'll say yes.

Jon and Kevin meet me for brunch at my hotel in Union Square, and we all exchange bear hugs. Jon and Kevin both live in Brooklyn, and even though it's a short flight from Chicago to New York, we don't see one another more than a few times a year. I'm envious of their proximity to each other. I have lots of buddies in Chicago, but for some reason, I don't have a best friend.

They look great. Jon's silver fox hair is swept back in a more fashionable cut than he usually wears, and he looks like he's added a few pounds of muscle to his slender physique. I'm sure all his students have crushes on him. Kevin's grown a rather dapper mustache, waxed at the corners, and his huge Tom Selleck frame is clad in one of his *looks*—a fashion editor to his core, he always wears *looks*—today's involving a frayed asymmetrical sweater and leather pants.

"So how is the illustrious Sarah Louise?" Jon asks.

"The dream and the vision," Kevin intones.

"I miss her," Jon says. "And I've only met her once."

"I miss her, and I haven't even met her," Kevin says.

I grin. "We should fix that. Maybe I'll bring her here for our engagement trip."

"Oh God, why?" Jon groans, wrinkling his nose. Jon notoriously hates New York, despite having lived here since graduating college.

"So where are we going first?" I ask them.

"Roman & Roman," Kevin pronounces. Kevin took it upon himself to spearhead my search as soon as I mentioned I wanted to propose. "They specialize in antique engagement rings. Beautiful stuff. Highly unusual pieces. You'll love it."

"Sounds perfect," I say.

We finish brunch and amble through the Union Square greenmarket. I love the smell of farmers markets, the fresh flowers and dirt. I'll have to take Sarah Louise here. She thinks she's not a New York person, but I bet she would be if we came together.

A woman with a chic blond pageboy greets us as soon as we walk into the jewelry store. "Kevin!" she says, moving in for a hug.

"Seth, this is Adair," he says. "We go all the way back to my days at *Iconic*. I had her pull some pieces for you."

"For Sarah Louise, right?" she says with a warm smile. "Kevin told me all about her and I think I have some options that might be perfect."

She leads us through the wood-paneled, minimalist space to a small room with a case of glimmering rings in black velvet waiting on a table.

She pulls out a platinum ring with a large, round center stone. "This is an estate piece. Rose cut, two carats. Incredibly classic."

Kevin makes a noise like he's having an orgasm. "Want," he moans.

"That's pretty," Jon says.

"I'm not sure," I demur. Something about it seems too much. Like it would make more of a fuss on Sarah's finger than she might be comfortable with. "It might be too . . . statement."

Adair nods like she knows what I mean. She puts it back and pulls out a much smaller ring with a diamond surrounded by green sparkly rectangles.

"Art deco," Adair says. "Brilliant cut, flanked by these four exquisite emerald baguettes. So delicate—look at the filigree along the edges."

"Ooh, I love that," Jon says. "Reminds me of the Chrysler building."

"Right?" Adair laughs. "I often suggest art deco pieces for people whose taste is a bit more quiet—the style is so striking, but delicate."

This ring is cool, and definitely all wrong for my girlfriend. Sarah Louise is a midwestern girl. She is plains and cornfields and natural platinum hair. She does not want a green engagement ring, art deco or not.

Adair shows me ring after ring. I learn about Asscher cuts and Old Mine cuts and look at something called a Fancy Yellow diamond that costs $78,000.

"I think she'd want something more . . . un-yellow," I gulp out.

A new tray is brought in.

We look at a half-carat solitaire that seems stingy, and infinity rings that look more like wedding bands than engagement rings. I like them all. But none of them is quite right.

What keeps occurring to me is that these rings are ever so slightly too specific. I keep imagining them on the hand of someone like Molly Marks— someone who might not want a ring at all until she saw these, full of history and character.

I can see Sarah walking into this store and thinking she wouldn't want to wear someone else's ring. I can hear her saying, "Oh, but what if they're bad luck?"

"You know, I'm just not sure she would want something used," I say apologetically to Adair.

"He means *antique*," Kevin says, horrified.

"I get it," she says, "don't worry at all. You might check out Trinket, in Williamsburg. Lots of super pretty pieces. Most of it's a little more modest, which is what it sounds like she might want."

I nod, although I'm not sure she *would* want modest. She's a public defender but she appreciates nice things. Her friends certainly wear substantial rocks. And I don't mind buying her something expensive.

Still, Kevin seems to think this is a very good suggestion. We hop on the L train and take it to Bedford Avenue in Brooklyn. All the people look like they live in a different city from the one we just left. They are not just fashionable, they are *outfitted*, ready to see and be seen at 12:30 p.m. on a random Saturday.

"Didn't you use to live here?" I ask Jon. "Wasn't it all guys with lumber-jack beards in really tight jeans?"

"Uh, yeah, back before I got priced out in like 2010. Now it's all finance bros and models."

Jon is a middle school teacher. He does not truck with finance bros and models.

"I have a bad feeling about this," I say. "Sarah would hate it here."

Kevin shushes me. "If you're not careful you'll end up with one of those big boring Tiffany rocks."

Tiffany.

Yeah.

I instantly get the bad feeling that what Kevin considers big boring rocks might be *exactly* what Sarah Louise would want.

We edge our way into the jewelry store, which has old-fashioned gilt signage on the window and is about the size of my foyer in Chicago. Everything in it, including the salesgirls and the crowd of mostly women browsing, are tiny. Jon is slight enough to fit in unobtrusively, but Kevin and I take up about 80 percent of the remaining space.

The twenty-year-olds who work here ignore us, so we just browse. Adair was right that this stuff is pretty, but it's also aggressively dainty. Some of the rings seem deliberately too-small, like they might be more befitting a child than a grown woman. Some are just bizarre, like a tiny opal set in the mouth of four interlocking snakes.

I can imagine Sarah being confused and disappointed if I bought her one of these.

Even more vividly, I can imagine Molly Marks laughing at them. Thinking them affected and twee.

I don't know why I keep thinking about Molly. I haven't spoken to her since she dropped me off at the airport in LA.

Probably because something about that day hurt. I got on a plane and put on a legal podcast and spent the four and a half hours back to Chicago trying not to remember the way her face crumpled when I said I'd met someone.

The way I'd wished, just for a moment, that it hadn't been true.

"Do you want to see anything here?" Kevin asks me.

"I don't know," I say. "It all seems a bit . . ."

"Precious?" he supplies.

"Yes!"

"I agree—this doesn't feel in keeping with the way you've described Sarah."

We leave the store, and I feel like I can breathe again.

"Listen," I say. "I think maybe we should go to Tiffany."

Kevin looks at me like I have stabbed him in the heart.

"A lot of her friends have rings from there," I say before he can object, "and I know she likes them, and I just want to get her something she likes."

"Sounds like the right move," Jon says. He turns to the street and flags down a taxi. "Tiffany, on Fifth Avenue," he says firmly to the driver.

"Maybe afterward we can have tea at the Plaza," Kevin grumbles, squeezing in next to me. "Take a carriage ride through Central Park."

"Sarah would love tea at the Plaza," I say, trying to explain who she is. "And carriage rides in Central Park. And going to the top of the Empire State Building. She's not cool. And I love that about her."

Jon pats my knee. "You don't have to apologize."

"Tiffany is very classic," Kevin allows grumpily. "I'm being a snob."

We walk into the store, and I let out a breath. Immediately I know that I'm right, surrounded by all that iconic robin's-egg blue. Sarah Louise will see the box alone and squeal with delight.

We find a sales associate, and I quickly pick out an oval halo ring with a diamond band in an expensive-but-not-ludicrous price range. I hand over my credit card and receive a bag in return.

Jon and Kevin clap when I hold it up in the air.

I smile, but I feel strangely flat.

I try to corral my thoughts to the appropriate image: Sarah Louise, diamond ring sparkling on her French-manicured hand, crying with joy.

But instead, I keep imagining Molly Marks, seeing the Tiffany blue and rolling her eyes at me. "How creative."

I'm relieved when Kevin says, "I'm starving. I want a burger."

"Let's go to P. J. Clarke's," Jon suggests. "It won't be too busy yet."

We walk the fifteen minutes to Third Avenue, and I begin to worry about losing my little blue bag filled with thirty-thousand dollars' worth of diamonds.

"Should I tuck this into my underwear or something?" I muse. "Does New York still have muggers?"

"Here, give it to me," Jon says. "I'll put it in my tote."

I hand it over and feel strangely lighter.

We get to the restaurant, which is already noisy with midtown types speaking over each other at the bar. It reminds me of happy hour at the spots in Chicago near my office, and I feel more like myself. We order beers and I pound mine while waiting for my burger.

"You all right, chief?" Jon asks, eyeing my second glass as it arrives.

"Great!" I say, reflexively.

But even with a buzz I feel glummer than a guy who just bought his girlfriend an engagement ring should.

"What's Alastair up to?" I ask Jon, to change the subject.

He and Kevin exchange an odd glance.

"I don't know," Jon says. "We . . . broke up."

"What? When?"

"Just before Christmas."

"And you didn't tell me?"

"Well, I wasn't ready to process it. We'd been talking about getting engaged for so long, but he wanted to open things up and I felt uncomfortable about it, so we decided to take a break. And then . . ." He shoots another glance at Kevin.

"We actually have some news for you," Kevin says. He takes Jon's hand over the table. "We're together. Like . . . *together* together."

I put down my beer midsip.

"You guys! What? How long has this been going on?"

"Since New Year's Eve," Kevin says. "We didn't want to tell you if it wasn't going to be anything serious."

"So it's serious?"

"We're moving in together at the end of the month," Jon says with a shy smile. "As soon as my lease is up."

"Oh my God, you guys. Wow. I'm so happy for you." I raise my glass. "To love! And to happiness!"

Maybe it's just my second beer hitting me on an empty stomach, but I feel much happier now. Like the news of my two best friends finding love together has made me more joyous than planning to propose to my own girlfriend.

"You know who called this?" I say. "Molly Marks."

"What?" Kevin laughs.

"Yeah. At the reunion. She said she thought you two had a spark."

"I guess she noticed it before we did," Jon says.

"Oh please," Kevin says. "I had a huge crush on you already. You know that."

Jon smiles at him. "What I meant is, I've had a huge crush on you for my entire adult life. I just didn't know it was reciprocated."

"It's *much* reciprocated."

They lean over and kiss.

They look right together. Natural. Relaxed.

I wonder if I look that way with Sarah.

But I don't want to think about Sarah, because the person in my head right now is Molly. And how I'm losing the bet, one to two.

And how she'll make fun of me relentlessly if she finds out.

And how much I want her to.

CHAPTER 19
Molly

His name is Sebastian Stone, née Tom Lovell, and he is the hottest man I've ever spoken to, let alone slept with.

We met at the premiere for my friend's movie. He walked up to me and asked if anyone had ever told me I look like Demi Moore, whereupon I immediately decided to sleep with him.

He's twenty-six. An actor. Not the aspiring kind—he's on a network show about teenage girls who solve crimes. He wants to pivot to action movies. He's never seen my films. I don't watch his show.

He works out for two to four hours a day and eats ungodly quantities of chicken breast. He gets spray tans and highlights and facials. He laughs about how I hide from the sun and don't dye my hair. He likes to play with my grays in bed, wrapping them around his manicured fingers and calling me his hot-ass crone.

He has a French bulldog named Milo he is sometimes photographed walking. The photos end up in the "stars, just like us" section of supermarket checkout line tabloids. He doesn't set up these photo ops, but he also doesn't avoid the celebrity-friendly coffee shops the paparazzi hang out in front of. Once, we were pictured together in a magazine holding hands while walking up Sunset and drinking twelve-dollar cold brews. The headline was SEBASTIAN STONE'S OLDER WOMAN. I framed it.

He lives in West Hollywood, on a high floor of an expensive condo tower. He doesn't own a car. It's a forty-five-minute drive, minimum, to get to his neighborhood. He's been to my house three times and questions why I would want to live in a place with no gym or private pool. He wants me to move to Beverly Hills. He laughs when I tell him I'd rather jump out of his high-rise.

We are an opposites-attract cliché, I'm aware, but you see: there's the sex.

I'm a professional writer and I'm not sure there are words to describe what he's capable of. I think it's something to do with his core strength and his young man's vigor. He loves to be between my legs. He loves to be inside me. He loves the taste of my skin. He loves to hold me up in front of mirrors and pin me against headboards and hitch me against trees. I've had more orgasms in the last three months than I have in the last three years.

He's the best antianxiety sex I've ever had. My life is a shambles, but I haven't popped a benzo since we met.

Currently, Sebastian is getting a massage at our hotel in Cabo San Lucas, where we've gone for a long weekend. Sebastian is treating, so he picked the hotel, and while it's luxurious, it seems to have been designed entirely for the sake of photo ops. It's difficult to navigate the walkways without running into scantily clad influencers having their pictures taken. I feel schlumpy and undermaintained in my boho white caftan. Everyone else is wearing, like, neon dental floss.

I flag down my waiter and order another margarita to my lounge chair. The sun is too intense for me to strip down and go in the pool, so I've been hunkered beneath an umbrella in my enormous sun hat for hours, dragging the umbrella around to fight the movement of the ever-encroaching sun.

I'm glad to be alone. Sebastian and I arrived a day and a half ago and have spent approximately every minute together since leaving Los Angeles. It's our first couple's trip, and the long stretches of time when we aren't either eating a meal or having sex are beginning to exhaust me. Sebastian is smart, in his way, but we don't have that much in common. In LA this is not a problem, since we rarely spend more than a night together. Here, I'm beginning to feel the conversational coffers run dry.

My phone chirps with a message notification, and I put down my book. I've been trying to spend my vacation not fixating on my phone, but reading an actual physical novel is harder than it used to be, now that most of my reading is done via apps.

Alyssa: Molls, how is vacay going?

Alyssa: I'm living for Sebastian's Insta posts

Alyssa: Do you know how many organs I would sell to go to a child-free resort?

Molly: There is actually one child here. A baby. With two nannies. And the mom has a dog she seems to love more than the baby, because she keeps sending the baby away and snuggling the dog

Alyssa: Sad

Alyssa: (BUT I GET IT!)

Molly: Rich people are wild

Dezzie: Molly, are you behaving wildly out of character and having fun?

I take a selfie of myself in my huge shades with my margarita in hand and throw it in the chat.

Molly: Poolside, baby

Dezzie: Where's your man?

Molly: Getting a massage

Alyssa: Getting along?

Molly: Mostly eating guacamole and fucking

Alyssa: STOP. I'LL DIE OF JEALOUSY.

Molly: He's a little boring though. We're running out of stuff to talk about

Dezzie: Talk about his abs

Alyssa: Or his penis

Molly: ALYSSA! When did you become such a pervert?

Alyssa: You do not even want to know how long it's been since I've had sex. Like five years. I'm not kidding

Dezzie: I think you're forgetting you have a baby under the age of two, so that's not possible

Alyssa: Immaculate conception

Dezzie: Wish that would work for me. I am so tired of having sex with rob for the purpose of procreation. If it doesn't work soon I'm buying a turkey baster

Alyssa: It'll happen

Molly: Keep trying!!! I need a mini dez

Alyssa: Or a mini Rob

Dezzie: LOL. An infant shuffling around in dockers and a concert tee from 2006? Can't wait

Molly: At least you HAVE a rob. Honestly you guys, this trip has me wondering why all my best relationships are sexual

Molly: Like, seb is nice and I enjoy his company in small to medium increments but mainly he's hot and we have amazing chemistry

Molly: I'm bored

Dezzie: I can answer that

Molly: Oh good

Dezzie: CUZ YOU AVOID DATING ANYONE YOU ACTUALLY LIKE

Alyssa: Not to mention when you accidentally do like them you break up with them immediately

I try to think of a sassy reply, but my text box is overridden by an incoming call. From, of all people, Seth Rubenstein.

I haven't spoken to him since we saw each other in Los Angeles. I have, however, spent a generous amount of time spying on him and his beautiful girlfriend on Instagram.

"Hello?" I say.

"Molly McMarks?"

"Speaking."

He chuckles. My mouth curves into a smile I can't hold back. I love the sound of his laugh.

"How the hell are ya?" His voice is ever so slightly soft around the consonants. Like he's tipsy.

"I'm a seven point five out of ten. Maybe even an eight."

"That's like a sixteen for a normal person."

"Sure is."

"What are you doing?"

"I'm in Mexico actually. Drinking margs in front of an infinity pool with a view of the ocean."

"For real, buddy?"

"For real, buddy."

"God, I'm jealous."

"Chicago's permanent winter got you down?"

"I'm in New York, actually."

"Oh yeah? What are you doing there?"

He laughs softly. "You don't want to know."

"Okey dokey."

"You're the only person left on Earth who says 'okey dokey.'"

"Nope. My mom says it."

"How is your mom?"

"She's great. Just sold a ten-million-dollar house on the bay. Working on my inheritance."

"You're going to be so rich. You can quit your job and live off the fat of the land."

"Excuse you. I'm an independent adult woman with a booming career."

A bent truth if ever there was one.

"I was just kidding," he says. "What are you working on?"

Ugh. I don't want to tell him, because this means acknowledging to myself how asinine my current project is. My father asked me the same question last week and I literally lied and said I'm between jobs rather than face his scorn.

But whatever. It's just Seth. He takes pride in my accomplishments like only someone who doesn't understand my downward trajectory can.

"I've been commissioned to adapt a third-rate young adult tearjerker that will premiere on some new micro-streaming app and be viewed mainly by sixth graders and those who have the taste of sixth graders."

"What do sixth graders taste like?"

"Chicken."

He laughs very hard.

"That was barely amusing," I say. "Are you drunk?"

"Mmmmm . . . maybe a little," he allows.

"Isn't it like seven o'clock there?"

"I started early."

"A special occasion? Or are you just a sad businessman drinking alone in some hotel bar?"

"Special occasion."

"Care to share?"

"Well, that's why I called you."

"Oh, I thought you called me because you're drunk and unrequitedly in love with me."

That just slipped out, probably because of the second margarita.

I screw up my entire face in humiliation and am infinitely grateful he can't see me.

He's quiet for a second. And then he laughs.

"Dream *on,* Karl Marx."

Ugh, relief. He's letting it slide.

"Don't call me that."

"Okay, Molly Malolly."

"Ew. That's my *mom's* nickname for me. Please don't impersonate my mother. Anyway, what's your news?"

I honestly have no idea what he's going to tell me. That Marian married her Cubs player? That he has an idea for a screenplay? That he's terminally ill and wants one last goodbye?

"You're winning," he says.

"Winning what?"

"The bet."

"Because you've finally admitted to yourself I won't be your date to our twentieth reunion?"

"No. Because Jon and Kevin are dating."

"What?" I yell so loudly that the YouTuber next to me interrupts her livestream and glares.

"I know." I can hear a smile in his voice.

"Aww, that makes me so happy!"

"Me too. Though I can't believe you were right about them."

I can. They are the rare fated couple on which all those "ships passing in the night" romances are based.

"I told you, I'm good at this," I say. "Are you with them right now?"

"I was all day, but I left to call you—oh *fuck.*" I hear scrabbling noises, then more curses.

"Seth? Everything okay?"

He expels a breath. "God *damn* it. I left something with Jon."

"Something important?"

"Yeah," he says, his voice strained. "Pretty important. Look, I gotta go."

"Okey dokey. Talk in six months?"

But he's already ended the call.

I immediately open my messages.

Molly: Guys

Molly: Wow

Dezzie: What?

Molly: Seth Rubenstein just called me

Dezzie: "Seth Rubenstein" lol. Like there's some other Seth

Molly: He called to say jon and kevin from high school are dating!

Alyssa: !!!

Dezzie: I always thought they had a thing

Molly: Me toooooo

I wish Seth were here so I could gloat to his face.

But he's not. Sebastian is here. And he is walking toward me, clad in a fluffy white robe.

He flops down next to me. "Hey, babe."

"Hey. How was your massage?"

"So great."

He removes his robe to reveal his perfect, massage-oiled musculature and takes his sunscreen, giant water bottle, and book out of his tote bag. He only reads self-help books about woo-woo shit like manifesting, as far as I can tell.

"What do you want to do for dinner tonight?" I ask. "Shall we go into town? I heard the food at Dahlia is incredible."

He puts his hand on my thigh. "Why don't we stay in and order room service?"

He means stay in and have sex in our suite. Which we also did last night.

This is not unappealing, but people can both eat food in a restaurant and have sex in one evening.

"Let's at least check out one of the restaurants here at the hotel," I counter. "The sushi place has omakase."

Sushi is one of the few foods Sebastian eats other than chicken breast.

He squeezes my thigh. "Sure, babe."

"I'll walk over and make a reservation."

It's nice to move my legs after an entire day rotting in the sun on a chaise lounge. I always think I like vacations where you do nothing but sit by the pool. And then, after about one day, I start losing my mind.

I make our dinner reservation with the concierge. And then, on impulse, I ask, "Are there any day trips or excursions you would recommend for tomorrow?"

"We're just at the end of the whale migration season," she says. "We offer a fabulous two-hour whale-watching trip that leaves at ten in the morning."

Whales! The marine biologist I aspired to be in fourth grade does a backflip.

"Fantastic. Can you book it for me? Two people?"

"Of course, madam."

I walk back to the pool, unnerved that a young woman called me "madam," but pleased with myself for concocting an adventure.

"So we've got a table for dinner at eight," I tell Seb. "And guess what?"

He looks up from his book on crystals, or whatever. "What, babe?"

"I booked us a whale-watching tour!"

He wrinkles his beautiful top lip. "On a boat?"

"Uh . . . yes."

"But I get seasick. And I thought you hated boats."

"I hate sailboats. And even if I didn't, I'd make an exception for *whales*. Come on!"

He gives me a kind smile. "Why don't you go solo and take lots of pictures."

"You *really* won't come?"

"Babe, I'll puke on the whales."

He returns to his book on self-actualization, or whatever.

I am speechless. What kind of man will not go on a whale-watching tour with his girlfriend?

A boring one.

Seb, I must finally admit to myself, is chronically boring.

I open my phone and pull up Seth's number.

Molly: Do you like whales?

Seth: Um, yes, I'm not a monster.

Seth: Why?

Molly: Just conducting an informal poll

Seth: To locate the sociopaths among your acquaintances?

Molly: Yep. So far i've only found one

Seth: Is it you?

Molly: I actually just murdered a whale, so

Seth: Presumably an endangered one.

Molly: Yep. A baby

Seth: Always stay true to yourself.

Molly: I'm a woman of principle

Seth: That's why I admire you.

I laugh out loud. Sebastian looks up from his book on astronumerology, or whatever. "What's so funny?"

"Oh, just . . . nothing. Whales."

He smiles at me indulgently. "You're cute. Want to go back to the room?"

I glance longingly at my phone, but Seb's already pulling me out of my chair.

The rest of the evening goes by predictably. We have sex in the shower. We eat sushi. (Sashimi for him, a twelve-course omakase for me, because it's important to *live,* even if your boyfriend is mortally afraid of carbs.) We go back to the room and have sex again.

I never thought one could grow so weary of fabulous sex.

I set my alarm and wake up early. Sebastian is gone—no doubt already at the gym. I grab a bacon torta at the breakfast cantina and head to the lobby to meet my tour group.

There are six of us: me and a family of five from Cincinnati. The parents are nice, but the children—three adolescent girls—look at me like I'm creepy for being alone.

"I'm here with my boyfriend, but he gets seasick," I explain to the mother, who has not asked.

"Oh, that's a shame. Too seasick for whales?"

"I know." I sigh. "I should probably break up with him."

She gives me a confused look.

"Just kidding!" I say.

She laughs politely and busies herself doling out sunscreen to her children.

We are led down to the beach, where a speedboat awaits us. The tour guide introduces himself and distributes life vests. Two men push us out into the surf, and then we're off.

I sit near the bow of the boat with the guide. "They're just a few miles off the coast today," he tells me. "It's a good day. Calm. They're feeding."

I nod and let the wind whip through my hair and the salt spray my face. Boating on the Pacific is different from the calm Gulf bays and intercoastals by my mom's house. This is more fun. I feel like Tom Cruise in a Michael Bay movie. I find myself grinning. Genuinely enjoying myself.

How novel.

The guide leaps to his feet. "Over there. Ten o'clock."

We all turn our heads to see a massive blue whale rise out of the water. She disappears, and then her tail breaks through the surf with a splash.

"Look, two more," one of the girls cries.

I whirl around to see them duck out of the water in tandem—one big, one small.

"It's a mama and her baby!" another tween cries.

We all grab our phones and wildly snap photos.

Then I stop, and just watch them—let the moment wash over me.

The guide grabs the wheel and turns the boat, and we spend the next hour finding whale after whale. Some of them approach us, curious. A baby shows off with a flip out of the water as her mother circles her protectively.

They splash us. They squirt water out of their blowholes. They do every single thing you could desire of a whale.

The family and I laugh and take pictures and by the time the hour is up even the daughters seem to like me. I can't remember the last time something felt so exhilarating.

I loved doing it for myself, but part of me wishes there had been someone to share it with aside from a family of strangers.

I tip the guide handsomely, say goodbye to the family, and walk toward the pool on wobbly, seafaring legs. I grab a chair, order a margarita, and collapse back to examine my haul of photos.

They are beautiful, and I open Instagram to post a few.

The first post I see is from @sethrubes.

He's sitting next to his gorgeous blond girlfriend in a park. They are holding hands, and there is a giant, sparkling ring on her finger.

It's captioned *@Sarah_LT just made me the luckiest man in Chicago. No, wait, the world.*

It has 563 likes, and the first comment beneath it is from the @Sarah_LT in question. *Can't wait to be your wife.*

I close the app, stricken, abandon my margarita, and fumble my way back to my suite to find Seb.

"Are you crying, babe?" he asks, emerging from the shower in all his glistening glory.

"It's nothing," I say. "I think I'm about to start my period."

"Aww. Come here and let me kiss it better," he says.

I bury myself in his chest and, for a minute, just let myself cry.

He wipes the tears from under my eyes and kisses me on both cheeks.

He really is nice.

I know that I'll break up with him as soon as we get back to LA.

I never do get around to posting the whales.

PART FIVE

June 2020

CHAPTER 20
Seth

I am a creature of movement.

I relish getting up at five in the morning to work out at my gym, and enjoy walking the two miles to my office, even in the frigid Chicago winters. (Except in the snow. I'm high energy, not insane.) I like to meet colleagues and clients for lunch at fashionable new restaurants (my treat), and to meet friends for drinks after work at the brass-bar, old-school pub around the block from my building. I like to go to the theater, the opera, the symphony, films. On the weekends, I like to hike and cycle and run long distances with Sarah Louise. I like to golf with my buddies. (I love dad sports.) I like to shop at the gourmet market and make elaborate meals, then vigorously clean the kitchen.

I like vigorous cleaning in general.

And I am a people person. An extrovert. I shoot the shit in the line at the grocery store and chat up strangers on airplanes. (I know. I can't help it.) I love to argue in court. I'm the life of the party, and if there is not a party happening soon, I throw one. My calendar is completely booked every day from morning 'til night, and if I happen to have a free spot, I fill it as quickly as possible.

I love this life, and I thrive on it, even if I'm antsy to replace all the karaoke bars and legal conferences with dad groups and playdates. But to manage the chaos, I need rigorous stillness when I'm not moving. Silence when I'm not socializing. A refuge of calm.

I keep my condo immaculate—all unobstructed views of the lake from the twenty-ninth floor, with clean marble countertops and sparse white furniture and dark, polished floors. I keep my office so organized that my paralegals are afraid to touch anything, and they should be, because a single stray paper destroys my focus and ruins my mood. My emails are sorted to such a degree of perfection that my assistant and I are almost in love, platonically. I keep my inbox at zero and my contacts relentlessly updated. When I'm not in meetings I work in silence, alone.

Movement and people, or silence and solitude. These are my modes.

A quarantine is thus custom-designed to make me psychologically implode.

I know that I am absolutely, magically blessed. I haven't lost anyone to Covid-19. My job is secure and I am able to work remotely in my home office. I am isolating with my fiancée, rather than alone. I do not have to homeschool children while trying to work.

But things are not ideal.

Sarah Louise sublet her apartment and moved in with me as soon as we got engaged. It would be odd not to live together before getting married. It made sense. I was excited.

I expected having to adjust to sharing my space, but I didn't expect it to give me claustrophobia. Sarah is a big personality—exuberant and chatty. She likes cozy spaces and has filled my apartment with photographs and knickknacks and throw blankets and pillows she embroiders while listening to podcasts because she has to be doing at least two things at once. She turns on the TV while working, because background noise helps her concentrate.

Shudder.

None of this is damning. In other circumstances, it would be endearing.

But without the hustle and bustle of our previously busy lives, we're on top of each other. We eat breakfast, lunch, and dinner together. She works from the guest bedroom and I work from my office. We Zoom, Zoom, Zoom. We watch television together in the evenings. We take turns on the Peloton. We talk until we run out of things to talk about.

We have run out of things to talk about.

I used to think we had everything in common. The law. Values. Exercise.

And we *do*.

But I also used to think we had a special spark. And for the life of me I can't figure out what it was, or where it's gone.

It's not that we fight. We're kind to each other. But we've stopped talking about anything that matters, except the grim, relentless statistics about Covid. We haven't had sex in a month. We don't make each other laugh.

And then last night, as we were both reading our his-and-hers copies of *The New Yorker* in bed, she turned over and gently took mine out of my hands.

At first, I thought she wanted to make love, and I felt a sense of dread wash over me, and then a sense of despair that this is how I felt about the possibility of touching my beautiful, sexy future wife.

"Honey, I'm tired—" I began.

"I need to tell you something," she said. "Rebecca is moving out of my apartment."

Rebecca is the tenant subleasing Sarah's old place until the lease is up.

"Oh yeah?" I asked. "Why?"

"She's tired of being alone in the city and she's going to move out to her sister's farmhouse in Wisconsin. Help with her kids."

"Ah, wow. That sounds nice."

It dawned on me that maybe Sarah Louise wanted to leave the city for a while, and I began rapidly calculating whether this would make things better or worse between us.

"So I was thinking I would move back into my place," she said, so quietly it was almost a whisper.

"*What?*"

She took my hand and squeezed it. "I know it must sound crazy, but I think we could both use more space. And, I mean, we're only twenty minutes apart, so it's not like we couldn't still spend time together."

Twenty minutes apart! The words were at once shocking and . . . strangely appealing. Perversely appealing. Treacherously appealing.

"What about, um . . . the whole living-together-before-we-get-married thing?"

"Well it's not like we can have a wedding anytime soon." She laughed weakly, and my hands began to shake.

"Sorry if I'm reading into this too much," I said. "But . . . Do you want to break up?"

She was quiet for a long time. "I don't know, Seth. Things have been off for a while. I know you've felt it too."

My instinct was to preserve her feelings by lying, to insist things are *amazing* and we are *madly in love*. But that wouldn't have been fair.

We've been overdue for a difficult conversation.

It was brave of her to start it. I'm not sure I ever would have.

"I know," I admitted quietly. "I'm not sure if it's the pandemic, or if it's us."

"I do love you," she said, her voice closer to her normal register. "But we might have rushed into all this too quickly. It's only been ten months since we met."

She's right. I was so excited to have the bachelor phase of my life be over. I was so eager to settle down.

I still want all of that. A marriage, a family. But I can't shake the feeling that this relationship is wrong.

That she's not my soul mate.

"I get it," I said, squeezing her hand. "It's been fast, and the circumstances took a turn. It's been really hard on us both."

"In a way the pandemic might be a blessing," she said. "If it weren't for Covid, we'd have rushed into planning a wedding, and gotten swept up in the excitement, and maybe wouldn't have had time to really be together."

It hurts me that being together is what made her feelings for me cool. Even if it's mutual, it's heartbreaking.

"Let's take some time," I said. "You'll go back to your place, we'll get some space. See what happens."

She was quiet for a while, gathering her thoughts. "Will that just drag out a breakup?"

I sighed. "Maybe."

"I just . . . God this is so hard. I wish this wasn't happening." She wiped away a tear.

I pulled her into my arms.

"Me too."

And then we made love—more tenderly than we have since we got engaged.

I think we both knew—know—that it's the last time.

That was last night.

I'm still processing as I wake up to the smell of her vegan, gluten-free banana muffins. She's in the kitchen, in her workout clothes, making fresh green juice.

"Hi, handsome," she says.

For a moment, I wonder if I hallucinated last night. If it was just my subconscious working through a problem my conscious mind refused to acknowledge was real.

Then I notice the suitcases by the door.

Jesus. She's leaving *today*?

"I reserved a U-Haul to pick up at nine," she says. She holds out a juice. It smells like cucumber and parsley.

I gape at her.

"You reserved a U-Haul in the *middle of the night?*"

"Yesterday," she says, looking at the juicer rather than at me. "Before we talked."

What do you say to that?

"Ah," is all I manage.

"I should be able to get everything packed up by the end of the day," she says. "Get out of your hair."

I go very still. "You're not *in my hair*, Sarah."

"That's not what I meant. Sorry, I just don't know how to act." She puts both of her palms on the kitchen island, leans forward. "Are you mad?"

"No. This is all just very sudden."

She nods. "I want to rip off the Band-Aid, you know?"

I suppose she's right. A few more days of cohabitation is not going to change the fact that another one of my relationships has failed.

"Okay," I say, "I get that. Why don't I go pick up the U-Haul while you start packing. I'll help you move back into your apartment, and then we can get Vinioso's takeout."

Vinioso's is an incredible red sauce joint by her place. Back when we were first dating, we spent many a night slurping up their spaghetti pomodoro over wine and delightful conversation. It seems like a fitting place to say goodbye.

"That sounds perfect," she says.

When I get back with the U-Haul, we spend the afternoon packing. Oddly, it's one of the happiest days we've had together in months. We laugh and make jokes and when she tries to pack up a pillow embroidered with a golden retriever, I demand she let me keep it.

"You despise it!" she protests.

"Stockholm syndrome. I can't live without it."

"Well in that case, she's yours."

By five, we've loaded the truck and driven to her apartment. Carrying up her bags and the handful of boxes with her stuff—mostly workout gear, photos, and books—takes less than twenty minutes.

We call in our order to Vinioso's and I don my mask to walk the few blocks to pick it up. I get a small pitcher of grab-and-go Manhattans as well—Sarah doesn't drink that much, and I have to drive the U-Haul back, but I figure one parting cocktail is a festive way to say goodbye.

When I return to her apartment, Frank Sinatra is playing—Frank was always playing at Vin's, back when it was safe to eat inside—and the table is set with a tablecloth and candles.

We exchange our favorite memories of our time together while we eat. We speculate on how our friends and families will react to the news—and hope they won't be sad for us, because we know we're making the right decision. As I eat tiramisu and she eats limoncello sorbetto, she takes the ring off her finger and slides it across the table.

"You should take this back," she says. "You can probably return it. I still have the box."

I can't imagine the sadness of going back to Tiffany and trying to return an engagement ring any more than I can imagine giving it to another woman. I bought it because I knew it would make her—specifically her, my Sarah Louise—happy. And it did.

The ring was never the problem.

"Please keep it. I want you to have it."

She smiles sadly and slips it over her right ring finger. "Thank you."

We both stand, and an awkward moment passes.

"Sarah Louise Taylor," I finally say, "I wish you the happiest imaginable life."

She squeezes me in a tight hug. "You too, Seth."

When I finally get home it's 10:00 p.m. and I'm emotionally exhausted. I put on cashmere sweats Sarah bought me and open my laptop. I figure I should start drafting an email to my family explaining what happened, even if it takes me a few days to send it.

I know if I try to call them, I'll break down, and they'll worry.

I know my brother, in particular, will be thinking *I told you so.* He never believed that Sarah was right for me, and warned me I was, once again, plunging into a serious relationship more out of a desire to be partnered than out of actual attraction to the specific person. We had a huge fight about it and didn't speak for three weeks. But he was correct. As always.

Instead of drafting my sad announcement, I scroll through a couple of work emails I don't have the emotional capacity to deal with and notice a message from my old college friend Mike Anatolian.

> From: michael_c_anatolian@netmail.co
> To: sethrubes@mail.me
> Date: Sun, June 21, 2020 at 4:06pm
> Subject: Favor?
>
> Hey there bud!
>
> How are you faring with the pandy? Hope to God all is well with you and Sarah and the fam.
>
> Wondering if you can do me a favor . . . my little sister is going to be a senior at NYU next year and she's freaking out about summer internships. She's a film major and had an internship lined up at a production company for the summer, but they've shut down due to Covid, and she's panicking. Long shot, but are you still in touch with that girl you hooked up with at your reunion? Becks is trying to find something she can do remotely in the film industry and I thought a screenwriter would have some intern tasks she could do from New York.
>
> No worries if that's awkward, just thought I'd ask since I don't run into too many artistes in finance.
>
> Anyway, how the hell are you?

Suddenly, at the thought of emailing Molly, I am a lot the fuck better.

CHAPTER 21
Molly

I am an inveterate loner. Total introvert. Taurus to my core.

Sitting in my house solo for a week and not talking to anyone except via text was, for many years, my dearest dream.

That was before solitary confinement became my enforced reality.

As it turns out, all that alone time that's so nice when it's a break from social engagements and meetings becomes something like torture without those things to break it up. My house, formerly my sanctuary, has begun to feel like a prison.

The novelty of catching up with friends online has faded. No, I don't want to play virtual poker with six people from college. No, I do not want to join another online movie club. No, I don't want to go on a blind date via Zoom.

I want to take meetings, where I can do a stressful song and dance to sell my writerly prowess to producers who don't care about my craft or singular voice. I want to go on a date, where I can make out with a stranger over craft cocktails. I want to go to a restaurant, where I can eat food served to me by an overly friendly human who keeps interrupting my conversation to ask how everything is tasting. I want to go to a spa with my friends, where we can be naked and oblivious to germs and gossip about mutual acquaintances.

I want to see my mom. I want to stop watching cable news in a fugue state of anxiety and despair. I want to know less about virology and case positivity rates. I want to stop worrying about the people I love dying.

I want another human being to touch me.

My psychiatrist upped my meds, but there is only so much Lexapro can do for chronic isolation and mass trauma.

It doesn't help that the film industry has slowed to a standstill. Offers for new projects have dried up. No one's buying anything.

Which does not stop me from staring at my email all day, hoping for something more promising than recipe chains from my mom, alerts from Facebook, and junk mail from dying clothing retailers. Or bills. Please, God, no more bills.

It's not that I'm broke. I have savings and I still get residuals, however dwindling, from the movies I wrote. But I'm also not optimistic about my future earning power. I'm truly beginning to circle the drain in my career.

When I "made it" as a screenwriter in my twenties, I thought my success was only the beginning. That my gift very obviously spoke for itself, and that I would become a brand, able to command better and better jobs and make ever more money.

But I've never been able to repeat the success of those first movies. My name is not a hot commodity. And with Hollywood at a complete standstill, there aren't a lot of opportunities to redeem myself coming up anytime soon.

It keeps me up at night.

Today is no different. I wake up and force myself to pour an iced coffee and take a quick walk around the block before opening my laptop and silently repeating my daily mantra: *Please let there be an offer. A nibble. Anything other than more silence and rejection.*

No dice.

Which means another shift at my new day job of sitting on my couch and watching reruns of Bravo shows while eating cereal directly out of the box.

My phone rings ninety minutes into my busy day of reality television, and I drag my attention away from women pouring wine on each other, wipe crumbs off my hands, and pick it up.

It's my dad.

Returning my check-in call from three days ago. A quarterly rite in which he discusses his latest placements on the bestseller lists, recaps his most recent vacations, inquires after my career, tacitly deems it pathetic, and offers me money.

It's a great bonding ritual.

"Hi, Dad," I say, settling back into the cushions.

"Hey, toots," he says.

There is a loud screech from somewhere on his end of the call.

"Hear that?" he asks. "Macaw."

"A macaw? Where are you?"

"The Keys. My pal Kimbo has a private island with a bird sanctuary. Celeste and I are here for a month."

"Jesus, did you fly? Is that even allowed? Aren't you worried about Covid?"

"Sailed."

I shouldn't have asked.

"Anyway," he says, "what's shakin'?"

I look from the muted television to my box of children's cereal.

"Oh, just doing a little work."

"What on?"

"Uh, a spec script."

"Rom-com?"

"Yep."

"Sounds like you have some time on your hands."

Ah. We've reached the part about my wasted potential earlier than expected. I don't know why I initiate these calls, other than that if I didn't, I'd be fatherless. It's strange how you can crave the attention of the people with the most power to hurt you.

"Well, yeah, things are slow here, obviously," I say. "Production being shut down. I'd think the Mack Fontaine stuff is on hold too, no?"

"Eh. I'm not worried. The latest one is already in post."

"That's lucky."

Never put it past my father to be unscathed by a global economic shutdown.

"That's why I'm calling, actually," he says. "We're in development for *Busted,* and we just fired the writers."

Busted is one of my dad's most popular novels. The plot is about a model who hires Mack Fontaine to expose a corrupt plastic surgeon after he botches her boob job. Obviously, because no one can resist Mack, she also has a torrid affair with him.

"That's too bad," I say, unsure what this might have to do with me.

"They weren't nailing Diane," he says, referring to the character with the leaking implants. "My producer thinks we need a woman to write it. Make it sexier."

I wish I could tell you this is the first time my father has referred to his work as sexy.

"That makes sense," I say. "It might be a nice change of pace. You don't see a lot of female-written action movies."

"Yeah, well, I thought maybe you'd want to throw your hat in the ring, since you love the book."

I do not love the book. I will allow that my father's novels have a lurid appeal, but they are decidedly not for me. Of course, I would never say that to him. He assumes I think he's a genius. He assumes that of everyone.

This does not change the fact that I'm stunned. He has always dismissed my work. I assumed he thought I was a bad writer.

"Wow," I say, unable to help myself. "That's . . . thanks for thinking of me, Dad. That could be really cool."

"Well, never say you didn't follow in my footsteps for nothing."

"What would you need from me to pitch?"

"A treatment, to start."

"Yeah. Okay. No problem. When do you need it?"

"No rush. Things aren't moving quickly, with the virus. We're still talking to directors."

"Okay. Well, I'll get started right away. I'm excited."

His wife calls his name, and the phone goes muffled for a second.

"Gotta go, kid. Tennis."

"Okay. Love you, Dad."

"Yup. Bye."

The line goes dead.

I feel a strange tension at the corners of my face.

A *smile,* you might call it.

My father has made me *smile.*

I try not to let this feeling get too big, because it's never good to get your hopes up where Roger Marks is concerned. But I can't help it. I'm *flattered.*

He thinks I can write a fucking action movie. Be trusted with his precious Mack Fontaine. Given how highly he thinks of his work, this is no small compliment.

I grab my laptop to email my agent and manager letting them know of this development.

My heart nearly stops when I see the name at the top of my inbox.

Seth.

I haven't talked to him since he got engaged.

I had to mute him on Instagram, because every time he posted a picture of himself and his beautiful, wholesome, seemingly perfect-for-him-in-every-way fiancée, it made me sad.

And I have enough making me sad.

Still, I click on his email faster than you can say "bad idea."

> From: sethrubes@mail.me
> To: mollymarks@netmail.co
> Date: Mon, June 22, 2020 at 11:12am
> Subject: Whale hello
>
> Hiya Marks.
>
> How are you faring during these dark times? I really hope that you're okay, and your family is okay.
>
> I was wondering if I could ask for a favor. A friend of mine has a sister studying film at NYU whose summer internship fell through due to Covid. She's looking for something she can do remotely, and I thought maybe you might want some help from a smart college kid for the summer? I'm pretty sure she'll do anything you want, even if it's just proofreading your drafts. No worries whatsoever if you're not interested—just thought I'd ask.
>
> Let me know how you're doing. Thinking of you.
> -Seth

Hmm. The tone is rather somber (fittingly) and matter-of-fact. Still, it's nice to hear from him.

I have absolutely no need for an intern, but I suppose I could scrounge up some tasks to help out his friend. I remember how desperate I was for any foothold in the business in college. If I'm your best inroad to fame and fortune in film I worry for you, of course, but still. I'm better than nothing.

I click reply.

From: mollymarks@netmail.co
To: sethrubes@mail.me
Date: Mon, June 22, 2020 at 11:20am
Re: Subject: Whale hello

Hey!

I'm okay! It's kinda lonely out here for a spinster, but I'm enormously
grateful that my loved ones are okay so far. And on the bright side,
I never imagined I'd be blessed with such a varied and glamorous
collection of face masks.

How's your family? Isn't your sister-in-law an emergency room
doctor? I hope she's okay. Can't imagine the stress of that.

I'm happy to help out your friend's sister. Things are quiet on the
film front right now, as you might imagine, but I'm sure I can find
some stuff for her to do for a few hours a week. Give her my email
if she's interested.

By the way, I saw the news about your engagement! Congratulations!

Cheers—
Molls

I click send before I can second-guess myself or labor over line edits, and
draft the note to my reps.

By the time it's sent, I hear the ding of a new message.

From: sethrubes@mail.me
To: mollymarks@netmail.co
Date: Mon, June 22, 2020 at 11:51am
Re: Re: Subject: Whale hello

I'm sure you look very glamorous in a face mask. I just look like a
bank robber.

But in all seriousness, I'm so sorry you're lonely. I've been having the opposite problem—feeling trapped with not enough space. I'm pretty sure quarantine is awful any way you slice it. I know it's not a feeling unique to me in any way, but I hate this so much.

Thanks for asking about Clara. She is indeed an ER doctor. She's been quarantining in a hotel for two months to keep the kids and Dave safe. Miserable situation—working like crazy, missing the boys, seeing horrible shit day in and day out. But at least she hasn't gotten sick. She's hoping that now that there's more proper PPE it will be safe to go home soon.

As for the internship, thank you so much. Her name is Becky Anatolian and she is going to be so pumped to work for such a rock star. I'll connect you by email.

And thanks for your kind words on the engagement. But actually . . . Sarah Louise and I just broke up. (Like, she moved out yesterday.) So I'm still processing . . .

Anyway, I'm so glad you're doing okay, and thanks again!

Oh my God.

Shit.

I shouldn't have said anything about the engagement. It's not helpful to know this. I feel horrible that it makes me feel . . . joy?

Ugh, *Molly.*

But it does. It makes me feel joy.

The joy is not borne out of schadenfreude. No part of me wants Seth to be heartbroken.

It's the part of me—the immediate, lizard-brain, pure id part of me—that wants Seth to be . . . available. That wants him to be held in reserve in case I decide that I want him for myself.

Or, perhaps the better word is "admit." "Admit" that I want him for myself.

Not that it's any more possible than it ever has been. I mentally repeat the reasons why I should not care about this foolish yen: we are separated by the better part of a continent in an unending pandemic in which it is not safe to take a commercial flight; he's *one day* into a breakup; he's wholesome and nice and I'm . . . the kind of person who feels joy when someone tells me they just broke off an engagement.

So I don't reply.

I step away from the computer, fill up my water bottle, grab a mask, and go outside for a walk.

Usually, I hate walking in my neighborhood, as the hills make my calves burn, but I can't sit in my house. I need to move around to force out the adrenaline. I feel like I just did three grams of cocaine. (I've never actually done cocaine because I'm convinced I would like it so much that I'd instantly get addicted, but my understanding is that three grams is, like, enough to kill an elephant.)

Mercifully, it's a breezy June day in LA—high of seventy-four. The kind of perfect weather we were promised in Southern California before global warming began to turn it into an uninhabitable fireball. I speed-walk up and down the street, dodging groups of children and unleashed dogs, plotting out what to write back to Seth.

Obviously, I cannot in any way express my relief or communicate romantic interest. Aside from the fact that it would make me seem insensitive, selfish, and possibly batshit insane, I'm not trying to be a rebound. And anyway, that's not what anyone wants to hear in the immediate aftermath of a failed relationship.

What I need to be is kind.

Express sympathy and an open ear should he want one.

In short, I need to act like a better person.

Back home, I go right for my laptop.

From: mollymarks@netmail.co
To: sethrubes@mail.me
Date: Mon, June 22, 2020 at 12:45pm
Re: Re: Re: Subject: Whale hello

God, Seth I'm so sorry to hear about your breakup. I can't imagine dealing with that right now.

Are you okay? I'm here if you need an ear.

Love,
Molly

I pause for a minute, come to my senses, and delete the "Love, Molly" part. I consider changing "love" to "xo" but that feels too casual given the subject matter. I can't think of anything better, so I hit send.

And then I stare at my inbox for the next hour while mindlessly eating more cereal.

From: sethrubes@mail.me
To: mollymarks@netmail.co
Date: Mon, June 22, 2020 at 2:06pm
Re: Re: Re: Re: Subject: Whale hello

Thanks for asking, Molls. I am . . . shell-shocked.

It was Sarah's idea. Which is not to blame her—ultimately I do think it was the right decision, and that she was brave and clear-sighted for calling it, rather than letting it drag on. But I'm reeling from how abruptly it ended. (She floated it Saturday night and moved out on Sunday.)

The thing is, I thought we were really good together. Actually, we *were* really good together. At least for a while.

She's a public defender and she inspired me to finally get my act together and start the nonprofit legal clinic I'd been spinning around in my head. I've got a great group of law students helping domestic violence victims with family court. Your friend Rob is actually referring clients—nice guy.

Anyway, then we got engaged, and what's kind of funny is that the day I bought the ring I immediately lost it. Accidentally left it with Jon and Kevin. Had to race in a taxi to Brooklyn to track it down. Now I can't help but think that was a sign.

But so, once we were engaged we moved in together and Covid started almost immediately, so we've been right on top of each other for months. It got claustrophobic. Maybe if we'd had more space it would have gone differently . . . I don't know. Maybe we got to know each other better and realized we weren't as compatible as we thought. In any case, it just wasn't working.

In my heart, I think if this broke us up, it wasn't meant to be. I'm glad it happened before we were married or had kids together.

I want to marry the love of my life, you know?

Still fucking hurts though.

Anyway, this is probably more than you want to hear!

Thanks for listening to/reading my meanderings.
-Seth

I read his email four times. The line I keep getting stuck on is *I want to marry the love of my life.*
He fucking deserves that.
I want to be there for him. I immediately write back.

From: mollymarks@netmail.co
To: sethrubes@mail.me
Date: Mon, June 22, 2020 at 2:20pm
Re: Re: Re: Re: Re: Subject: Whale hello

This sounds so painful. Even if it wasn't meant to be, endings suck. And one day's notice is . . . tough.

I'm going to indulge in some earnestness for a moment: you deserve someone truly incredible. You are one of the best people I know.

You'll find the love of your life. And she'll be a very lucky woman.

Which is why, every once in a while, I wish she were me.

My fingers are typing faster than my brain, and so it takes me a second to realize what I've written.

No, Molly.

No and no and no and *no*.

I delete that last line with pure horror and reread the whole email to make sure I didn't say anything else that will expose my longing for him.

I click send.

But getting the email off my desktop doesn't change the truth.

I *do* wish I was the love of Seth Rubenstein's life.

CHAPTER 22

Seth

All day, ever since I sent my "I regret to inform you I won't be getting married after all" email, I've been fielding texts and phone calls from well-meaning friends and relatives.

My mom sobbed and wondered how anyone could leave her perfect boy.

My dad said I'll find someone else pronto, because I'm a catch.

My brother said Sarah wasn't right for me and, "as he's told me many times before," I need to break this pattern of too-fast relationships.

Kevin said he'd had a bad feeling ever since I bought the "basic" ring.

Jon said Kevin is callous and lamented that they can't come visit me because it's too dangerous to fly.

But the person whose words comforted me the most was actually Molly Marks. "You're one of the best people I know."

It's not that the sentiment is so true. It's that Molly doesn't give compliments often. She's so rarely sincere, and when she is, she really means it. Reading those words from her made me remember the last time we saw each other. How she invited me to stay with her. How she looked so disappointed when I told her about Sarah, and then embarrassed that I could see her disappointment.

And I know that I'm twenty-four hours out of a relationship. But I find myself wondering if she's single.

I can't *ask* her. She'll think I'm nuts.

But when she said she knows I'll find the love of my life, part of me thrummed with this wild thought: *What if I already have? What if it's you?*

I want desperately to respond to her note—to keep the conversation going—but I have no idea what to say.

Instead, I respond to Mike Anatolian.

> From: sethrubes@mail.me
> To: michael_c_anatolian@netmail.co
> Date: Mon, June 22, 2020 at 2:27pm
> Re: Subject: Favor?
>
> Hey dude! Good to hear from you. All is well with me and the fam—health-wise, anyway. Work is slow but that clinic I mentioned is going well and keeping me busy. As for Sarah . . . long story. Give me a buzz soon and we'll catch up.
>
> Molly is down to offer an internship to Becky. Have her email me and I'll connect them.

I get an email from Becky within minutes.

> From: bma445@nyu.edu
> To: sethrubes@mail.me
> Date: Mon, June 22, 2020 at 2:35pm
> Subject: Internship
>
> Dear Mr. Rubenstein,
>
> Thank you so much for your help in connecting me with Molly Marks. I am really looking forward to meeting her and I am beyond grateful for your help.
>
> I hope this isn't too forward, but I have another idea to propose. I've been volunteering for a women's shelter in NYC all throughout

college, but it's currently closed due to Covid. As you can imagine, this is incredibly heartbreaking and so dangerous for our clients in abusive situations. Mike told me about your legal clinic, and it sounds incredibly inspiring and dearly needed. If there is any volunteer work I could help with remotely, I would really love to help out.

Thank you again, and kind regards,
Becky Anatolian

What a nice kid.

And what a nice distraction from my obsession with Molly's relationship status.

I dash off a note back.

From: sethrubes@mail.me
To: bma445@nyu.edu
Date: Mon, June 22, 2020 at 2:46pm
Re: Subject: Internship

Hi Becky!

Wow, what a kind offer. I'm definitely going to take you up on it. We could use help with screening interviews, which we conduct over video chat. These are to help us ascertain whether we can help potential clients, or if we need to refer them elsewhere. I'm going to have our intake coordinator reach out to you to see if it's a good fit. And I might have a few cases I could use some support on with research, if you're interested in the legal side of things.

In the meantime, I'll connect you with Molly.

All the best,
Seth

I open another window and start typing.

From: sethrubes@mail.me
To: bma445@nyu.edu; mollymarks@netmail.co
Date: Mon, June 22, 2020 at 2:48pm
Subject: Molly, meet Becky

Hi Molly and Becky,

I wanted to send you a note so you have one another's contact
info. I'll let you take it away with introductions.

Happy writing!
Seth

Whew.

The miasma of failure hovering around me since I woke up this morning
is dissipating in this sea of emails.

My inbox makes a friendly little ping, and the thread from Molly turns
bold with a fresh message. There's a paper clip icon—she's attached something.

I open it.

I'm greeted by a picture of a baby whale mid-backflip in a sparkling
turquoise sea.

From: mollymarks@netmail.co
To: sethrubes@mail.me
Date: Mon, June 22, 2020 at 2:53pm
Re: Re: Re: Re: Re: Re: Re: Subject: Whale hello

Thanks for the intro to my young amanuensis.

Thought you might want something to cheer you up.

(Took this right before I broke up with my last boyfriend. Made me
happier than he did.)

I slam my fist down on my marble coffee table so hard I yelp in pain.
But who cares, because Molly is *single* and moreover she *volunteered* that

information. Is she reading my mind? Is she telling me this because she feels the same pull that I do?

I whip out my phone because this calls for more immediacy than emails provide. I don't even care if I look psychotically eager.

Seth: Thanks for the whale content!
Molly: Nothing like baby whales to soothe the pain of a breakup
Molly: And i have A LOT MORE where that came from

I was not going to ask about her breakup, but I feel like maybe she wants me to? Or at least won't mind, since she keeps mentioning it?

Seth: Was your breakup bad?
Molly: Not really . . . We weren't in love or anything

Weren't in love! She is talking to me about *love?* She is admitting she sometimes *feels* it? I have to restrain myself from hitting the coffee table again.

Molly: It was more the timing . . . We broke up RIGHT before covid
Molly: So i've been alone, basking in my own charming company for four months
Molly: And as much as I pride myself on being a self-sufficient introvert curmudgeon, it turns out that I like human companionship
Molly: Also sex. Could have done with some sex to pass the time

SEX? Not to be a teenage boy about it, but SHE SAID SEX???

Seth: There's always cam boys
Molly: Who needs cam boys when dick pics are free?

Oh my God, she went *there?* I suddenly feel like I'm punching above my weight class in terms of escalating flirtation. But I try to reply as blithely as possible.

Seth: There is indeed a robust dick pic economy
Seth: Something to console myself with on the lonely nights to come
Molly: Receiving dick pics?

Seth: Distributing them
Molly: I do not for one second believe you have ever sent a dick pic
Seth: I have
Seth: Only tastefully and upon request
Molly: I zero percent believe you
Seth: Why?
Molly: Because you're like a civilized courtly gentleman from 1849

I no longer feel like a teenage boy. I feel like an adult man with an absolutely rock-hard erection. And if Molly thinks I don't know how to sext, she has failed to understand the concept of "gentleman in the streets, freak in the sheets," despite having witnessed me embodying it in real life.

So I am going to remind her.

Seth: That's not what you said when I came on your tits

There is not immediately a response bubble to indicate she's typing, and I instantly worry that I offended her. I bite my lip, stressed-out, as she finally begins replying.

Molly: LOL
Molly: That doesn't count. You were drunk and i took advantage of your
    impaired sense of decency

Oh, girl, it is on.

Seth: My cock didn't see it that way
Seth: Three times
Molly: You counted
Seth: Fuck yeah I counted
Seth: Still think about you when I jerk off
Seth: All beautiful and wet and whimpering my name
Molly: Do i make you come?
Seth: So fucking fast
Seth: Except when I edge it out so I can think about you longer
Molly: How hard are you right now?

Seth: So. Fucking. Hard.
Molly: Prove it

I'm stone-cold sober but I feel drunk. I open my jeans. Pull them off. My dick is already poking out of my boxer briefs, wet at the tip. I position myself so that she gets a little bit of my abs along with my cock, because I'm a generous man.

I take a moment to switch to black-and-white mode before snapping a pic, because I was not lying about being classy when distributing homemade pornography.

I hit send.

Molly: Fuck
Molly: I want to watch you touch it

I literally throb at the loins. Jesus Christ.
I've never sent a *video* before.
But I want to.
I'm going to.
And I want something in return.

Seth: I'll show you mine if you show me yours
Molly: Deal

I prop my phone up against my laptop and fumble a bit with it until I get a reasonably flattering angle. And then I go for it. I'm thinking of her touching herself while thinking of me, and it takes about one minute to come all over myself.

A lot.

At length.

It is fucking obscene. I've never sent anyone anything like this in my life, and my heart is pounding at the idea of her watching it.

But, yeah. I really fucking want her to.

I drag the file into the messenger app, triple check I'm sending it to the right person, and hit send.

The preview of it lands in the box and I'm so turned on by the fact that she's going to see it that I know I'm going to have to make myself come again in a matter of minutes so I don't die of lust.

And then a video pops up beneath mine. The preview image is of her breasts. Breasts that I spent so much time holding and stroking in high school that they are like dear, treasured friends. Extremely hot treasured friends.

I click on the video, and it's Molly from the breasts down. She's sitting on her bed propped against a mound of pillows and there is a pink vibrator beside her.

Jesus Christ.

She starts by playing with her breasts—stroking them, twisting her nipples. Her hands travel down to her thighs, which she brushes airily with her fingers, teasing herself.

I grab my cock, which is already obtrusively hard again, and begin working it as I watch her—but not too fast. I don't want to finish before she does.

She spreads her legs to show me her pussy and rubs two fingers into it. I can hear her wetness. She reaches for the vibrator, presses a button, and it begins to whirr. It's like sexual ASMR. I could get off on the audio alone.

But I don't have to, because she puts the vibrator to her clit. I can hear it buzzing, hear her sigh of pleasure, hear her breath turn into little moans, hear her whispering "oh fuck yeah, oh *fuck.*"

Her hand reaches out and pulls her camera closer to her pussy, and I can see up close how swollen and red and wet it is and I want to taste it so bad I put my own finger in my mouth and pretend it's her. I stop stroking my cock because I'm going to come if I don't, and it throbs against my stomach, like it's angry to be left alone.

This is an ache unlike anything I've ever felt. My groin is literally pulsing.

She grabs another toy from somewhere off camera—a dildo in the shape of a sparkly, purple, generously proportioned penis. Slowly, she eases it inside herself. I cannot believe what I'm seeing. She's on her knees now, with the cock up between her legs, thrusting against it, and she puts the vibrator over her clit.

I can tell from the way her moans are coming, fast and high-pitched, that she's about to come, so I grab my dick and start stroking myself in time with her. And then she cries out so loud it's almost a scream—"oh Seth, oh God, *fuckkkkk.*" I close my eyes and explode all over my thighs and stomach.

I nearly black out with it.

I spend a full minute panting.

When I open my eyes I see that underneath the video in the message app she's typed a single thing: a little whale emoji, water spewing out of its blowhole.

It makes me laugh.

But I'm still emotional.

I can't believe she did this for me, shared this incredible, intimate, personal thing with me. I grab my underwear off the floor to wipe myself off, pick up my phone, and call her.

She answers on the first ring.

"Hey," she says. Her voice is barely more than a sigh.

"I'm . . ." My own voice is raspy, and for a moment, I'm at a loss for words.

"Me too," she whispers.

"Thank you," I say. For someone who uses his words for a living, I am wildly incoherent. "I've never . . ." I get out. "I'm, like, *moved*, Molly."

She laughs softly. I can picture her lying in bed, naked and boneless from that orgasm, smiling up at the ceiling.

"I thought you might need a pick-me-up," she says.

"That was a lot more than a pick-me-up."

She laughs again. It sounds shy. A register I haven't heard from her since we fooled around in high school.

"I've never sent anyone something so . . . explicit before," she says. "Was it too much?"

"Too *much?* Baby, I want to fly across the country and fuck you so senseless you have to quit your job because you don't have time to do anything but scream my name."

"I don't technically have a job at present," she says. "But that just gives me more time for screaming."

I can hear a smile in her voice.

For a moment I'm tempted to actually do it. I could take my chances double-masking on a plane. Or I could drive for two days to LA. But I wouldn't want to get sick, and then get her sick. So I just say, "I'll keep that in mind."

"What are you doing for the rest of the day?" she asks.

"Probably watching your video and masturbating," I say. It's sort of a joke but probably also true.

"Me too," she says.

We both laugh.

"Hey," I say. "Your email meant a lot to me."

"Aww."

Her tone is unreadable. I decide not to press it. "So how are you doing these days?" I ask.

"Hmm," she says slowly. "Fine, I guess."

"Fine's not so great."

"Is anyone so great?"

"Not especially."

"I'm slowly losing my mind from being so isolated," she says. "But I feel like an asshole complaining about it, since no one in my family has gotten sick and I have savings to float me until film comes back."

I hate to think of her alone in Los Angeles. I find that city lonely enough even when I'm just passing through. Quarantining there sounds desolate, even with the better weather.

"Do you have a bubble?" I ask.

"Yeah, sort of. Some girlfriends and I hang outside. But it's not quite enough to keep me from being sick of my own company. I'm considering getting a dog, and I don't even like dogs."

"You like cats."

There is a pronounced satisfaction in knowing this about her. In having institutional knowledge that dates back to her teens.

"I know, but dogs are more sociable and less likely to be snatched by coyotes."

"Ah. We don't have many coyotes in Chicago. Maybe you should move here."

"You have blizzards, Seth. Stop bragging."

"Snowstorms are great for cozy winter sex. In front of the fireplace. With a nice full-bodied cab on the coffee table and a view of the city all the way to the lake."

"You present a compelling argument for life on the tundra."

"Well, I *am* a lawyer."

"I need to shower," she says. "But this was . . ." She trails off, searching for the word. "Fun."

I could do with a more effusive descriptor—like "mind-blowing" or "life-changing"—but I'll take what I can get.

"Can I call you again?" I ask.

"Yeah."

I smile. "Good."

"Good."

There's a click, and she's gone, and my face hurts from smiling.

CHAPTER 23
Molly

I put my phone down beside me and look at myself in the mirror across from my bed. I'm naked, surrounded by sex toys, and grinning.

Seth is single. And he's so incredibly hot.

But more than hot, he's . . . known to me. I *know* him. I *like* him.

And I want him to call me again. I want him to call me all the time.

My excitement feels so new and tender that I don't want to tell anyone what happened—not even Dezzie and Alyssa.

I want to protect Seth. He just broke up with someone, and to outside eyes it might seem disloyal or desperate to fall into the virtual arms of an ex. But I also don't know how to explain the intimacy of what happened.

It feels intensely private. Just for us.

I clean my toys, take a shower, and tidy up my room. I have a burst of energy that manifests in a desire to clean my house, which I do with unusual gusto and attention to detail. I clean it like I would if Seth were visiting. Seth has always been one of those people who can't tolerate mess.

I wonder what his apartment looks like. I wonder what he's doing right now.

Probably working. Which is what I should be doing.

I grab my laptop with more purpose than usual.
My only new email is from my new "intern," Becky.

> From: bma445@nyu.edu
> To: mollymarks@netmail.co
> Date: Mon, June 22, 2020 at 3:06pm
> Re: Subject: Molly, meet Becky
>
> Dear Miss Marks,

I shiver in horror at this salutation. Does she think I'm seventy years old?

> I cannot overstate my gratitude to you for this opportunity. I hope
> you don't mind if I take a moment to express my awe at your
> talent and body of work. *Careless* is one of my favorite films of
> all time, and I can't believe how young you were when you wrote
> it. I am so excited to learn from a woman with your tremendous
> accomplishments.
>
> I'm attaching my CV. Please let me know the best way to get
> started.
>
> All my best,
> Becky

I'm going to have to get young Becky cursing and writing four-word
emails or she'll never make it in this town.

> From: mollymarks@netmail.co
> To: bma445@nyu.edu
> Date: Mon, June 22, 2020 at 3:15pm
> Re: Subject: Molly, meet Becky
>
> Hi Becky—I'm excited to work with you. Let's get started with a
> phone call—say, Wednesday after 10am PT? Let me know your
> avails.

And if you call me Miss Marks again you're fired ;)
-Molly

As I have no further emails, this constitutes work for the day. I place an Amazon order for *Busted* so I can reread it, then resume my *Real Housewives* marathon while daydreaming about Seth.

I wonder if he'll call me tomorrow. Wake me up with sweet words.

I go to bed with my ringer on, so I don't miss it if he does.

But in the morning, I wake up with no missed calls.

Instead, there is a string of texts from my mother.

Mom: Good morning my darling baby.

Mom: I had a dream about you last night. We were shopping in Miami for your sixteenth birthday. You got that sheer lime-green shirt that always made your armpits stink. Do you remember that shirt? HA! And then we fell down a sewer.

This is not the kind of sexy content I was hoping for.

Mom: I miss you.

Mom: Someone at Publix yelled at me and Bruce this morning for wearing masks!

Bruce is the man she's been seeing. They met when she sold him a mansion a few houses down the street from hers. Over the course of the pandemic, her "I" has slowly morphed into "we" as they've spent more and more time together. I guess now they are at a "shared trips to the grocery store" level of courtship.

It's cute.

Mom: Can you believe it?? YELLED.

Mom: No one here will take precautions. We are all going to get the plague.

Mom: Are you sleeping?

Mom: Call me when you're up!

Mom: If you want to.

Mom: Love you!-Mom

I putter to the kitchen to make tea. I call her back while I'm waiting for it to steep.

"Hellooooo!" she sings on the first ring. She always answers the phone like she just drank six Red Bulls.

"Hi, Mom."

"Have you heard the news?"

"I just got up."

"At *noon?*"

She gets up every morning at six to work out on her twenty-year-old elliptical and is on to her work emails by seven, including on the weekends. She found the lackadaisical schedule of a creative professional horrifying even before Covid. Now that I have nothing pressing to do, she thinks I'm basically in a coma.

"It's barely nine a.m. here," I say. "Relax."

"You're sleeping your life away!"

"I have nothing to get up for!"

"Go for a walk! Maybe you'll meet a husband."

She's still harassing me to find love. Like she thinks I purposely avoid it. Like she didn't do exactly that for nearly two decades.

"Don't make me hang up on you," I say.

"Anyway, have you heard the news?" she asks.

"You *just* asked me that."

"Seth Rubenstein was *left at the altar,*" she stage-whispers. "I heard from Jan Kemp at the store that—"

"Seth was not left at the altar," I interrupt, rubbing my eyes. "His fiancée broke up with him."

"Jan says he's heartbroken!"

"How would Jan know?"

"She's best friends with Bonny O'Dell," my mother says triumphantly.

Bonny O'Dell is Seth's parents' next-door neighbor.

I know that I should sidestep this conversation, but I have not had caffeine and my wits are not yet fully about me.

"I heard it was amicable," I say.

"Heard from who?" she asks suspiciously.

"Uh . . . Seth."

There is a long silence.

"Seth Rubenstein?" she asks.

"Um, yes, Mother. The Seth that we're talking about."

"Why were you talking to Seth Rubenstein?"

"We're friendly. He emailed me about something else, to ask a favor, and it came up."

"Baloney."

I can't help it. I burst out laughing.

"What are you talking about, baloney?"

"A man doesn't just email asking for some favor the day he's left at the altar."

"Which, as we've established, did not happen."

"You be careful with him. He's slippery."

"Oh good God. He's maybe the least slippery person I know. Why do you have this axe to grind with him?"

"Because he's a divorce lawyer. Have you ever heard of one single nice divorce lawyer?"

"Well, luckily his job is utterly irrelevant to your life."

"Not if he's emailing my daughter to drown his sorrows."

"Okay, Mom. He's madly in love with me. You figured it out."

I will not deny that the idea of this makes me giddy.

"Oh, he is for now, maybe. Until he *divorces* you and *ruins your life.* Which is his *career.*"

"Okay, Mom. Thanks for the tip. I guess I won't marry him after all."

"He deserves to get left at the altar, now that I think about it," she says, really on one now.

"Yep. Deserves to be in jail, actually. I have to go."

"You do not," she counters.

"I do. Love you, Mom. Bye."

I hang up and shake my head. But I am the slightest bit pleased that she thinks there's something going on between the two of us.

My phone buzzes again with a message from Dez.

Dezzie: OMG have you guys heard about Seth Rubenstein????
Alyssa: No!
Alyssa: What happened?
Dezzie: His fiancee left him
Alyssa: During quarantine???

Dezzie: Yes! Rob called him with a referral for his nonprofit this AM and
    Seth was apparently despondent

I do not enjoy hearing this. Poor Seth. However, I can't help but feel that
his mood would be improved if he called me to whisper sweet nothings.
I do not share this sentiment with my friends.

Molly: I heard. really sad. I feel bad for him
Dezzie: You should text him with your thoughts and prayers
Dezzie: And boobs
Alyssa: Well maybe not right away with the titties
Dezzie: True, you gotta have some chill
Dezzie: But this is your time to shine
Molly: OMG you guys WTF??
Alyssa: You deny you two are in love?
Molly: um yes
Dezzie: Puhleeze every time I mention him you get all tragic
Molly: Do not. Stop slandering me
Dezzie: Okay well in other news rob has been acting weird
Molly: Weird how?
Dezzie: He keeps insisting on going in to his office even though it's
    closed, like he can't stand to be in the house with me
Alyssa: He might just be stir-crazy? Personally, I would kill to be able to
    go to an office. Murder. With bare hands
Dezzie: I don't think it's just that. He's been snappish
Dezzie: Like permanent PMS
Dezzie: And drinking too much. Even for him. Our recycling bin is
    shameful
Dezzie: Makes me nervous cuz we're gonna start IVF whenever the clinic
    reopens and it's bad for sperm
Molly: Ugh i'm sorry! Have you talked to him about it?
Dezzie: He won't admit anything is wrong
Molly: I wonder if it's stress from his job?
Alyssa: Thinking the same thing. I'm sure he's dealing with kids who've
    lost people. Must be absolutely godawful
Dezzie: You're right. It's def been tough for him

Dezzie: Probably being paranoid

Dezzie: Anyway gotta go

Molly: Love you dez. Call if you wanna talk more!

I'm tempted to reach out to Rob with a friendly "pay attention to your wife, how bout?" text. Normally he wouldn't mind—he calls me all the time with questions about what to get her for her birthday or to tell me when she's in one of her dark moods so I can check in—but I don't want to meddle in their marriage if it's something serious. It gives me a bad feeling that he's checked out, since he's usually the type of guy who leaps around for her attention like a puppy. Plus, he drinks too much in the best of circumstances. The idea of it getting worse is . . . not good.

I'm distracted from this by a new text from Seth.

Seth: Can you talk?

I break out into such a big smile my lips feel unfamiliar on my face.

I go to my bedroom, change out of my ratty T-shirt into a tank top that shows off my cleavage, and put on a little makeup. Then I FaceTime him.

It rings out a bit and I wonder if he doesn't want to chat face-to-face, but then he answers.

He looks ragged.

His eyes are bloodshot, his hair is mussed, and he hasn't shaved. It's sexy, but I know this is not a great sign for a person of his disposition. He's not the kind of guy who walks around in sweats.

"Hey," I say.

He gives me a sad, tight-lipped smile. "Hey, Molls."

That big, unfamiliar grin falls right off my face. He does not look happy to see me.

But maybe he's just tired.

"How are you doing?" I ask tentatively.

He puffs out a breath. "Um. Not great."

I didn't expect him to be great, but after last night I didn't expect him to look this torn up either.

"What's going on?" I ask in my most sympathetic tone.

He sighs.

"I can't stop thinking about last night."

"Me neither," I say softly.

He closes his eyes. "And I feel so guilty."

My stomach drops.

"I think I made a mistake," he goes on.

I lick my lips. My mouth has gone dry. I don't want to ask, but I must: "You mean, breaking up?"

He scratches his face with the back of his hand, scrunching up his eyes. He looks *so* miserable.

"No," he says, to my profound relief. "It's the right thing to do. But it's just so sudden, you know?"

I nod, trying to keep my face neutral.

"And after yesterday, it's like all I want to do is see you. Talk to you."

Oh, thank God. I really thought this was going in another direction.

"Yeah. Me too."

"But, Molly, I am *two days* out of an engagement."

Relief turns to dread. His voice is full of self-loathing. I don't know what to say.

"And obviously we didn't do anything wrong," he says, "and it was enjoyable—"

I grimace at my most intense orgasm ever being described as "enjoyable."

"But I just feel like maybe this is all too much, too soon."

"Ah," I say.

He gives me an aggrieved look. "I don't mean you—I mean me. I need to stop jumping into every single little thing like a relationship is a life raft."

"Every single little thing?"

I feel ill.

"Fuck. I didn't mean it like that. You're not—you mean so much to me, Molly."

I'm touched to hear him say this. Even though I know in my bones that what comes next is going to be brutal.

"But I need to be alone right now, figure out why I keep doing this, you know? Jumping into things."

"Yeah. That makes sense," I force out.

"And it's not fair to drag you into it. It's my mess, and I don't want to mix you up in it."

What is sad about this is that I know he would not be saying it if he didn't feel like I do. That there is something big between us. Too big. At least for him. At least for right now.

Which is why I can't fight it.

"Don't worry about it. I totally understand."

He rubs the stubble on his chin, looking exhausted. "You do?"

I do. I don't want to, and I hate it, but I do.

"Yeah. It makes sense to have unresolved issues and to want to work through them."

He closes his eyes and inhales deeply. "Molls, I feel like I used you."

I laugh softly.

"You didn't use me. If anything, I tricked you into performing sex acts on camera for my own selfish gratification."

"You didn't have to trick me, Molls. And I don't regret it."

"Me neither."

He nods. "Okay. Well, I'm sorry about this. I really don't want to send you mixed messages, or hurt your feelings, or—"

I can't stand this pitying tenderness. I have to make him stop before I burst into tears. So I slap a wry smile on my face and hold up my hands.

"Whoa," I say. "It was just cam sex, dude. We're not dating or anything."

That isn't true, of course. It wasn't just cam sex, at least not for me. But I don't want him to think that I'm going to sit at home, pining for him. I do have dignity. And I won't make him feel guiltier than he already does.

But he looks taken aback. Injured, almost.

"I guess it just meant something for me," he says. "And that's the problem."

I don't say anything. I want to cry.

He gives me that tight-lipped smile again.

"Bye, Molls."

And with that, he ends the call.

PART SIX
July 2021

CHAPTER 24
Molly

Florida in the dead of summer would not be my first choice for a wedding. I am, after all, on record as someone who avoids group celebrations in general, and I also firmly believe that the Gulf Coast is only habitable November through February.

But Jon and Kevin's wedding is special. At the risk of being mawkish, it represents more than a celebration of their romance. It's a celebration of the chance to live life again. And for that, I will endure all the double-masked transcontinental flights and suffocating humidity you can throw at me.

And tonight, the eve before the blessed event, I am soaked not just in sweat, but also in the pleasure of being with my best friends. Reuniting with Dezzie and Alyssa after not seeing each other for eighteen months is transcendent.

Except for the presence of Rob.

We're sitting on the patio of a restaurant, and he is speaking way too loudly to our waitress.

"Another old-fashioned, sweetheart," he says, rattling the ice in his empty crystal tumbler at her.

Dezzie gives him a dirty look. We've been here forty-five minutes and he's already two drinks in. That's not counting the two martinis he had at Alyssa's mom's cocktail hour. His consonants are already muddy. It's seven o'clock, and he's basically slurring.

"Don't call her sweetheart," Dezzie hisses.

"She likes it," he says in a much too loud voice.

The server gives us all a tight smile. "Coming right up. Can I get anyone else anything?"

The rest of us shake our heads.

Ryland leans back in his chair. "It's so nice to be at a restaurant without three screaming children."

He's obviously trying to clear the air, but Dezzie's glare doesn't lift.

"Yeah, much more relaxing to be here with only one screaming child," she says, her expression trained on her husband.

"Are the kids having fun with their cousins, Ry?" I ask.

"Who cares?" Ryland jokes. "I'm having fun. This is the first time we've been child-free in"—he gestures like he's checking a watch—"seven years?"

Alyssa groans. "It certainly feels that way."

"If you're sick of your kids, why did you have a third?" Rob asks.

We are all silent for a moment, taken aback.

Dezzie has worried about Rob's change in attitude for months, and Alyssa and I have been increasingly concerned about the two of them. But this is far worse than I imagined.

"I love my children more than anything, Rob," Alyssa says evenly. "But the older kids are doing virtual school and need our constant supervision, and Jesse is still in diapers. We're both working full-time from home with no childcare, in close quarters. It's been very stressful."

"She means it's been like Dante's ninth circle of hell," Ryland says, putting an arm around her.

"Yeah well, at least no one *died*," Rob says.

Alyssa's face goes ashen.

Ryland leans in. "What the fuck did you just say?"

"I said I'm sorry you've been inconvenienced by having to watch your own children when people are dying," Rob says. "In my job—"

"I lost my *mother*," Ryland interrupts. "We couldn't even say *goodbye* to her because she was isolated in the *hospital,* okay? So shut the fuck up about my kids *dying*."

Alyssa takes his hand and stands up. "Come on, babe. Let's take a walk."

"Shit, my bad, my bad," Rob says thickly. "Sorry, man. Sit down. I didn't know."

"I *told* you," Dezzie says.

"Well, I forgot!"

Ryland, who is among the most good-natured people I know, is visibly vibrating with rage. He lets Alyssa pull him up, and they wordlessly make their way through the crowded restaurant toward the doors.

"Really nice," Dezzie says to Rob.

He doesn't look at her.

"I have to take a piss," he mutters, rising.

This leaves Dezzie and me alone at the table.

Of course, this is the exact moment the entrées arrive.

Neither of us touch the food.

"Jesus. You weren't kidding," I say.

She puts her head in her hands.

"I know. Sometimes he's completely sweet and normal, and then sometimes he's . . . this."

"Do you think it's still from all the Covid shit?"

"I honestly don't know. I mean, he has a lot of young clients who've lost people. So I think that's why he snapped at Ry. Not that it excuses it."

"No. That was out of control."

"And obviously the isolation and fear and all of that take a toll," she goes on wearily. "His doctor put him on Prozac but . . ." She trails off. "Obviously it's not working."

I reach across the table and take her hand. "I'm so sorry."

"It's really beginning to drain me, Molls. He's just so erratic. Drinks *so* much." She starts to tear up. "I don't know how much longer I can take this. He can be so mean."

I walk around the table and wrap my arms around her.

"I'm so sorry, my love," I murmur.

"I keep hoping it will get better." Her voice breaks. "I love him so much, you know? And I know he's in pain—I can *see* it—but he's not bringing it to me. He's turning away from me. And I don't know if it's to protect me or if he just can't bear to talk about it, but I feel like I'm losing him."

"Have you guys thought about therapy?"

"He won't go. With me or alone." She wipes away a tear and sniffles. "And

I feel awful complaining about my marriage when so many terrible things are happening to other people. But, we're finally starting IVF next month and I'm worried that—"

Just then Rob reappears.

"Food! Hell yeah!" he says, as though he doesn't notice I'm holding his crying wife.

I glare at him, which must provoke some level of compunction because he says, "You all right, babe?"

"You need to apologize to Ryland and Alyssa," Dezzie says.

"Roger, dodger." He plops back down in his seat and tears into his steak.

I squeeze Dez and return to my chair. The sage and butter sauce on my ravioli has already started to congeal.

Alyssa and Ry return, hand in hand.

"Hey, I'm sorry," Rob says to them immediately. "I was totally out of line."

"Yes, you were," Ryland says, in an icy tone that makes it clear he doesn't want to discuss it.

We finish the meal awkwardly. I try to smooth over the tension by chatting about Marian's recent wedding to her baseball player (an intimate family-only ceremony featured in *People* magazine) and showing off pictures of Gloria and Emily's twins (who are so adorable they've made me wonder if *I* should have a kid).

As soon as we've paid the check, Dezzie tells Rob they should get back to her parents' house before they fall asleep. Alyssa, Ryland, and I decide to take a walk and get ice cream.

"I'm worried about Dez," I say as soon as she and Rob are out of earshot. "She started crying while you guys were gone."

"Poor thing," Alyssa says. "What in the world is going on with Rob?"

"Could have strangled that fucker," Ryland mutters.

Alyssa squeezes his arm.

For the millionth time, I marvel at how good they are together. How they radiate quiet, steadfast love.

I'm skeptical that love like theirs happens for many people, and even more skeptical that it might happen for me. I think it's a rare gift that my dear, gentle Alyssa deserves.

But it makes me wish I had a relationship like that. One in which there is a safe, private world between the two of you.

We wend our way through the tourists, past boutiques that all seem to sell pastel sundresses and Tommy Bahama shirts exclusively. The air smells and feels like my childhood—sweet and thick. As we get closer to the ice cream shop (an iconic local establishment called Miss Malted's) the sidewalks are packed with couples and families happily licking the towering, melting, soft-serve cones Miss M's is famous for.

"Ry, did you know Alyssa used to work at this ice cream parlor?" I ask.

She groans. "I ended up with three cavities that summer."

"Hey guys!" a familiar voice calls from somewhere up ahead of us.

Seth's voice.

I stop walking. My entire body stiffens as he comes into focus.

I knew he would be here, of course.

I've tried to prepare myself.

But I don't have a playbook for how to behave in front of a person you can't stop missing.

He's with the whole Rubenstein gang—his parents, brother, sister-in-law, and two nephews.

"Hey yourself, Rubenstein," Alyssa shouts, bounding ahead to greet him.

"Oh my word, it's Alyssa and Molly," Mrs. Rubenstein cries, elbowing her way past her sons to give me a hug. "Girls, how are you? It's been so long!"

She wraps her arms around Alyssa, and then turns to Ryland. "And who is this handsome young man?"

Ryland offers her his hand. "Ryland Johnson. I'm Alyssa's husband."

"Barbie Rubenstein, and my husband, Kal. And this"—she gestures at her other child—"is our son David and his lovely wife, Clara. And of course, you must know Seth."

"Nice to see you, man," Ryland says.

"I'm Jack," the little boy on Seth's shoulders shouts before Seth can reply. He bonks the top of Seth's head for emphasis. "Tell them I'm Jack."

"My apologies, Jack, how rude of me," Mrs. Rubenstein says with mock gravity. "Friends, this is my grandson, Jack, and that handsome gentleman is his brother, Max."

"I'm four," Jack yells, loud enough to wake the dead.

"I'm six," Max provides shyly, like he is obligated to furnish this information after his brother's announcement.

Mr. Rubenstein drops Max's hand and squeezes my shoulder. "Why, if it isn't Miss Molly Marks. My goodness, doll, how long has it been? Twenty years?"

I smile, because Mr. Rubenstein always called me doll, and I've always loved Seth's family.

"Just about," I say. "It's so good to see you."

Mrs. Rubenstein grabs my hand. "Molly. You look amazing. How is your mom? Happy and in good health, I hope? I always see her signs in town."

I laugh. "She never met a park bench she didn't want her face on."

"So what brings you all to these parts?" Mr. Rubenstein asks.

"Jon and Kevin's wedding," Alyssa says.

"Oh how lovely!" Mrs. Rubenstein exclaims. "We'll be there too. Except for the boys, of course."

"I didn't realize you were coming," Seth says to me, taking his nephew off his shoulders and setting him down gently on the sidewalk.

"Somehow I made the list," I joke.

He winces. "Oh, no—sorry, I didn't mean I'm surprised you're invited—I just know you hate weddings. And Florida. Figured you'd probably skip it."

It's a fair assumption. Normally, I probably would have. After all, a pandemic is a pretty good excuse to avoid mushy emotions under white tents.

I certainly don't offer the truth: I partially came to see him.

We haven't talked in over a year, not since he cut off contact last June. I've carefully avoided bringing him up to my friends. I muted him on social media. I've done everything in my power not to pour salt into the wound he left.

But I still think about him every day.

There is never a time I check my email that I don't hope I'll get one from him.

It's pathetic.

"Uncle Seth, Uncle Seth, knock knock," Max says.

"Who's there?" Seth asks.

"Beets."

"Beets who?"

"Beats me!" Max shouts.

Seth shoots me an amused glance. "Maxie here is the family comedian," he says.

"So I see." There is something very charming about a child enjoying the fuck out of a knock-knock joke. I bend down. "Hey, Max," I say. "Knock knock."

His eyes light up. "Who's there?"

"Goat."

"Goat who?"

"Goat to the door and find out."

He guffaws. "I never heard that one!"

"You should steal it, bud," Seth says. "Very elevated comedy."

"Well," Alyssa says. "We were on our way to Miss M's. I don't suppose you all want to—"

Dave's finger goes up to his lips and he shakes his head in what I gather is a parental gesture for "don't mention ice cream."

Alyssa flashes him a thumbs-up.

"See you at the wedding?" I ask.

"See you tomorrow, doll," Mr. Rubenstein says.

"See you tomorrow, doll," Jack echoes.

Ryland watches them walk away.

"Stop staring," I hiss at him.

"You mean the way Seth was staring at you?"

The fact that they noticed makes me happy.

"Doth my eyes deceive or did you just attempt to charm a *child*?" Alyssa asks.

"I think she was trying to charm his uncle," Ryland says dryly.

I consider how to respond to this. Then I laugh. "Do you think it worked?"

CHAPTER 25

Seth

"What a knockout," my dad exclaims as soon as Molly walks away. "Is she single, Sethie?"

"You recall she broke his heart and sent him reeling into a yearslong depression, right Dad?" Dave asks.

"Yes, but is she *single?*"

"I don't know," I say. "I haven't seen her in years."

This is, of course, a lie. But being harassed by my parents on potential romantic prospects is a pastime I try to avoid.

"Text Jonnie. See if Molly's bringing a date to the wedding," my mom says.

In fact, I would like to text Jon to ask why he didn't tell me she was coming. If he had, I might be mentally prepared. Instead, I feel unsteady. (Emotionally, that is. I'm not weaving around on the street. Unlike many of the tourists currently stumbling out of the Daiquiri Deck.)

"Leave him alone, Ma," Dave says.

"Can we go swimming when we get home?" Max asks.

"It's late," Clara says. "You can swim all day tomorrow."

"With Uncle Seth?"

Clara gives me a wry smile. "You'll have to ask Uncle Seth about that."

"Please, Uncle Seth?" Max asks.

"Sure," I say. It is, after all, too hot here to do anything except lounge in a pool. I love Florida weather, but even I have my limits when it comes to ninety degrees with 100 percent humidity. "We have to swim first thing though, guys, because the adults have a wedding to get to."

"Early morning swim with these monsters?" Dave asks. "You know they wake up at six."

"Duty calls," I say.

"He said doody!" Jack screeches.

I don't get much sleep.

The boys take "first thing in the morning" literally. They are in my room jumping all over me by six fifteen. It is only thanks to Clara's maternal negotiation skills that I secure time to drink coffee and do a ten-minute meditation before putting on my trunks and cannonballing into a morning of mayhem.

The boys are a blast, if you don't mind physical violence. All squirt guns and pool noodle fights and attempts at underwater "shark attacks" that result in surprise dunkings. I attempt to engage them in a wholesome game of Marco Polo, but they're having none of it. They want me to throw them up into the air instead. I oblige, and it gives me a moment of nostalgia.

Molly, chasing me around Gloria and Emily's pool almost two years ago. Molly, impulsively asking me to go to Joshua Tree.

Molly, showing me her most vulnerable self.

I wonder if she still thinks of me.

I detach myself from the boys and go inside to shower and catch up on some work emails before it's time to get dressed. At two thirty I put on the linen suit Jon and Kevin have required for this event and gather with my family to meet the chauffeured SUV we've rented to squire us to and from the wedding. We arrive at the venue—an opulent, pink stucco 1920s mansion built to look like a Venetian palazzo, right on the bay.

We walk over a marble terrace and down into the gardens, which are surrounded by massive, knotty banyan trees protruding from the earth like self-contained jungles.

A young woman hands out feathered, Jazz Age–style fans, which we cool ourselves with as we mill about in the crowd. I spot Marian sitting near the front with Javier.

And then, behind him, I see Molly arriving with Alyssa and Ryland. She's in a gold-beaded flapper dress. Jon and Kevin requested we wear white linen or gold Roaring Twenties attire, and no one here has done it better than Molly. I've never seen her so dressed up, or looking so elegant.

I catch her eye, and she smiles at me. I'm about to walk over to say hello when a chime rings out over the speaker system, our cue to take our seats.

Jon and Kevin look incredible as they walk down the peony-lined aisle together, holding hands and beaming. They radiate the magnetism of two people madly in love.

I want what they have.

I want it so badly I have to take deep breaths and remind myself to focus on this moment, *their* moment, so I don't get lost in my own longing.

The music stops and the officiant—a poet friend of the grooms—welcomes everyone and says some beautiful words about commitment and love.

My mother notices how emotional I am and starts *rubbing my back.*

I shrug off her hand like a four-year-old and am glad Molly is sitting a few rows ahead of us, so she didn't see.

And then it's time for the grooms to say their vows.

Jon goes first. Though he's shy by nature, he's also a teacher, accustomed to being in front of surly teens all day. He speaks directly to Kevin without notes.

"I met you when we were fourteen and immediately knew I loved you," he says. "But because we were kids, it took me a couple of years to figure out that the feelings I had for you were more than just friendly. But I knew. I knew even then, in high school, as we goofed around and studied (or skipped studying) and applied to college, that you were more to me than a dear friend. You were my *person.* My very best person."

I remember their bond during those years, their gentleness with each other. There was a coupled quality about them. A way in which they shared a shorthand and always cracked each other up into near hysterics.

I was the third in our little group, but it was always clear that they were closer.

"Once we left for college, and both ended up in New York," Jon goes on, "I realized that what I felt for you was romantic. And that terrified me. Because you were my best friend. My rock. My safe place. The person who could calm me down when I was anxious, make me laugh when I was sad, fill up my heart when I was lonely. You were the person who knew all my secrets."

His voice catches. "Except one."

He pauses, collects himself. "I couldn't tell you that one because I was so afraid that you would feel awkward or crowded and push me away. That I would lose you forever.

"So I kept my secret, even though there were so many times—*so* many times—I was tempted to take a chance and tell you how I felt. But the timing never seemed right. You would be in a relationship, or I would. You would be too busy with work, or traveling abroad. I always had an excuse not to tell you."

I can hardly breathe. It's like Jon is speaking my own heart. I glance over at Molly to try to see if these words are reminding her of me the way they're reminding me of her. Her gaze is trained on Jon. I see her wipe away a tear. Molly Marks, *crying* at a wedding. It's so out of character I almost laugh. And I hope—I *hope*—part of it is because she sees us in this story.

I hope she's crying for us.

"And then one day," Jon goes on, "in the dead of winter, during a snowstorm, there was a knock at my door. I was fresh off a breakup, making cookies for New Year's Eve, planning to eat them alone in front of the TV. I wasn't expecting a soul."

He puts his hands on Kevin's shoulders and grins at him.

"And it was *you*. And you were carrying a bouquet that you'd put a plastic bag over to protect the blooms from the snow. I laughed, asking what you were doing buying flowers in this weather, and you took off the bag and handed them to me. They were white peonies. My favorite. Not even remotely in season. So delicate, yet you'd protected them from the cold. I reached out to take them so I could put them in water but you took my hand and stopped me.

"My blood went cold. I was afraid you were going to tell me you were moving, or sick.

"And instead you said, 'Jon, you're my soul mate. I love you.'"

I begin to cry in earnest. Big, silent tears roll down my cheeks, competing with the sweat.

"And all I could say back," Jon continues, "was 'I love you too.' What you said was so simple, and so true, and it changed my life forever. So, Kev, today my own vow is simple and true. I vow to be your soul mate. I vow to love you too."

I sneak another glance at Molly, who is beaming at them with wet eyes.

And I just think: *yes*. I need to be brave, like Kevin. I need to trust her to hear the truth, like Jon.

I need to tell her I'm in love with her.

And whether she believes in soul mates or not, I need to prove to her she's mine.

CHAPTER 26
Molly

I suppose I should make a confession.

Part of the reason I hate weddings and baptisms and anniversary parties so much is that their pageantry works on me. I hate to experience emotions, at least in public. And here I am, mopping up my mascara with my pinkies as I follow the crowd up the stairs to the terrace where the cocktail hour will be held.

I feel conspicuous. I feel off-brand. I feel like a sap.

"Molly," Dez whispers in my ear. "Are you *still* crying?"

I elbow her away, sniffling, as I try to collect myself. Even for me, this is excessive. But those vows—especially Jon's—hit me right in the gut.

And how could they not?

A speech about two people who met in high school, who loved each other from afar, who were always in the wrong place at the wrong time? Not to center myself at someone else's wedding, but those vows could have been written about me and Seth.

I still don't believe the soul mates part. I don't believe happy endings are guaranteed, even for people who deserve one as much as Jon and Kevin.

But I believe that what Kevin did was brave. I want someone to stand in my kitchen cradling frozen peonies and tell me what I'm too cowardly to profess myself. And *that* is why I'm crying.

I dodge away from my friends and make off toward the bathroom. It is mercifully cool inside, and, even more mercifully, empty.

I sit in a stall and collect myself. And then I stand in front of the mirror and touch up my makeup. I wipe away the evidence of my sadness and swipe over it with concealer. I refresh my red lipstick like it's armor.

My phone vibrates with a new email, and I decide to check it while I wait for my face to de-puff.

I swallow. It's from my dad.

The development process with *Busted* got derailed because of more Covid delays, and I thought he was probably going to ghost me on it after I sent the treatment. But four months ago, to my utter shock, he said he liked it, and asked for a script. I sent that at the beginning of May and haven't heard anything back.

I texted him to say I'm in town, hoping that would prompt an update. Usually he at least replies to my texts, even if it's to blow me off. That he's been radio silent probably means this email is bad news.

> From: rog@rogermarks.com
> To: mollymarks@netmail.co
> Date: Sat, July 17, 2021 at 7:15pm
> Subject: script
>
> Molly—Loma and Cory like your script. (I do too.) They want to meet in LA to discuss. Cassie will send times.
>
> Afraid I'm not going to catch you this trip—I'm out of town—but I'll take you to dinner after the meeting.

Holy fucking shit.

I start shaking, and laugh to myself like a crazy person in the bathroom alone.

I feel absurd for letting this affect me so much, but that casual aside—"(I do too)"—I've basically been waiting for that my whole life.

His email is quickly followed by another from Cassie, his long-suffering assistant, with a series of dates and times for next week.

I choose a week from Monday at 1:30 p.m. and write an email to my dad that I carefully construct so as not to convey too much excitement or expectation.

From: mollymarks@netmail.co
To: rog@rogermarks.com
Date: Sat, July 17, 2021 at 7:25pm
Re: Subject: script

Cool, glad to hear it. Sorry to miss you in FL but see you soon.
M

I'm giddy as I walk back outside to rejoin cocktail hour.

"You okay?" Alyssa asks when I spot her standing alone on the terrace. "You look . . . suspiciously happy."

"Never better. Love a smoldering evening."

"You're the smoldering one, with those lips."

I smack them at her. "All the better to ravish you."

"To ravish *someone* anyway," she says, glancing over at Seth, who appears to be introducing his family to Marian's celebrity husband.

"Stop staring at him," I hiss.

"Why?"

"Because it's embarrassing. You're being conspicuous."

She snorts. "Maybe you should be more conspicuous and stop pining."

"I was pretty damn conspicuous last year, if you recall."

She and Dezzie have come to know all about my exuberant sexual performance, and the way it was politely rejected.

"That was different," she says. "He was just out of a relationship. You should go talk to him."

I know she's right. He is, after all, a huge part of the reason I came to this wedding.

But despite my good cheer, I feel a little demoralized where Seth is concerned. Wounded that he never reached out after last year. I can't help but read it as a sign that he thought about what he wanted, and I wasn't it.

I need him to take the first step.

But I'm glad that my good news has given me this boost of confidence tonight, of all nights. I hope he notices my shine.

"Where is everyone?" I ask, changing the subject.

"Well." Alyssa sighs. "Rob and Dezzie are having an argument about what time they need to be at the airport tomorrow. They disappeared somewhere. And I sent Ryland off to get us some drinks. Shall we mingle?"

We make our way toward Jon's parents to congratulate them. Jon's mom was our fifth-grade teacher, and his dad was the dean of our high school. From there we run into Kevin's siblings, and before long it's time to go in for the reception. Kevin's family has always been quite prosperous, and I suspect they are paying for this evening, because everything is lavish, from the frescoed ceilings, to the mountains of white peonies, to the 1920s-style brass band playing jazz standards.

I take a sip of champagne, happy to be with my friends in such a beautiful environment. The vibe even seems to work on Rob, who pulls Dezzie onto the dance floor as soon as the grooms are done with their first dance. Alyssa and Ryland are close to follow. Which leaves me at the table with Marian and Javier, who are so busy canoodling they don't notice I'm alone.

I survey the room for someone to talk to and see that Seth is leaning against the bar, staring at me. He looks good in his white linen suit, albeit rangier than the last time I saw him, like he's lost muscle—maybe since gyms have been unsafe for so long. Thank God I never worked out to begin with.

"Dance?" he mouths, pointing between himself and me.

He is so handsome I almost want to say yes.

But I shake my head. "I can't," I mouth back.

He pouts. Which he should not, as he knows I'm a terrible dancer. If I attempt it, I will topple over and kill Jon's and Kevin's elderly relatives. Manslaughter by foxtrot.

Still, I'm happy that he asked.

Happier still when he saunters across the room anyway.

"Molly Malone," he says in greeting. "Get up. You have to dance with me."

I stay put. "Please. You know I'm not going to do the goddamn Charleston, or whatever."

He looks out at the sea of linen- and gold-clad guests who all seem to know how to do complicated steps to old-timey music. "Come on. Look how much fun they're having. I'll teach you."

"No. I'm too uncoordinated. I can't even do the electric slide. I can't even do *workout* videos."

He laughs and raises his hands in defeat. "I suppose I do recall you falling over when we had to waltz at Porter Carlisle's debutante ball."

"Yep. Right into her grandma."

"Hmm. Is there anyone we hate here? We could weaponize you."

"Perfect crime."

"Fine. But come outside with me. We can watch the sunset."

We stop at the Prohibition-themed bar and Seth orders us French 75s. I take a sip of mine as we walk outside, and it's tart with lemon and sharp from brut champagne, and it cuts through the humidity nicely.

"Classy joint," I say, gesturing at the mosaic floors of the terrace and the elaborate balustrades setting off the bay, which is pink, reflecting the sherbet sunset.

"You know this place was built by a circus impresario, right?" he says.

"Circus impresario. Is that still a job?"

"Looking for a career transition?"

I gesture at the lavish mansion behind us. "Seems like it pays pretty well."

"Not worth the risk of getting eaten by a tiger."

"Do you remember when that tiger tried to eat Roy from Siegfried and Roy?"

"Of course. You were perversely obsessed with it."

"Because it was like an Edgar Allan Poe story."

"Maybe you should talk to your therapist about your lingering Siegfried and Roy schadenfreude."

"Oh, come on. The tiger was named Mantacore. Imagine owning a *tiger*, naming it *Mantacore*, trapping it for *years*, and then expecting it *not* to eat you."

He laughs. "I've missed your cultural observations."

"Yeah," I say softly. "It's been a while."

I don't add: you could have had all the dated early-aughts references a man could ever want. Because I was right here.

Waiting for you.

Something flashes in his eyes. "I know. I wanted to reach out to you but I . . ." He shakes his head, like he's at a loss for words. "I'm sorry."

For a second, we just look at each other. Neither of us speaks.

This would be the moment, in one of my scripts, where he says how much he's missed me.

But he doesn't. He looks away.

I remind myself that the beats of romance are narrative devices. Not real.

"So," I make myself say. "What have you been up to for the last year?"

He blows out a breath, very obviously grateful that I changed the subject. "Oh, you know. Working. Doing yoga. Sitting around in my lake house listening to Cat Stevens and crying."

"Sounds healthy."

He nods. "Yeah, well, I've been working through some stuff. Meditating. Writing in my journal."

He says it like he's telling me a secret.

"Oh?" I ask. "Anything about me?"

He nods.

"Most of it."

I swallow.

"Like what?"

"Like how much I miss you."

I stare at him.

I can't believe it.

He's doing the romance beat.

"Like how much I regret always being in the wrong place at the wrong time," he continues.

He squeezes my hand. I can barely breathe.

"Are you single, Molly?" he asks.

"Yeah," I whisper.

"Good," he whispers back.

He moves in and puts the faintest trace of a kiss on my cheek. Out of the corner of my eye I see his brother through the glass doors, and I blush. Dave isn't looking at us, but still, I don't want to be spotted.

"Not here," I say.

I grab Seth's arm and lead him down the terrace steps. A few hundred feet away there's a cluster of banyan trees. They're eerie in the fading light, casting shadows across the grass. We walk through the grove made by their trunks to a picnic table in a clearing under a canopy of hanging roots. We can still hear the band and the murmur of conversation, but we're hidden from the party.

I sit down on top of the picnic table and Seth comes and stands in front of me, his shins pressed against mine.

I open my legs to make room and pull him toward me. His kiss is soft and tastes like lemon. It's sweet, and slow, and it reminds me of the way we kissed in high school, in the early days of our relationship, before we knew what we were doing. I felt so drawn to him and yet so clumsy. So afraid of getting it wrong that I almost didn't want to risk it.

I feel that way now.

I pull away.

"Seth, I'm scared."

"Oh Molls," he says tenderly. "Why?"

"Because I don't want to ruin it."

He comes and sits beside me on the table.

"What do you mean?"

"I feel like last time, when we were texting"—I don't say "sexting," but I assume he knows what I mean—"I made things weird. And I don't want to do that again."

"Molls, if you mean your video . . ."

I nod. I am not ashamed of my sexuality, but that was one of the few times I have extended myself like that. I feel a bit bruised that it led to him severing contact, even though intellectually I know that the circumstances, not the video, was the reason Seth needed time.

I'm hurt, but also embarrassed to be hurt.

"Molls, it had nothing to do with the video. If you knew how many times I've watched that video . . ."

"You saved it?"

I saved his as well. I keep meaning to delete it, but it makes me so, um, let's say, *amorous* that I can't make myself do it.

"Baby," he says. "Even thinking of it has me . . ." He takes my hand and puts it over his groin. I look down in shock, because he has a full-on erection. I can see the outline lewdly through his pants.

I bury my head on his shoulder, feeling cleansed of all the horrible shame I've been harboring.

"Okay," I say. I rub my hand over him and he hisses and closes his eyes. It's thrilling.

I do it again.

He catches my hand in both of his, lifts it up, and kisses my thumb.

"If you keep doing that I'm going to ejaculate all over my nice linen pants and embarrass myself in front of my family."

I giggle.

"Remember in high school how we would dry hump in your room and you would—"

"Get wet spots on my jeans? Yes, Molly. I *do* remember that. Thank you for the reminder."

"God, we were so horny."

He looks down ruefully at his erection. "Not much has changed on my end, I'm afraid."

"If you could feel how soaked my—"

He claps a hand over my mouth.

"Now you're just torturing me."

I am, but I'm also trying to distract from the tension between us. The unspoken feelings. The vast question of what, if anything, comes next.

Which is childish.

If I want this, I need to actually be an adult and face my own fears.

"I think we need to talk," I say.

Seth nods. "Yes."

He looks like he's organizing his thoughts to speak, but I gather my courage.

"I've really missed you."

His face does this beautiful thing. The light begins in his eyes and then travels down to his mouth, which spreads into a smile so wide it shows all his teeth. The lines around his eyes crinkle into little rivers of happiness. It's an expression of absolute, unguarded delight.

"I've missed you so much, Molls. Come here."

He opens his arms and I pivot my hips and we wrap ourselves around each other.

In the distance, the music ends and a man's voice requests that everyone return to their seats for a toast from Kevin's father.

"Oh shit," I say. It's too early to sneak off. "We should probably go back. I don't want to be rude."

He nods and offers me his hand to help me up.

"Also," I add, "I'm staying with my mom, so I'm not sure I can . . . um, not go home. I mean I *can* but it would provoke a conversation that I really don't feel like enduring."

He laughs. "Same here. But what are you doing tomorrow?"

"Sleeping off a champagne hangover?"

"Would you go on a date with me?"

The way he asks it has a trace of vulnerability. Like he's worried I might actually say no.

"Yes," I say. "I'd love to."

"Do you know what might be fun? We could go back to the place where we had our first date."

"That corny brunch place with the pancake bar? Is that still around?"

"Roberta's on the Cove," he says, grinning. "It's still there. I checked." He pauses. "I've been planning to ask you out all night. Just been gathering the nerve."

I love how boyish he seems. The part of me that knew him when we were fifteen, when he was so nervous to be with me in the beginning, lights up with recognition.

"Okay," I say. "Elaborate pancakes with retirees it is."

He squeezes my hand. "Can I pick you up at eleven?"

I nod. "I'll text you the address."

He puts his hand on the small of my back as we walk back to the terrace. When we reach the stairs, he stops me and puts a kiss on my temple.

"See you tomorrow, Molly."

"Yeah. See ya."

And you know what?

I can't wait.

CHAPTER 27

Seth

I wake up blessedly late, a little bleary from a night of Prohibition cocktails, and give thanks that my nephews are already in the pool with their parents, leaving the house relatively quiet.

I throw on clothes and go to the kitchen, where my parents are drinking coffee and reading the newspaper on their iPads.

"Good morning, honey," my mom says. "Want some breakfast?"

"No, I'm okay."

"Are you sure? We have bagels and lox and I can make eggs. Or grits? Or I have—"

"Don't worry about me. I'm actually going out. Dad, do you mind if I use your car for a few hours?"

"But Seth!" my mother cries. "Why go out when we have so much food here?"

I knew it was a mistake not to rent my own car. But my parents always protest that I don't need one, that I can always take one of theirs. "Why spend the money?" my mother beseeches.

They then proceed to monitor my comings and goings and insist on accompanying me on every five-minute journey to the grocery store.

Normally I find their clinginess endearing; in my family, hovering is a love language. But today I have sixteen-year-old jitters and don't want to be observed or explain myself.

"I'm meeting a friend," I say.

"Oh, who?" my mom asks.

I really, really don't want to tell her.

Obviously she can instantly sense this, and is on me like a bloodhound.

"Is it someone we know?"

"Yep. Molly Marks," I say as nonchalantly as possible.

My mom glances at my father, whose eyes are carefully trained on his newspaper. I can feel the excitement building in her as she says, with conspicuous calm, "Oh, that's nice. I *thought* I saw you go outside with her last night."

I cough. I hadn't realized we'd been spotted. I'm shocked my mother has kept it in this long. And I hope and pray she didn't see all the sexually charged embraces.

"We didn't get much time to catch up, since I was squiring a certain mother around the dance floor all night," I say. "We decided to grab brunch for old time's sake."

There's no reason why a grown man can't consume room-temperature eggs with an ex for perfectly friendly and casual reasons. But my cheeks are red.

I know that she knows.

"Ah. Why don't you take my car?" she says. "It's comfier than Daddy's."

Her sudden lack of interest in my plans doesn't fool me. She always pretends to be bored when she thinks she's got something good. I know exactly what's going to happen. She'll play it cool, and then scream-whisper to my dad that I'm *going on a date* as soon as she thinks I'm out of earshot.

I like this dynamic exactly as much now as I did when I was sixteen.

"Thanks," I say pleasantly. "When do you need it back?"

She gives me a beneficent pat on the hand. "We'll use Daddy's if we need to leave. Take as long as you like."

"Thanks."

I grab her key off the hook, gather some supplies from the garage, and leave as fast as I can.

My parents live on a golf course on the inland side of town, and Molly's mom is out on one of the islands, so it takes me thirty-five minutes to get to her behemoth waterfront house. (I will not call it a McMansion, because no McDonald's franchise would ever spend so much money on fake-Spanish turrets.)

I stop and press the call button at the gated driveway.

"Hello?" a woman's voice says. It has to be Molly's mom. "Is that Seth?"

"Yep, hi there."

"Come in."

She doesn't sound enthusiastic.

The gates open and I drive past an ornamental gatehouse to the main residence, which is perched on a massive lawn verdant enough to rival the golf course in my parents' development.

I park my mom's car next to a shiny rose-gold Mercedes G-Wagon that likely cost as much as the down payment on a home.

I am happy for Mrs. Marks that she's done so well, but this place is so lavish it's comical. I suspect it makes Molly cringe every time she looks at it.

Molly opens the (double-height, stained glass) doors before I have a chance to knock.

She's wearing a short, fluttery dress and beige platform sandals with little straps that tie around her ankles. I immediately want to spend all day tying and untying those little straps.

"Hiya," she says briskly. "Let's go. Can you drive?"

I lean in and give her a kiss on the cheek. "Gladly."

"Wait!" a voice cries. Molly's mother comes rushing out of the house, barefoot in a floor-length hibiscus-patterned dressing gown.

"Seth," she says in greeting, looking me up and down.

Molly audibly sighs. "Mom, I told you, we have to go. We have reservations."

"What's five minutes? I just want to say hello."

She stares at me expectantly, like she's waiting for me to do the honors.

"Hello, ma'am," I say obediently. "How are you?"

Molly groans. "Don't call her ma'am."

I can't help it. It's an instinct left over from my terrified high school boyfriend days.

"I'm very well, Seth. Thank you for asking. And you?"

"Also very well."

We all stand in uncomfortable silence.

"You satisfied he's not a serial killer, Mom?" Molly finally says.

"Molly tells me you're a lawyer in Chicago," Mrs. Marks says, ignoring her daughter.

"Yes, for going on ten years now," I say nervously.

"A *divorce* lawyer," she adds, glaring. I feel like an undeserving boy sniffing around for more of her too-good-for-me daughter's attention. A familiar feeling.

"Uh," I say, hoping to change the subject. "My parents mentioned your business is thriving—they see your signs all over."

Her face softens slightly.

"Oh don't say that in front of Molly. She hates my signs."

"Well you do put them on *city buses*," Molly retorts.

"Anything to increase your inheritance, dear daughter," Mrs. Marks says. "Who knows if your father will leave you anything."

She glares at me, like Roger Marks being an asshole is *my* fault.

"So morbid," Molly groans. "Anyway, we have to go."

"When will you have her back, Seth?" Mrs. Marks asks.

Molly barks out a laugh. "Enough, Mom!"

"It was absolutely lovely to see you, Mrs. Marks," I say. "But Molly's right. We're running a little late, and you know how Roberta's is at brunch."

"Have fun," she says, clearly hoping we won't.

She stands in the driveway glowering as Molly and I get into the car.

"Jesus," Molly says under her breath. "Sorry about that. You'd think she'd never seen a *person* before."

"Good to know she still hates me," I say through my smile.

"It's not you. She hates all lawyers. You know, because of what happened with my dad."

She clears her throat, suddenly seeming uncomfortable. "You kind of dodged a bullet though. Ever since she got a boyfriend she's been obsessed with me dating. Usually if any man comes within four feet of her washed-up spinster daughter she's offering to pay for an engagement ring before she even gets his name."

"You *aren't* a washed-up spinster."

She pulls down the passenger-side mirror to inspect her face. "I suppose I'm a moderately well-preserved spinster."

I reach over and snap the mirror shut. "Come on, Molly. You're beautiful."

She seems surprised.

"I live in a city of twenty-year-old sylphs and people spending all their money attempting to pass for twenty-year-old sylphs," she says. "I'm an old maid comparatively."

"Then maybe you should leave that devil city," I say. "Go somewhere where your good looks are appreciated."

"Where, like Chicago?"

I blush at the realization she thought I was suggesting she move to my city. (Not that I would mind if she did.)

"Nothing wrong with Chicago," I say. "You could be near Dezzie."

She smiles. "It would be nice to be near Dezzie. And closer to Alyssa. I sometimes feel very far away on the West Coast."

"Would you really move?"

"Well, now that everything's gone virtual it would be easier. But I do like LA. I've been there so long that it feels like home."

This is completely understandable, but I won't lie that I wish she was itching to move.

"Would you ever leave Chicago?" she asks.

"Maybe. If I had a good reason. I'm a member of the New York State bar. And I guess it wouldn't be that hard to qualify somewhere else." Like California, I don't add.

"Wouldn't it be difficult to leave your firm?"

Suddenly I wonder if we are talking about *us,* without directly talking about it. The potential viability of our relationship. So I give it serious thought.

"I have a good reputation as an attorney in Chicago, and that brings in a lot of business. But I've been thinking lately that I might want a change. I could make a lateral move and build up a practice somewhere else, or maybe start my own firm. People get divorced all across the globe."

"Yeah, at an alarming rate. Makes me wonder why anyone gets married."

"Because getting married is romantic when you're in love," I say.

She's quiet for a moment.

"Huh," she says. "I've genuinely never thought about it like that. I think I almost *agree* with you."

Good.

I pull into the parking lot of Roberta's. It's a little out of the way, a few miles down the island from the public beaches, in an older, 1960s-era building with wall-to-wall glass windows. My parents used to take me and Dave here for birthday brunches. And when Molly first agreed to go out with me in high school, I wanted to take her somewhere special. This, to my teenage boy's mind, was as special as it got.

As we walk in, I'm tempted to put my hand on Molly's back, but I don't. All the attraction and intensity of our conversation last night feels distant, because I'm so nervous about the conversation I want to have with her now.

The maître d' is wearing a three-piece suit, and the tables are decked out in stuffy white cloths and crystal wineglasses. The room is populated primarily with groups of older couples drinking mimosas, and families with hyper children running around with plates of Mickey Mouse–shaped pancakes heaped with chocolate sauce and whipped cream.

It's a little like a retirement home, and it's making me question my choices.

At least we get a table near the windows, with a view of the lagoon behind the restaurant. If you're going to dine in an assisted-living facility, you should be able to do it while looking at swans.

"This place is insane," Molly whispers as soon as the maître d' is gone. "Like, I remember it had the elaborate buffet and the omelet and pancake stations. But were there always ice sculptures?"

"No. And I think the chocolate fountain is new."

Our server comes to take our drink orders—an oat milk cappuccino for her and a lemon ginger tea for me. (I'm too jittery with nerves for caffeine.)

"We don't have oat milk," the server says apologetically.

"Oh. Almond milk?" Molly asks.

"We only have, you know, milk milk," the girl says.

"Right. Okay, milk milk it is."

We opt to order off the à la carte menu rather than risking the buffet. "I don't want to catch Covid from a sausage link," Molly says.

Once ordering is out of the way, there is nothing to do but . . . talk.

I'm so nervous I could throw up.

And so I just plunge in.

"Well, thank you for agreeing to come here with me today," I say. I immediately cringe at this bizarrely formal choice of words.

Molly nods gravely. "Why, it's my pleasure, sir. Thank you for your kind invitation."

Her mockery actually puts me a bit more at ease. Gentle ridicule has always been her way of expressing affection.

"I wanted to apologize that I haven't been in touch this past year."

"You already did that last night. It's fine."

I shake my head. "No, it was shitty. And I should tell you a bit about why."

She frowns. "Okay then. I'm all ears."

"Right. Good."

She looks at me expectantly. I feel awkward and clumsy talking about this. I'm so used to being the positive, optimistic, everything-all-figured-out guy. It's hard to admit being adrift.

I dive in anyway.

"Well, after Sarah Louise left, I had, um, a bit of an existential crisis." I glance up at Molly to see if she's recoiling at this admission, but her face is neutral. She nods at me to go on.

"It wasn't because of the relationship ending or anything like that," I say quickly, "but because I realized I have this pattern of plunging into relationships one after the other, with no time in between to breathe or reflect, because I want that fairy-tale love story. The wife, the kids, the white picket fence."

She nods again, listening intently. She does not seem surprised or horrified to hear any of this. It shores me up a bit.

"And honestly," I go on, "it was late coming, because Dave has been pointing this out to me for years. But I guess it can take a while to understand your own patterns, even if you're aware of them on some level, you know?"

"Yeah," she says. "I do."

She says this emphatically, like she identifies with it. I haven't articulated this thought to anyone before, and it's a huge relief to be taken so seriously.

"I realized I set this arbitrary timeline for myself that was meant to be motivating but was actually causing me to sabotage myself. Because I kept pursuing people who weren't right for me but who fit the model in my head. And it's almost like I've been talking myself into loving them, to speed things along.

"And what I realized is I've been choosing women based on a set of criteria. And consequently, I keep cultivating relationships that disappoint me, and then wondering why I always end up alone. And then I get that antsy feeling and the cycle repeats." I look into her eyes. "And I'm so, so tired of it."

"So what *do* you want?" she asks softly.

"I want to stop planning and obsessing about everything being perfect and just be with the person I adore. And that person . . ."

She stares back into my eyes, waiting for me to finish.

"Molly, that person is you."

CHAPTER 28
Molly

I wanted this.

I wanted it *badly*.

But now that I'm getting it, I feel so overwhelmed that I wish I had taken an Ativan.

I am not accustomed to being spoken to this sincerely. This romantically.

I'm not sure anyone has been so earnest with me about wanting a relationship since, well . . . Seth. In high school.

Say something, I beg myself. I can see he's putting everything he has on the line, and I can't just sit here nodding. This is the kind of scene I write. I should be able to find the right lines.

But I don't have any.

So I just blurt out the truth. "I adore you too."

And it must be the right thing, because he lets out maybe the world's longest breath. "Did you really just say that?"

"Yeah," I whisper.

His eyes are glistening. He reaches out for my hand and kisses it.

It's so sweet, and it's harrowing to be the object of such sweetness. My every instinct is to make a joke of the emotion in this moment.

But Seth deserves better.

He deserves the same sincerity he has given, like a gift, to me.

So I don't deflect. I don't break eye contact.

And sitting in the intensity of this moment, just *feeling* it, is beautiful.

But it's also unbearable.

It's making my heart slam into the walls of my chest.

There's a reason I make stupid jokes when things get emotional. Stupid jokes don't make your throat close.

Please don't have a panic attack, I beg myself. *Please don't have a panic attack.*

"Hey," Seth says, his face drawing tight with concern. "Why do you look so upset?"

I look down at the table. I'm mortified that I can't be who I need to be in this moment. The girl he deserves.

"I'm really scared," I confess.

"Oh, Molls," he murmurs. He stands up, walks around to my side of the table, and puts his hands on my shoulders.

His touch is such a relief. I lean back against him and close my eyes.

"Hey," he says, stroking my hair. "Don't be scared. This is *good*. This is *happy.*"

I reach for his hand and put it against my cheek. Its coolness is a balm against my flushed skin.

"I'm okay," I say. "Thank you." I take a very long sip of my ice water.

"I think this calls for something a little stronger," Seth says.

He beckons our server and whispers into her ear. As they confer, the food comes, and I'm grateful for the distraction.

I still feel overwhelmed. But I can do this.

With him, I can do this.

Seth returns to his seat, and I begin carving into my crab Benedict.

"How is it?" he asks.

"Good. Crabby. How's yours?"

He got—wait for it—Mickey Mouse pancakes.

"Good. Mousey. Want a bite?"

I shake my head. "I don't eat rodents."

"Some might say crabs are the rodents of the sea."

"Ugh. Let me enjoy my crustaceans in peace, please."

Our server comes back with a tray of bright pink cocktails garnished with huge, red, rock-candy suckers and neon bendy straws.

"Are those . . ."

"Shirley Temples!" Seth announces. "Just like our first date here."

"Can I have vodka in mine?" I ask our server.

"Way ahead of you," Seth says.

We clink our glasses.

"I guess it's not surprising that I'm freaking out," I say. "Do you remember how anxious I was on our first date?"

"Yes. Even though we were friends and we'd already made out."

I shrug. "Making out is fun. It's the dates that are stressful."

He grins. "Would you like to leave and make out?"

"No, I'll eat my crab like a big girl."

"Good. Because these Mickey pancakes are ridiculously delicious."

I feel better now that my panic is out in the open. More normal. Normal enough to air the question that has been plaguing me since last night.

"So, not to be too forward," I say, "but how do we . . . how would it work, if we were to try to be together?"

He meets my eyes. "I don't know, honestly. I've never dated anyone long-distance. I think we just . . . *try.*"

"Would we be, um . . . exclusive?" I manage to squeak out, even though I'm worried even asking this will make me seem needy.

He just smiles.

"I'd like to," he says. "But I'll take you any way you'll have me."

Good. I can't imagine the agony of having to share him.

"I guess we could visit each other, now that flying is viable," I venture.

"We could go on trips," he says.

"Do you really have a lake house?" I don't remember hearing about it before last night.

"I do. I bought it after Sarah and I broke up. So I could hole up like Thoreau and contemplate the nature of existence."

"Did you know that Thoreau lived like a five-minute walk from his mother, and she would bring him food?"

"Lucky Thoreau. My place doesn't even have DoorDash."

"Where's the house?"

"Lake Geneva, in Wisconsin, about ninety minutes outside of Chicago. It's pretty small—two bedrooms. But it's right on the water. Good kayaking."

"You would not want to put me on a kayak."

"I would absolutely want to put you on a kayak."

"I don't even like sailboats. I definitely do not want to ride in something with oars."

"You're in luck. Kayaks don't have oars, they have a paddle. I'll take you out on the lake when you visit. Show you some good ol' wholesome midwestern fun."

"I prefer Paris and Hawaii."

"Oh, come on. I'll feed you cheese curds. I bet you've never even seen a cheese curd."

"The word 'curd' has to be among the most revolting in the entire English language."

"Cheese curds and summer corn and cool dips in the lake on hot days. You're going to be in heaven."

I smile at him. That actually sounds wonderful. "I would like to see your place."

"What are you doing next weekend?"

"Working, sadly." I have that meeting with my dad and his producers on Monday, and I don't want to be jetlagged for it.

"Cancel it," he says decisively.

"Whoa tiger." I laugh. "I actually do have a job. I can't just gallivant around the hinterlands of America on short notice."

"Is that a yes?"

"Let's look at our calendars and find a date." I pause. "It's funny that I've never seen you in your own environment. Like, I've never been to your apartment."

"I'm dying to go to your house. I bet it's so girly and cute."

My house actually is girly and cute.

"I bet yours is full of doilies and cats and those wood blocks that say *it's wine o'clock somewhere*," I joke.

"Yep," he says. "And dead bodies."

"That goes without saying."

Seth asks for the check and I get up to go to the bathroom.

I take in my reflection in the mirror.

Usually I feel critical of myself, but right now, in this moment, I think I look pretty. Maybe it's just the lighting, or the flattering color of this dress, or the way my hair turns wavy in the humidity.

Or maybe I'm seeing myself through Seth's eyes.

I consider refreshing my lipstick but then decide it's pointless. I want to kiss Seth with these lips, and I'm not sure how he'll look in Nars Jungle Red.

"Ready?" he asks when I get back to the table.

"Yep. Where to next?"

"It's a surprise."

He takes my hand and we walk out to the parking lot. We make it as far as his mom's car. I push him against the door and kiss him.

The last dregs of anxiety I've been harboring melt away once his arms are around me. "You," my body thinks. "You."

"Mommy! Eeeeew! They're kissing!" a little boy cries.

"Knee that kid in the balls," I whisper to Seth.

He laughs into my hair, pulling me closer.

We make out for what must be five minutes, until we're both sweaty and sticky from the heat.

I step away and rub my mouth with the back of my hand.

"Let's go to a hotel," I say.

Seth shakes his head. "Nope. I have a whole day planned for us."

And he does. Our next stop is the aquarium where we went on our second date. We wander through dark rooms, past otherworldly floating jellyfish and tanks boasting schools of angelfish, butterfly fish, and prehistoric-looking monsters called porcupine fish. It's both captivating and deeply creepy, in the way of all aquariums.

We step out into a room with a giant sea turtle lolling in a huge, open pool, and then to something called the Shark Room, which I drag Seth through quickly. I do not fuck with sharks. This leads us to the aquarium's most famed inhabitants: two giant manatees.

"I can't decide if they're cute or hideous," Seth says, taking in their roly-poly bodies and snubbed snouts.

"Both," I say.

"They kind of look like swimming pigs with no legs," he muses.

"I'm sure they think the same thing of you."

"They eat seventy-two to eighty-four heads of romaine lettuce a day," an attendant informs us.

"Yum!" Seth enthuses.

We exit into the gift shop. I head for the doors, but Seth calls for me to wait. He's standing at a counter inspecting marine life–themed jewelry.

"I want to buy you a present," he says.

"I'm good on fish jewelry, actually."

"No woman can *ever* have enough fish jewelry." He flags down the cashier. "Do you have any of these necklaces with whales on them?"

I can't help but smile.

The cashier looks confused. "Sorry, no . . . we don't have whales in Florida. But we have these with manatees, dolphins, and starfish, in all the birthstones."

"Well, manatees are like the whales of the bay," he says authoritatively. "We'll take one of those. In—" He turns to me. "What's your sign, babe?"

"Taurus," I say reluctantly.

"Taurus, please," he says to the cashier.

"How lovely," she says, plucking a necklace from the counter. "Shall I wrap it up for you, or would you like to wear it out?"

"She'll wear it out," Seth says. He takes the necklace and delicately slides it under my hair and around my neck.

"Cubic zirconia," he says admiringly to the saleswoman. "Don't you just love it on her?"

"Beautiful," she agrees. "It really catches the light."

I roll my eyes at Seth, but I take the charm in my hand and rub it with my thumb. It gives me that feeling you get when you pick out a crystal at a rock shop. You know that its supposed powers are probably bullshit, but it still makes you feel better to touch it.

"Thank you for my bauble," I say as he hands over his credit card to the tune of $34.99. "I'll treasure it."

"For you, my lady, the finest jewelry the ocean-trinket industry can muster."

We stroll back into the heat toward the car.

"Can you guess where we're going next?" he asks me.

"The hotel?" I say hopefully.

He chuckles. "Come on. Think harder."

The memory of our third date comes back to me. "No way," I say.

"Yes way," he counters.

"I'm not dressed for fishing," I protest, looking down at my rather chic outfit. "And we don't have poles."

"Au contraire," he says, popping open the trunk to reveal two fishing rods and a small cooler. "I stole my dad's."

"What's in there?" I ask, pointing at the cooler.

"Kal Rubenstein's finest cold brewskies, babe," he says. "Get on in, it will be fun."

We drive over a bridge to a fishing village and stop at a tackle shop by the pier. Seth runs in and emerges with a big bucket of bait fish. I carry the bucket and he hauls our gear out to the pier. There's a pelican chilling on one of the posts, and some wizened old fishermen casting lines.

"Notice how no one else appears to be on a date here?" I ask.

"Too bad their boyfriends aren't as creative as me."

"Are you my boyfriend?" I ask softly. I don't know why this word feels so freighted, since we've spent the past few hours reliving our youthful romance, kissing, and discussing trips we can take together while we feel out being a couple.

But it does.

"I want to be," he says.

I feel a slow grin overtake my face. "I think I want that too."

He reaches out and draws me to his chest.

I burrow there.

I feel eyes on us, and look over Seth's shoulder at a pair of burly, tanned men openly ogling us as they wait for bites on their lines.

"They're staring at us like we're the catch," I whisper.

"Yeah. We better get down to business," Seth says, drawing away. Apparently public displays of affection on a pier where people routinely gut fish are a bit too sappy even for him.

Snapper are biting, and we catch a few small ones we throw back. And then Seth gets a giant tug on his line and has to really fight to bring it in—so much that the fishermen guys crowd around us to give him advice.

"Step back and brace your shoulders," says an old man with a tobacco-stained beard.

"Don't tug so hard, you'll snap the line," commands a younger guy with a deep sunburn.

Seth struggles for what feels like forty-five minutes until the creature breaks above the water. We all cry out encouragement as he reels in . . . a very small, very mad, hammerhead shark.

"You caught a fucking *shark?*" I squeal, taking one million pictures with my phone.

I don't fuck with sharks, as stated, but I'm still impressed that my dude *caught one with a fishing pole.*

Seth shoots me a smug grin, holding the writhing, furious creature up for a portrait. The fishermen help him remove the hook from the shark to throw it back, though not before a few of them pose for pictures with it too. We give away the rest of our bait and walk back to the car.

We drive five minutes to an outdoor oyster bar so old that my grandparents took my mom here when she was growing up. Seth orders two dozen oysters on the half shell, which come with a bucket of saltine crackers and cocktail sauce so full of horseradish it nearly burns my face off.

The sun has moved behind the clouds and a big gust of wind blows over the stack of napkins in front of us. All of a sudden, I smell petrichor.

"Uh-oh," Seth says. He peers out at the horizon, where you can already see rain pounding the ocean in the distance.

"It's going to pour," I say.

We ask for our check, but every other person at the bar has the same idea. By the time we pay there's a crack of thunder, and then the sky erupts.

"Should we make a run for it?" Seth asks.

I grab his hand. "Come on."

We sprint out from under the cover of the bar to his car, getting utterly soaked in the process. Water is dripping down my arms, my hair, my nose. His shirt is clinging to his chest. We dive in and slam the doors behind us.

Seth reaches in the backseat for some towels and hands me one.

"You've thought of everything."

"I'm trying to impress you. And I was hoping we could make out on the beach later. I guess we'll have to scratch that one."

I pull him close, and kiss him. "We can make out in the car."

Necking in a steamy car, with the windows fogged up and rain slamming down, gives us an air of privacy. Were it not for the console between us I would be in his lap. And were it not for the presence of children at the oyster bar, my mouth might be there instead.

But keeping things PG-13 has its own erotic appeal. By the time the storm stops I am dying, actually *dying,* to have sex.

"Let's go to a seedy motel," I pant. "There's that place that charges by the hour off the highway. I'm slutty enough to find it hot."

"Hold that thought," Seth says.

His phone has been lighting up with notifications. He checks his messages and turns to me, looking sly.

"My family is going out to Heron Key for dinner. They'll be gone for a few hours. Do you know what that means?"

I shake my head.

"My childhood home has no parents."

His childhood home was the locale of many of our horniest nights.

"You really want to bone me in a twin bed?"

He nods gravely. "I *really* want to bone you in a twin bed."

I can't deny that this holds a certain nostalgic appeal. Plus, as much as I fancy myself charmed by roadside motels, Barb Rubenstein's sheets are far less likely to have bed bugs.

I laugh and shake my head. "Okay, Rubenstein. Let's go."

His parents' house is exactly as I remembered it. A large, pleasant split-level in a gated community built on a golf course.

It still smells the same way it did in high school—like clean counters and Seth's mom's beloved peppermint tea.

"Feels like home," I say.

"I'm sure my parents would be happy to have you move in."

"Great, I'll consider that."

"Want anything?" Seth asks. "Water? Wine? One of my mom's three zillion diet sodas?"

"Just you."

"As you wish, my lady."

He takes my hand and escorts me to his bedroom. His parents, remarkably, have not redecorated it in the two decades since he left home. It still has his twin bed with its madras print bedspread. His bookshelf brimming with sci-fi paperbacks. Even his old desk, with the bulbous turquoise iMac he used in high school.

And his bulletin board, tacked with the same snapshots that were there the last time I was in this room. Seth with his friends from space camp. Seth with Jon and Kevin, grinning and sweaty in their soccer uniforms. Seth and Dave, wearing Minnie Mouse ears at Disney World.

And then there are the ones of Seth and me. Our official portrait from homecoming. (I look distinctly uncomfortable, and he looks like he's having the night of his life.) The two of us sitting side by side on towels at the beach, tangle-haired and laughing. And the one I always loved the most: the two of us standing in his backyard, his arm casually thrown around my shoulders as

I lean into him. We're both smiling, squinting a bit against the sun. We look so happy to be near each other. So in love.

I untack the picture and take a closer look. "I can't believe you've had these in your room all these years," I say. "Weren't your girlfriends hopelessly jealous of me?"

"Yes, my girlfriends were all kept awake by the torment of my eternal love for my sophomore year homecoming date."

"As they should have been. Look at us now." I pull him toward the mirrored closet door so we can admire our reflection.

"They look pretty good together," he says.

"Very sexy against the backdrop of your *Ender's Game* poster. I'm sure your exes couldn't resist you ravishing them in here."

"*You* never could," he says. "And actually, when I bring girlfriends home we sleep in the guest room. I'm only staying in here because Dave and the kids are here, too."

"Okay but for real, why didn't your parents change your room? This place is like the Seth Rubenstein Museum."

"Never got around to it, I guess. Or maybe they just pine for the days when I was a snotty eleventh grader."

"You were never snotty. You were the Platonic ideal of a teenager. You made the rest of us look even worse than we were."

"And you," he says, leaning in to smile at our photos on the bulletin board, "were so beautiful." He turns to me and moves my hair out of my face. "Almost as beautiful as you are now."

He opens his arms and I step into them and he pulls me on top of him and we collapse down onto his bed. It groans under the weight of two rabidly horny adults, and I hope it doesn't break as he pulls me on top of him and I open my legs to feel his erection. The friction of the bulge in his jeans through my panties makes me want to cry—both from how good it feels to be connected to him in this way, and from the corporeal memory of grinding against each other in this bed, frantic for each other's bodies but too afraid of getting caught by his parents to take off our clothes.

Emotion is not a feeling I am used to experiencing in the lead-up to sex. Or during it. Or afterward.

Emotion gives me panic attacks. In contrast, sex gives me the kind of dopamine rush I usually have to pay good money for at the pharmacy.

It's a *relief* from emotion—a way to lose myself.

But here, in Seth's embrace, with the pressure of his lust raging up against mine, I'm not lost.

I'm overcome.

"I've missed this, baby," he murmurs.

"Dry humping is still surprisingly hot," I manage to get out, shuddering under him.

"Only cuz I'm so good at it." He's grinning, but his voice is breathy and I know this is driving him crazy too.

"Well, you did have years of practice," I say, grabbing his ass and drawing up my hips to get a better angle.

"Who said I ever stopped?" he says, really giving it to me.

"Oh yeah? Is this your signature move?"

Talking is helping me not to come, but he groans, and I love it.

"Jesus fuck," he says, lifting himself off me. I'm bereft at the loss of that pressure. Until he slides his hand into my panties and slips a finger inside me.

"Not to brag," he whispers. "But I recently learned how to do hand jobs."

"Nah. You were always pretty good at it."

I lean up and kiss him, devour him, dying.

So many feelings overwhelm me. How he taught me to feel this way. How easily I feel myself becoming raw, wanting to let him break me open. How he knows how to touch me, even though we've only slept together once, because his body still remembers mine from all those years we made each other ache.

I come so quickly I'm embarrassed.

"Shit! Sorry!" I gasp out, shaking.

"What's wrong, sweetheart?" he asks, between covering my face with kisses.

"I want you too much. It's like a sickness."

"I think I know the cure for that," he says.

"What is it?"

"How about," he says, "you roll over and I fuck you until you can't see straight."

God, the *mouth* on this man.

I oblige, and he growls as he pulls off my underwear, throws it on the floor, unzips himself, and slides into me.

It's fast and hard and everything I need. It's us, but with the advantage of experience. Urgent and rough, fueled by Seth's filthy mouth and our insane need for each other, yet somehow still tender.

When it's over we collapse down onto his pillows, still clothed and panting, and he pulls me close and spoons himself around me.

I can't stop smiling.

"You are shockingly good at that," I say.

"Shockingly? Do I not exude sexual prowess?"

"You're very sexy," I say honestly. "I'm just not used to nice boys who rail me senseless doggy-style in their childhood bedroom."

"It's usually mean boys who rail you in their childhood bedrooms?"

"Yep."

He nibbles my ear. "No one should be mean to you."

"What will you do if they are?"

"File frivolous lawsuits against them in civil court."

I wrap my fingers through his. "That shouldn't arouse me, but it does."

"Oh yeah?" he murmurs. He presses himself against me, and he's still hard.

I guess some things *haven't* changed since high school.

"Yeah," I say, hitching my hips to rub against his erection.

He rolls over so he's on top of me, propped up on his forearms.

"Let's get you out of that dress."

We take off each other's clothes, and I allow myself to ogle his body.

"Exercise fucking works," I say, running my hands over the muscles of his shoulders and down his abs to the borderline ostentatious V of his hips.

"Are you being nice to me?" he asks.

"I'm trying to sweet-talk you into having sex with me again."

"Oh, weird," he says. "It worked."

This time it's slower. By the time we both come I am, to use a metaphor that befits this room, Play-Doh.

We cuddle up together, naked, and put the blanket over us. It barely fits. He has to wrap himself around me to avoid falling off the mattress. Our breath has slowed, and I can feel his heartbeat.

It might be the best feeling in the world.

He kisses my jaw.

"Molly," he whispers in my ear, squeezing me a little. "I'm in love with you."

My breath catches.

I go completely still, waiting for the panic to wash over me.

But when my heart flips over, it's not with anxiety.

It's with joy.

"I love you too," I say.

We lay like that, basking in warmth and contentment, until I get drowsy. Seth glances at his phone.

"They'll probably be gone for another hour or so. Want to take a quick snooze before I drive you home?"

I nod, and he sets an alarm and gathers me up.

We drift off together, heartbeats in sync.

And when I awaken, it's not to the beeping of an alarm.

It's to a child's voice shrieking, "There's a *girl* in Uncle Seth's *bed!* And she's *naked!!!*"

CHAPTER 29
Seth

"Max, close the door," I say, bolting up. He can't hear me, because he's screaming with a level of horror that would make you think an asteroid just hit the house.

"*Max,*" I yell. "*Close* the *door.*"

His eyes go wide and he freezes, then slams it shut. I hear him running down the hall, still shouting about the woman in my bed.

Said woman has buried herself completely under my tiny blanket, where she is currently laughing so hysterically the bed is shaking.

I lean back against the mini headboard and burst out laughing too.

From the living room, I can hear my sister-in-law trying to quiet her son's hysteria. It doesn't seem to be working, because I catch the sound of Jack joining in.

"So much for a clean escape," I say. "Sorry. I don't know how they're back already."

She reaches for my phone and checks the time. "Probably because your alarm didn't go off. It's nine forty-five."

"Shit. Let me see that?"

Turns out I set the alarm for 8:30 a.m., not p.m.

"Admit it," Molly says. "You did this on purpose so I would have to do a walk of shame in front of your entire family."

"Okay. I admit it."

She flicks me on the shoulder.

"So, what's the move?" she asks.

"Uh, first we get dressed. Then we go out and act like absolutely nothing in the world is weird about this."

"Great. That should be easy."

She slips her sundress over her shoulders and I shimmy on my pants. We gather up all her belongings.

"You ready for this?" I ask her.

She takes a deep breath. "Yes. Can't wait."

I open the door and we walk to the kitchen.

My entire family is there. The boys are eating orange Popsicles, which I suspect they were bribed with to get them to stop yelling. But at the sight of us, Max's eyes bug out of his head.

"That's the girl!" he cries. "The one that was naked!"

"Guys, this is Molly," I say, putting my arm around her. "You met her the other day. She's my girlfriend."

My mother drops the sponge she's holding onto the kitchen island and puts her hand over her mouth. My dad inclines his head at me with a huge smile. Dave gapes at me like I've announced I'm quitting my job to become a professional hang glider. Max and Jack both squeal "Eeeeeeeeew, girlfriend!"

Only Clara seems to have her wits about her. "Hey, Molly," she says pleasantly.

Molly smiles at my assembled family members. "Hi."

Clara gathers her sons and corrals them out onto the lanai, from which their shrill protests of disgust are less deafening. I walk over to the refrigerator and fill two glasses of water.

"Sorry," I say, handing one to Molly. "We were looking at old yearbooks and lost track of time."

Dave snorts. "Sounds like they were pretty good yearbooks."

"Very good," Molly agrees.

"Did I hear you say 'girlfriend'?" my mother asks, glancing across the kitchen at my father as if to say *is this really happening?*

"Yep," I say.

"Seth!" she cries, beaming. "Why didn't you tell us?"

"Hot off the presses," I say.

My mom rushes over and gives Molly a big hug. "I'm so happy for you two."

"Seth is a lucky man," my dad says.

Dave has politely wiped away his instinctive horror. "Welcome to the family, Molly," he says.

Molly grins at him. "Honor to be nominated."

My mom holds up an enormous bag of leftovers. "Would you two like some hush puppies?"

"No," I say quickly. I'm sure Molly is dying to get out of here.

"Actually yes," Molly says. "I'm starving."

"Oh good," my mom says. "We also have tri-tip and mahi and—here, I'll make you a plate."

"Thanks," Molly says.

"Do you want a plate, Seth?" my mom asks.

"I'll share Molly's."

"I was just about to open a bottle of pinot," my dad says. "Care for a glass?"

"Sure," Molly says.

And then my parents are dishing up food and pouring wine and leading us out to the patio.

Clara has managed to distract the boys by taking them for a night swim. The pool is lit up pink, and their splashes and cries of pleasure create a resort vibe, like we're all on one big family vacation.

I try not to fixate on the idea that someday that could be a reality.

"So, Molly," my dad says. "When are you heading back to La La Land?"

I realize I have not yet thought to ask this question myself.

"My flight is first thing in the morning," she says.

"It is?" I ask, crestfallen.

I assumed she must be staying longer, seeing family.

"Yeah. I've been here all week."

My parents and Dave are clearly picking up on my disappointment.

My mother stands up suddenly. "Kal, Dave, why don't we grab our suits and join the boys for a family swim."

My nephews hear this and immediately start screaming, "FAMILY SWIM! FAMILY SWIM!"

"All right, all right," Dave yells at his children. "Let's not wake up the astronauts on the moon."

"I guess you need to get home to pack," I say to Molly. I try not to show how bummed I am, but I am not at all successful.

"Sorry, I should have thought to say something. I just . . . got caught up in the moment."

"Don't apologize. I'm just sad we have to say goodbye already."

She nods. "I know. When are you leaving?"

"Friday."

Today is Sunday. I'd been looking forward to a week of family time, but after the day we've just had—very possibly the best day of my life—the idea of being here without her is as appealing a prospect as swallowing sand.

Molly's phone buzzes. She grabs her bag and glances at it. "Shit. It's my mom. Passive aggressively asking if you abducted and killed me."

"Not yet. But I plan to on the way home."

"Oh good. I'm tired of this mortal coil."

"Well, shall we call it a night?"

She nods. "Yeah, I should spend a little time with her before I pack up. Let me say goodbye to your fam."

We wave goodbye at Clara and the boys and intercept Dave and my parents in the living room. Molly hugs them all, which is somewhat amusing to watch as they are all in their bathing suits.

And then we are back in my mother's Volvo, cruising down dark suburban streets, trying to get Molly home before curfew, just like we're sixteen again.

I put on Elliot Smith, because it evokes sadness and Los Angeles and I wish she wasn't going there.

"Jesus, Seth," Molly says, flicking the volume down. "Let's not wallow in misery."

"I'm going to miss you. I'm still reconciling what to do about how much I'm going to miss you."

She strokes my neck. "It's going to be awful," she says.

That she agrees makes me feel better. Until she adds, "Maybe this isn't a good idea."

I tense up.

"What?"

"Trying to be . . . something. Maybe it's better as a dream than an emotionally wrenching logistical nightmare."

"How would that be better?" My voice is too loud, too appalled. She leans away from me, closer to the door, like she's startled.

"It's just that we've had this one perfect day. Maybe we should—"

I pull the car over, put on my hazards, and turn to face her.

"Molly, why are you saying this?"

She takes a shallow, ragged breath, and I know she is on the cusp of a panic attack. I want to hold her, to physically squeeze the anxiety out of her, but we're separated by a console and both wearing seat belts.

"I am going to ruin this, Seth," she says. "I know myself and I will freak out and hurt you, and then you'll realize you can't be with me and I'll miss you for the rest of my life."

"Baby," I say gently. "Is that what you really think?"

"Yes! I'm so fucking *squirrelly*, Seth. You have no idea."

I laugh hoarsely through the knot in my throat. "Actually I do have an idea. I want you anyway."

She's quiet.

"I've wanted you for twenty years. You know that, right?"

She sniffles. "Yeah. Me too."

"And I know you have your issues, and so do I, and I know this won't be easy to do long-distance. But we *have* to try. Otherwise, what a waste."

"Okay," she whispers. It's almost a sob. It guts me.

I reach out for her and crush her hard against my side. She puts her head on my shoulder. In the rearview mirror I can see silver tearstains on her cheeks.

I must fix those tears. We've been through too much for this day to be sad. The matter is not up for debate.

"I have an idea," I say.

"Yeah?"

"What if you don't go to LA tomorrow?"

"I can't stay, Seth. I'm already on the verge of killing my mother."

"Then what if we both leave? We could get a flight to Chicago and drive out to my lake house. Just the two of us. Spend the week together. Make plans. Figure out how to do this for real."

"You're serious?"

"So serious."

"What about your family?"

"I'll tell them I have to go see about a girl."

I hold my breath.

"I'd have to be back in LA by Saturday afternoon," she says slowly. "But you know what? Fuck it. It's better than nothing. I'll look up tickets."

"Hell yeah."

I pull back onto the road and she grabs her phone and runs through departure times. She's purchased our tickets before we even make it to the bridge to the island. She has to remind me not to speed because I'm so high on joy and adrenaline that I accidentally go fifty in a twenty-five.

I make out with her in the car in her mom's driveway.

When she gets out, I jump out of the car after her and make out with her again in front of her mom's door.

I sing at the top of my lungs to the radio on the way home.

I dance a little as I inform my parents I'll be leaving early.

And by eight thirty in the morning, I'm meeting Molly on the curb of the departures terminal of the airport.

"You sure this is a good idea?" Dave asks me as he stops the car. "I know you're happy but this is . . ." He pauses and I know he's searching for a diplomatic word. "Sudden."

I see my girl, hair glinting in the morning light, and wonder how he could think this is anything but the beginning of a fairy tale.

Still, his concern for me is touching. He was never a particularly doting older brother when we were kids, but no one is there faster or feistier when I need him. I love with my heart on my sleeve. He loves with his fists out.

"I'm positive," I tell him. "Don't worry about me."

He nods and claps me on the shoulder. "All right. Well, call Mom when you get there. She'll worry."

"Will do. Thanks for the ride."

I grab my suitcase from the trunk, wave goodbye at Dave, and all but run to Molly.

"Morning, beautiful," I say, pulling her into my arms and smelling her delicious hair.

"Good morning to you," she says. She lets me stand there and nuzzle her for longer than I expect.

I bury my face against her cheek to hide the pure glee of my smile. Because what I know from her standing here in public, snuggling me, is that she *likes* me.

I know she said she loved me, which is perhaps the highlight of my adult

life, but sometimes affection is just as hard to earn as ardor. So it floods me
with warmth that I can tell she's happy to see me. That she enjoys my nearness and my company.

I have forgotten so many times in my string of relationships that *like* is
just as necessary as love.

We check in for our flight and drop off our bags. We're just past security,
walking to our gate hand in hand, when Molly stops short. I almost trip.

I glance back at her, and she's pale. Devoid of any of the lightness she
exuded thirty-five seconds ago.

"What's wrong?" I ask.

"Oh. Nothing. Just . . ." She points to the line at the coffee kiosk.

There, standing with a very pretty redheaded woman, who looks to be
about twenty-five, is Molly's dad.

Roger Marks was always a striking man—tall and lanky with hollow
cheeks and pale blue eyes. In his golden years, his thick snarl of hair has gone
white, his face is craggier, and he's cultivated a suntan so deep and leathery
he looks like a Cuban cigar. You could imagine him robbing tombs in Egypt,
or filming culinary adventure shows in Thailand—or, what he actually does,
I imagine—writing lowbrow detective thrillers on a sailboat in Florida while
drinking aged rum on the rocks.

He must sense our eyes on him, because he looks up and scans the terminal.
Molly waves. He squints, like he's trying to place her.

In his defense there's a glare from the skylights, but it still takes him a
startling amount of time to clock that the Molly-size person walking toward
him calling "Dad!" is his daughter.

You can tell the moment he recognizes her because his face goes totally
slack. He looks pained. No. He looks *caught*.

He lifts up a hand but does not sacrifice his place in the line to greet her.
Which tracks. He never inconvenienced himself to see her when she was a
traumatized teenager. Why should he start now?

I hate him.

I've always hated him.

But I hate him more because I see the eagerness in her walk, and I see him
just standing there with dread on his face.

I rush to catch up with Molly, clenching the handle of my bag like it's a
baseball bat. I will beat Roger Marks senseless in this airport if he is not kind
to his daughter, my precious TSA-Pre status be damned.

"Well hi," Molly says to her father. "Didn't expect to see you here."

"Hey, toots," he says, because he's the kind of man who calls women "toots." He leans forward to accept a kiss on the cheek, which he doesn't reciprocate. "What a coincidence."

"Yeah," Molly says. "I thought you were out of town. Just getting back?"

"Just leaving, actually," he says. "Quick jaunt to Barbados. Golf tournament."

"Ah," Molly says slowly. "And, um, who's this?"

The young woman is staring down at the floor with wide, horrified eyes, as though she has just noticed a roach walking over her foot and can't look away.

"Savannah," Roger says to her, "this is my daughter, Molly."

The girl looks up and very briefly glances at Molly's eyes. "Nice to meet you, Molly." She has a slight southern accent and a tremulous voice. She is either quite shy or quite terrified.

"Nice to meet you, too," Molly says.

There is a very, very long pause.

"And who might you be?" Molly's dad asks, offering me his hand with a jovial, back-slapping energy that has appeared out of nowhere. He seems very eager to turn the conversation away from his trip and his travel companion.

"Seth Rubenstein," I say. I wait for him to register that I dated his daughter for most of her teenage years, but he evinces no recognition.

"Pleasure to meet you, Seth. Roger Marks." He says this like he knows I will recognize his name from the entire shelf of neon-covered hardbacks emblazoned with it at the newsstand fifteen feet away, and is pleased to give me a chance to meet a celebrity.

"You've actually met," Molly says. "Seth was my boyfriend in high school. Remember?"

"Ah, of *course*," he says, though he is very obviously lying. "Nice to see you again, Seth. Where are you two headed?"

"Chicago," Molly says, in a timbre I have never before heard her use except when she's trying not to sound upset. "On our way to Wisconsin."

This would be a natural point for Roger to ask his daughter why she is going to the Midwest with her high school boyfriend, but he is not moved to inquire.

"Looks like we're next in line," he says. "Can I get either of you a coffee?"

I want to ask for an iced quad dirty chai coconut-milk latte just to make him spend ten minutes waiting around for it, but this interaction is clearly excruciating for all involved, so I restrain myself.

"No, we're good," Molly says.

"Well it's great to run into you, tootsie," her dad says with forced warmth. "I'll see you in Los Angeles."

"Yeah. Sounds good," Molly says, with the same unconvincing brightness. "Have fun on your trip."

She steps in for a hug just as he turns to the cashier to start ordering.

It's like watching a kitten be hit by a car.

"Oh, whoops," she says, nearly colliding with Savannah. I can hear humiliation in her voice, but Roger is too busy giving a teenager instructions on how long to brew his espresso to notice.

I want to grab him by his big stupid hair and bash his face into the plexiglass counter.

She begins to walk away, but I remain planted.

"Asshole," I say under my breath.

Roger turns around. "Excuse me?" he says.

I shake my head in disgust. "That's your fucking daughter."

"Seth, come on," Molly says, tugging at my hand. "It's fine."

"You can't give your own daughter a hug? Maybe act like you're halfway happy to see her?"

"Enough," Molly hisses. "Don't do this."

"Sorry, Dad," she says over her shoulder. "See you in a week."

She pulls me away and doesn't look back as she walks quickly in the direction of our gate.

I put an arm around her but she shrugs it off. "That was humiliating," she whispers. I assume she means her father's profound apathy at seeing her, but she whirls around to face me head-on. "Don't ever do anything like that again, do you understand?"

Oh, shit. She's mad at me.

"I'm sorry," I say immediately. "You're right. It wasn't my place to step in."

"No. It wasn't."

I can tell by her tone she wants me to drop it, but I can't let it go.

"It's just that I can't believe him," I say. "He lied to you about being out of town? And who was that girl?"

She shakes her head, stone-faced. "Who knows. Not his wife. It doesn't matter. It's not worth getting into it with him."

But it *is*. I want her to be as incensed as I am. To flay into that bastard with her poison dagger tongue. To storm over to Hudson News, grab the latest Mack Fontaine book, and whale on him with it.

"Baby," I say at a much quieter volume. "Why should *you* protect *his* feelings?"

"Because he's my father," she says flatly. "At the end of the day, I want a relationship with him. And we've been getting along. I'm writing the next Mack Fontaine movie."

I'm astounded that she would trust him enough to work with him on anything, let alone on one of his sleazy PI movies, but I know that isn't my business.

"Okay. I get that. But you can still be angry with him for how he treated you."

"That's just what he's like. I'm used to it. I have my mom. It's fine."

But it's not. I can see in her complete lack of affect that she has disappeared somewhere inside herself. I *despise* it.

I pull her into my arms, but she stays rigid. It's like hugging a piece of driftwood.

"Listen to me," I say. "I pity him. Because his daughter is one of the most extraordinary people I've ever met. And he blew it. And he knows it. That's why he's like that. Because he failed you, and he's ashamed."

She takes a deep breath.

"Yeah? Well, he's where I get it from."

"Get what?"

"Being a selfish remote asshole with a cruel streak."

I'm taken aback. "Molly, you are none of those things."

"Yes, I am," she says flatly. "I'm built just like him. I'm cold and cynical and I hurt people."

Before this moment, I have never truly understood the meaning of the word *aghast*.

"You are absolutely not," I say, wanting to sear it into her brain. "I'm not even entertaining—"

"No? Sarcastic writer throws away great guy, ghosts him for fifteen years? Sound like anyone we know? Remember when you said I'm a bolter? Well bingo. Learned it from the best."

"Molly, I was *awful* to say that. No one is only their past. No one is just one thing."

"Yes, I'm sure I'm all the colors of the goddamn rainbow, but I get my shitty parts from my dad. Relationships freak me out, and I check out and run away and hurt people who care about me. And I know how that feels, because he fucking did it to me, okay? He still fucking does. And if you are wondering how you fit into this, as a nice person with feelings who *loves* me, so am I."

Her pupils are dilated, and I can tell she's catastrophizing. Condemning herself to a character trope that I'm partly responsible for casting her in.

She's writing the end of our story before it even begins.

"Molly?" I say. "We all make mistakes, and we all have baggage. It doesn't make you a bad person. It makes you human."

Tears well in her eyes. "Thank you for saying that. But I'm not sure this trip is a good idea. I'm not going to be good for you."

I shake my head. "No. Sorry, kid. You are exactly what's good for me."

"I don't want to treat you like that. I don't want to hurt you. I'm so afraid of myself." She's not crying, but her whole body is clenched, like she's using every muscle she possesses to hold it together. "I don't want to lose you again."

"Baby," I say, squeezing her with my entire life force, "I won't fucking let you."

And I know, when she goes limp and starts to cry into my neck, that she's willing to try to believe me.

CHAPTER 30
Molly

I'm so glad Seth didn't let me flee at the airport. Because if I hadn't gotten on that plane, how would I have ever known that he murmurs words in his sleep?

They aren't in English. He speaks a made-up language in his dreams.

He wakes up with the sun at 6:00 a.m. and goes out to the deck to meditate. When he's done, he takes a morning kayak, or goes for a run around the lake. He comes home dewy with exertion and takes a shower. And then he returns to bed and kisses me awake.

He won't let me out of bed until he's made me come at least two times. It isn't hard. My body is in a permanently heightened state around him. I want, and want, and want.

He makes me breakfast every day. Eggs scrambled with juicy tomatoes and fresh basil, topped with feta. Yogurt with homemade granola—a fragrant mix of cinnamon and pine nuts and oats and ancient grains—served with a dollop of blueberry jam. His grandmother's drop biscuits with cheesy stone-ground grits. Raspberry-studded pancakes saturated with melted better and doused in maple syrup he heats up on the stove.

He never lets me help him. Other meals we prepare together, but breakfast—he makes me that alone.

While he cooks, I putter around, trying to read him from his possessions like they're tea leaves. His house is spare and airy, an A-frame cottage with big glass windows that look out onto the lake. The furniture is more rustic than I expected—a leather Chesterfield couch that's been allowed to age. Rewired vintage lamps. Hand-woven rugs. A farmhouse table he keeps piled with candlesticks and teak bowls of fruit. Every item in the house, from his vintage board games to his cookbooks to his yoga mat, has a specific home. He never leaves anything out of place.

Occasionally, Seth has to carve out time to deal with work. At first, I brace myself to hear him talk about divorce and alimony—trigger words. But once I hear him counseling clients with patience and compassion—delivering hard truths about the dissolution of their marriages or good news about negotiations over custody of their children—I realize I've been wrong about his job. I still don't love it, but it requires empathy and kindness and insight into human nature. It suits his better self.

He's also funny and collegial with his team as he discusses cases and assigns responsibilities and makes decisions. I hear his calls with lawyers on the other side—unfailingly upbeat and polite even when he rejects their demands and shreds apart their arguments. I marvel at his competence. I understand how he can afford a lake house.

He still loves music. When he's not on calls or videoconferences he always has it on. He wasn't lying about his predilection for Cat Stevens, which I find endearing. He's given me a new perspective on the discography of Elvis; the man had bangers. Despite Seth's best efforts, I still hate The Rolling Stones. We both love Etta James. He thinks it's funny to play NSYNC when we get in bed, and I have to steal his phone to turn it off.

The first night, I tried to listen to lullabies in my earbuds to lull myself to sleep. He gently plucked them from my ears and put my playlist on the speakers. Every night, we fall asleep to them together. Sometimes he croons them in my ear.

In the afternoons it's hot and humid and we go swimming in the lake. Afterward we lie on towels and read books we bought at the secondhand store in town. He picked out a pile of sci-fi paperbacks—the same kind he loved in high school—and tears through them one by one. He reads expressively, smiling at the good parts, furrowing his brow when things get tense. I pretend to read a dog-eared collection of Alice Munro stories, but mostly I peek at Seth and ponder my good fortune.

I try not to think about my father, or work, or Los Angeles—the ticking clock we're both aware of. The fact that this is temporary.

We have five days, I tell myself. *Three more days. Still one last night.*

We come home damp and sun-sated, have lazy sex, and take a nap.

Seth loves shopping. He loves to take me to the natural grocery store to buy hand-ground peanut butter and nutty bread. He knows the vendors at the farmers market, and proudly introduces me to them: "My girlfriend, Molly." He's friendly with the girls who own the local wine shop, and they point him toward bottles of ruby-tinted pinot noirs and skin-fermented orange wines that remind me of the sun.

At night, Seth grills lake-caught fish and midwestern steak while I make us herby salads and summer corn. We open wine and eat on the deck under the July sunset. When darkness finally falls, the sky's so clear you can see the Milky Way.

Seth talks about our future. We should try long-distance for six months, he says, and take stock. FaceTime every day. See each other in person at least once a month.

He brainstorms places we could meet—places neither of us have ever been, where we can make new memories together. Santa Fe. Yosemite. Orcas Island to see whales.

He wants to see my house, and burrow in my stuff.

I still think about my dad. I think about how he and my mom were high school sweethearts, and that didn't stop him from destroying their relationship. I think of how he still cheats, sheds marriages like last season's clothes. I think of all the nice guys I've bailed on, back before I stopped dating people who might care if I leave them.

Instead of quietly obsessing, I talk to Seth about it in the dark.

He's tender in hearing out my fears, but optimistic. We love each other, he reassures me. We know each other. This can work.

He writes a gratitude list in his journal every night before he brushes his teeth, and makes me do it too.

I'm thankful for mornings listening to Chopin as the smell of toast and pesto drift around me in a sunlit cabin.

For lake water crisping up my hair.

For a job that lets me disappear into this momentary life.

For sex on the deck at midnight when the stars are out and the neighbors are asleep.

I'm grateful, in a word, for Seth.

CHAPTER 31
Seth

Every time I hear Molly Marks softly snore beside me, my heart flips over. I wake up early just to hear the breathy rhythm of it. The proof of her beside me.

She sleeps in while I do my morning workout. But I know she gets up in secret to brush her teeth, because when I join her in bed after I shower her breath is minty fresh.

Her suitcase is such a mess I itch to fold and organize her clothes. (I manage to control myself.) But hanging from a hook on my bathroom door is a bag with neatly packed compartments of skin care products, sorted in the order she applies them. It takes her fifteen minutes every morning, another twenty in the evening. She says she doesn't meditate, but I think this is her version of it.

After she does the products, she smells amazing.

In fact, she always smells amazing.

The first morning we woke up together she said she didn't eat breakfast—"not to worry about her." Maybe, she said, she'd have a protein bar later. A protein bar! I made her scrambled eggs anyway, and it turns out she *does* eat breakfast if you make her something delicious, infused with love. Every day while I'm preparing it, I brainstorm what to make tomorrow, trying to top myself. Trying to use every tool at my disposal to make her associate me with sensuous delights.

She likes to wander around my place while I'm cooking, tinkering with this and that, asking me the provenance of furniture or books or records. She rifles through my possessions with an intense curiosity that flatters me, but also makes me slightly nervous. I hope she likes whatever she is finding.

Sometimes, when I have to work, she takes out her laptop and writes. She's the fastest typist I have ever seen, using the tips of her long nails to fly across the keys. It's as though her ideas have overtaken her body, transforming her into those flying fingers.

Yet she often complains of being stuck, or uninspired. "How can you say that when you write so fluidly?" I ask her.

"I delete a lot," she says. "I delete hundreds of thousands of words a year."

Imagine that. Hundreds of thousands of words, gone. I wish that I could have them.

At night she asks me questions about my cases and my clients. I never share identifying details, but we talk about the law, the issues that my clients face. "I'd rather never marry than get divorced," she says.

"That's why you have to marry your soul mate," I say.

She looks away.

I have yet to get her to agree that I am hers.

I will never stop trying.

Every day Molly makes us lunch, and every day it's exactly the same thing: a giant mound of dark, curly kale generously massaged with a pungent garlic-Parmesan dressing, topped with avocado, grapes, pepitas, and grilled chicken breast. She calls it The Salad, and eats it directly out of the bowl with her fingers. She claims The Salad is meant to be consumed with one's bare hands. I find this point of view questionable, and consume my portion on a plate with a fork, but I like watching her daintily pick out just the right piece of kale and lick the dressing off her fingers.

After lunch, we grab towels and sunscreen and books and walk down to the beach. Molly always wears an enormous sun hat embroidered with the words BEACH MILF in hot pink cursive, which she stole from her mother in Florida. We go into the lake together and frolic. If there aren't too many kids around to scandalize, we'll wade deeper and make out—just like we did in the ocean in high school. Molly is naughty and touches me below the waist. I do not allow things to become too hot and heavy, because we are in the land of decency, but I enjoy her daily efforts to tempt me to submit to a public hand job.

When I go back to shore she goes for a swim, and I watch her figure cutting back and forth across the water in the distance and think *we have five days. Three more days. Still one last night.*

Usually, when we get home . . . let's just say I get something better than a hand job.

When I don't have more work after our siesta, we play gin rummy. It was Molly's suggestion—it's her mom's family's vacation game of choice—and at first, she beat me every hand. Then, after humiliating myself two nights in a row, I googled "Gin Rummy Strategies" and realized I was committing to my cards too early. Now we are evenly matched, and she is outraged every time I win. Beating Molly Marks at something has always been one of life's great pleasures.

We make dinner together and drink good wine from my friends' little shop in town. (The two owners, Meg and Luz, quit their jobs in Milwaukee to be local booze purveyors, and sometimes I wish I had thought of it first.) Molly is fantastic at assembling sides and salads. (But never The Salad. The Salad is only for lunch.)

I'm so in love. I'm so happy. I try to play it mostly cool, because Molly gets anxious when I'm emotional. In a way, it's worse than high school, because she's had two more decades to perfect her defenses against love. But when it happens—when she gets panicky—she lets me hold her.

She lets me stroke her hair and help her breathe.

She trusts me.

And I'll take that.

Because I don't want this to be a fling. I don't want this to be another one of Seth's Doomed Impulsive Love Affairs™. I don't want it to be the thing that makes Molly finally stop talking to me for good.

Before we go to bed, I make her join me in writing in a gratitude journal.

I'm thankful for the sunshine that warms our skin.

For lullabies that soothe my girl to sleep.

For the lake that helps us relearn each other's bodies.

For a chance never to stop learning Molly Marks.

And I'm grateful for this hope.

This chance to hope, and hope, and hope.

PART SEVEN

November 2021

CHAPTER 32

Molly

It's two days before Thanksgiving and I'm scouring my perennially unkempt house. It always takes everything I have to prepare my home for Seth, a man who folds his socks into stackable rectangles and has a toothbrush just for grout. After five months of going back and forth between each other's houses I am mostly inured to his shrieking at the appearance of stray crumbs and his habit of bleaching my sink. But this is the first time we've spent a holiday together, and I want it to be perfect.

I take a break to check my email. I'm waiting to hear back from my dad and his director on the latest draft of *Busted*. I sent it weeks ago and haven't gotten any notes. The director, Scott, usually responds right away. The radio silence is making me uneasy.

But there's nothing—just some emails about other, smaller projects I've been working on—so I commence the dreaded task of steam-mopping my floors.

My phone rings—Dezzie—and I pounce on it, eager to wail to a sympathetic ear about my fear of being judged dirty by society's most hygienic man.

But she's sobbing.

"Oh my God," I say. "Babes. What is it?"

She doesn't say anything. She makes a noise like she's suffocating.

The first thing I think about is Seth. They're both in Chicago. Maybe something's happened to him, and she's been tasked with telling me. Every day, now that we're so close, visions flash before my eyes of losing him. A plane crash. A car wreck. An undiagnosed heart defect. So many things that could strike at any moment to take this unexpected joy away from me.

"Dezzie!" I say. "What's wrong? You're scaring me."

"It's Rob," she chokes out.

I feel a sharp, shameful relief that whatever horrible thing this call is about, it's not Seth. And then an overwhelming wave of guilt that this is my reaction to my best friend's hysteria. I'm seeing more horrific visions. I think of Covid. I think of cancer. I put my fingers on the table and press them down to make myself talk instead of spiraling.

"What's wrong? Is he okay?"

"He's leaving me."

"Wait, what? Leaving *you*?" I'm sure I heard it wrong.

I have frequently entertained the thought that Dezzie might benefit from taking some time apart from Rob, who has continued to devolve from a goofy model husband into an erratic, booze-soaked stranger. It never once occurred to me that he might leave *her*.

"He got some woman pregnant, and he's filing for divorce," she says raggedly.

I stare at my phone like it's radioactive.

"What the *fuck*? Rob *cheated* on you?"

"Yes! With some woman from his grad program. He said it was just a fling, but now that there's going to be a baby, he needs to try to make it work. With *her*."

All I can think is: no. No, no, no. This cannot be happening to someone I love.

Not to Dezzie, of all people.

She's about to start her second round of IVF. She and Rob refinanced their house to pay for it. I suspect her desire for a child is the reason she's stayed with him this long.

That, and she loves him.

However difficult their marriage has become, there are years and years of love between them.

I want to fly to Chicago and stab him in the neck.

"I'm going to die," she gasps out.

No, Rob is. Because I am going to murder him.

But I bite that thought back because it isn't what she needs to hear right now.

"Oh, honey, no you're not," I say. "It's going to be okay. You have me and Alyssa and your parents and all your friends and we love you so, *so* much and we will be there with you every step of the way, no matter what happens."

Even as I say it, I know it might not be enough. It took my mother years to glue herself back together after my dad left her. Two *decades* to trust another man.

When someone you've been with for so long turns on you—changes into something unrecognizable—it makes you question your own reality. What did you miss? What did you do? And if it can happen once, what will keep it from happening again?

"I don't know what to do," Dezzie says hoarsely. "He's just gone, Molly. He literally took a duffel bag and left. Just like that."

I flash back to my dad's BMW pulling out of the driveway. Of standing in the front yard sobbing, begging him not to leave. Thinking that what was happening could not possibly be real. Praying he would see my desperation and realize his mistake and turn the car around.

He didn't.

They don't do that.

They just fucking break your heart and go.

My hands are shaking.

"Dez?" I say, trying to keep my voice calm for my friend. "Listen. I know exactly what to do. First, do you have any herbal tea? Chamomile?"

"Tea?" she wails. "What the hell, Molly?"

"Process-oriented tasks are calming!" I tell her, marshaling my years and years of therapy. "You're going to make yourself a cup of tea and we're going to talk this out, okay? Can you do that?"

"Yeah," she says, after a long pause. "I guess."

"Good. I'll wait. Put me on speaker."

"Fine. Hold on."

I hear her fiddling around in her kitchen. Hear water running, then the electric kettle roaring. Hear her crying.

"Okay, I made the stupid tea."

"Good girl. Now I want you to inhale the steam off the top of the cup while I count to five. All right? Deep inhales, deep exhales, all the way from your belly."

"I should have called Alyssa."

"I promise, this will help. Deep breaths. Do it with me." I model breathing as I count. "One. Two. Three. Four. Five."

I hear her following my breath. I count it out again. We repeat this over and over, until her crying slows.

"Okay," she says shakily. "I feel calmer. Thank you."

"Good. Now, before you do anything else, you need to call Seth. I'm going to text you his work number."

While I've been counting, I've also been having visions of my mother losing her house. My rich dad hiding his money. This isn't the same situation, but I know that Dezzie and Rob have debt. And if Rob can cheat on her and leave her, he can also hire a scumbag lawyer who can ruin her financially.

Maybe *this* is the reason I've fallen in love with a divorce attorney. I still don't trust them as a species, but I trust Seth. I know he is honorable and good at what he does. I know he will protect my friend.

Dezzie whimpers. The sound is pure pain. "Oh God, Molls," she says, "this is a fucking nightmare. It's Thanks*fucking*giving, how am I supposed to—"

"Stop. Seth will know exactly what to do, okay? Will you call him?"

"Yeah," she says weakly.

"And, while you're doing that, I'm going to book a flight to Chicago."

"No, don't. My parents are already planning to come. They'll be here tonight."

"Then you'll have all of us."

"No, no, you have your trip with Seth."

We'd planned to drive to Joshua Tree for the long weekend. Seth wants to cash in on my pining-era impulsive invitation to take him there. He says that was the first moment he realized I might really feel something for him.

"Are you sure?" I ask Dezzie. "Seth will understand. We can stay at his place and all spend the weekend together."

"I'm sure," Dezzie says.

"Okay, love. Call Seth and call me back."

As soon as she hangs up I put my head on my kitchen table. I'm still shaking.

Dezzie and Rob. My God.

Happy endings, man.

Just when you think they might exist . . .

It's terrifying, because things with Seth are getting really, really serious. I've watched myself fall for him, knowing my feelings are getting out of hand, and let it happen anyway. *Enjoyed* it happening. Sometimes I find myself randomly smiling and staring off into space, daydreaming about a life with him. One where we move to the same city, get married, maybe even have a baby.

I've begun to let myself wonder if we're safe.

But no one's ever safe. Because if this can happen to Dezzie and Rob, it can happen to anyone.

I send Seth a text.

> **Molly:** Hey babe—dezzie is going to call you at work. Make sure to pick up. It's important

I wait two minutes. He doesn't reply.

He always replies.

Intellectually, I know he must be in a meeting or already on the phone with Dezzie, but it rattles me. I attempt to return to cleaning, but I can't focus. Trying to prepare your home for a romantic visit from your boyfriend seems really fucking tasteless in the midst of your best friend's life unraveling.

And I keep getting lost in my own memories of the day my dad left.

He'd taken me out for breakfast, to Denny's, which was our special place. He ordered chicken fingers for breakfast—a childish habit of his I'd always found hilarious. My pancakes came and he took a sip of coffee and told me, casually, that he'd be moving out that day. "Your mother and I are getting a divorce."

At first, I thought he was kidding. My dad liked to be funny, and my mom was often the butt of his jokes. In retrospect that's a telling detail, but at the time I was a daddy's girl and thought it was charming when he mocked my mother to amuse me. Our shared sarcastic sensibility was our special bond. My mother's sincerity and warmth and easily hurt feelings weren't on *our* level.

But that morning, there was no punch line—unless you consider him telling me he was moving into a beach condo with Coral Lupenski, the twenty-two-year-old daughter of my dentist, funny.

I began to suspect I'd been on the wrong side of history.

It was confirmed when we got home and Mom was locked in her bedroom, sobbing like she might die, and his only response to this was to roll his eyes and tell me she was "being hysterical" and that he'd left money for pizza in case she stayed "a basket case all day." Which is when the true panic set in.

When I realized he was leaving *me* too.

I started yelling. I said this was pathetic, that you can't just leave your wife for some bimbo because you'd gotten famous.

He said—because he is a bad writer who traffics in stale clichés—"All good things must come to an end, toots." Then he grabbed his keys and walked out the front door.

I couldn't not follow him.

I begged him to take me with him and, when he didn't even respond, collapsed bare-legged in my cutoffs on the sharp crushed shells of our driveway as he drove away.

And the worst part was that in the aftermath, during the deepest, scariest part of my mother's depression, when she stopped making meals and barely showered and refused to see anyone except my grandparents, I kept wanting *him* to fix it.

I wanted my father.

He and I had been so close. I would get waves of despair so intense I'd almost pass out from them, and I wanted to call him and tell him I felt like I was dying, that I needed him to rub my back and tell me it was going to be okay—but he was the reason for the despair in the first place. He was the reason it would never be okay again. At least not for a very long time.

And I know that *this*—this ache for someone who has irrevocably destroyed their ability to comfort you—is how Dezzie is feeling. The person whose love she most craves isn't there for her because he's the one who is causing her the pain.

I want to take her in my arms and hold her. I want to give her everything that Rob gave up.

My phone rings, and it's her.

"Dez?" I ask. "Did you get a hold of Seth?"

"Yes." She sniffles. "He can't help me."

"*What?*"

Seth is one of Chicago's premier divorce attorneys. *Of course* he can help her.

"Babe, back up," I say. "What do you mean?"

"He said he can't represent me because Rob already came to him this morning and tried to hire him. He says he's 'conflicted out,' even though he didn't accept the case."

"Wait. Rob told him about this and Seth didn't fucking *tell* you?"

"I don't think he can? Legally? I don't know. He gave me the numbers of a couple other attorneys he said are good."

"Jesus." I am flooded with a sudden, all-consuming feeling of betrayal. "I'm going to call him right now and talk to him. I'll get him to do it. There must be a way."

I hang up before she can say anything, and speed-dial Seth.

He picks up immediately.

"Hey," he says in a somber tone.

"Please tell me it isn't true that you refused to help Dezzie."

"Whoa," he drawls out. "Refused to—I told her—wait. What's going on? Are you upset with me?"

"Yes," I hiss. "I am extremely upset with you."

I drum my gel nails aggressively on the table, glad they are long and spiky for the satisfying clack they make.

"I didn't refuse to help her," he says. "I can't really say anything beyond that—conversations regarding legal matters are confidential—"

"Oh, please," I interrupt. "You can't invoke attorney-client privilege if you won't take her as a client. And I can't believe you didn't tell her right away when fucking *Rob* showed up at your fucking *office*."

He sighs.

"Molls, I've been devastated all morning, but my hands are tied. It would be completely unethical for me to share that information. And I would love to represent Dezzie, but Rob got to me first. We've been working together on the nonprofit, so he thought I'd take the case. But obviously I would never represent him against Dez, so I said no. Unfortunately, the fact that he consulted me means I can't represent her either."

He's being so patient and reasonable that I want to throw the phone at the wall.

"Why can't you make an exception?" I shout. "You've known Dezzie for decades. She's my *best friend*."

He sighs. It sounds awfully long-suffering. Like *I* am the problem here.

"Like I said, it's unethical. I feel terrible, but there's nothing I can do to change that."

I have no words.

Oh, wait. I do: "You're fucking over my friend."

"No, I'm not," he says, in his firmest lawyer voice. "She's my friend, too. And I've given her the names of the best people in Chicago. She's going to be in very good hands, whoever she chooses."

I don't say anything. This does not deserve a response.

"Molls, I have a client waiting. I'll call you in an hour, okay?"

"Yeah. Fine. Whatever."

I hang up the phone before he can say goodbye and call Dezzie back.

"Hi," I say. "I'm really sorry but I can't get him to change his mind. He says it's a matter of ethics and he's being completely intransigent."

"It's fine," she says. "I understand."

She might, but I don't. He's a senior partner at his firm. He can't bend the rules one time? If not for her, then for me?

"Molly," Dezzie says. "Really, it's fine. He was nice and super apologetic."

I force myself to take a deep breath.

This is not about me and Seth.

This is not about my dad.

I'm just having an emotional reaction on behalf of my friend that I will no doubt have to apologize for later.

"How are you feeling?" I ask Dezzie. "Have you called the other lawyers?"

"Not yet."

"You should do it right away, before people leave the office for Thanksgiving. Get to them before Rob does."

"I know. I will in a minute. I just feel completely discombobulated."

"Have you talked to Alyssa?"

"No. I feel like she's going to say I told you so."

"God, Dez, no. Alyssa would *never* do that. Besides, she didn't predict this."

But Seth did.

In our bet.

The thought gives me chills.

"I know Alyssa thought I should leave him," Dezzie says. "She basically implied it when we took the kids to Six Flags last month. And she was right."

"Well, she'll certainly wish she'd been wrong."

Dez puffs out a breath. "Honestly, I'm just glad I found out before I got pregnant."

"Yeah. Bullet dodged."

"Huge bullet." She pauses. "You are so smart, you know that?"

I'm taken aback. "What do you mean?"

"You've never given a real fuck about men. Never arranged your life around romance bullshit. I used to think you were pathologically cynical, but now I think you're a genius. Rejecting all these toxic institutions."

It's not great to be called pathologically cynical by someone who has known you since elementary school, but I try not to get tripped up.

"What toxic institutions?" I ask, though I suspect I know.

"Marriage. Love. 'Til death do us part bullshit."

She sounds so brittle.

She sounds like me.

I hate to hear it.

Seth has opened me to the possibility of these things. I'm not sure I fully believe in them. But for him, I want to.

"Dezzie, love is not a toxic institution," I say. "I certainly don't reject it. And as for marriage—some people seem to enjoy it. Who knows."

But she's not listening.

"You don't set yourself up to let other people upend your life," she's saying. "You protect yourself. And I used to think it was a little cowardly, to be brutally honest. But now I'm really fucking jealous."

"Um, I'm not sure whether to be offended or flattered right now," I admit.

"I'm sorry," she says. "I shouldn't rant at you. I know things are going well with Seth, and I'm really happy about that. I'm not trying to, like, poison your optimism. I just know you always keep one eye open, and I feel idiotic that I didn't do that too, especially after the last year with Rob. Like, I should not be blindsided, but I feel like I've been hit with a truck when I wasn't even walking near a road."

"I really think you should let me fly out. Or meet you somewhere."

"Dude. *No.* You and Seth are doing your first Thanksgiving. I'm not going to fuck that up."

"He can stay his ass at home. I'm so pissed at him."

"Don't be mad on my account. I get it. He was really sweet on the phone."

I sigh. I know I'm going to have to let go of this anger, but at the moment it feels good and right.

It's probably not fair to Seth.

But it's real.

"What can I do to make you feel better?" I ask Dezzie, trying to remind myself that this is not about me.

"Nothing," she mutters. "Unless you want to kill Rob."

"I do want to," I say. "I've been fantasizing about it all morning."

"Me too. I was thinking I might use a pastry blender."

"Gory. I love it."

"I'm going to call Alyssa now," she says. "Face the music."

"Okay. Call me whenever you want. I love you."

"Love you too, Molls."

I spend the next few hours rage-cleaning. Using a previously untouched vacuum cleaner attachment to suck God only knows what from the interior cracks of my couch. Magic-erasing fingerprints from light switches. Dusting the bulbs in my lamps. It calms me down. By the time I'm done my fury has dissipated, at least a bit.

I strip my bed and put on the brand-new sheets I bought for Seth's visit, and even pre-washed and dried for optimal softness. I sage every room and burn palo santo—giving the house the official smell of LA. I go out and buy fresh flowers to arrange on my table and then secure provisions to take with us to the desert. I splurge on good cheese and charcuterie and briny olives and rosemary-fennel crackers from my favorite *fromagerie*. Cornish game hens to roast in lieu of turkey. Two kinds of potatoes and fresh thyme and cracked pepper and cream for my mom's famous gratin. A cranberry-orange pie speckled with shiny flecks of demerara sugar. Eggs and bacon and carrot cake muffins for breakfast. Whiskey and Seth's favorite pinot and ingredients for a special Thanksgiving cocktail with cranberries and sloe gin. Candles. A big cooler and two bags of ice to transport my haul when we make the two-hour drive tomorrow.

I shop myself into something numb enough to feel like forgiveness.

Seth calls me back just as I'm pulling into my driveway.

"Hey," he says. "Sorry, I got sucked into client calls all afternoon. I just arrived at the airport. Are you okay?"

He sounds almost frightened.

I feel terrible.

"I'm fine. And I'm sorry for being tough on you earlier. I was just disappointed."

"It's okay," he says. "You're an amazing friend."

I would not credit my behavior to being amazing. More like traumatized. But I don't argue. "Thanks."

"Are you still picking me up from LAX or should I grab an Uber?" he asks.

"Of course I'm picking you up. I can't wait."

I hear him smile. "Me neither. See you tonight. I love you."

"I love you too," I say.

And I do.

I'm still shaken up, but I do.

CHAPTER 33

Seth

Normally the feeling I get when I'm about to see Molly after weeks apart is elation so intense it makes me borderline manic. But tonight, there's a dull, painful pressure behind my eyes as I roll my suitcase past baggage claim and confront the hot cloud of exhaust fumes outside LAX.

I've been upset all day, ever since Rob showed up in my office with his gross fucking bombshell.

The timing could not be worse.

It's unspoken, but a lot rides on this trip.

It was Molly's idea to spend Thanksgiving together, just us.

She hasn't said it, but she's testing out being my family.

And I want to graduate with honors.

I know it's fast, and that's my old, problematic pattern. But I spent a year working through that, alone, and this feels different. I've wanted this woman since I was fourteen years old.

And the Thanksgiving invitation feels like a bookend to the time she invited me to Joshua Tree: her own Molly way of telling me she wanted me the way I wanted her.

We've spent a lot of time these past months talking through our respective issues. My history of overeagerness, her fear of people leaving out of the blue, which drives her to do it first. I've taken pains not to leap at making this permanent before she's ready, to give the relationship time to breathe. I can tell she's been doing work not to flinch from my love. To let herself trust that it's real, and hers. That I'm not going anywhere.

But her anger over the Dezzie thing has me anxious. Divorce is a tough subject for her under any circumstances, and Dezzie is one of her dearest people. I wish I could use my skills to rescue both of them.

I can't.

As an equity partner, it would be egregious to break the ethics policies I'm in charge of upholding. I adore Dezzie and will give her all the emotional support she needs, but I can't be her legal counselor.

I text Molly my location and she says she's two minutes away. I strain to see around the bend, waiting for that first glimpse of her car.

There she is. My girl.

And—thank God—she's grinning at me.

She jumps out of the car as soon as she finds a place to stop and runs to me and throws herself into my arms.

I kiss the top of her glossy, clean-smelling hair.

"Hi, baby."

"Hi," she whispers.

We hold each other for a few seconds longer than is socially acceptable in a competitive parking situation. Her nearness makes my headache feel a little better.

She pulls back and takes me in. "You look exhausted," she says.

"Long day. Lots of lawyering to get done before my big California adventure."

She refrains from making a barbed comment about not lawyering for Dezzie, to my profound relief.

"We'll get you nice and rested," she says. She kisses my cheek and then grabs my bag and stashes it in her car. I hop into the passenger seat and she navigates through the serpentine traffic snarled around LAX.

Molly drives like it's an art form. She's not aggressive, but she's skillful—elegantly weaving across six lanes to reach an exit that comes out of nowhere, making room for cars about to get cut off without disrupting the flow of traffic, maintaining conversation as she zips along the steep, winding mountain roads that lead up to her house.

Her authority behind the wheel is sexy. I can't wait for her to drive us to the desert. I hope the route is really difficult.

"Home sweet home," she says, pulling into the driveway of her small, white, Spanish-style house. It's surrounded by purple bougainvillea bushes and cacti that shoot up from the earth like jaunty flower-capped erections. The air smells like jasmine.

It's so her. I love it here.

Inside is a mix of dark wood and comfortable white linen furniture. The floor has Spanish tile and the rooms lead into each other through archways original to the 1920s house.

She's already lighting scented candles on every surface, making the rooms glow.

"Want a snack?" she asks.

"Yes. I'm famished."

She leads me into her yellow kitchen, with light blue cabinets that have vintage crystal knobs she found on eBay. The care she has taken to restore her house, and the pride she takes in telling me about it, is dear to me. It's another one of those unexpected facets I've discovered about her as we've gotten to know each other's adult selves.

I fantasize about buying a rambling old Craftsman and fixing it up with her. Somewhere with a big yard and plenty of fruit trees. A home of our own.

"Toast?" Molly asks.

She has learned about my midnight toast habit. "Yes, please."

She puts some bread in the toaster—the sourdough I like from the farmers market in her neighborhood—and leads me out the door onto her patio. We stand there, holding hands, staring out at the glimmering lights of Los Angeles. There's a slight breeze blowing and the air is cool, but not cold. The smell of my toast wafts from the kitchen and I inhale deeply and kiss the temple of the woman who knew to make it for me.

It is in this exact moment I know I can really do it: I can move to Los Angeles.

"I never get tired of this view," I say. "I've missed it here."

"It's only been three weeks."

"Felt like three months."

She squeezes my hand.

We go back inside and she slathers normal butter on one slice of the toast and peanut butter on the other and mashes them together into a saturated mess, just how I like it. I take my signature sandwich and devour it over the sink. It's so much better when she makes it.

When I finish, I tidy up the counter.

She watches with a wry look. "Finished, inspector?"

"Yes. Take me to bed."

We walk to her room—a pretty, girly space with white velvet drapes and a queen-size bed with a puffy stack of pillows that I immediately want to nestle into after my long day of work and travel.

I grab Molly with both arms and pull her down onto the duvet. "Come here, kid."

She lets me wrap my entire body around hers and squeeze her like I'm an overly exuberant squid. Her body feels small and soft and heavenly beneath mine.

"Thank you for having me," I say into her hair. And I mean thank you for loving me. Thank you for the honor of welcoming me into your life.

She laughs. "My pleasure, Miss Manners."

Still no mention of Dezzie. I wonder if I should bring it up. But Molly seems relaxed. I don't want to ruin her mood.

I drown her in more kisses from her eyes to her throat. She squeals and pushes me off.

"You're crushing me!"

"I can't help myself. You're so crushable."

"You're so cheesy."

I yawn. "I'm so tired." It's eleven p.m. in Los Angeles, making it one a.m. in Chicago.

"Are you going to conk out on me, Rubenstein?"

"No. I'm going to take a shower in your adorable bathroom. And *then* I'm going to conk out on you."

"I'll get you a towel."

I enjoy washing my hair with Molly's shampoo, the bottle of which identifies the name of the familiar, intoxicating scent of her hair—*neroli*. I slather myself with her eucalyptus soap, which floods the shower with the scent of spa treatments. The luxuriousness of her bath products makes me question my own affinity for drugstore brands that profess to smell like "man."

I come out of the bathroom with a towel around my waist, releasing a cloud of fragrant steam into the hallway. Molly is waiting on her bed. She's changed into a white, gauzy, floor-length nightdress that reminds me of a virginal Victorian maiden about to get corrupted by a sexy ghost in a candlelit attic.

"You smell like me," she observes.

"I know. I can barely resist myself."

She gestures at the night table on "my" side of the bed. (Molly is dogmatic about sleeping on the left, no matter where we are.) "I got you some water and Advil PM, in case you're too wired to sleep."

She knows me well.

"Thank you, my queen." I hang my towel over a hook on the back of the door and climb naked into her bed.

I turn to face her and run my finger along the lace cuff of her nightgown. "Am I allowed to see what's under your Jane Austen getup?"

"The lady is feeling a bit chaste tonight. Do you mind?"

The uncomfortable thought flickers up again that she might still be pissed about Dezzie. I'm always harassing Molly to talk through her anxieties. It's bad form on my part not to broach this, even if I'm a little scared to.

"That's all right," I say. "But, Molls?"

"Yeah?"

"Are you still upset? Over my not being able to represent Dezzie?"

She stiffens. "A little," she admits. "But I do understand. I think?"

"I would do it for you in a heartbeat if I could. For both of you."

"I know. I don't want to be unfair to you. I guess it's just this terrible reminder of all the ways things go wrong. Even for people who were happy."

I hold her tighter. I know this is bringing up everything that happened with her dad.

"And I was thinking about how your whole life is dealing with stuff like this," she says. "And telling myself, okay, maybe this is the universe's way of showing me that your job is a positive thing, that I don't have to feel guilty about it, that you can help my friend. But when you said you couldn't, it was like *of course not*. How stupid of me."

I hate to hear this. My career is one of the few things about myself I can't promise to change for her, and it saddens me that she might always feel conflicted about what I do—that it might be a tension we just have to live with.

"I get it," I say. "I wish more than anything that I could fight for her. Not to be selfish, but I feel like this was an opportunity to prove myself to you, and Rob ruined it. But Dezzie will find a great lawyer—we'll make sure of it."

Molly leans over and gives me a peck on the lips. "You don't have to prove yourself to me, Seth. But I have my issues, and they don't go away just because I love you."

Oh God, the relief to hear those words.

"I love you too," I whisper back.

I hold her in my arms until her breath slows, grateful that we've survived our first real fight as a couple.

In the morning, I wake up before her and sneak off for a run. (It's much harder in her mountainous neighborhood, and I can see why she refuses to do it.) When I get back, she's already dressed. She waves off my desire to cook her breakfast—she wants to take me to her favorite Mexican diner for horchata and chilaquiles to fuel us for our journey.

I order mine the way she recommends—half mole sauce, half verde, with a runny egg on top. The owner knows her and calls her *mija,* and suddenly I wish we were staying in Los Angeles instead of going to Joshua Tree—I love seeing her in her world.

But if things go the way I hope they will, I'll have the rest of my life to do that.

The drive to the desert is at first flat and bright and nondescript, and then becomes beautiful. The brown earth sprouts thousands of tall white windmills. The roadway opens up into rugged mountains. After about two hours I catch my first sight of a Joshua tree. I've never seen one in real life before, and I marvel to Molly at the way their branches divide over and over into Seussical formations. We drive down a road evocatively named Twentynine Palms Highway, past a rugged town with a mix of old-timey saloons and hipstery boutiques and strip malls and abandoned shacks, until Molly turns off the highway and navigates down a series of unpaved roads to a gate with a wooden sign reading JACKRABBIT RANCH.

"This is us," she says. She hops out, fishes a key from the back pocket of her jeans, and unlocks the gate to let us in.

Molly's friend Theresa sent me pictures when I was making my secret arrangements for the weekend, but I'm still blown away by how perfect it is. The yard is thick with mature Joshua trees and spidery ocotillo cacti. The front yard is landscaped with a beautiful rock garden and a bench big enough for two lovers to make out under a starry sky. I happen to know that if you drive about a thousand feet past the entrance there's a second gate, which leads to a guesthouse. Theresa usually keeps it closed during the winter, but she sent me the keys on the sly.

"How big is this place?" I ask, because I don't want Molly to know I already sleuthed it out.

"Ten acres," she says. "Theresa bought two parcels next to each other in the aughts for nothing and renovated the old 1950s bungalow that was here originally. It's amazing. Just wait."

We grab our bags and unlock the screened-in porch. The house is low to the ground and seems to be made entirely of wood-paned windows with views of the trees. Everything inside looks hand chosen to feature in an *Architectural Digest* article about retro chic.

"This is amazing indeed," I say.

"You'll be pleased to note there's a fire pit."

Molly knows from our Wisconsin days that I'm a bit of a pyromaniac.

We unload culinary delicacies out of the cooler and into the old-fashioned SMEG fridge in the kitchen. I admire the milky green dishes stacked on the shelves, which Molly informs me are called "Jadeite" and are "ungodly expensive." She says this with such covetousness that I mentally note to find her a Jadeite kitchenware collection of her own.

"Are you ready to go to the park?" Molly asks.

"Yep."

"Great. Put on your hiking boots. I'm just going to check in on Dez real quick."

She goes into the bedroom and closes the door. I hear soothing tones coming through the wall, though the words aren't distinct.

"How's Dez?" I ask when she emerges.

"A little better today," Molly says. "She managed to get ahold of one of those lawyers you recommended and has a consultation lined up for Monday."

Thank goodness. I texted all three of them to see if they could squeeze in a call, but it's so close to the holiday that only one—the fearsome Geneva Bentley—was still in the office.

"I'm so glad," I say.

"Me too. Ready to go?"

We drive ten minutes to the entrance of the national park, and Molly pulls in at the trailhead for what she calls a "normal people hike," a short, flat loop through boulders that leads to Skull Rock. (A rock, she helpfully informs me, that looks like a skull.) Then, to "honor my desire for punishing exercise," we drive to another trail and spend two hours trekking up and down a mountain.

The hike is vigorous and the view is beautiful, and I'm exhilarated with fresh air and endorphins by the time we get back to the car.

"We should get out of here before it starts getting dark, but I want to take you to my favorite place first," Molly says.

"If it's your favorite place, it's my favorite place."

"You're a real cornball."

"I do live in the Midwest. Home of corn."

For now.

We drive through groves of Joshua trees as the sun begins to set, turning the surrounding mountains purple.

Molly stops at a parking lot with multiple large signs warning of bees. I look around warily.

"Molly?" I say.

"Seth?"

"Is this a prank to try to kill me?"

"Are you allergic to bees?"

"No, but I'm scared of bee attacks. Like any sensible person."

She waves this off. "It's worth the risk. Trust me."

We get out and walk toward the entrance of a trail through a giant maze of cacti.

"Cholla cactus," she explains.

The plants are waist-high and ombré, with brown roots that grow up and out into a spectacular shade of yellow. From afar they look fat and fuzzy, like Muppets, but up close the spikes seem like they could kill you. They seem like they *want* to kill you.

"Aren't they beautiful?" Molly asks.

She is beautiful. The golden hour sunlight is radiating against her hair and making her skin luminous. But what I really love is the serenity on her face.

She's so happy here.

And I am so happy to bask in her happiness.

I can see that however shaken she is by Dezzie and Rob, she's not consumed by it. There's room for joy, too.

"So Molls," I say, forcing my voice into a casual calm I in no way feel. "I have a surprise for you."

"Oooh. What is it?"

We're wandering the gardens, and I steer her toward a viewpoint where there aren't any other people.

"I set up some meetings on Monday," I say. "With law firms."

"Oh yeah? What about?"

"About potentially interviewing. For jobs here."

Her eyes go wide. And not, it is instantly apparent, with joy.

"Whoa," she says. "Wow. Why didn't you tell me first?"

"Because I wanted to surprise you," I say carefully. "I thought it would be . . . good news?"

She squints at me. "So you're thinking of moving here?"

She doesn't sound excited—more like confused.

That's okay. I can fix confused.

I put my arm around her waist. "Babe, the past five months have been the happiest of my life. I love you, and I want to be where you are."

She nods slowly. "I love you too, Seth. But that's a really big change for you, just to be closer to me. Like, a huge commitment."

"That's the idea," I say softly.

"What about your nonprofit?"

"We've been thinking about expanding beyond Chicago. I'd love to do something similar in LA."

She gives me a strained smile. "Okay. We can talk about it more. Let's see how your meetings go."

I decide not to tell her I've already done a series of Zoom interviews with both firms I'm considering. That this is basically a chemistry visit to help me decide which one to choose.

But then she reaches out, pulls my head down and kisses me.

"Sorry," she says. "I'm just on edge. I think it could be great. Can you imagine, getting to see each other every day? You're amazing to even consider it."

I'm not amazing.

I'm madly in love.

"I just want to be with you, Molls. Any way you'll have me."

"I want you all the ways," she says. "Let's go home and get on that."

CHAPTER 34

Molly

I'm getting better at recognizing my moments of self-sabotage. I'm proud of myself for course correcting.

Of course I shouldn't panic at the idea of Seth exploring jobs in Los Angeles. Nothing is set in stone, and it could be incredible if he moved here. We can't be long-distance forever. I love our marathon phone calls and romantic trips to see each other, but there's always an undercurrent of sadness: I always, always miss him. Even when we're together, I know it's temporary, and I miss him in advance.

I should not let my unease over Dezzie's crisis ruin what should be a beautiful moment.

What she said on the phone about love is what my therapist would call "reactive." An understandable point of view given the circumstances, but not one I should internalize.

Still, I woke up at 4:00 a.m., my body's customary brooding hour, so rattled I never fell back asleep. Instead, I let my mind turn over all the ways Seth and I could fail each other, or hurt each other, or be mortally wounded and die. I know I'm catastrophizing. But catastrophizing is a means of preparation. A way to pre-break your own heart, before someone else does it for you.

In daylight, though, I'm better able to accept that anxiety is not reality. So

I take Seth's hand, lead him back to the car, and kiss him for all I'm worth. Kissing him always makes me feel so much better.

"Want me to drive?" he asks. I think he can tell that I'm wobbly.

"No, I'm good."

We pull out, and I drive fast over the desert roads, which are nearly empty, given the holiday and the hour. It's six o'clock by the time we get back to town, and I'm starving.

"Fancy moseying down to the saloon, partner?" I ask Seth.

"I could eat an entire jackrabbit."

"I think jackrabbit would be gamey and tough."

"Just how I like it."

It's usually hard to get a table at the saloon at night, but the town is sedate this close to Thanksgiving, and we're seated right away. We proceed to order every fried thing on the menu—pickles, onion rings, wings—plus burgers.

Seth gets up to go to the bathroom and my fingers itch to text Alyssa about him potentially moving here. I'm excited and terrified and it would make me feel better to unpack it with her. But I don't. Telling Alyssa would distract away from Dezzie's crisis, and that doesn't feel right. Plus, it's not like this is happening immediately. There will be plenty of time to work through my feelings with my friends.

And anyway, maybe it's healthier if I work through them with, you know, Seth.

"There's a stuffed roadrunner in the men's room over the urinals," he informs me when he gets back. "I felt like it was checking out my dick."

"Well, I'm sure he was impressed."

"Yeah. My dick is *way* bigger than a roadrunner's."

"Do we have to speak of roadrunner dick? I'm trying to eat fried pickles here."

"Oh, sure. What kind of dick do you want to talk about?"

I smile at him and wipe aioli off my mouth with the back of my hand. "The dick who didn't tell me he's considering moving to LA."

"Excuse me!"

"I'm just kidding. I was thinking about it more. How do you think it would work? Would you move into my house?"

He looks *delighted* to be having this conversation.

"Maybe to start?" he says, like he hasn't thought about this, though I'm sure he has a whole PowerPoint somewhere. "And then we could see how it feels and whether we need more space?"

"I wouldn't want to give up my house," I say quickly. My house, in my name, is my security. I learned that the hard way from my mom. "But maybe I could keep it as a rental. And we could buy a bigger place somewhere nearby. Hmm, but traffic. Where are the firms you're talking to?"

"Downtown."

"Oh, that's only twenty minutes away if you time it right."

He nods. "Yeah. I looked into it before I reached out to them. I know how you feel about going to the West Side."

I've lived in Northeast LA the entire time I've been on the West Coast, and at this point anywhere west of Silver Lake feels like it might as well be in Patagonia.

"Did you tell your parents about this?" I ask.

"Only Dave."

"Is he rabidly opposed?"

I know that Dave still doesn't trust me, even if Seth won't admit it.

"He thinks I should do what makes me happy. And you make me astonishingly happy."

Astonishingly happy. Sometimes I am so in love with this man it makes me woozy.

We can do this, I think. *You, Molly Marks, can do this.*

"Will you have to retake the bar?" I ask.

"Yeah. But I'm really good at standardized tests, as you know."

I do know. He got a perfect SAT score. Still galls me to this day.

Suddenly, I'm excited. Genuinely happy for the first time since I heard Dezzie's news.

"I'm really grateful you're considering this," I say.

He's midsip of beer, and his eyes widen over his glass. He comes up for air with a froth mustache. "You are?"

"Yeah. I mean, we can't keep commuting back and forth like this forever. And I know it would technically be easier for me to move to Chicago, since I can write from anywhere."

"But you love it here. The more I see you in your zone, the more I know it wouldn't make sense for you to leave. I want you to be somewhere you're happy."

"Maybe we can get Dezzie to move out here."

His eyes are so bright and happy. It feels like we're *actually doing this.*

We finish our meal and go home and make love.

Afterward, Seth lights a fire in the fire pit while I call Dezzie. She doesn't pick up. She must be sleeping.

A very selfish part of me is glad. I want to be there for her, but I don't want to diminish the loveliness of this night with sadness. I want to snuggle up with Seth under the stars.

And I do.

We go to bed early and sleep in 'til the luxuriant hour of 10:00 a.m. Seth's arms are around me when I open my eyes. He didn't get up to go running, which is unusual.

"You're here," I say happily.

He pulls me tight against him. "I'm here."

We hold each other for a while, and then he goes to make breakfast. I look at my phone and see a text from Dezzie asking if I can talk.

I go outside to call her.

"Hey, love," I say when she picks up. "How are you doing?"

Her voice is a croak as she tells me how poorly she slept, how much she misses Rob even though she hates him.

"Molls, I just want him to come back. Isn't that sick?"

"Oh, sweets. It's not sick. You still love him."

"But I should *despise* him. I *do* despise him."

"Two things can be true at once. They probably will be for a long time."

Her mom comes and grabs her to help with cooking, and I promise to call her later.

Which is my cue to start cooking too.

I go to the kitchen, where Seth has left me coffee, a plate of bacon, and a muffin, like an angel. I munch on it and muse over what to do first. I need to pull the hens out of the brine and stuff them, shell beans, make garlic butter, braise the cranberries . . . I get lost for an hour in food prep, humming to myself, content.

In the living room, Seth is FaceTiming with his family, who are at Dave and Clara's. I can hear the boys screaming through the phone all the way from the kitchen. I smile to myself as Seth giggles with them.

"Hold on," he says. "I'm going to put Molly on."

He walks in with his entire family peering out from his phone.

"Happy Thanksgiving, Molly!" they chorus.

"Happy Thanksgiving to you!"

"Doesn't Molly look so cute stuffing apple slices up the butts of tiny chickens?" Seth asks.

"Molly would look gorgeous stuffing any butts," his dad says.

I choke. "Is that a sex joke?" I mouth to Seth.

He makes a horrified face. "I think so," he mouths back.

"Grandpa said butts!" Max screams.

"Lucky you," Clara say dryly.

"All right, fam. I gotta help Molly with butt stuff," Seth says, pinching my ass. "We miss you."

"Love to you both!" Barb calls.

Seth hangs up, laughing. "Pure chaos over there."

"Are you regretting not going?"

"Not even a little bit," he says, wrapping his arms around me and kissing my neck. "Now, what can I do to help?"

I put him to work peeling and slicing potatoes for the gratin while I grate cheese and chop onions. Cooking elaborate meals with Seth is a joy. Maybe, I think, as I watch him squint at the potatoes to cut them as thin as possible, I really do want this.

Full-time.

Full stop.

Forever.

"Spuds chopped, chef," Seth says, presenting me with a cutting board of potatoes sliced with such precision they're nearly translucent.

"Beautiful work."

"Is it weird that I'm sad we're not making green bean casserole? Are you sure we don't want green bean casserole?"

"I told you. No beige, cream-of-mushroom-soup-based foods are allowed."

He sighs tragically. "Your loss, McMarkson. What else can I do?"

"We're good for now."

"Mind if I explore around the property? I'm a little antsy since I didn't run."

"Of course."

I focus on assembling the layers of the gratin, adding dots of butter and sprinkles of flour and pepper and salt and thyme and Parmesan. It's meditative, and I feel content.

I put it in the oven. That's the last of my prep, so I decide to call my mom.

"Hello, darling daughter!" she trills into the phone. "I'm hosting lunch for Bruce's family and we have a houseful at the moment. Can I call you back in a few hours?"

"You little scamp! You didn't tell me you were meeting his family!"

She giggles. "Surprise!"

She finally introduced me to her boyfriend when I was in Florida for Jon and Kevin's wedding. He's a soft-spoken retired financial advisor with kind eyes who dotes on my mother and told me about all her latest sales achievements with so much pride and excitement I wonder how she ever fell for my dad.

Look at us. The Marks women, in healthy relationships with men we love.

"Okay, Mom," I say. "Let me know how it goes. Love you."

Just as I end the call, I get an incoming one from my father.

Well that's out of character. He usually doesn't even text on Thanksgiving, let alone phone me. Things have been polite, if a bit strained, since the scene at the airport, which we've tacitly agreed to pretend never happened. When I saw him in LA we stuck mostly to business—him not asking about Seth, me not inquiring about Celeste.

I did not try to hug him.

But he's had surprisingly detailed notes on my drafts of the screenplay, and I can't help but take a certain satisfaction in his close attention to my work. Apparently, it took a script to get me a seat at the table when it comes to receiving his respect. I wish simply being his daughter would have conferred that privilege. But he is who he is.

"Hi, Dad," I say. "Happy Thanksgiving."

"Thanks, toots. Same to you."

"What are you doing to celebrate?" I ask.

"We sailed down to Key West. We're not turkey people."

I'm not sure if he means Celeste or Savannah, so I just say, "No, me neither. I'm making Cornish game hens."

"Will you be serving it with Kathy's artery-clogging gratin?"

I breathe through this dig at my mother. "And a shitload of wine."

We can at least agree on wine.

"Well, listen, toots," he says. "I wanted to give you a quick update on *Busted*."

Ah. That would explain why he deigned to call. Trust Roger Marks to materialize with demands at the rudest time possible. At least I can stop worrying about it.

"Hold on, let me grab my notebook," I say, brushing flour off my hands.

"No need," he says. "I'll make it quick."

I get a bad feeling. When it comes to his vaunted work, he's never quick. "Okay. What's up?"

"Scott has decided to go in a different direction."

I relax. Just more revisions. I don't mind. Editing is my favorite part of writing.

"No worries," I say. "Should we set up a call to discuss it, or will he send notes?"

"Top-line is he thinks your version is too feminine. So you can stand down."

"Stand down?"

There's a very, very long pause.

"Lion Remnick is going to take over from here."

Lion Remnick is a leading writer of superhero movies, car chase movies, and other movies in which things frequently explode. He's not even a hack. He's good at it. He's the kind of person whose success I compare with my own, and come up short.

It's not shocking for a script to change hands midway through development. It's happened to me plenty of times before.

But this script is for my *father*.

"Wait, is this Scott's decision?" I ask, my voice shaking. "You're an executive producer. He can't just fire me if you don't agree with him."

"I do agree with him," he says flatly. "In fact, if you must know, I've had misgivings since the previous draft, and Lion became available unexpectedly, so—"

"So you brought on someone else behind my back? Because I'm too *feminine?* Isn't that why you hired me in the first place? To write a woman who wasn't just a stick figure with botched boobs?"

"Look, Molly, it's show business. I shouldn't have to tell *you* it doesn't always work out." The implication being, of course, that nothing of mine has worked out in a while. Not that he would be impressed with another rom-com even if it had.

"Are you serious, Dad?" I yell into my phone.

"You'll still get paid your fee, of course," he says calmly. Like this is about money.

"I don't care about my fee. I care that my own father is *firing* me on Thanksgiving."

"It's not personal, Molly," he says with a long-suffering sigh. "I have to do what's right for the franchise."

I shake my head at my own reflection in the kitchen window, because I need *someone* to join me in marveling at how offensive this is.

"Okay, it might not be personal to you. But does it occur to you that it's personal to me? Do I register to you as a human being at all?"

"We can talk about this later, when you've calmed down."

The suggestion that I'm being irrationally emotional makes me feel irrationally emotional.

I'm not done with this conversation. I am sick to death of being rejected by this man. And for once, I don't want to make a joke or flee the conversation or numb out with Xanax and wine. Maybe it's Seth's fault—his insistence on communication. Maybe it's Rob's fault—I've had enough shitty men for one weekend. But I want to air my fury. I want to let my father know he's not off the hook for hurting me.

"No, wait," I say. "I have a question for you."

He sighs. "And what's that?"

"Why didn't you take care of me?"

"What—"

"When you left."

"Excuse me? Where is this coming from, Molly?"

"I suppose it's coming from two decades of biting my fucking tongue while getting hurt over and over."

"Don't be dramatic," he snaps. "I know the divorce wasn't easy on any of us, but—"

"You left me with Mom. Who you *knew* was losing her mind and could barely take care of herself, let alone your thirteen-year-old. And you just *left* me to deal with it."

"If I recall, you didn't want to see me."

"Yeah, I was a *kid* and you broke my heart. It was on you to fix it. And you didn't even try to get partial custody."

I'm not sure I've ever admitted to myself how much that devastated me.

"The situation was more complicated than that, as I'm sure you can imagine now that you're an adult," he says.

But I can't. If I had a child, I'd put on steel-toed boots and chain mail to fight for them. I'd salt the fucking earth.

"Seeing your kid is not that complicated," I say. "You *abandoned* me. You *never* have my back. Not even with your preposterous movie."

"I'm not abandoning you. This was a professional arrangement with the attendant uncertainties that entails, and if you're not enough of an adult to handle it, it just proves we're making the right decision."

"The 'attendant uncertainties'? My God, you're such a dick."

"That's *enough*," my father yells. "Happy Thanksgiving, Molly. I'm hanging up."

The line goes dead.

I throw the phone on the counter, hardly able to breathe.

I hate him. I hate him so much. I hate that his love is conditional. That he doesn't give a shit about me. That he always fucking leaves.

But then, is that surprising? They all fucking leave.

The phone starts buzzing.

Unbelievably, my first thought is that it must be my father calling back to apologize, because hanging up on me is brutal even for him.

But, of course, it's not.

It's Dezzie.

I don't want to answer it. I want to lie down on the cold kitchen floor and cry.

But she needs me, and I love her, so I pick up.

"Hey, my love," I say, trying not to betray how upset I am. "How are you?"

"Horrible," she says in a thick, hoarse voice. I can't tell if she's been drinking or crying or both.

"Mad," she goes on. "Mad, bad, sad."

"I'm sorry," I say. "Did you have lunch with your family?"

"Yeah. They're being sweet. Which almost makes it worse. I don't want pity."

"I know exactly what you mean," I say, thinking of Seth. I don't want his sympathy about what just happened with my father. He already had his hackles up about me working for him. I can't stand to think of the look in his eyes when he finds out he was right to be wary. He'll be apoplectic. My pain is too raw to handle his anger too.

I've felt enough feelings this weekend to last me the rest of my life.

"Don't ever get married, Molly," Dezzie slurs. "Promise me. Make me a blood oath."

I think of my father, pulling out of the driveway in his shiny BMW, leaving me sobbing and my mom catatonic. I think of Rob, fucking some woman while trying to get his wife pregnant.

And I think of my boyfriend, who abets men just like them. My boyfriend, who spends every day of his life helping people turn on each other, abandon their promises. My boyfriend, who is perfect until, inevitably, he's not.

The reality of this makes my heart pound in my chest. It makes me want to sob.

I've been trying so hard to believe that what I feel for Seth won't end in my emotional slaughter.

But it's pretty hard not to see today's bitter truth: *the more you trust, the more you stand to lose.*

"Don't worry, Dezzie," I say. "Refraining from marriage should not be a problem."

"Good. Because I don't ever want you to feel like this. I don't want anyone to."

"Me neither, my friend."

She yawns. "I had too much wine. I think I need to pass out."

"Okay. Take a nap. I'll call you tonight."

CHAPTER 35
Seth

I'm giddy.

While Molly was cooking, I walked over to the other gate and let in the crew I hired. They're silently setting up the lights in the front yard. I need to distract Molly until it's time for dinner.

I go in the house, which smells amazing. "Damn," I call. "Whatever you're doing in there—"

But I see Molly and stop talking.

She's slumped at the table, nursing a glass of wine and staring at something on her phone.

"Hey," I say. "What's wrong?"

She looks up at me. She seems hollowed out.

"Nothing," she says. "Sorry. Dezzie called and I got distracted. She's in pretty rough shape."

That would explain why she's upset.

Fuck.

I wonder if I made a mistake by not reconsidering this when there was still time to change course. It did cross my mind that the circumstances are less than ideal, given everything going on with Dezzie. But we were having such a beautiful day yesterday, and Molly seemed so happy to be together, and so excited about the possibility of me moving, that it seemed silly to second-guess myself.

In any case, it's too late to change course now. There are already six men in the driveway erecting the set I designed.

And I have an idea to cheer Molly up.

"You know," I say, "if you want, we can drive back early tomorrow and grab a flight to Chicago. You might feel better being with her. And I can help her prep for her meeting with the attorney."

Molly looks up at me with sad eyes. "You would do that?"

"Of course."

"What about your interviews on Monday?"

I shrug. "I'll reschedule them."

I know these firms want me, bad. They'll wait.

"Wow," Molly says. "It would be so nice to surprise her. Let's do it."

"I'll look at flights after dinner."

She smiles, and her whole face looks brighter—like she just got an extra four hours of sleep.

I relax. My plan is still fine.

"The food smells amazing," I say. "I'm excited for your feast."

"Thanks," she says. "I have every intention of blowing your mind with my culinary prowess."

"You can blow me anytime, babe."

She groans.

"Hey, I saw a deck of cards in the dining room," I say. "Want me to beat your ass at gin?" I want to keep her occupied so she doesn't find a random reason to go out into the front yard for the next half an hour.

"I'm a little tired. Didn't sleep well last night. Would you mind if I lie down for a bit before we eat?"

Even better. The bedroom is at the back of the house, where there's no chance of her hearing anything.

"No," I say, "of course not."

"Okay. I just put the chicken in. The oven's on a timer, so you don't need to do anything."

"Got it. Get some sleep. I'll set the table."

I text the event coordinator to let her know we'll be starting a little later, but this is actually good, because it gives me time to make the table romantic as fuck. I'm grateful to my mother that she forced me to learn where all the forks go. I'm the George Clooney of tablescapes.

I rummage in the sideboard and get to work arranging place settings. I find some Jadeite candlesticks and set up long white taper candles for a perfect, flickering ambiance. We need a centerpiece, so I snatch a towel and some scissors from the kitchen and go outside. I cut a bunch of green limbs from a flowering creosote bush with pale yellow blooms, which I arrange around the candlesticks.

The effect is festive and pretty, and the creosote gives the room an earthy scent, like the aftermath of a rainstorm.

I change, to look nice for dinner, then pace around, jittery and excited. Molly sleeps longer than I was expecting, so I occupy myself with texting holiday wishes to everyone I know. When she finally emerges, she's wearing a cozy sweater and her makeup is fresh. She'll look so cute in our pictures.

"How was your nap?" I ask.

"Restorative. And I'm starving. Are you ready to eat?"

"Yep."

"Okay. I just need to blanch the beans. Sit down. I'll serve you like a proper little wifey."

Wifey. Pleasure surges through me. I send a text to give the ten-minute warning, light the candles, and hope I don't fall apart from nerves and give myself away.

Molly walks in holding a tray with two little golden hens surrounded by rosemary sprigs.

"Why Miss Molly Malone," I say. "I can't believe you've been hiding your poultry-cooking ability all this time."

"A lady has to have her secrets."

She carries out the rest of the food, and I snatch the bottle of pinot she opened and pour us each a glass. And that's my cue.

Time to change our lives.

Let's fucking do this.

"Before we begin," I say, "let's say what we're grateful for."

She smiles. "You and your gratitude lists."

"Hey! It's Thanksgiving! If ever there was a day for gratitude lists—"

"Okay, okay, you start."

"Well, first and foremost, I'm grateful for airplanes, because they take me to see you," I say.

She rolls her eyes, but she's smiling. "Very creative."

"Gratitude is not a creative writing assignment. It's a mindfulness practice."

She nods like *yeah yeah*.

"May I go on?"

"Please."

"I'm grateful to N95 masks for keeping us safe when we travel to meet each other. I'm grateful for frequent flier miles, which keep us from going broke. I'm grateful for beds, perfect for—"

"Okay, Casanova. I get it. You're grateful for sex and travel."

"Sex and travel with *you*," I clarify.

"Are you done?" she asks.

"I'm just getting started."

"Of course you are."

"I'm grateful for the national park system," I say, "for giving me an adventure with my woman. I'm grateful for cholla cacti, for making her eyes light up like a kid's. I'm grateful for sauvignon blanc, because of the way it makes you agree to dance with me, even though, I will admit, you are terrible at it."

"Is this a roast?"

"Only a little bit. To keep you honest."

"Is it my turn now?"

"Nope. I'm grateful for cabins in little lake towns, where I spent some of the happiest days of my life. For high school reunions, for giving me a second chance with you. For all the wrong relationships that made me see this is the right one." My voice cracks a little. I'm getting emotional, but I'm determined to get through this without crying.

Molly's face has grown tense. She's watching me intently.

"Seth," she says, "I love you, but the food is going to get cold. Let's eat."

But I'm in it now. I couldn't stop even if I wanted to.

And I don't want to. I only want her.

I take a deep breath. "I'm grateful for all the years we spent apart, because they helped us become the people that could be together."

In the distance, I can hear the music starting, right on time. She hears it too. She looks at me with this terrible expression. "Okay," she says. "What's going on? Seriously."

There is flight in her eyes. Like she knows exactly what's going on and is frantically running through her options for making it stop.

My stomach turns over. I have never prayed harder than I am in this moment, hoping this will turn out okay.

"I think it's coming from outside," I say in a voice much calmer than I feel. "Let's go look."

Molly stays planted. "What are you doing, Seth?"

"Come on," I say, forcing a grin and taking her hand. "There's something I want you to see."

She doesn't move. There's a wild look in her eyes, like she's a cornered animal.

"Baby," I say. "Just trust me. Come on."

She lets me lead her through the living room and out onto the front porch. In the yard, in a clearing among the Joshua trees and ocotillos, a string quartet is seated in front of a ten-foot-high screen projecting a starry night's sky. At the sight of us, they break into "I Found a Love" by Etta James.

It's one of our songs. One we played over and over at my cabin that first week we spent together.

Lights that I had brought in from LA go on all around us, projecting vertical beams into the sky.

Molly covers her mouth with her hand. Her eyes are filled with tears. In the darkness, I can't tell if they're happy ones. All I can see is the sheen.

I rummage in my pocket for the ring I bought her at Roman & Roman. It's an antique Georgian-era cluster of diamonds forming a flower on a delicate gold band. It reminds me of the charms on the many strands of necklaces she always wears.

"Baby," I say raggedly, "I'm so grateful I get to share this holiday with you. For the chance to make new traditions with you. And for the chance to honor old ones. Like this one."

I bend down on one knee.

At that cue, the lights begin to change colors, projecting a swirl of beams into the sky. Behind the musicians, the projector lights up with images of fireworks. (The real thing is illegal in Joshua Tree; this is the best I could do.)

"Molly Marks," I say. "I'm so grateful I found my soul mate. Will you marry me?"

The music swells and tears stream down Molly's face.

I reach out for her left hand. It's limp, and clammy.

She pulls it away.

I pause, the ring dangling in midair.

She puts the back of her hand to her cheek, like she's guarding her fingers from me.

Her eyes are wide and focused just beyond me, on the lights.

My body is growing cold, because I know this isn't good, this isn't happy, this isn't the way things like this are supposed to go. But my dumb smile is still on my lips, and my dumb lights are still going nuts, and a question I thought I knew the answer to is still in my eyes.

"Stop looking at me like that," she says. There's true anguish in her voice. "Please, don't ask me. I can't. I just can't."

She turns around and runs inside.

CHAPTER 36

Molly

The music stops abruptly, but the house is eerily lit from all the lights outside. It feels like an FBI raid in here.

Seth follows me. He still has the ring in his hand, clenching it so tightly in his fist I hope it doesn't break the skin.

All I want is a rewind button. Some way to signal to him, five minutes ago, that he should not be asking the question he just asked.

Some way to not be living in a reality in which all I can do is hurt the man I most want to protect.

But I can't help him, because my heart is thundering with one word: *no.*

No. It throbs behind my temples, in my chest, huge and certain and punishing and as much a part of me as an organ.

"Molly?" Seth says hoarsely.

I shake my head. Tears are running down my cheeks.

When people talk to you with that sound in their voice, and you are at fault and you can't make it better, there is no recovering.

"Please," I say, backing away.

He stops moving. He looks like he's going to fall over. He braces one hand against a bookshelf.

"It's okay, Molls," he says, in a voice that makes it clear that it is not okay, will never be okay. "I get it."

But it doesn't matter if he does because the *no* is getting bigger, enveloping me like it's a sleeping bag I'm zipped inside, suffocating me.

I need Seth to hold me, hug me, settle me down, make this go away.

But he can't. He's the reason I can't breathe.

I crouch down, gasping.

Fuck.

Fuck, fuck, fuck.

Seth rushes over to me and gets on his knees and puts his hands firmly on my shoulders. "Molls," he says urgently. "Look at me."

His eyes are filled with kindness.

Jesus, I don't deserve him. I never did.

"Baby, you don't have to panic. Everything's fine."

I shake my head, unable to speak.

"You're doing the thing," he says soothingly. "The bolting thing. And you don't have to. You're safe with me."

But he's making the wrong assumption. He's thinking that I don't already know what's causing this panic. That when I see the pattern, I'll calm down. He's imagining I've grown. That I can believe what he says about safety.

But I can't. My heart is thirteen years old, and I can't.

"I am doing it," I say, through my tears. "You know me so well."

He lets out a ragged laugh. "Yeah. I do. And that's why—"

I cut him off. "And if you know me that well, then you should also know I was always going to do this. It's just how I'm built."

"Molly, that's not true—"

But it is true. There is no conceivable future in which the answer to his question will be anything but no. I used to worry that he'd leave me because I'm too cynical or too mean for him, but really it's me who is going to leave, who was *always* going to leave, because I love him too much to ever stop being scared.

"Stop, please," I say. "Please. Let's not drag this out."

"Don't talk to me like that," he says sharply, like the words are being excavated from his soul. "We can take all the time you need. Fuck, Molly, I'm sorry. I timed it wrong, I see that, I understand, but you don't have to answer right now."

"I answered."

His face tightens. I can see him beginning to believe this is real.

"Let's just call this fifteen minutes ago, when things were good," I say quietly.

He looks like I've stabbed him and he's holding the wound, refusing to believe in the blood even as it drips through his fingers.

"*Call* it? Do you mean, like, *us?*"

"Yeah. I'm not ever going to be your happy ending, and I don't want to live under a ticking clock. So let's just hit the pause button at the part where it was perfect."

The last trace of gentleness flickers off his face.

"We're not in a fucking rom-com, Molly."

"No. You're right. We're in Joshua Tree, on Thanksgiving. And I'm grateful, however this has ended, for the time we spent together."

I think I've cobbled together a sentence that sounds right. The kind of thing that he would say.

But his face contorts in pain, and I realize he's reading my earnestness as mockery.

"Right," he says shortly. "Beautiful. Thanks for that."

CHAPTER 37

Seth

Molly Marks once said, after that first night we slept together, that I would always love her more than she loved me.

I guess she was right.

I turn away from her and lunge for the front door. Cold desert wind whips against my face and makes the tears beading on my lashes sting as I stagger out into the yard.

I hate that I'm crying. Not because there's any shame in it—I'm a crier, God knows—but because I thought I'd be tearing up with joy right now. I thought Molly would be in my arms, wiping the drops from my cheeks and teasing me for being so emotional.

The string quartet is still there, instruments poised, watching me for a signal, like there might be a redo.

I tip them and tell them to pack up.

The devastated way they look at me is humiliating.

I walk around the house to the fire pit and fumble in my pocket for my phone. I need to talk to someone.

I call Dave.

It rings a couple of times, then goes to voicemail. Right. It's getting late on the East Coast, and he's probably bathing his kids or cleaning up the kitchen with his wife, who loves him. A phenomenon it is looking likelier and likelier that I will never experience.

I don't leave a message because Molly has ingrained in me that voicemails are annoying. Presumably, they are even more annoying when the person who leaves them is crying.

I guess I'll just sit out here all night with my throat aching and the wind pushing smoke into my eyes, alone.

But then my phone vibrates.

I've never been so glad to see my brother's name.

"Hey," I say.

"Yo!" he says excitedly. "How'd it go?"

My composure completely breaks down at the sound of his voice.

"Dave," I sob.

"Jesus," he barks. "What's wrong?"

"She said no. And she broke up with me."

I clench, waiting for him to say she doesn't deserve me, or that he knew she would do this, or that he's going to kill her.

But he just says, "How soon can you get to Nashville?"

The idea of being there with him and my family is like someone turned on the lights of a Christmas tree in a dark room, making it glow.

That. I need that.

"I could probably get there by tomorrow night," I say.

"Book a flight. Right now."

He's terse, as always, and it's comforting. The commanding confidence of an older brother who knows exactly what to do.

"Okay," I say.

"Hey, Seth?"

"Yeah?"

"You're going to get through this. It'll never feel as bad as it feels tonight."

His kindness cracks me open.

"I love her so much, Dave," I sob.

"I know, buddy. I know."

"What do I do?"

"Cry it out. Drink some water. Go to sleep. Text me with your flight info and I'll pick you up."

I nod. This is all sensible. These are things I can do.

"Are you going to tell Mom and Dad?" I ask.

"Do you want me to?"

I certainly don't want to do it myself. They love Molly. They'll be crushed. And then they'll be furious at her. And for some reason, I can't stand the idea of that.

"Yes, please," I say.

"Then I will."

"Okay."

There's a pause.

"You don't deserve this, bud," Dave says.

Tears slide down my cheeks. It's not about what I deserve, or what Molly does, but it's nice to hear those words.

"Okay. I'm going to go now."

"Get some rest. We'll see you tomorrow."

I close my eyes and take a deep breath. I imagine myself sitting on a stool at the island of Dave's kitchen, the boys yelling about LEGOs over my shoulder, eating leftover green bean casserole. It's something to hold on to. I just have to keep it together until then.

And you know what?

I will.

I'm not going to sit here shivering. I'm going to go through the motions of being a functional adult and see if they make me feel like one.

I walk inside through the kitchen. It's an ungodly mess. Which is good. If there's one thing I know how to do on autopilot, it's clean.

I roll up my sleeves and throw myself into the solace of soap bubbles and scrubbing.

It takes forty-five minutes to clean up, and Molly never materializes. When I walk into the dining room to begin clearing off the table, she's sitting there, slumped in a chair with her eyes closed.

"Are you awake?" I ask, because her back is to me.

"Yeah," she says.

"Do you want food? Or should I put it away?"

She still doesn't look at me. She just shrugs. "Toss it."

"I'm not tossing out an entire Thanksgiving dinner."

"Fine," she says. She stands up and turns around, and she looks like hell. My impulse is to take her into my arms, despite everything.

But I don't.

Instead, I watch her pick up a fork and stab it listlessly into the gratin pan. She eats two bites of cheesy potatoes and swallows them like she might gag. Then she digs into the breast of one of the Cornish game hens with her fingers, rips off some meat, dabs it into cranberry sauce, and eats that. She plucks a single green bean out of the serving bowl and forces that down too.

"Okay," she says. "Do what you want with the rest."

This display pisses me off.

"Why are you acting like a child?"

"Because I am one," she says tonelessly. "I'm an emotionally stunted person. That's what I've been trying to tell you."

I don't argue with her. I don't have the energy. Instead, I clear the table. I wrap up the leftovers and shove them into the fridge. Maybe I'll eat something later, if I feel less like vomiting.

She comes into the kitchen. She's hobbling like she's in pain.

I'm glad I'm not the only one who physically hurts.

"Sorry," she says, without clarifying what she's apologizing for. Breaking up with me? Eating petulantly with her hands?

"Yeah," is all I say back.

"Thank you for cleaning."

"Well, you cooked."

She crosses her arms and hugs herself.

"I'm going to go to bed."

It's 7:00 p.m., but I don't argue with her.

"We'll leave first thing in the morning," she says.

"Yeah," I say. I'm already dreading the two-hour drive back to Los Angeles.

"I'm booking a flight to Nashville," I say. "Do you still want me to get you a ticket to Chicago?"

She shakes her head. "I'll figure it out."

"Fine. I'll sleep in that other bedroom. Good night."

"Night," she says.

I grab the bottle of red wine and take it to the smaller of the two rooms. It has twin bunk beds, which feels demoralizing enough to fit the occasion.

I wash Advil PM down with the wine, wincing for my kidneys, and pass out so fast I wake up with my uncharged phone on my chest, ravenous and with no idea where I am, at 5:00 a.m.

The whole thing comes back to me. My eyes ache from crying.

Fuck this. Fucking fuck this whole thing.

I pillage the refrigerator, still wearing my clothes from last night. I eat my Thanksgiving dinner cold, in the dark, directly out of the serving dishes, and then throw the rest in the trash. I don't bother making coffee. I'm wide awake on despair.

I take a shower. Molly is up when I emerge, sitting with her knees tucked under her on the couch. She looks as gray and drawn as I've ever seen her. I don't think she slept.

Her overnight bag is sitting by the door.

"Ready whenever you are," she says.

"Let me just grab my stuff."

I go back into the tiny room to get dressed, and notice that I left the ring sitting on the desk, next to my sweater.

I don't want to touch it, but I can't just leave it in some random person's house in Joshua Tree. I throw it into my suitcase, shove in the rest of my shit, and walk back to the living room.

She's already outside, packing up the car.

"Got everything?" she asks, when I put my bag in next to the cooler.

"Yep. My flight's at twelve thirty out of LAX. Can you drop me at the airport?"

She nods.

We drive back in complete silence.

At the airport, she doesn't get out of the car.

She just looks at me, with bloodshot eyes, as I step onto the pavement.

"Bye, Seth," she says, like it costs her everything she has to speak those two syllables.

"Bye."

As it comes out of my mouth, I realize this is probably the last time I'm ever going to see her. So I lean over and kiss her cheek one last time.

"You win the bet," I say into her ear. "Romance is bullshit."

She starts crying.

I don't care.

I grab my bags from the back and walk away. I glance over my shoulder when I reach the doors to the terminal.

Her car is already gone.

PART EIGHT
December 2021

CHAPTER 38
Molly

I've always considered writing an act of commerce. I don't journal. I don't pour my soul into autobiographical novels or write personal essays processing my life through the lens of, like, butterfly migrations or ghost towns in Texas. I write bullshit screenplays for money. That's it.

It is therefore odd that at this moment, when I've been fired from my job and broken up with my boyfriend and have nothing but time to work on my flailing career, my overwhelming impulse is to write something that isn't for sale.

It's a speculative fantasy occurring in a world uncannily like our own. It's called *Better Luck Next Time*.

You'll recognize the story. Two exes, a divorce attorney who's a hopeless romantic and a rom-com writer who doesn't believe in romance, make a bet at their high school reunion: whoever can more accurately predict the outcome of five relationships before their twentieth reunion must admit that the other is right about soul mates.

It might be the most marketable thing I've ever written—that elusive mainstream script my agent has been harassing me to produce for years. But I haven't sent it to my agent.

I'm writing it for myself.

In a rom-com, this would be the black moment beat, where I'm forced to look inside myself to understand my failings so I can grow into the partner Seth deserves.

But I don't think that's what this is. Understanding my failings was never the problem.

It's the growth I can't hack.

I panicked when Seth proposed, predictably. It was shortsighted, predictably. Had it not been for the shock of Dezzie's divorce and the sting of my father's indifference, maybe I would have said yes.

But it wouldn't have mattered.

Saying yes would not have changed the fact that there's a terror of love buried inside me like a land mine, and it would have erupted eventually. The closer you get to the blast radius, the more inevitable it is that you'll be hit by shrapnel. And Seth's heart was so close that sometimes I still imagine it beating beside me. That low, safe, soft thrum.

Maybe it was a blessing that it only took me five months to destroy us. Had our relationship gone on any longer, would the fallout even be bearable? Because, as it is, it's a wake-up-in-the-middle-of-the-night-and-can't-breathe kind of loss. A cry-in-the-shower, then sob-in-the-car, then weep-at-the-grocery-store heartache that seems to get worse every day. I am mourning Seth Rubenstein. And I'm grieving the woman who, for a few months, thought she'd healed enough to trust herself with him.

And so as a gift to myself, I'm writing *that* woman's story. The happy ending I wish I could have had in real life.

A text rolls in, and as I do every time my phone buzzes, I hope it's Seth, then realize it's not going to be, then hate myself for continuing to have this impulse, then don't want to look at the message at all. Were it not for my desire to be there for Dezzie, I might just silence my phone for good.

It's from Alyssa.

Alyssa: Daily check in

This is her new ritual to reassure herself that I'm still alive.

Molly: Fine. Breathing. Go about your day
Alyssa: Report stats

I obediently tap out the proof that I'm doing the basics of functioning.

Molly: Slept 5 hours
Molly: Ate food
Molly: Put on sunscreen, so extra credit
Alyssa: 5 hours is not enough sleep!
Alyssa: What food?
Molly: Froot loops
Alyssa: Doesn't count. At least make TS!!

(She means The Salad.)

Molly: Stop worrying I'm fine
Alyssa: You're not. CALL SETH

Not a day has gone by when she hasn't demanded I call him, in all caps.

"You'll feel better if you clear the air," she tells me. "You guys loved each other too much to let it end like this."

"Loved" is inaccurate phrasing. What I feel for Seth could never be in past tense.

And I know Alyssa is right. I owe him more than silence.

But I can't bring myself to make the call. I'm too scared of what he'll say.

"An open wound can't heal," Alyssa says, like she's a doctor and not an accountant.

But I don't want to heal. I don't want to let go of this ache. My devastation is all I have left of Seth.

Thus, the script. It's my way of keeping him with me. Immortalizing my love for the person I can't stand to keep, or to lose.

I'm up to the break into Act III—the point in a rom-com when one of the lovers, despite having been thwarted in their desire for the other by various obstacles for the past seventy minutes, decides to try one last time.

The scene begins at a destination wedding in Bali. (It's a movie, after all; I've taken some creative liberty with the set pieces.) Our lovers, Cole and Nina, run into each other during the toasts. Up until this point, despite some near misses, their old flame for each other hasn't gotten a chance to ignite. They've been in other relationships, or in mourning for them, or angry at each other, or denying their attraction. But now, finally, they are both single. And tonight, they can't take their eyes off each other.

Cole asks her to dance to "Can't Help Falling in Love." (In my fantasies, our movie has the music budget for Elvis songs. Also, I can dance to them without falling over.)

It's electric. Nina melts as Cole whispers the pivotal words in her ear: *I'm carrying a torch for you.*

They go home together. And this time, it's right.

She's softer now, ready to open her heart to him. He's out of fucks, ready to go for broke and try to make her see she's his soul mate.

They run away for a week to a beautiful house on the coast of Maine. (Which has cliffs, and is therefore a bit more cinematic than Lake Geneva, with all due apologies to Wisconsin.)

We flash to a montage of Cole and Nina falling in love: holding hands as they walk the bluffs above the ocean, looking for whales. Having lazy sex on a rainy day while Etta James's "I Found a Love" plays in the background. Singing along with lullabies before bed.

Cole proposes. *Love might not be perfect,* he says to Nina. *But I know this: we're perfect for each other. You're my soul mate.*

I think you know what she says here. The line writes itself:

I don't believe in soul mates.

She's too scared.

She leaves him.

She breaks his heart.

And then we switch to her POV, a week later.

Like me, she's all alone, and she's miserable.

Like me, she can't stop thinking about the person she left.

Like me, she knows she's made a mistake.

But unlike me, she's in a rom-com.

So she decides to be brave.

When I'm done, I'm crying.

I wish I were Nina.

I wish Seth were Cole.

I wish our ending could have been like this one: poignant and redemptive and beautiful.

I have an overpowering feeling, as I type "THE END."

I want Seth to read it.

He loves my movies—probably more than anyone else on this earth. And I know, if we were still together, he would delight in the idea of making one out of our story. He'd treasure this artifact of our love. He'd watch it over and over. Memorize all the lines. Lord it over me that he wrote the best ones himself.

My phone rings—my mom. I'm leaving in the morning for Florida. She probably wants to confirm for the third time when to pick me up from the airport.

"Hi," I say.

"Hiiiiiii my Molly Malolly," she trills.

She hasn't called me that in a long time. It's her special nickname for me, and it's so like the goofy names Seth calls me, and I miss him so much, and I'm so disappointed in myself, and so exhausted from this last month of 4:00 a.m. wakeups, and so unmoored by what I just wrote, that I burst into big, ugly tears.

"Molly!" my mother cries. "Honey, oh no! What's wrong, sweet girl?"

"It's Seth," I warble. "I really, really miss Seth."

"Oh, sweetie," she says. "I wish I were there to give you the biggest hug. But you'll be here soon and I'll take such good care of you and we'll have a wonderful Christmas and it will all be okay."

"I know," I choke out. But I can't stop crying.

"I fucked up, Mom," I say. "I'm just like Dad."

I hear her take a sharp breath. "No. You are *not*. How can you say that?"

"I'm not good at love."

"My darling," she says instantly, with great authority, "that is not true. If anyone on the planet should know, it's me."

"Mommy, I leave people, like he does. I throw them away."

"Molly, listen to me. Your father leaves people because he is not capable of loving them enough. You left Seth because you love him so very much. You are the *opposite* of your father."

"I broke his heart," I choke out.

"And you broke yours, too. And my love, I know you're scared, but I really, really do think you should tell him how you're feeling."

"I don't think that's a good idea."

"If I remember correctly," she says, "you didn't think it was a good idea when you broke up with him after high school either."

This makes me feel worse. I hate thinking about that time.

I woke up in the middle of the night dying to call him for months. I took to getting blackout drunk just to sleep. I lost my virginity to a twenty-four-year-old ski instructor and then slept with a string of older men, thinking that it would dull the pain. It didn't. The stress was so intense that clumps of my hair fell out and I stopped getting my period.

"And so you spent about two years regretting your decision and missing him," my mother continues, "calling me sobbing every week, all the while refusing to try to make up with him. And you knew he was hurting, because all your friends told you, but you couldn't bring yourself to say that you'd gotten scared and made a mistake. When you could have just told him, and fixed it.

"And I feel very guilty about that, Molly," she says softly. "Because I wasn't in a healthy place myself back then. I was so negative about anything having to do with relationships, and I dismissed what you were feeling as puppy love. I wish I'd been able to help you through it better. I think I'd have encouraged you to try again."

"Mom!" I protest, my voice raw and hoarse. "We were eighteen. Of course we broke up. I was going to be sad either way. It's not your fault."

"That might be so," she says. "But you know what? I think you both stayed a little bit in love with each other all those years. And that's why you fell so hard again. In fact, I think he's the only boy you've *ever* loved."

I lose it completely.

My mom murmurs into the phone, like she's soothing a baby, and I just listen to her and cry. When I've tired myself out, she says, "Sweets, call him. The worst thing that can happen is that you're right, and he doesn't want to hear from you, and you'll stay just as sad as you already are."

"I'll think about it," I say. "I'm sorry for being a mess."

"You can be as messy as you want. I'm your mother. And, Molls? Loving you has been the honor of my life. I'm so sorry I wasn't there for you when you needed me."

Her words send a chill of recognition up my spine. Because that's how it felt, to be the person Seth Rubenstein loved. An honor. And it was an honor to love him in just the same bone-deep, lifelong, weak-at-the-knees desperate way he's always loved me.

And when you love someone like that—when they love *you* like that—you owe them something. Maybe your relationship ends, but that doesn't mean the connection between you just breaks.

I've been telling myself I don't deserve to get Seth back. And I don't. But that misses the basic point.

I need to apologize for *hurting* him.

For lashing out to avoid my terror of losing him. For panicking at how much I love him and want him and need him. For seeing my mistake and doubling down on it, because I'm so afraid he won't want me back.

If I apologize, I risk learning he can't forgive me.

That I've finally hurt him for good.

But just because the results won't be fairy-tale perfect doesn't mean you can't try your best to be vulnerable.

When you hurt someone, you do what you can to fix it.

When you're scared, you do what you can to be brave.

"I love you, Mommy," I sniffle into the phone. "I have to go, okay? There's something I need to do before I pack up."

She hangs up, and I reopen the screenplay.

Fuck it.

I'm going to do the grand gesture beat.

I drag the screenplay file into my email and address it to Becky. She's proven such a worthy intern that I've hired her as a part-time assistant.

From: mollymarks@netmail.co
To: bma445@nyu.edu
Date: Wed, Dec 22, 2021 at 4:01pm
Subject: Can you proofread this?

Becks—attaching something new. Can you give it a read for typos and make sure the formatting, etc. is right? I need it back before NYE. Thx!

CHAPTER 39
Seth

I will spare you an accounting of what the last month of my life has been like. Let's just say when I got to Nashville, I cried so hard I threw up.

Don't feel bad; it's been weirdly galvanizing.

The silver lining to getting my heart put through a garbage disposal is that I've been converted to Molly's way of thinking: I now know, once and for all, there is not a woman waiting to make my life perfect and meaningful. I can't count on another person to do that. I can only count on myself.

So I'm opening my own firm.

I've moved quickly. I've already lined up two founding copartners and arranged the financing. We've hired an office manager, and with his help, we'll be up and running by March. At that point I'll resign from my firm and take my clients with me.

If that seems devious, well, maybe Molly was right to distrust divorce lawyers.

At least I can console myself by giving back to my community.

My nonprofit is expanding. I've been working closely with Becky Anatolian and some law school friends who now work in New York to get a new branch up and running there, staffed by Columbia and NYU law students.

Becky's been such a rock star as a volunteer that we asked her to lead the effort to open the new office.

I'm waiting for an email from her regarding a location in Brooklyn she just went to look at with our Realtor.

I'm about to leave my office for the airport—I'm visiting my parents in Florida for New Year's, to avoid the despair of spending it alone—when Becky's address pops up in my inbox.

> From: bma445@nyu.edu
> To: sethrubes@mail.me
> Date: Thurs, Dec 30, 2021 at 10:41am
> Subject: As requested . . .
>
> Hey Molly! Hope you are having a good time in Florida! I'm attaching the proofed screenplay. Let me know if you need anything else.—Becks

Attached is a file called BLNTFinal_BAedits.FDR.

Obviously, this email was not meant for me.

Obviously, it was meant for someone named Molly.

Obviously, the Molly in question is Molly Marks.

Becky must have entered my email address accidentally when she sent this.

I know it's wrong to open something that isn't meant for you. I should let Becky know she sent it to the wrong person and delete the email.

But, yeah . . . I'm not doing that.

I forgive myself under the circumstances and click the attachment.

My computer doesn't recognize the file.

Fuck.

I google .FDR extensions and figure out that this is a screenplay written in a software program called Final Draft, which I don't have.

My assistant pokes her head in the door. "Your car is waiting. You should probably leave now if you don't want to be late for your flight. Google Maps says the traffic is bad."

"Okay, thanks, Pattie," I say, trying not to reveal that I am in a state of emotional crisis.

I grab my suitcase and rush downstairs to my car.

"O'Hare?" the driver asks.

"Yeah," I say, buckling up.

As soon as the car starts moving, I buy the Final Draft app and reopen Becky's email.

When I click on the attached file, a screenplay pops up.

BETTER LUCK NEXT TIME
BY MOLLY MARKS

INT. WHITE TENT - NIGHT

NINA MACLEAN (mid-30s, world-weary) is sitting alone at a banquet table in a white tent on a beach. It's decorated with over-the-top tropical decor: think fake palm trees and baskets of flip-flops. Above it all is a sign: WELCOME SEA VIEW HIGH SCHOOL CLASS OF 2003!!!

FORMER CLASSMATES are on the dance floor grinding to a late 1990s rap song.

COLE HESS (mid-30s, charming) makes his way toward Nina from behind.

Nina flags down a waiter just as Cole approaches.

                    NINA
               (TO THE WAITER)
       Another glass of prosecco, please.

                    COLE
               (TO THE WAITER)
       Make that a Negroni, with an extra splash
       of Campari. Nina likes things bitter.

Nina and Cole lock eyes. These two have history.
He sits down in an empty chair next to her.

> COLE
>
> How have you been since you broke my heart
> fifteen years ago? Still out there drowning
> kittens and making toddlers cry?

> NINA
>
> Not to mention embezzling retirement funds
> from the elderly.

> COLE
>
> Weird, given you always sucked at math.

> NINA
>
> Funny. Actually, I write screenplays. Rom-
> coms.

Cole bursts out laughing.

> COLE
>
> That's a bit ironic, don't you think? You
> always hated anything that had to do with
> love. I should know.

> NINA
>
> I always liked money. And they pay well.
> What do you do?

> COLE
>
> I'm an attorney. Family law.

> NINA
>
> Oh my God. You're a divorce lawyer?

Holy shit.

Is this about *us?* Did Molly write a screenplay about *us?*

This is what she's been doing while I wake up in the night unable to breathe? Turning our love into *punch lines?*

I'm shocked she's able to keep hurting me, given how wretched I already feel, but I shouldn't be; no one was ever able to twist the knife like Molly Marks.

I should stop reading this out of self-preservation, but I can't bring myself to.

I'm rapt as Nina and Cole start flirting and arguing over who knows more about love. They pick five couples to bet on, including themselves.

My car reaches the airport and I force myself to stop reading long enough to get through security. At the gate, I get in trouble for staring at my phone and holding up the priority boarding line.

I can't help it. I see words we've said to each other on the page, verbatim. *You make me astonishingly happy,* he tells her. *You'll find the love of your life, and she'll be a very lucky woman,* she tells him. And my heart goes into hummingbird mode remembering how it felt to say and hear these things. Knowing these moments are burned into Molly's memory the same way they're burned into mine.

My anger has sharpened into something more complex. This bittersweet feeling of resentment and nostalgia and joy, all at once.

I rip through Act II, and just like me and Molly, Nina and Cole run into each other at a baseball game and have a great time. But at the end of the night, when she tries to kiss him, he tells her he's in a relationship.

She acts cool, but as soon as he leaves, she sobs with her head against the steering wheel of her car in the parking lot, surrounded by raucous tailgaters lighting streamers and setting off firecrackers so loud that her windows shake.

I think of that day in Molly's car, after the baby shower. Her face when I said I was seeing someone. I knew she was disappointed. I didn't know she was crushed.

But it's here: she was *crushed.* She never mentioned that to me. I guess she wouldn't have. She doesn't like to share her vulnerabilities.

Instead, she writes them into her characters.

And the character she wrote? Nina? She's pining. And Cole doesn't see it. He gets engaged to the wrong woman, and he doesn't see it. He "takes time to heal" when that relationship ends, even though Nina is right there—and he *still* doesn't see it.

I always felt like I was the one doing the chasing. But I realize, reading this, that Molly was chasing me too. That I hurt her, deeply, in ways I couldn't help any more than she could have helped hurting me.

That she may have broken us up when I asked her to marry me—but she also waited for me. For *years*.

It makes me want to gather her in my arms and tell her I'm sorry for being so dense. For making her wait for what she could sense was right all along.

I keep reading. Cole and Nina run into each other at a friend's wedding. They're both finally single. They fall for each other with all the tenderness and passion that we did.

And then, standing on a cliff in the rain as they're watching for whales, Cole gets down on one knee and proposes.

He tells Nina she's his soul mate.

I clench.

Molly writes rom-coms, but I have a terrible feeling this isn't one. That it's what she calls a "rom-traum"—the twist on the genre, where the love story is doomed.

Don't do it, I mentally plead with her. *Don't make them suffer like we have.*

But in my heart, I know what's coming.

Nina says she doesn't believe in soul mates.

She leaves Cole in Maine.

I frantically scroll down, praying what comes next is not the words THE END.

There are still fifteen pages left in the script.

I'm dying.

We see Nina mourn. *I fucked up,* she tells her best friend. *But I don't deserve another chance.*

TELL HIM, I want to yell at her as I read this. JUST TELL HIM.

There are four pages left, and I can barely breathe.

We switch to Cole's POV. He and his best friend are making plans to attend their twentieth high school reunion. *Is Nina coming?* the friend asks. *No,* Cole says. *She hates this kind of thing. And she won't want to see me.*

And he's right. When they arrive, she's not there.

Despite knowing she wouldn't be, Cole is flattened. But just as he's walking out, someone taps the microphone on the stage.

It's Nina, standing up there. And she's looking right at him.

Five years ago, she tells the crowd, *I did something really stupid. I told Cole that true love was a fairy tale. That soul mates were bullshit made up by the Hallmark Industrial Complex. We made a bet over it, in fact. If he wins, I have to admit that happily ever afters are real. And if I win, he has to admit that true love is a fantasy—a pit stop along the road to heartbreak.*

Well, I'm here to say that maybe neither of us was right. Relationships carry joy and pain. Sometimes big loves fade. Sometimes rocky ones recover. Sometimes life brings unexpected twists. All we can count on is cherishing what we have, and trying like hell to be good to each other.

All we can do is be brave enough to believe in love, and to fight for it.

Cole, I know I messed up. I know I was cowardly, and I hurt you. But this is me, fighting for you. And if you'll give me another chance, I'll fight for our happily ever after for the rest of our lives.

He doesn't even need to think. He runs across the room, dodging gawking classmates, and leaps onto the stage.

They kiss like their lives depend on it.

Sorry you didn't win the bet, he whispers.

I don't care about the bet, she says. *I only care about you.*

He swings her around as the classmates all cheer for them.

THE END

By now I am full-on weeping. The man next to me ignores this for a few minutes and then finally looks over at me.

"You okay, dude? Need a whiskey or something?"

I shake my head.

"Sorry," I sniffle. "I'm fine. Just really happy."

And I am.

Because Molly had it in her to write this.

Our happy ending.

But I'm also crying because this screenplay breaks my heart all over again. It proves that this woman knows in precise emotional detail what caused our relationship to collapse. She sees both the ways we have loved each other, and the ways we have failed each other. She gets that neither of us was right about love—her version pessimistic to the point of nihilism, mine optimistic to the point of parody. And rather than talking this out with me, and trying to make our relationship work, she wrote a perfect movie about it.

This script proves that she pursued me, loved me, grieved me. And yeah, it's an idealized version of us, with a fairy-tale ending that is too pat and tidy to stand up to real life. And yeah, like she's always saying, the story ends at the good part, at the peak of their happiness.

But I would watch the hell out of the sequel, when things get messy, and they work through it. I want the part where they bicker over her never putting the dishes away and his obsession with vacuuming. When they fart in front of each other and talk openly about pooping. When they're sleep-deprived and shaky because they have a colicky baby, or bereft over the decline of a parent. I want to watch them live out the pleasure and sadness and tedium and comfort and joy of a partnered existence.

Because I never needed the rom-com part of our relationship.

I was living for the part you *don't* freeze in amber. The love and the pain and the mess.

And instead, I'm getting this. The most profound emotions of my life, packaged into commercialized fiction. The sweet things I did, amped up into swoony details to make you fall vicariously in love with the dude in the movie. Our most tender moments, turned into heart-clenching dialogue. Our foibles, simplified into predictable character flaws that we'll overcome in 110 minutes.

Part of me is so hurt that *this* is what she chose to do with our love story. Idealizing it instead of trying to fix it. Selling it instead of living it out. That sliver of me is tempted to simmer in my resentment until this movie comes out in three years, and then write an aggrieved open letter calling her out for monetizing my pain behind my back. Sue her for exploiting my life rights without my permission. Get her back for how much losing her cost me.

But that's not how I'm built.

In my heart I think there's something at work here more important than ambition or money. I think writing this script is how Molly is trying to heal.

I know, in my soul, that we love each other in a way I've never experienced, and doubt I'll ever experience again.

Our love wasn't a romantic comedy.

I didn't expect it to be.

All I ever wanted was her.

But what am I supposed to do now? Reach out, just to get rejected again? Receive another lecture on how I don't understand that fiction is fake?

As much as I want to storm her door and demand that she try again, I can't be the one on my knees.

Not again.

But I hope.

I hope, and hope, and hope.

CHAPTER 40
Molly

"Molls, do you have any Aleve in that stockpile of pills you travel with?" Alyssa moans.

"Or morphine?" Dezzie asks. "I think I might need actual morphine."

I peel myself out of my sleeping bag on the floor of my mother's attic. My body feels like I slept in a trash compactor.

"We are officially too aged and infirm for sleepovers," I say as I limp toward the bathroom.

When the three of us concocted this plan to have a post-Christmas slumber party at my mom's, we did not think through what might happen to a thirty-six-year-old body sleeping on a hardwood floor.

"We should have gotten air mattresses," Alyssa says. "I think my hips are bruised."

"Well, it was fun," I call through the open bathroom door. It was the first night I haven't spent fully obsessing about Seth since we broke up. "And look, I found some Advil."

We pass around the bottle like we're sharing ecstasy at a rave.

"Do I hear the pitter-patter of little feet?" my mom calls from downstairs.

"We're up," I call back.

"Oh good. I'm making waffles."

We shuffle down to the kitchen, where my mom is standing in a palm-tree-print caftan shoving whole oranges down her $3,000 juicer.

"I covet this kitchen," Dezzie says as she hobbles to a barstool.

"You can come over and cook with me anytime," Mom says. "*Someone* here will only make the same boring salad."

Dezzie and Alyssa both burst out laughing.

My mom slides us a pitcher of orange juice. It's perfect. Florida does two things better than California: white-sand beaches and citrus.

"So how was you girls' Christmas?" Mom asks, pouring batter into the waffle iron.

"Chaotic," Alyssa says. "Eight cousins careening around my dad's house. The tree fell over twice. I thought my stepmom was going to take the whole gang outside and start performing executions."

"I bet they love spending time with the grandkids," my Mom says, looking at me pointedly. "Some of us may never know."

All three of them have been doing this all week. Making veiled references to their mutual belief I should go after Seth.

I haven't told them my plan to fly to Chicago when I leave here.

How I'm going to have my script printed and bound. How I'm going to show up on Seth's door on January 1, his least favorite day of the year, with this piece of my heart in my hand, and ask him to read it.

I *want* to tell them. I'm in agony, wondering how he will receive me when I show up, and all I want to do is pepper them with questions about what they think will happen.

But if I add anyone else's hopes and fears to my own, I might lose my nerve.

I have to do this alone.

I shrug at my mother. "Maybe you and Bruce should adopt some preschoolers."

The two of them got engaged on Christmas Eve, surrounded by me and Bruce's kids. I'm so happy for her. For them. It's amazing to see my mom as half of this head-over-heels, heart-eyed couple. Bruce captains her speedboat, and she buys all his sun-protective sportswear, and they walk back and forth between their two mansions all day in their flip-flops. They're adorable.

"Did you have an okay holiday, sweetie?" Mom asks Dezzie gently.

Dez smiles. "You know what? Surprisingly, it was really fun. I thought it would be hard to get through Christmas without Rob, but honestly, after Covid it was so nice for us to all be together that it was okay."

My mom takes Dezzie's hand from across the kitchen island and squeezes it. "Good riddance." She lowers her voice. "And how's the divorce going?"

"Mom!" I protest. "She doesn't want to talk about that!"

"No, it's fine," Dezzie says. "So far so good. I have a fierce-ass bitch attorney, and as soon as I'm divorced I'm going to marry *her* because I love her so much."

The email alert on my iPad dings and I reach for it.

"No phone thingies at breakfast," Mom says, snatching my tablet. She's on a mindfulness kick and keeps hiding all my devices.

I snatch the iPad back.

"I need it for work."

"It's New Year's Eve!" she protests.

"No rest for the wicked."

In truth, I have no work. I'm waiting on tenterhooks for Becky to send back a clean copy of my screenplay so I can get it printed out for Seth this afternoon. My flight to Chicago is first thing in the morning, and I want to have it professionally bound before I leave.

Becky's name is at the top of my email. Finally.

> From: bma445@nyu.edu
> To: mollymarks@netmail.co
> Date: Fri, Dec 31, 2021 at 8:44 am
> Subject: As requested . . .
>
> Hey Seth!

I get chills at the sight of his name.

"What the fuck?" I say out loud.

"What is it?" Alyssa asks, concerned.

I hold up my finger and read on:

> The space is perfect—even better than the pictures. The Realtor
> said the owners would be open to us renovating it to our specs.
> The deadline for the lease application is January 3, so we should

make a decision ASAP. Let me know if you want to move forward. Hope you have a great New Year's in Florida!—Becky

"Holy shit," I murmur.

My mom flicks flour at me. (Flicking food at people is a trait I inherited from her.)

"Tell us what it is, goose!" she says. "And stop cursing."

"It's no big deal," I say, trying to get control of my pulse. "Uh . . . I got an email that was meant for Seth."

"Seth *Rubenstein?*" Mom asks.

"There is no other Seth," Dezzie says. "You know there is no other Seth."

Alyssa puts her hand on my shoulder. "You okay?"

"Yeah. No worries," I say. "Just surprised me."

"What does it say?" Alyssa asks.

"Not much. Some business thing. But, I guess he's here. For New Year's." Which, of course, ruins my plan.

I must look as distressed as I feel, because the kitchen goes uncomfortably quiet.

"Didn't his parents always have a big New Year's Eve party?" Alyssa asks.

"Yeah. With all their golf friends. We crashed it once," Dez says.

"Maybe that's what you should do, Molly," Alyssa says softly. "I bet he'd be happy to see you."

But I can't go to the Rubensteins' in this state. I can't even watch slightly emotional television commercials in front of other people without freezing up in embarrassment. Giving my big speech in front of Seth's parents or, God forbid, Dave, would be like attending all the weddings and christenings and funerals in the world while naked and shivering.

"I don't want to talk about Seth," I mutter.

Alyssa, Dezzie, and my mother are all staring at me sadly, with looks that vary between "I feel bad for you" (Alyssa), "I'm worried you'll never be happy" (Mom), and "You are the stupidest woman in the world" (Dezzie).

"Oh my God, stop it!" I say. "It's fine. I'm fine. Can we eat?"

"Yes," my mom says. "Help me carry this stuff to the table."

She hands out plates heaping with waffles, eggs, and bacon and we gather around the breakfast nook. She's set up fancy bowls of whipped cream, maple syrup, strawberry sauce, and sprinkles. God, I love her for the sprinkles.

We all eat and chat about our plans for the night. Mom and Bruce are hosting a disco-themed cocktail party. She bought me a slutty dress for the occasion. Alyssa's dad and stepmom are watching the kids for her and Ryland so they can go out to dinner at a little bistro downtown. Dezzie is driving to Miami to go to a party with her sister.

We inhale approximately eight pounds of waffles each, and then the girls pack up to go. While they're busy, I open my email and reply to Becky's mis-addressed note.

> Hey Becks—I think you sent this to me by mistake. Also—have you had time to look at that script I sent yet? Need it ASAP.

I go upstairs and wash my face. I look like hell—five years older than I looked a month ago. Dezzie and Alyssa come into the bathroom behind me. They both put their arms around me, and we squeeze each other in a three-way hug.

"Ménage à trois!" Dezzie says in a creepy French accent—which she's been doing every time we all hug since we were ten and she learned what it meant.

The joke still kills.

"Can you drive us back?" Alyssa asks. "Ryland just texted, and apparently Jesse had a meltdown over having to put on shoes before going outside, and it sent Amelia into a rage spiral because *she* was wearing shoes, and now all hell is breaking loose."

I laugh. "Yeah. Let me throw on some clothes."

We pile into my mom's car and blast a shared playlist of our favorite songs as we head into town. I drop Alyssa off first. Dez and I pop inside to say hi to Ryland and the kids (who are indeed in devil mode) and quickly retreat back to the car.

"Damn," Dezzie says. "I want kids so bad and then I see that and my ovaries shrivel."

"I'm sure they'll be angels again in fifteen minutes."

"At least they're cute, even when they're having rage blackouts."

"I know. They even make me want one."

She gives me a pained look. She knows I would want a baby with only one specific person.

I pull into the Chans' driveway and go inside with Dezzie to say hello to her parents. Mrs. Chan insists on sitting me down and having me update her on the last year of my life. Which is hard to do in a fashion that leaves out Seth, who I will very certainly cry if I mention. I tell her about Los Angeles fire season instead. Floridians love that. Distracts them from their hurricanes.

Once we've caught up, I give Dez a big hug and get back in the car.

At home, my mom is flitting around with Bruce and her party planner, so I am able to dodge her and go upstairs and truly panic about my plan unraveling. I anxiously check my email to see if Becky has replied yet, but she hasn't. Not that it matters. If he's here, I can't go ahead with surprising him tomorrow. I wonder if it's a sign that I should not be doing this. That I should leave him in peace.

Downstairs, the doorbell rings.

I look out the window and see, of all people, my father, carrying a giant bouquet of lilies.

The fuck?

Oddly, my brain fixates on the lilies, rather than the inexplicable fact of his presence here. Either he doesn't remember my mother is allergic to them, or he is planning to use them to suffocate her in her own home.

I walk to the staircase and lean down to hear what's being said.

"Is Molly here?" Dad asks. "I texted her and she didn't reply, but I know she's usually in town for the holidays so I thought I'd try . . . I would have called but I don't have your number."

My mother sneezes.

"First of all, Roger, get those things out of my face. I'm allergic."

"You are? Sorry. I didn't know."

"You absolutely did know. We were married for twenty years."

She takes the bouquet out of his hands and hurls it at his car.

This is absurd but very satisfying, and I giggle.

"Secondly," she goes on, "if my daughter wanted to see or speak to you, she would have replied to your text. If she did not, we can both safely assume she doesn't want anything to do with you. And after that stunt you pulled on Thanksgiving, I can understand why."

"I did not 'pull a stunt,'" he says, using exaggerated air quotes. "I addressed a simple business matter. But I admit it was poor timing, and I'm sorry she got her feelings hurt."

"You're sorry she 'got her feelings hurt'?" my mom asks, returning his air quotes. "What a heartfelt apology. I'm sure she'll be very touched."

I don't want to watch her strangle him, so I walk downstairs to put an end to this.

"Hi, Dad," I say, taking my mother by the elbow and moving her out of striking distance. "What are you doing here?"

He reconfigures his face to something approximating the serious, self-important expression he wears signing books.

"Hello, Molly." He gestures out at the lilies. "I brought you flowers, but your mother threw them in the driveway."

"She has a severe lily allergy. You should know. You were married for twenty years."

He ignores this and reaches into his breast pocket. "I also brought your Christmas present."

He produces a check, folded in half.

I don't take it. "No thanks. I have my lucrative Mack Fontaine kill fee, remember? Why are you here?"

He sighs in a long-suffering way. It's like he's imagining there's an audience observing us who's on his side, ready to sympathize with him for the hostile reactions he's getting from these two women he was obviously justified in leaving.

"I wanted to tell you that I'm sorry you're upset about the movie," he says.

It is not my job to train him how to apologize without blaming the injured party for their feelings, so I just give him my best dead-eyed stare and say, "Do you really think this is about the *movie?*"

"It's about you being a terrible father, Roger," my mother says, shoving her head back into his eye-line.

"Mom," I say, "why don't you get back to hanging your tinsel and let me talk to Dad?"

"Fine. But don't let him bring down your mood."

That's pretty close to impossible, given that my mood is about a one out of ten already.

"I love you, Molly," my father says, in the stern tone of someone correcting a dog that won't be trained. "And I know you are struggling in your career—"

"Oh my God—"

"But you can't expect special treatment. How does that make me look, to keep you on out of nepotism when you weren't cutting it? There are other ways I can help you. If you need money—" He holds out the check again.

"For fuck's sake," I explode. "You truly don't get it, do you? I wasn't excited about the movie because of the *money*. I was excited because I thought it meant you *respected* me. That you were acknowledging my existence as more than someone you're obligated to take out to lunch when you pass through LA."

"That's not fair," he says. "I want to see you. You're my daughter."

"I'm your daughter on your terms when it suits you. Have been since I was thirteen."

His distinguished crow's-feet pinch together in agitation.

"Look, Molly," he says. "I know you think I wasn't there for you, but I did try to visit you when you'd let me. I paid for your schooling. I allowed you to stay in my ski house by yourself after graduation."

My impulse is to slam the door in his face. But I think of Seth. Of how he forced me to articulate my feelings.

"Is this supposed to be your vindicating little speech before our tearful reconciliation?" I ask. "Because I think you'll need to do some more soul-searching."

He runs his hands through his iconically messy white hair, making it even more iconic.

"Fine," he says. "You know what? You're right. After a while, I didn't try as hard to see you. Perhaps that was a mistake. But you disliked my wife, you were sour with me whenever you agreed to meet, and I thought I'd do us both a favor and not force it. Frankly, I thought you wanted it that way."

"It's not just in the past, Dad. You hardly ever contact me, and when I reach out, half the time you blow me off. It hurts me when you do that."

"Well, then you should understand that it hurt me when you blew *me* off."

"Do you mean when I was in *middle school?*"

"I've said that I'm sorry, Molly. I don't know how many more times I can."

I'm over this. I want him to leave.

"Okay," I say. "I accept your apology."

He nods nobly. "Good. I appreciate that. Moving on, let's try a fresh start. Why don't you come over for brunch tomorrow? We can take the sailboat out. A new tradition."

I wince at how badly teenage Molly would have wanted him to think up this idea.

But this Molly—grown-up Molly—isn't risking herself for a dollop of his attention.

And she fucking hates sailboats.

"It upsets me to see you right now," I say. "It's not a good time."

He purses his lips. "That's your choice. But remember it next time you want to fling my so-called neglect in my face."

"Will do. Bye."

I start to close the door, but he puts his foot in the doorway to stop me.

"Are you serious?" I ask.

"Do not slam this door in my face. I'm your father."

"But you aren't!" I cry. "That's what I'm saying. So can you leave me alone now? Do you really want to ruin another holiday?"

He stares at me like he really, truly, cannot comprehend my anger. And then he removes his foot. "I'll wait for you to contact me, since you clearly don't want to talk."

He turns around and stalks back to his car, abandoning the lilies where they lay.

"*Fuck* that guy," I say as I close the door.

"Yeah," my mom calls, rushing in from the living room. "Fuck that guy!"

Bruce follows her with the party planner, wearing a concerned expression. "Molly honey," he says, "I don't like to wish ill on others. But fuck that guy."

"I don't know who you're talking about," the party planner says, "but fuck that guy!"

My mom gives me a hug. "Are you okay, sweets?"

"Yeah. But that was exhausting. I'm going to try to take a nap so I can be my sparkling self for your party."

"Good idea," she says. "No one likes a grump."

"I know. That's why no one likes me."

She puts a big sloppy kiss on my cheek.

"I like you, Molly Malloly."

Upstairs, I throw myself onto the bed and my back rejoices that I'm on a mattress rather than a thin layer of acetate on a hardwood floor.

I am so, so tired.

I don't know what to do about Seth. I don't know what to do about my father.

All I know is this: I have to change my plan.

I don't want to be Roger Marks.

It's as cowardly to expect Seth to see a screenplay as an apology as it was misguided to believe that my father's offer of a career opportunity proved his love for me.

I need to stop doing what my father would do: writing a check to prove his affection instead of loving me in real life. What is my script except my own form of that check? *Here, please accept this piece of paper in lieu of me telling you how I actually feel.*

Maybe writing the screenplay was just for me.

What I need to do is go to Seth and simply say that I love him and want him back.

I can sleuth out from Kevin when he's going back to Chicago and meet him there. Say what I need to in private.

Fix this.

For now, I need sleep.

I grab an eye mask and pass out in minutes.

I wake up to my mother knocking on my door.

"Molls? You awake? It's almost seven o'clock. Guests are arriving at eight."

I've been asleep for nearly four hours.

"Sorry," I call groggily. "I'll take a shower and get dressed."

"Take your time. You can make a grand entrance in your party dress."

I wince, thinking of the short, spangly number she said she found at Saks but that looks more like something you'd get at Forever 21.

Whatever. Fuck it.

Besides my mom and Bruce, no one I care about is going to see me tonight. I might as well dress myself up in Bratz doll cosplay. I go for it. Shimmery hot pink lips, fake lashes, stilettos, push-up bra, the works. By the time I start hearing the doorbell, I look hot. Entirely out of character, but hot.

I grab my phone to check my messages before I go downstairs, since I've been incommunicado all afternoon. There's one from my mom from an hour ago asking if I'm up. And there's a new email from Becky.

Just the knowledge that Seth's name is going to be in it is enough to make my heart beat faster. I consider deleting it, but it has an attachment. I grit my teeth and click it open.

From: bma445@nyu.edu
To: mollymarks@netmail.co
Date: Fri, Dec 31, 2021 at 4:44 pm
Re: Re: Subject: As requested . . .

Molly! I am SO sorry—I mixed up two emails I had queued, and
I mistakenly addressed this one to you and the one for you to
Seth Rubenstein. Which means . . . I accidentally sent him your
screenplay. I'm SO embarrassed. I'll send him a note asking him to
disregard it. It's in Final Draft so I doubt he opened it anyway.

I'm sorry again!!! I feel terrible!!! I'm attaching the proofed version
for you here.

This cannot be real.

I deserve bad things for what I've done, but not this.

If Seth reads that file without context, he's going to think that I'm trying
to make a movie out of what happened between us. Profiteering off his broken heart, without even asking him if it's okay.

He's going to hate me so much I can't stand to think about it.

I try to tell myself that he's the most ethical person I know, and that no
matter how curious he was when he saw the attachment, he wouldn't want
to invade my privacy by opening it.

But he's also human.

Of course he's going to open it.

And I can't stand it—the thought of him reliving the best parts of us, and
the worst, without knowing I wrote it for him.

I think about what I yelled at my dad: *Do you really want to ruin another
holiday?*

I can't do that to Seth.

Fuck Chicago. Fuck what his family will think of me. Fuck the cold,
grinding fear in my heart.

I run downstairs trying not to fall out of my four-inch stilettos, slip out
the door past the tipsy Marks Realty clients calling my name, and steal my
mother's big, ridiculous SUV.

CHAPTER 41
Seth

I have resolved to be cheerful for New Year's Eve.

Buoyant, even.

I will cast off my annual dread of the last night of the year and lose myself in the melee of my parents' dearest friends and golf rivals. I love schmoozing with retirees. The mid-60s seems like a fun age.

Plus, my mom, who eschews the trappings of bourgeois elegance when she entertains, is serving all of my favorite norm-core party foods. Chicken fingers. Deviled eggs. Cocktail wieners. I adore cocktail wieners and you just don't see them at parties anymore.

So I'm cruising through this backyard shindig with a smile on my face. I'm circulating on the pool deck, downing way too many tubular meats. I'm chatting up Sue and Harry Gottlieb about their grandkids. I'm flirting with Pris Hernandez, who I've had a crush on since she taught AP Spanish in high school. I'm wearing my Happy New Year's crown. You *can't* be depressed in a sparkly crown, even if it's a little too small and bites into the sides of your head.

And you know what? My good mood is not entirely an act.

Because I'm holding Molly's screenplay in my heart.

I'm still sad that this is how she chose to express her love for me. But my hope overpowers my pain. Maybe I'm deluding myself, casting my usual rose-colored tint on the possibility that passion and tenderness can overcome fear. After all, Molly always said that rom-coms bring the fake happy endings that don't exist in real life.

After all, I haven't heard a word from her in a month.

But I just can't bring myself to believe that in an autobiographical script, her character's grief for the loss of our relationship wasn't based in real mourning.

And as my shaky heart reverberates with this emotion, I discuss doubles tennis with a pair of retired dentists.

"It used to be impossible to get on the courts, and now you can't even set up a good round robin," Dr. Steele complains.

Dr. Yun nods. "Everyone left for pickleball."

Dr. Steele is about to say something scathing about pickleball, judging from his facial expression, but then he freezes.

He's staring at something behind me.

He elbows Dr. Yun. "You see her?"

Dr. Yun slowly nods, as if in a trance. "Yowza."

I glance over my shoulder to see what they're ogling.

It's a disco ball.

Or, at least, a woman wearing a dress the approximate size of a disco ball—the shortest, tightest, sparkliest dress I've ever seen outside of a Katy Perry video. Her legs are long, set off by towering silver stilettos. Her dark brown hair is down to her ass.

She's Molly.

My Molly.

Emanating such a glow that if the dentists were not groping her with their eyes, I'd think I was hallucinating.

But she's real.

She raises her hand at me and waves.

She looks terrified.

My heart turns over.

Whatever happened between us, I don't *ever* want to see Molly Marks looking scared.

I wave back and walk toward her.

Time slows down, just like in the movies.

One of *her* movies.

"*Seth*," she mouths.

"*Molls*," I mouth back.

And just as I'm close enough to take her hand—

I trip over an umbrella stand and fall directly into the hot tub.

Like, with my entire body. *Kablam*. Neck-deep in the stew.

I catch myself just in time to avoid smashing my skull onto a Baja shelf. A scrum of sixty-somethings converges around me, screeching in alarm.

Molly's face looks like a very beautiful, heavily made-up version of Edvard Munch's *The Scream*.

She runs toward me, elbowing her way through the retirees, and kneels at the side of the tub, to which I am clinging for dear life.

"Oh my God, Seth!" she cries. "Are you okay?"

"I'm calling 911," Dr. Yun shouts over the din.

"No, no, I'm fine," I rasp at him. My voice is hoarse from emotion and the hot, chlorinated water that went down my windpipe. "Just wet. And embarrassed."

Molly offers me her hands and I take them and she helps pull me up.

But I'm chest-deep in burbling water, and the incredibly goyish salmon-colored chinos my mother insisted I wear to this party weigh me down, making me clumsy.

I slip again, and this time I take Molly down with me.

Her sparkly body flies forward, knees first, and she topples into the water with a scream and a huge, 104-degree Fahrenheit splash.

We both clamber for the sides of the spa, limbs twisted, trying not to drown each other. My baggy pants are getting caught on her spiky heels. Her sequins are scratching my bare forearms.

"Are you okay?" Molly gasps, once she's gotten herself somewhat righted.

"Fuck," I say sharply, though my mother would not approve of me cursing in front of her friends. "I think I just sprained my ankle."

"At least hot water is good for injuries?" she offers feebly, her hair tangling around her shoulders as it ripples in the jets.

She wipes water out of her eye, and a false eyelash lands on her cheek.

I delicately remove it and hold it up to the light cast by the tiki torch. "Make a wish."

She starts to cry. "I already did."

And I hope, I *hope*, that she means the wish is me.

"What are you doing here, Molls?" I ask softly. "Or, should I call you . . . Nina?"

She sucks in a breath through clenched teeth. "You read the script."

I nod. "Are you here for notes on the ending?"

The pink of the hot tub lights shines against her sequins, turning them rose gold. "Well, falling into a hot tub *would* be a good set piece to punch up the draft," she says.

"I like your script the way it is."

She shakes her head. "I'm *so* sorry, Seth. I wrote it for you, not to sell. I was going to give it to you to say that I'm sorry."

My shoulders relax at these words. I knew it. I *knew* she wrote it for us.

I pull her into my arms. It is very painful to move, but this is the best I've felt in a month.

Still, she said the script was an apology. Not an attempt to get me back.

Apologies in relationships are often goodbyes. As the king of failed relationships, I should know. So I ask the question that's been haunting me:

"Molly? How much of the ending is true?"

"The ending?"

"The part where you pine for me. Regret leaving me. Want to come back to me but fear I won't want to see you."

"Oh. The dark night of the soul."

"Jesus, it was that bad?"

"That's technically what the beat is called when the girl has to either brave up, or lose the love of her life."

Those words knock the wind out of me.

"The love of her life?"

She looks into my eyes. "Yeah. The love of my life."

And then I marry her in that instant and we have fourteen kids and establish an eternal celestial kingdom in heaven, no questions asked.

Or I would. This is all I've ever wanted to hear.

But she's not done talking.

"Seth, I am so, so sorry. It's not an excuse but . . . I was so scared. I never thought I was wired to fall in love this hard, and I couldn't stand the idea of losing you. So I sabotaged it. Again. And I hurt you."

I want to comfort her in this moment, but my throat is too raw. I just shake my head.

"And I don't expect you to let that go, or take me back, or trust me," she says. "But I had to come here, because I'd never forgive myself if I don't tell you that you are my person, and I'm madly in love with you, and I'm going to regret what I did for the rest of my life. And if I had a chance to do it over, I'd choose—"

Her voice breaks off.

"What would you choose, sweetheart?" I whisper.

"I'd choose my soul mate. If he'd have me."

But she knows I'll have her, because I've already grabbed her and pressed her against my chest as hard as I can without hurting her and am murmuring, "I'll have you, I'll have you, I'll have you."

Slowly, consciousness of the forty pairs of spying eyes—many of them wearing hot pink "2022!" novelty glasses—dawns on us.

"Hmmm," I say. "I think they're getting off on this."

"We do probably look like we're doing some kind of strange pseudosexual baptism ritual," Molly says. "But I guess that's my fault for falling on top of you into a hot tub."

"Oh, baby," I say. "Do you think I've gone a single day without hoping against hope that you would appear in a slutty dress and fall on top of me into a hot tub?"

"I'm grateful for your love of pratfalls," she says.

Jesus, this girl. Always, with the lines. You'd think she writes sappy movies or something.

"What else are you grateful for?" I ask.

She laughs shakily. "I'm grateful for assistants who send the wrong emails. I'm grateful your parents have lived in the same house for thirty years so I know their address. I'm grateful for screenplays that say what I didn't have the courage to in real life. And I'm grateful for sweet boys who believe in happy endings."

I kiss her.

"I'm grateful for you, Molly. I'm just grateful for you."

And that's how our rom-com ends.

The camera zooms in on the lovers, and the credits roll over a montage of their beautiful life.

But that's not the end of our story. That's not even the end of our night.

The camera isn't rolling for the part when we dry off and go into the guest room and cry in a guttural and asthmatic way that is more medical than cinematic.

The bloopers are playing on-screen, but in real life I'm telling her how scared I am that if we get back together she'll keep leaving me, and she's sobbing and saying she knows, that she's scared of it too. She's admitting that my job gives her anxiety she's not sure she'll ever make peace with. I'm telling her I don't know how to reassure her. That I can't chase her down for the rest of our lives.

That we'll just have to love each other, and trust each other, and nurture this treasure—this absolute witchcraft—that we're so blessed to have.

That we'll just have to hope.

But I still believe that some loves are fated.

And I know that Molly Marks is the love of my life.

PART NINE

PALM BAY PREPARATORY SCHOOL
TWENTIETH REUNION

November 2023

CHAPTER 42
Molly

If you ever find yourself hosting an event that requires a rented white tent, you can be certain that I, Molly Marks, will be dragged there by my husband.

Sometimes, even if we haven't been invited.

"I love shit like this." Seth sighs happily as we walk underneath a banner that proclaims in pink, swirly letters:

**WELCOME TO YOUR 20TH REUNION,
PALM BAY CLASS OF 2003!!!**

"Calligraphy!" Seth enthuses. "Fun!"

"Don't troll me," I say, pinching the underside of his wrist with my nails. But I'm smiling.

Because we made it back here to this beach where we used to explore each other's bodies as teenagers, getting sand flea bites clear up to our hips. Back to this tent where, fifteen years later, Seth Rubenstein deigned to let me sit next to him even though I once broke his heart.

We made it back here, together, just like he predicted. His prophecy— "It's Gonna Be Me"—fulfilled.

Marian Hart waves at us from her station by the place cards. "Welcome, lovebirds!" she squeals. "How's married life?"

"Transcendent," Seth says.

"I just heard the news about your movie," she says to me. "I *love* Kiki Deirdre!"

She means *Better Luck Next Time,* which Seth convinced me to sell, and which was snapped up and fast-tracked for production by Kiki, one of the few remaining A-list movie stars who can still carry a rom-com into box office glory. They are casting the role of Cole right now. Seth is gunning for Javier Bardem, who he says is the only living actor who might be able to capture his raw sexual magnetism. When I explained that Javier is both too old and too Spanish for the part of a midthirties Jewish lawyer from Florida, he told me to "expand my world-building." Notes like this are how he earns the executive producer credit he negotiated to compensate him for his life rights.

If the movie is as big as we're hoping, it might even out-earn the next Mack Fontaine, netting me an effusive text from my father reading "Congrats, toots." (We're on speaking terms again, though I did not attend his fifth wedding.)

Marian turns to Gloria, who's trying to find her name in the pile of place cards.

"Aren't these two adorable?" Marian says, gesturing at us. "I always knew they'd end up together."

"Oh?" Gloria deadpans. "I'm shocked that anyone would have Molly. Even him."

I give them a high-wattage smile. "Seth likes my bad attitude."

Seth leans over and smacks a kiss on my cheek. "I *really* like it."

Marian hands us our place cards. "You guys are at Table Four. I sat you with Jon, Kevin, two girls from the tennis team, and Steve Clinton."

"That weird billionaire guy?" I ask, genuinely excited.

"Some might argue he's normal and you're weird," Gloria says.

"You look stunning, Marian," Seth says, pointing at her pregnant belly. "How far along are you?"

"Only twenty weeks, but you wouldn't know it. Triplets!" She gives us a "can you believe it?" face and actually, of course, I can, because she and Javier detailed their fertility journey on *Good Morning America,* where they are fixtures, now that he's retired from baseball and she's parleyed their domestic bliss into a multimillion-dollar lifestyle brand.

"How are your twinsies?" Marian asks.

"Hell on earth," Gloria says, "but we love them anyway."

They get into a conversation about parenting multiples. So far, we are only parenting a cat, so Seth grabs our place cards and leads me away.

"If I recall," he says, "you prognosticated that Gloria and Emily would be broken up long ago. And look at them. Parents to twin monsters."

"If I recall," I counter, "you said Marian would be married to Marcus by now. Yet here she is, bearing an entire litter of children to the world's most famous outfielder."

"Marcus seems happy anyway," Seth says. We both look over to where he and his hot professional golfer girlfriend are chatting with Chaz, the standup comedian.

"Hmm, Rubenstein," I say. "We're tied, one to one."

"Nope. Remember how you thought Dezzie and Rob would stay married forever?"

"RIP Rob," I mutter. He's not dead, just dead to me.

Not that Dezzie cares anymore. She's tossing back a Palm Bay Preptini with Felix, the chef with whom she started one of Chicago's buzziest restaurants and is marrying in April. Alyssa and Ryland walk over to them, hand in hand. No couple in this whole room looks more natural together than Alyssa and Ryland.

Seth and I were both right about them. That makes me happy.

"At least I didn't think Jon was gonna end up with that guy Alastair, like you did," I say.

"Alastair had a British accent," Seth says. "I *love* British accents."

"I guess he's the one that got away. Sorry you're stuck with me instead."

"Well actually, don't be sorry," Seth says. "Because you're here at our twentieth reunion with me as your date."

"Oh *ho ho*, no you don't," I say. "You predicted we would *sleep together* the night of our twentieth reunion. You have no idea if you'll be so lucky."

"I think I will," he says into my ear. "You can't resist me after you get started on those Preptinis."

"All right, Rubes," I say. "I'll award you a provisional victory, but only because I want that hot, hot—"

He holds up a finger. "Not so fast. Do you remember what you have to say to me, since I win?"

I make my face very sour. I hate losing.

"Soul mates exist," I recite in the voice of a hostile Muppet.

"Good girl," he says. "Though I could do without the tone."

I sigh. "*Soul mates exist*," I say in a sexy baby voice. "Is that better?"

He scowls. "I worked hard for this. For *years*. Don't make it creepy."

I grab his face and put a kiss on his lips, leaving a smear of red on his cupid's bow. "Okay," I say softly. "You were right, Seth. Soul mates exist."

"Thank you, Molly," he says. "I know defeat is hard for you."

"Actually, it works out," I say. "Because, on the upside, apparently soul mates exist. And somehow, I got lucky enough that you're mine."

ACKNOWLEDGMENTS

A few months after I finished this book, we lost my beloved Grandma Pat. She was the person whose lurid Fabio-bedecked paperbacks got me into romance as a disturbingly young child, and she made sure to stock signed copies of all my books in the library of her retirement community, where her closest and most salty friends could pass them around and marvel at the sex scenes. She never got to read *Just Some Stupid Love Story,* but so much of it is inspired by the place where she lived and helped to raise generations of our family that I think she would have gotten a kick out of it.

That place, as you may have gathered, is Florida. I would like to acknowledge my peculiar home state for shaping me into a person who knows more than she ever wanted to about hurricanes, circus culture, grifters, mosquito-borne illnesses, heatstroke, red tide, plagues of escaped anacondas and alligators in swimming pools. My dear Sunshine State, your politics make me so sad lately, but I would not be the person I am had I not grown up in your bathwater seas beneath showstopping sunsets, and Seth and Molly would not exist without you.

Seth and Molly would also not exist were it not for my husband, a dazzling creature who showers me in adoration I in no way deserve and who was one of the original readers of this book, twice. Thank you for making it possible for me to sit on the couch writing romance novels all day, and for thinking it's impressive instead of utterly slothlike. I am still madly in love with you, even after forty-five years. No notes.

And thank you as well to my whip-smart and indefatigable agent, Sarah Younger, without whom I would be a lost child instead of a semifunctioning writer. Nothing perks me up like your red lips on FaceTime, nothing improves my books like you demanding that I instill swoonery into the text, and nothing keeps me going like you fighting for me. I am also so grateful to NYLA mastermind Nancy Yost for her encouragement and wise counsel, and for foreign rights genius Cheryl Pientka, who so devotedly and skillfully got this book into the hands of readers around the world.

The book in your hands would not be what it is without the editor of my absolutely wildest dreams, Caroline Bleeke, who sliced through it with surgical precision to make it one hundred times sharper, cleverer, and more heartfelt. I am so grateful for your vision, tenacity, and delightful emails.

I am also so thankful to Sydney Jeon for shepherding me through production and to Shelly Perron for the rigorous copyedit and encouraging asides. I'm grateful to the whole team at Flatiron for giving this book such a great home—thank you to Bob Miller, Megan Lynch, Malati Chavali, Claire McLaughlin, Maris Tasaka, Erin Kibby, Emily Walters, Jeremy Pink, Jason Reigal, Jen Edwards, Keith Hayes, Kelly Gatesman, Katy Robitzski, Emily Dyer, and Drew Kilman. And a massive thanks to Vi-An Nguyen for designing the gorgeous cover.

One of my main occupations in my day-to-day life as a writer is threatening to quit writing, and I might have succeeded by now without the support of my writerly sisters-in-arms. Erin, Kari, Alexis, Emily, Kelli, Melonie, Nicole, Susan, Susannah, and Suzanne—you are not just my pocket friends, but my family. Thank you for filling the existential void, bat by bat. And thank you to my platonic wife, Lauren, for helping me to understand how to craft romcoms in the first place. Our Baby prepared me to write this book, and our wine-soaked nights keep me sane. And ta, indeed, to my beloved Claudia: guru into the UK publishing world, best cook, best time on Whatsapp, best transatlantic friend.

I am also so grateful for my family, who my dear father, on whom Roger Marks is not in the slightest way based, will be very annoyed to see me call the Dirty Doyles in this text. You are so funny and loving and supportive, you speak a language all your own, and I adore writing about family because of you. I'm sorry that all your cats pale in comparison to mine, and I love you to the ends of the earth, except when you are beating me at Settlers of Catan.

No painfully long acknowledgments section would be complete without a word of devotion to all the brilliant romance writers who keep upping the game of what this genre brings to the world. Molly Marks can doubt love stories all she wants, but you make me believe in them and aspire to write them better. Thank you for inspiring me, for making me more ambitious, and for being evangelists for a world of fiction that holds, nurtures, and delights its readers like no other.

And finally, thank you to everyone who has read this book, and all my books, and books in general. Authordom is a strange, lonely calling, and your enthusiasm, kind words, hilarious social media posts, dizzying annotations, and careful reviews make it so, so worth it. None of us authors would be here without you, and I doubt many of us would want to.

ABOUT THE AUTHOR

Katelyn Doyle is a writer based in Los Angeles. *Just Some Stupid Love Story* is her debut rom-com. She also writes as the *USA Today* bestselling historical romance novelist Scarlett Peckham.

Recommend *Just Some Stupid Love Story*
for Your Next Book Club!

Reading Group Guide available at
www.flatironbooks.com/reading-group-guides